Praise for the novels of Deirdre Martin

"A great contemporary r̶... ...-
acters and a setting that I ... ...e

"Erin is a character a female reader can be proud of."
—*Fresh Fiction*

"As usual, the romance is top-notch! Fans of second-chance love
stories will delight in Rory and Erin's reunion as she puts him
through the wringer just a bit, making their eventual happiness
just a tad bit more fun!"   —*Romance Junkies*

"This series is such a delight to read . . . Martin really knows
how to write about sexy, athletic, attractive men!"   —*Fic Talk*

"An enjoyable book in an amazing series."
—*Guilty Pleasures Book Reviews*

"*Breakaway* is a smash hit! The eleventh installment of Deirdre
Martin's Blades [novels] proves this series just keeps getting
better and better! This one's a must-read."   —*Joyfully Reviewed*

"This story will enchant you from start to finish."
—*Coffee Time Romance & More*

"Readers will cheer as Rory works on his chance at redemption . . .
Breakaway is a sassy treat filled with intriguing, lighthearted
characters and tons of sexy fun. Don't pass this one up!"
—*Romance Reviews Today*

"This contemporary mainstream romance is absolutely perfect. I
hated the mere thought of putting it down . . . I don't think I can
rate this book high enough."   —*Night Owl Reviews* (Top Pick)

continued . . .

Power Play

"Contemporary romance doesn't get much better than this."
—*All About Romance*

"Deirdre Martin has another hit on her hands."
—*Romance Reader at Heart*

"Sparkling banter and a couple with red-hot chemistry."
—*Romance Reviews Today*

Just a Taste

"Another victory for Martin." —*Booklist*

"Be prepared to get a little hungry . . . Pick up *Just a Taste* for a tempting read you won't want to put down."
—*Romance Reviews Today*

Chasing Stanley

"Martin has a way of bringing her dissimilar characters together that rings true, and fans and curious new readers won't want to miss her latest hockey-themed romance." —*Booklist*

The Penalty Box

"[Martin] can touch the heart and the funny bone."
—*Romance Junkies*

"Martin scores another goal with another witty, emotionally true-to-life, and charming hockey romance." —*Booklist*

"Fun, fast." —*Publishers Weekly*

continued . . .

Total Rush

"Deirdre Martin is the reason I read romance novels."
—*The Best Reviews*

"Martin's inventive take on opposites attracting is funny and poignant."
—*Booklist*

"Martin depicts the worlds of both professional hockey and ethnic Brooklyn with deftness and smart detail. She has an unerring eye for humorous family dynamics [and] sweet buoyancy."
—*Publishers Weekly*

"Makes you feel like you're flying."
—*Rendezvous*

Body Check

"Heartwarming."
—*Booklist*

"One of the best first novels I have read in a long time."
—*All About Romance* (Desert Isle Keeper)

"You don't have to be a hockey fan to cheer for *Body Check*."
—*The Word On Romance*

"A dazzling debut."
—Millie Criswell, *USA Today* bestselling author

Titles by Deirdre Martin

BODY CHECK
FAIR PLAY
TOTAL RUSH
THE PENALTY BOX
CHASING STANLEY
JUST A TASTE
POWER PLAY
WITH A TWIST
STRAIGHT UP
ICEBREAKER
BREAKAWAY
HIP CHECK

Anthologies

HOT TICKET
(with Julia London, Annette Blair, and Geri Buckley)

DOUBLE THE PLEASURE
(with Lori Foster, Jacquie D'Alessandro, and Penny McCall)

Hip Check

Deirdre Martin

BERKLEY SENSATION, NEW YORK

THE BERKLEY PUBLISHING GROUP
Published by the Penguin Group
Penguin Group (USA) Inc.
375 Hudson Street, New York, New York 10014, USA

Penguin Group (Canada), 90 Eglinton Avenue East, Suite 700, Toronto, Ontario M4P 2Y3, Canada
(a division of Pearson Penguin Canada Inc.) • Penguin Books Ltd., 80 Strand, London WC2R 0RL,
England • Penguin Ireland, 25 St. Stephen's Green, Dublin 2, Ireland (a division of Penguin
Books Ltd.) • Penguin Group (Australia), 707 Collins Street, Melbourne, Victoria 3008, Australia
(a division of Pearson Australia Group Pty. Ltd.) • Penguin Books India Pvt. Ltd., 11 Community
Centre, Panchsheel Park, New Delhi—110 017, India • Penguin Group (NZ), 67 Apollo Drive,
Rosedale, Auckland 0632, New Zealand (a division of Pearson New Zealand Ltd.) • Penguin Books
(South Africa), Rosebank Office Park, 181 Jan Smuts Avenue, Parktown North 2193,
South Africa • Penguin China, B7 Jiaming Center, 27 East Third Ring Road North,
Chaoyang District, Beijing 100020, China

Penguin Books Ltd., Registered Offices: 80 Strand, London WC2R 0RL, England

This is a work of fiction. Names, characters, places, and incidents either are the product of the author's
imagination or are used fictitiously, and any resemblance to actual persons, living or dead, business
establishments, events, or locales is entirely coincidental. The publisher does not have any control over
and does not assume any responsibility for author or third-party websites or their content.

HIP CHECK

A Berkley Sensation Book / published by arrangement with the author

PUBLISHING HISTORY
Berkley Sensation mass-market edition / February 2013

ISBN: 978-0-425-25115-7

PRINTED IN THE UNITED STATES OF AMERICA

10 9 8 7 6 5 4 3 2 1

ALWAYS LEARNING   **PEARSON**

Acknowledgments

Special thanks to:
    Sinead Noel, for letting me pick her brains about eight-year-old girls.

Additional thanks to:
    Mark.
    Kate Seaver, the most patient editor on earth.
    Miriam Kriss, the best agent any writer could hope for.
    Fatin Soufan, Dee Tenorio, Eileen Buchholtz, and Binnie Braunstein.
    Mom, Dad, Bill, Allison, Frankie, Aine, Jane, Dave, and Tom.

1

"*Hey, Saari: who's* the cute blonde you parked with Lou?"

Esa took his time answering Ulf Torkelson's question as he stood in front of his locker, briskly rubbing his head with a towel. He couldn't believe it had taken one of his teammates this long to ask about Nell. Maybe they didn't want to distract him before practice. As if he wasn't distracted already.

Heads had turned when he'd walked into practice with her. How could they not? Thankfully, Nell was oblivious to his teammates gawps and glances. For some reason, it was Lou Capesi who held her attention. Since Lou was an expert on only two things, publicity and food, Esa assumed he was entertaining her with stories of his gourmet adventures.

Esa draped the towel around his neck. "The blonde's my niece, Nell."

"She visiting?" Ulf asked.

"No. She's living with me now. I'm her legal guardian." Saying it aloud made it feel all the more surreal.

The reaction in the locker room was akin to a sparkler being blown out, postpractice adrenalin plummeting to bafflement. The only people in the Blades organization who had known about Nell were General Manager Ty Gallagher, Coach Michael Dante, Lou, and Rory Brady, his best friend on the team.

Esa sat down on a bench. "Fire away, guys," he said, even as his guts filled with dread. "Ask anything you want. I think it'll be easier to just get it all out of the way right now."

His teammates glanced at each other apprehensively. No one said a word, so Esa broke the ice. "You're all thinking: 'Esa, taking care of a kid? What the fuck—?' "

"Pretty much, yeah," Tully Webster admitted. "Is she living with you for good?"

"Until she turns eighteen, I guess." Esa anticipated the next question and decided to ask it himself. That way, he wouldn't have to go deep into details that hurt too much. "Why is she with me? Because my sister died in a plane crash last year. Remember?"

"Oh yeah." Tully looked ashamed; clearly he hadn't remembered at all.

"So the kid's dad bit it, too?" Ulf asked casually, slicking his armpits with deodorant.

Eric Mitchell looked at the hulking defenseman with more than his usual disgust. "Jesus Christ. Do you have to be so insensitive?"

"What?" Ulf whined, looking around the locker room for support. "Saari told us to ask questions!"

"Yeah, okay, maybe that wasn't such a good idea," Esa said, half jesting. He felt drained, and not just from practice. The stress of his life changing overnight was taking an immediate toll.

"Here's the deal: my sister, Danika, was single; Nell's dad is someone she selected from a sperm bank. Even though I'm Nell's legal guardian, when Danika died, her best friend, Leslie, and I thought it would be better if Nell stayed with her, since it meant not uprooting Nell from London. Plus, Leslie has always been like a second mother to Nell."

Esa sighed deeply. "Unfortunately, Leslie just took a job that involves a lot of travel to Asia. We decided that the best thing for Nell was that she come here. That's it."

"That's it?" Jason Mitchell repeated incredulously, pulling a Blades sweatshirt over his head. "Does this Leslie know you know shit about kids?"

Esa's hackles went up. "I'm not a fucking moron, you know. I can figure it out."

"How old is she?" Ulf asked.

"Eight."

"Same age as you mentally," David Hewson pointed out to Ulf.

"Dude." Teammate Tully Webster looked at Esa like he was delusional. "No disrespect, but you don't seem the single parent type. Single uncle type, I mean. She's an eight-year-old *girl*. You're a professional hockey player whose number one hobby is chasing tail."

"No, it could work out," Ulf interjected. "When this happens in the movies the uncle is usually some crabby old bastard, and the kid is scared of him. But in the end, they get really close and love each other." He looked at Esa. "So don't worry. There's always a happy ending."

Esa stared at him. "You're a Swedish idiot."

"He's just trying to be helpful," Rory pointed out quietly. *Thank Christ for Rory*, Esa thought. If he and his wife, Erin, hadn't been there for him when he found out Nell was going to be his, he'd probably have lost it completely.

Esa looked at Ulfie, who was clearly hurt. "Sorry, man."

Ulf grunted begrudgingly. "You can be a real Finnish fuck, you know?"

"Look." Rory's voice turned serious as he slipped his wedding ring on. "I think we should try to support Esa with this."

"Who the fuck are you, the Irish Dr. Phil?" Eric mocked affectionately. He patted Esa on the shoulder. "Anything we can do, bro. You know that. You need to learn how to do a French braid? I'm your man." He jerked a thumb at his brother, Jason. "You want to know which Barbie dolls she might like? This douche bag is the expert."

Esa rose, too tired for a clever comeback. He noticed that Tully Webster's expression hadn't changed: he was still looking at him with disbelief. "What's the problem?"

Tully just shook his head. "You have no clue what you're getting yourself into."

Esa slammed his locker shut. "Everything will be fine." That ended the conversation. Leave it to Tully to be the voice of doom. Just because Tully had two kids, it didn't mean he was the world's expert on child rearing. A bunch of the guys had kids. Hell, Coach "Mikey the Merciless" had kids and he hadn't given Esa a hard time. Yet.

There was just one problem: Tully was right. Esa had no idea what he was getting himself into. He couldn't remotely imagine what life with an eight-year-old little girl was going to be like. He and Nell knew each other a little bit, but they weren't especially close. He saw her once or twice a year, when he went to visit his sister. Yet for some inexplicable reason, Danika had wanted Nell with him.

It didn't make sense. He could understand her not making their parents Nell's guardians. For one thing, it involved moving the poor kid to Finland and forcing her to learn a whole new language. For another, his parents were strict and impatient, with about as narrow a world view as an ayatollah. They weren't the warmest people, either. But why hadn't Danika left Nell to Leslie? Shit, "left" was the wrong word. It made Nell sound like she was a lamp or some family heirloom.

Nell was the most precious thing in Danika's life, and she was close to her Aunt Leslie. Didn't it make more sense to make Leslie Nell's legal guardian from the start? So what if she wasn't a blood relative? Danika had no illusions about what Esa's life was like. Did she think making him responsible for Nell would tame him, turn him into some kind of domesticated beast? Those were the last things he wanted right now— domestication and responsibility. Nell was a great kid, but he resented the way she had been thrust upon him. He felt like a shit thinking that, but it was true.

Still, he was determined to honor his sister's wishes and give it his best shot. He just hoped he didn't screw up Nell too much in the process.

2

"Saari, hold up."

The sound of his coach's voice behind him caught Esa by surprise as he left the locker room. Usually he and Rory departed together, but today Esa had to swing by Lou's office to pick up Nell. Rory didn't see what the big deal was if he came along, but Esa just felt it was better he fetch Nell alone. The kid had only been in the country three days and he'd already dumped her on Lou, as if she didn't already have enough trauma in her life.

Esa had been lingering in the locker room, dragging his feet going to fetch her. The thought filled him with dread. What were they going to do the rest of the day? She'd had jet lag for a day and a half, so he'd been off the hook for a while. Yesterday he'd brought her to FAO Schwartz at the suggestion of his doorman. But he had no idea what to do next.

Esa stopped, waiting for Michael. "What's up?"

"What's up?" Michael sounded incredulous. "You're taking care of an eight-year-old kid, that's what."

"Don't have much choice," Esa replied with resignation as they started down the neon-lit hallway toward the elevators.

Michael was scanning his face. "Esa, this is serious shit. You know that, right?"

"Of course I do," Esa replied with irritation. Jesus. He might not be a family man, but he wasn't a complete idiot.

"You two close?"

"Not really," Esa said. The admission pained him. He'd been a shitty uncle and a shitty brother. He should have visited Nell and Danika more. He should have spent more time with his sister, period. Having Nell with him brought home the fact that Danika was really dead, and he'd never see her again.

"I saw Nell a couple of times a year."

"But do you get along?" Michael's brown eyes were probing his, making it tough to run from the truth. One thing about Coach Dante: he had a knack for getting you to cough up info. Maybe because he really cared.

"Yeah," Esa said uncertainly. "I mean, I know she likes me. I like her: she's a good kid."

"A good kid who's been through a lot," Michael pointed out quietly.

Esa was silent. He and the coach continued walking.

"Did you have anything set up for her when she arrived?"

Esa glanced at him. "What, like her room?"

Michael nodded.

"Yeah. Leslie—my sister's friend—sent a bunch of stuff over before Nell came: some clothes, books, DVD's. I bought her pink sheets. The woman at Bloomingdale's said little girls liked pink. And purple." Esa paused. "She seems to like it."

"When does the nanny start? Where is she going to school?"

Esa stared at him blankly. *You asshole*, he thought. He kept meaning to get around to taking care of both, but for some reason, he kept forgetting. Forgetting on purpose, Rory would say. Thinking that if you don't do it, it'll make Nell go away.

Esa knit his eyebrows together, feigning deep thought. The corridor suddenly felt endless. "I have to double-check."

Michael laughed softly. "*Madonn'*, you haven't even hired a nanny yet, have you?"

"I've been busy."

"What? Continent hopping and flirting your ass off in trendy bars?"

"Hey, I'm doing the best I can here, okay?" Esa retorted.

He knew he deserved the rebuke; what kind of moron neglects enrolling a kid in school and lining up care? Answer: one who wanted to pretend his life wasn't going to be pulverized into something unrecognizable.

"Saari, the school year starts in two weeks, and preseason starts in three. You have to move fast." Michael looked thoughtful as he smoothed back his thinning black hair. "I might be able to help you on the nanny front."

"Yeah?"

"Yeah. Theresa has two clients—a really famous acting couple—who are moving out to L.A. Their longtime nanny wants to stay put."

"Why doesn't the nanny want to go?"

"Her family's here."

That bode well. Loyalty. It meant she'd take care of Nell for as long as he was a Blade.

"Theresa's met her and said she was nice," Michael continued.

Theresa was Michael's wife. Together with Ty Gallagher's wife, Janna, she ran FM PR, one of the top PR firms in Manhattan with clients ranging from professional jocks to the rich and famous. Michael wasn't supposed to, but he was always feeding the guys tasty morsels of gossip that he got from Theresa. Which was why the next question out of Esa's mouth was, "Who's the couple?"

Michael glanced behind them to make sure they were safe, then told him.

Esa was floored. "Wow."

"I know. Real prima donnas. So she'd be used to dealing with rich assholes like you." He didn't seem to be kidding. "Want me to ask Theresa about her?"

"Hell, yeah. Tell Theresa I'll pay the nanny whatever she wants. If she could start at the weekend, that would be great."

"Saari, you have to meet the woman and interview her first. She's not Mary freakin' Poppins, just turning up on your doorstep like magic."

Esa's heart sank. "Right."

"I'll talk to Theresa, and if the woman is interested, I'll have Theresa pass her info on to you. Sound good?"

"Sounds great."

"Well, the more I can get you focused on the ice this season, the better." Esa knew what was coming. "You have to kick it up a notch. You were good last year, but you weren't great, and we need great. I need you to be great. Ty needs you to be great."

Esa deflated. "Yeah, I hear ya."

As if taking on Nell wasn't enough, he was in the last year of his contract, and according to his agent, the Blades seemed in no hurry to re-sign him. It would be nice going into the season knowing this was taken care of. Blades' management dragging their feet was one more distraction he didn't need. His life had gone from simple to complex overnight, and he hated it.

*   *   *

Esa found Nell sitting at Lou's desk, her eyes glued to his computer screen as her fingers flew across the keyboard. She looked so serious sitting there in the office chair, a beat-up old wooden number that Lou refused to part with. He had no interest in "ergonomics or anything of that bullshit." The chair he'd started with decades back was fine with him. The only change was that now, because of his bad back, he sat on a couple of pillows, too.

Nell hadn't noticed Esa yet, which gave him a chance to study her. Christ, she looked so much like his sister, with that long, long blond hair and big blue eyes.

But she differed from Danika in one fundamental way: she didn't laugh or smile very much. Esa knew this was a recent development. He remembered one Christmas at his sister's a few years back when Nell had been giggling her head off, watching a cartoon about some horrible kid who's always pulling pranks on people. It was hard to believe she'd turned into the intense little girl sitting in front of him.

"Hey." Esa joined her at the computer, peering over her shoulder. "Looking at anything good?"

"I'm researching Italian restaurants in the San Francisco area for Mr. Capesi." Nell's voice was quiet but lyrical; "posh," as his sister would say. Esa agreed: she sounded like Keira Knightley.

"How many times do I have to tell you?" Lou asked

affectionately as he waddled over to his desk, giving Esa the stare of death before turning his full attention to Nell. "You don't have to call me Mr. Capesi. You can call me Lou."

Nell looked up at Esa from beneath her long, blond lashes, unsure of what to do. He could see she was desperate not to misstep.

"It's okay to call him Lou," Esa assured her.

"Lou," she repeated as her eyes sparked to life. "A boy in my school once had a hamster named Lou. He escaped from his cage and got run over by a mail lorry."

"What the f—what's a lorry?" Lou asked.

"A truck," Esa supplied.

"I'm not surprised the hamster got run over," said Lou. "Lous don't always have the best of luck. Anyway, that's what you call me from now on," he told Nell. "Sounds a helluva lot better than Mr. Capesi, doesn't it?"

Nell nodded. Maybe it was wishful thinking, but Esa swore he detected a faint smile on her lips. She liked Lou, she was comfortable with him. That was a good sign.

"What have you got her researching restaurants for?" Esa wanted to know.

"Whaddaya think? Me and the missus are headed out to Frisco for a long weekend in October. I want to make sure we hit the right places."

"You couldn't look this up yourself?"

"I wanted to help him," Nell interjected.

"She sees I'm busy, she's a good kid, she wants to help," Lou finished for her. "Right, doll?"

Nell nodded, looking pleased with the explanation her tough talking, morbidly obese translator had given.

"There you go," Lou said to Esa, as if it were self-evident.

Esa smiled at Nell. Tentative, he put a friendly hand on her shoulder, but only for a moment, since he didn't want her to be uncomfortable. She'd been so stiff when he'd hugged her at the airport it had actually hurt his feelings. Better not to push.

"Ready to go?"

Nell nodded yes, but she didn't move. *Fuck*, Esa thought. *She's as enthused about going with me as I am with taking her.*

"Before you go," Lou said to Nell, while continuing to

murder Esa with his eyes, "I just need a minute to talk to your uncle about something."

Nell's eyes remained on the screen. "Me, right?"

"No," said Lou. "Just stuff."

Nell shrugged indifferently and went back to Googling restaurants. Esa followed Lou through the PR department's outer office and out into the hall.

"I know what you're going to say," said Esa, "so let me apologize in advance: I'm sorry for asking you to watch Nell. I know it was wrong, but I didn't know what else to do."

"Hey, she's a great little girl, lucky for you. But you can't fuckin' do that again, Saari. It's not right. You couldn't get the Leprechaun's wife to look after her?"

"Erin works, you know."

"Oh yeah, I forgot: sorting out old pictures or some shit—"

"She's an *archivist*, Lou," Esa corrected impatiently.

"Besides, I wanted Nell to see me while I practiced. She's only been here three days. I thought it might be a bit much to let someone else watch her when—"

Lou held up his hand. "Stop. I know you, Saari. I know the way you think, and I know what you think about. Worrying that deeply about your niece's mental state isn't you. Admit it: you had no idea what to do with her, so you brought her to practice with you."

"Yeah, maybe." Lou turned on his trademark glare. "All right, yes."

"What're you going to do with her the rest of today?"

"I don't know," Esa said miserably.

"Of course you don't, because you hot shit, Finnish pricks don't know anything."

"This hot shit, Finnish prick agreed to pose in the buff for some 'Hockey Hunk' calendar for you," Esa pointed out tersely, the mortification of the photo shoot rushing back to him. Never again.

Lou was shaking his head in reprimand. "You have to do more stuff like that, Saari. I've told you for two goddamn years: more PR, less fucking around."

"I don't 'fuck around,' Lou. I like going out with beautiful women. How is that fucking around?"

"It's not just the women. It's the whole bachelor ethos."

"I'm a bachelor!"

Lou tilted his head in Nell's direction. "Yeah? Well, maybe you should cut back. You owe it to the kid, at the very least."

"Right," said Esa, fighting resentment.

"Anyway, the babysitting . . ."

"Look, Lou: it's Friday. I'll have a nanny by Monday. I swear."

Lou looked skeptical. "Yeah? What're you going to do? Buy one at Bloomingdale's?"

Esa ignored Lou's remark. "The coach has a lead on one. If she's interested, I can talk to her tomorrow and this whole issue can be wrapped up by Sunday."

"What if you don't like her?"

"I'll like her."

"You don't know that."

"Jesus Christ, why are you being so negative?" Esa snarled. "Theresa's met her and said she was nice."

Lou just grunted. Esa got the sense he was almost disappointed that hiring a nanny might be easy for him, that somehow Esa didn't deserve it.

"Thanks for watching her," Esa said to Lou. He was genuinely grateful.

"Yeah, well, don't make me do it again," Lou muttered.

"I've got to ask, though: what the hell were you talking to her about at practice that held her so rapt?"

Lou stifled a burp. "What do you think, you *cidrule*? You."

3

"*Thanks for stopping* by on such short notice, Michelle."

Michelle Beck smiled as Theresa Falconetti ushered her into her corner office at FM PR. When Theresa called, Michelle's assumption was that the Karles were trying to make an appeal to her, through Theresa, to reconsider moving to L.A. with them so she could continue being their nanny. She was surprised when Theresa told her she knew of another nanny position that might suit her well. Michelle was intrigued: She'd planned to take advantage of her severance package and take a little time off before trying to find her next job. But she decided she'd be foolish not to hear what Theresa had to say.

"Can I have Terrence get you anything?" Theresa checked with a cordial smile. "Water? Some coffee? Tea?"

"Nah, I'm fine."

Mention of FM PR's receptionist didn't exactly fill Michelle with the warm fuzzies since, when she'd walked through the door, Terrence had given her outfit not the once-over, but the twice-over, his gaze haughty from behind his frame-less spectacles. She could have sworn she heard Terrence murmur a disapproving, "Tsk, tsk," under his breath. She wasn't rich and famous like FM's clients, but it wasn't like she'd shown up looking like some slob, either.

Michelle sat down on Theresa's couch, quickly taking in the office, which was dominated by a wall lined with photos of Theresa's famous clients, including Michelle's former employers. Just as in real life, the Karles' teeth were blindingly white, their smiles brimming with self-confidence and charm from their tanned, unlined faces. Michelle smiled sadly to herself; she'd loved taking care of their kids, though the couple themselves had often put her nerves to the test.

"Let's talk about this nanny position," Theresa began, joining Michelle on the couch. "It's for one of the players on the New York Blades, Esa Saari. Ever heard of him?"

Michelle vaguely recognized the name: her friend Marcus worked as a dog walker for a woman named Delilah Gould, who was married to Jason Mitchell, one of the Blades. Michelle inwardly chuckled about how New York's social connections could sometimes resemble those of a small town. She was pretty sure she'd heard Marcus mention Esa Saari, which probably meant he was handsome. Marcus never missed a chance to talk about hunky hockey players.

"Sort of," Michelle answered.

"I'll assume you're not big on reading the gossip pages, then," Theresa replied wryly.

"Not all the time."

Looking at Theresa, Michelle thought to herself: *Maybe I do look like a slob*. Theresa was tall and thin, with a long, curly mane of dark hair. Her makeup and manicure were perfect, her business suit impeccable. But Michelle's feelings of inadequacy slowly faded as she reminded herself that one of the perks of being a nanny was that she didn't have to get dressed up for work.

"He's a winger. His speed is what—" Theresa started, then stopped with a sheepish smile. "I'm sorry. I always assume everyone knows about hockey."

"Oh, I know about hockey, believe me," Michelle chortled. "I grew up in a house with two rabid Islander fans."

"I won't hold that against you," Theresa joked, "or mention

it to my husband. Let me cut straight to the chase: Esa is single, and he's just gotten custody of his eight-year-old niece."

Michelle shifted uneasily, not sure if she wanted to know the answer to the question she was going to ask. "What happened to his niece's parents?"

"Her mom, Esa's sister, was single. She used a sperm donor." Theresa's eyes skimmed the portrait of her own family on her desk. "She died in a plane crash."

"Oh, God, how awful."

"I know," Theresa agreed quietly. It wasn't hard to see that at this moment, the mother in her took precedence over the businesswoman. "Anyway, Esa needs a nanny now. As in *now*."

"Live-in?"

Theresa nodded. "Michael said his place is nice. Really big. It's on the Upper East Side."

The locale didn't concern Michelle as much as her potential employer.

"What's Esa Saari like? Do you know?"

Theresa hesitated. "He's a great hockey player."

"Theresa."

"He's an egomaniac who's perpetually on the prowl."

Michelle frowned. "Sounds great."

"A lot of the single guys on the team are."

"A lot of single guys in general are," Michelle said. "Is he a jerk? Because frankly, I'm done working for jerks."

A knowing look passed between them regarding the Karles, who often mistook Michelle for the family servant rather than the children's caretaker.

"I don't know Esa well enough to answer that," Theresa replied honestly. "I know he works hard on the ice and is a great player, I know women fall at his feet, and I know he loves it that they do. I don't think he'd be around very much, to be honest."

Michelle considered this. A largely absentee employer could be a definite plus, depending on the circumstances. But Michelle wasn't sure she wanted to be around a bigheaded jock at all, especially a womanizing jock. Last but not least, she'd never been employed by someone single.

"Have you met the little girl?" Michelle asked.

"No. Her name is Nell, by the way. Like I said, her mom died in a plane crash last year."

"*Last year?* Who's been taking care of her up until now?"

"Her mom's best friend. But the woman just got a job that requires a lot of travel, and since Esa is her legal guardian . . ."

A lump formed in Michelle's throat. "So, not only did her mother die, but the person she's been living with for a year is now passing her on to someone else?"

Theresa nodded sadly.

"That poor little thing," said Michelle, feeling like her heart might crack into pieces just thinking about it. There was nothing worse than a child in pain. Nothing.

"Are you interested?"

Michelle didn't hesitate. "Of course I'm interested."

Theresa looked profoundly relieved. "I'll tell Esa and have him call you ASAP. Maybe you two could set something up for tomorrow."

"That works for me."

Theresa inhaled, blowing out a deep breath. "Michelle, you're a lifesaver."

"And he's going to pay me like one, believe me."

"That won't be a problem," Theresa assured her, adding in a stage whisper, "Don't let him push you around about your salary."

"Trust me, there's no chance of that happening." Michelle stood. "I'm so glad you thought of me," she told Theresa, surprising herself. "My initial intention was to take a short break, but this sounds perfect."

"I'm glad you think so." Theresa rose. "I'll have Terrence give you Esa's number as well. That way if the Karles wave millions in your face and you do decide to move to L.A. with them, you can tell him the interview is off."

Michelle shook her head. "Not going to happen. I could never move that far away from my family. I don't think I'd like it. God knows *they* wouldn't."

"Oh, I hear you on that one, believe me," Theresa answered dryly. "My mother's still upset Michael and I didn't buy a house on her block."

Michelle laughed.

"Let me know how it all turns out, okay?"

"Definitely. Thanks again, Theresa."

"Thank *you* for not going to L.A. We'll talk soon."

Michelle nodded, heading out of the office. An eight-year-old girl whose mom had died? It was a no brainer.

4

At Lou's suggestion, Esa asked Nell if she wanted to go to the zoo. Her momentary hesitation told him she didn't, but she agreed anyway, probably because she wanted to please him. Esa was at a loss. Should they go anyway? Should he offer another option? That might make sense . . . if he had another option. He hoped that once they got there, she'd have a good time.

So off to the zoo they went. Nell loved it; he hated it. It was ninety-eight degrees, humid, and packed with noisy families. The hordes of screaming and misbehaving children, accompanied by yelling parents who seemed unable to control them, made him glad he didn't have kids. Then he realized: he did have one.

Nell had been drawn to the polar bears in the Polar Zone. She stood there for ages, watching their every move intently. Esa wondered what she was thinking, so after a while, he asked her, even though the question felt awkward to him. "You seem to like them a lot. Is it because they're so big?"

"No," Nell said thoughtfully. "It's because they look like giant teddy bears. They look like they'd be fun to play with."

"You can't play with them, Nell. They'll attack you and eat you."

Nell looked at him like the inept moron he was. "I *know* that."

Esa quit while he was ahead.

Despite the heat and the crowds, he was glad they'd made the trip, since it took up the better part of the morning and early afternoon. He had an appointment with his agent around five, but the evening with her stretched out in front of him, endless as decades. Clearly, he was going to have to cancel his date with the TV announcer Kendra Meadows tonight, which sucked. He really needed to go out and have a good time—*and* he wanted to get laid.

Esa was thrilled when he and Nell left the zoo, and she told him she was tired and just wanted to go home and read. But when they got back, Nell headed directly to her room and closed the door. Esa wasn't sure what to make of it. Is this something she did when Danika was still alive, go off into her own private world, not to be disturbed? Or was she sending him a specific message: "Go away. Leave me alone. I hate it here." Esa felt terrible. Terrible, incompetent, and inadequate. A small wave of resentment toward his sister rolled through him, and again, much to his shame, he found himself asking: why me?

He knocked on her bedroom door. "Nell?"

"What?"

"Uh . . . I have to go meet my agent. So—"

"I don't want to go. I want to stay here."

Esa hesitated. "I don't know if that's such a good idea." In truth, he thought it was a great idea, but knew he wasn't supposed to.

"I'm not a baby."

"Yeah, I know, but—"

"Please?"

Esa leaned his forehead against the door, unsure of what to do. "Okay," he finally capitulated, "if you don't leave the apartment."

"I won't."

"I won't be long, I promise."

"Okay."

He waited to see if she'd say something more, but she
didn't. His gut told him it wasn't the right thing to do; pain in
the ass though it might be, he should drag her with him to his
agent's office. But his head said: Yeah! Perfect! She's right:
she's not a baby. She's got food, a TV, nothing could possibly
happen.

Before he left, though, he was going to call Michelle Beck.
That was the name of Nell's nanny—or rather, the woman Esa
intended to hire as Nell's nanny. That she'd been vetted by his
coach's wife was good enough for him. He'd set up an interview for tomorrow morning. She wouldn't know it, but he was
just interviewing her as a formality. At least he'd be doing one
smart thing today. Or maybe two, depending on his conversation with his agent.

*   *   *

"Have a seat, Esa."

Esa sank back in one of the plush leather chairs in the
office of his agent, Russell Hedges. Hedges was with Winston,
Lyon, and Schell, a multi-sports agency that represented some
of the biggest names in sports. Hedges concentrated specifi-
cally on hockey, which was why, the minute gossip starting
going around the NHL that the Blades wanted Saari, Russell
had reached out to him in Finland. His European agent had
done his best for him, but both he and Esa knew that when Esa
was being scouted by the NHL, there would be an inevitable
parting of the ways. Esa needed to be represented by someone
who knew the NHL. Russell Hedges had set his sights on Esa,
and Esa was glad that he did. Eventually, Hedges got Esa a
three-year contract from the Blades for a total of $9.6 million.
But it ran out at the end of this season.

"What can I do for you?" Russell asked after they'd made
small talk for a few minutes. Esa always had a hard time
believing Russell hadn't once been a jock himself: the guy
was stone solid, with biceps that bulged beneath his custom-
made shirts. He carried himself like an athlete, too, with a
confident swagger.

"Help me not to lose my mind," Esa replied grimly.

"Talk to me."

"I had a little chat with Michael Dante today after practice.

He told me I really have to kick it up a notch this season. I got the sense he was hinting that management don't feel they're getting what they paid for."

Russell nodded. "And your contract runs out at the end of the season, and they've made no effort yet to re-sign you."

"That's the problem, in a nutshell."

Russell offered Esa a glass of water, which he turned down. "You know how this goes, Esa," he said, pouring a glass for himself. "Sometimes teams want to make players sweat. They think the pressure of playing for a contract could, consciously or subconsciously, lead to better performance. And God knows they don't like to open their coffers before they absolutely have to."

"I don't have time to sweat," Esa lobbed back. "I have a lot of stuff on my plate right now, and the less stress I have in my life, the better."

Russell peered at him worriedly. "What kind of stuff?"

"Personal stuff. Remember I told you my sister died last year?" Russell nodded. "Well, my eight-year-old niece just came to live with me. For good. Don't even ask who's been taking care of her the past year. It's too complicated."

Russell took a sip of water. "How about this: I reach out to Blades management and try to nudge them on the contract issue. I'll make it clear that we'd like this done sooner rather than later so it's not hanging over your head all season."

"That's exactly what I want. Tell them the better I'm able to concentrate, the greater the return on their 'investment.' "

"I'll contact them first thing Monday. Doesn't mean they'll get back to me right away."

Esa eyed him warily. "Yeah, I know the game."

"How's it going otherwise?"

It took Esa a split second to realize he meant Nell. "Okay. As well as can be expected, I guess."

"Have you got a nanny?"

"Starts Monday." *She doesn't know it yet, though.*

"That's got to be a relief."

"It is."

"I guess this means a big lifestyle change for you in a lot of ways," Russell continued casually.

"Let me guess: I'll turn into more of a homebody, which will be a big boon PR wise."

Russell shrugged. "Couldn't hurt. You know Kidco likes to portray itself as a family-friendly business. They might love the image of the party boy turning into a dedicated uncle."

"Amazing," Esa marveled. "You guys are all alike. I got the same thing from Capesi." He really didn't want to go down this road, so he headed toward the door. "I should run."

"Anything else you want to talk about before you go?"

"Nope. Thanks, Russ. Keep me posted."

"That goes without saying. Enjoy your evening, Esa."

"You, too, Russ."

Esa checked his watch. He'd been gone less than an hour. He had no doubt he'd get home and Nell would still be in her room, or maybe watching TV. He had no idea what to do with her tonight. Or what to do about dinner. Pizza, maybe.

There, that was one thing settled. Next he had to call Kendra Meadows and cancel their date for tonight. He'd shift it to tomorrow. By then, everything would be in place with Michelle Beck. He'd make sure of that.

5

The next morning Esa struggled with impatience, trying to keep busy until ten a.m. rolled around. He made oatmeal for Nell and himself, which she seemed to like. He showed her an article about the Blades in that morning's *Sentinel* that said he was one of the key players if the team was to have any chance of winning the Cup. Nell nodded politely, but as soon as she finished her breakfast, she asked to be excused. Esa had no problem with her parking her butt on the couch and channel surfing. But she didn't. She took a shower, and went back to her room to read. Was that weird? He had a vague memory of Danika reading a lot when they were young, teasing him about being a *tyhmä urheilija*, a dumb jock. Maybe Nell had inherited his sister's bookworm gene. Or maybe she was scared of him. Or didn't like him. Or thought he was a *tyhmä urheilija*, even if she didn't know Finnish. The idea of any of them hurt.

Esa checked his watch for the hundredth time that morning. Michelle Beck was due in five minutes. He tidied up his apartment a bit; he didn't want her to think he was taking care of a little girl in some kind of pigsty. He'd have to remember to tell her that he had a housekeeping service already. At precisely ten, the doorbell rang and he buzzed the nanny up to his apartment.

He opened the door to a petite woman with short black hair and green eyes with lashes that were, in his opinion, a little too mascara heavy. Not his type. He liked leggy blondes.

She extended a small hand to shake his. "Hi, I'm Michelle."

"Esa. Let me take your coat."

Michelle shucked her faded denim jacket and handed it to him. Her eyes were sweeping his apartment, making him feel a little self-conscious. "Wow. Nice place."

"Thank you." Esa agreed: he did have a lovely home, but it had nothing to do with him and everything to do with Danika, who'd told him that just because he was a cool NYC bachelor, it didn't mean he had to inhabit a "soulless lair of steel and glass." A whiz with catalogs and the net, she'd ordered him what looked like furnishings for a real home, with Oriental carpets and potted plants and comfy furniture. The only incongruity in the room was his massive sixty-five-inch wide-screen TV. It stuck out like a sore thumb, but he didn't care. When all was said and done, this was still *his* lair.

Michelle smiled politely. "Where's Nell?"

The question surprised Esa. "In her room reading."

"Oh." Michelle seemed disappointed. "I was hoping I'd get to spend some time with her today, if you decide to hire me."

You are hired, Esa thought. He smiled graciously. "Yes, of course. I just thought you and I might talk a little first. Coffee?"

"That would be nice."

The small woman followed him into the kitchen. He'd let Danika take care of that, too. English something style. Or maybe it was French. Whatever it was called, it had a wide-planked wooden floor, and in addition to the usual kitchen stuff, there was a wooden island in the middle of the room with a big rack of pots hanging above it. He always laughed at that touch since he never cooked anything that couldn't be made in a bowl in a microwave. White-windowed cabinets lined the walls. He'd been told he had an amazing amount of counter space. Maybe so. He'd never noticed.

"This is amazing," Michelle marveled.

Esa flushed with pride. "Thanks."

She gestured at the hanging pots. "You like to cook?"

"Sometimes," he lied. He went to the fridge, pulling out a half-empty bag of coffee. He also had two bottles of Finlandia chilling, and the virgin bottle of champagne he'd hoped to pop last night. He had milk there, too, for Nell to drink and to put on her cereal. He'd done pretty well in the food department for Nell, he thought, getting a bunch of things he was sure kids liked to eat: macaroni and cheese, brownies, hot dogs, soda, cold cereal, chocolate chip cookies, and some breaded chicken bits. He should probably take her to McDonald's.

Coffee brewed, he and Michelle sat down at the kitchen table. Michelle pulled a neatly typed sheet of paper out of her big leather shoulder bag and pushed it across the table to him. It was a list of references.

"Sorry I couldn't get this to you sooner, but Theresa said you were crunched for time, and I didn't get your e-mail address."

"No worries." He cursorily skimmed the paper and handed it back to her. "Very impressive."

"That's it?" Michelle looked slightly taken aback. "You're done?"

"You come highly recommended from Theresa Dante. That's enough for me. I need you to start tomorrow afternoon. I'll pay you whatever you want."

Michelle leaned forward as if she hadn't heard him correctly. "What?"

"I said I'll pay you whatever you want. To take care of Nell. You'll have your own room and bathroom. Locks on the door."

"Whoa, whoa, slow down a minute."

"Why?"

"We've got to discuss terms first. It's very important that we're both clear on a number of things. And we need to see if Nell and I are a good fit."

Esa looked at her over the brim of his coffee cup as he took a sip. "Whatever terms you want. Also, I'm sure you and Nell will be a good fit. She's a very nice little girl."

Michelle looked concerned. "We're not talking about a puppy here. We're talking about the care and welfare of a child."

Esa felt ashamed. "Yes, of course." He drank down more coffee, hoping to wash away some of his impatience. "What is it you need to know?"

"You're supposed to be interviewing *me*, not the other way around."

"Right. Of course." *Well, as you can see, you'll be working for an idiot.* Esa aimed for a serious look. "I guess I'm wondering: why are you a nanny?"

Michelle's face lit up. "I love kids. Always have. I taught first grade for a while, but it didn't give me the kind of one-on-one connections I wanted. Being a nanny lets me do that. It also pays better than teaching."

"Ah." As surreptitiously as he could, Esa checked his watch. He thought this "interview" would take all of ten minutes. Obviously it was going to run longer.

Michelle studied him. "You really have no idea what you're doing, do you?"

Esa hesitated. "Uh . . . no," he confessed. "Here's my problem: exhibition games begin in three weeks, and we're already hard at practice. Yesterday I had to bring Nell with me. I need someone in place now. I just . . ." He felt bad. ". . . I just don't have the time to spend with her."

Esa wondered what Michelle was thinking right now. Probably that he was a selfish, inept prick. Which happened to be the ugly truth.

Michelle took a deep breath. "Here's the deal," she began, tenting her fingers on the table, which made her look very professional. "I get two days and nights off a week. My only job is taking care of Nell. That means I don't clean or do *your* laundry. I will cook for Nell but not for you."

Esa raised an eyebrow.

"You look surprised."

"I am."

"Why?" Michelle's voice was polite, but firm. "You're paying me to take care of your niece, not be your chef."

Esa felt a flick of irritation. *Bossy little woman.* She was going to be in his employ, not the other way around.

"What—*exactly*—will your responsibilities be as Nell's nanny?" Esa enquired.

"Like I said, I'll make her meals. I'll get her ready for school in the morning, I'll take her to school if that's necessary, and I'll pick her up after school. I'll help her with her homework. I'll pick up after her, though that's something I hope she's already doing on her own. I'll take her to any extra-curricular activities or playdates she might have. I'll arrange for her to have playdates here. I'll discipline her as I see fit. I'll put her to bed at night. Basically, my promise to you is to keep her healthy and safe so that she can thrive."

Her eyes pinned his. Perhaps it was his own ignorance on the issue, but Esa felt as if she were challenging him, waiting for him to dispute some aspects of her job. She needn't have worried.

"How much do you want?"

Michelle looked uncomfortable. "There's usually a ball-park—"

"How much do you want?" Esa repeated, trying not to sound desperate. "Look, you're doing an extraordinary thing, helping us out on such short notice. I want to show you my gratitude."

"Fifteen hundred dollars a week," Michelle said, quoting a price even higher than she was earning with the Karles. "Plus all of the expenses I incur caring for Nell."

"Done," Esa said, immediately feeling lighter.

"I'd love to meet Nell."

"No problem."

Michelle got up from the kitchen table, expecting Esa to do the same. But he didn't move. "Aren't you coming with me?"

Esa looked bewildered as he took another sip of coffee. "Why?"

Michelle stared down at the kitchen floor. She needed a moment to collect herself before answering his asinine question. Finally she raised her head to answer, "To introduce us? So you can observe whether Nell and I are a good fit?"

Michelle couldn't decide whether Esa was unruffled or uncaring when he murmured, "I'm sure the two of you will get along fine. Her room is down the hall on the left." He gave her a small smile and started reading the paper.

Run, Michelle's instincts told her. *Don't take this job no matter how much he'll pay. Run far and fast. This guy's a self-ish, unfeeling idiot.* Which, unfortunately, was all the more reason to take the position. No little girl should have this putz as her primary caregiver.

* * *

Michelle put her ear to Nell's bedroom door, knocking lightly. It was important to respect children's privacy, especially in a situation like this, where the kid didn't know you. Michelle didn't want to overwhelm Nell or put her immediately on guard.

She heard a small voice pip "Come in," so she slowly opened the door. Michelle could tell that Nell had been on her stomach, reading, but was in the process of sitting up now that Michelle had entered the room. *Polite*, Michelle thought.

The first thing that struck Michelle was how gorgeous the little girl was, with gleaming blond hair and big blue eyes that were big enough to contain more than their share of pain. Not a trace of her uncle in her looks.

Michelle introduced herself with a small smile. "Hi, Nell. Is it okay if I come sit on the edge of your bed?"

Nell nodded.

Michelle approached the bed and sat down quietly, extending her hand. "I'm Michelle."

Nell shook her hand, though she did look mildly apprehensive. "My name is Nell."

Michelle cocked her head thoughtfully. "I know. I like that name. You don't hear it very often." She glanced at the book Nell was clutching in her hand, holding it as tightly as another child might hold a security blanket. "What're you reading?"

"*Little Women*," Nell answered reluctantly.

Michelle lit up. "I love that book! Who's your favorite March sister? Mine was Meg."

"I like Jo," said Nell, her clutch on the book loosening a bit.

"How come?"

"Because she has adventures. And no one tells her what to do." Nell looked at her shyly. "Why do you like Meg?"

Michelle sighed. "Oh, because she was beautiful. I was a little envious of her. I was kind of envious of them all, you know? Because I don't have any sisters."

"Me, neither."

"I do have a brother, though, named Jamie."

"My friend Casey has two brothers," Nell shared tentatively. "Nigel and David. David plays football and Nigel is a trainspotter." She wrinkled her nose in distaste. "Their room smells."

Michelle laughed. "Are they teenagers?"

"Kind of. Yeah."

"Teenage boys aren't always the best with hygiene."

Michelle scootched a tiny bit closer to her. "Do you know who I am?"

Nell looked at her blankly. "One of Uncle Esa's girlfriends?"

"No. I'm going to be your nanny! Didn't your uncle tell you I'd be coming here to meet you guys today?"

Nell shook her head. "No." Michelle had been here less than half an hour and already she was making a mental note to tell her new employer that you couldn't just spring stuff like this on kids, especially a kid in Nell's situation. What a jerk.

"Ever had a nanny before?"

Nell's expression turned wary. "No."

"But I bet you know people who have."

"Yes. My best friend Caro Moore, had a nanny."

"What was she like?"

"Lovely. She baked biscuits with us and all sorts of things."

"There's no reason why we can't bake biscuits."

Now she was talking Nell's language. "Honest?"

"Yeah! I'm moving in to take care of you. You'll probably get sick of me!"

Nell looked down at her bed, her index finger slowly tracing the spiral patterns covering the quilt. "I won't get sick of you," she said quietly.

"We'll have to help each other out and get used to each other," Michelle continued kindly.

"Okay." Nell's finger was still following the quilt's designs.

Michelle tapped her fingers on the bed. "You know, I was just thinking about your friend Caro. You miss her, right?" Nell nodded sadly. "Well, there's no reason why you can't call her." *Maybe even have her visit some time. God knows your uncle has the money to spring for plane fare.*

Nell was pop-eyed. "Really?"

"Why not?"

"I'd like that."

"Now," Michelle began cheerfully. "I'll be moving in tomorrow afternoon. In the meantime, could you do me a big favor?"

"What?"

"Could you make me a list of foods you love and hate? And all the stuff you like to do: dancing, writing, anything."

Nell looked thrilled.

Michelle leaned in close, as if imparting a secret. "Do you like nail polish?"

Nell looked at a loss for words. "I guess. I've never worn any."

"I thought it might be fun if tomorrow night, after I'm all moved in, we paint our fingernails and our toenails. What do you think?"

Nell nodded avidly. "I think it'll be fun."

"Oh yeah," Michelle agreed, as if it were a foregone conclusion. "It'll be great."

"Thank you," Nell said politely.

"You don't need to thank me." Michelle stood. "I'm going to leave my telephone number for you on the kitchen counter, okay? That way you can call me if you need me between now and tomorrow." She smiled at Nell. "I think we'll do okay together, don't you?"

Nell's fingers stopped tracing the quilt. "Yes."

"I'll let you get back to your reading. See you tomorrow."

* * *

"How did it go?"

Esa looked up from the sports pages of the *Sentinel* as Michelle reentered the kitchen. He'd actually been feeling anxious about her meeting his niece. What if Michelle didn't think she and Nell were a "good fit"? *If you're being paid enough*, he reasoned irritably, *shouldn't you be able to make things fit*? Well, in any case, he couldn't imagine anyone not liking Nell.

"It went well," Michelle reported. "She's a sweetie."

"Shy, I know, but I think once she gets to know you . . ." He swallowed uneasily. "She's been through a lot."

"I know. I'll take good care of her, I promise."

Michelle's promise prompted a painful moment of self-examination. Had he himself said that to Leslie before taking Nell? Had he even told Nell herself he'd take good care of her? He did remember telling her not to be scared. It seemed enough at the time.

"Do you need any help moving tomorrow?" he asked her. "I can rent a small moving van."

Michelle waved the idea away. "No need. My brother has a truck. I don't have that much stuff, anyway."

"Travel light?"

"You have to in my line of work."

"I promise you that by Monday morning, you'll have your own TV in your room. Also, towels, sheets, and such. If you want to make a list and call me with some items you need, I can make sure they're here."

"Thank you." Michelle glanced once more around the kitchen admiringly before looking back to Esa. "I think that's it. Is there anything else you want to ask me?"

Esa hesitated. "Yes. A favor."

Michelle was puzzled. "Okay."

"Would it be possible for you to unofficially start your job tonight? I have a date, and—"

Michelle laughed curtly. "You've got to be kidding me."

"Why?"

"I'm not here at your beck and call. I thought that was established. I have a life of my own, and I plan on keeping it that way."

Esa was taken aback. "I just thought—"

"That since I agreed to be her nanny, you were free from all childcare responsibilities?"

Esa was embarrassed. "I'm sorry." But inside, he was irked. *I'm allowed to have a life, too*, he thought. *That's one of the reasons you've been hired*.

"Apology accepted."

His miscalculation prompted a shift in Michelle's behavior: she was now all business. "I'll bring over a standard contract tomorrow for us to both go over and sign, if the terms are amenable to you. It'll lay out the duties we spoke of earlier, and some fine details we need to work out."

Esa rubbed his eyes. "That's fine."

"Anything else?"

"Obviously I'll cancel my date tonight," Esa muttered. "Nell and I can stay in and watch a movie."

"See? How hard was that?"

Harder than you know, Esa thought. *The woman I was going to go out with is smokin'.*

"What are you two doing the rest of the day?"

"I don't know." The idea of the hours, stretched out before him, made Esa queasy. "It's so hot outside . . . maybe I'll rent a car and take her to the beach."

"That sounds great." Michelle paused. "Does she have a bathing suit?"

"I don't know."

Michelle's expression changed once again; this time she was looking at him with pity. If anyone else dared look at him like that, he'd kill them dead with viper sharp words within seconds. But in this case, the look was warranted: he *was* pitiful.

"How about this," Michelle said helpfully. "For today, take her to the movies. On Monday, she and I will go through her closet and we'll figure out what she needs. Give me a budget and I'll take her shopping."

Sweet relief. Esa had actually been worrying about whether he'd need to take Nell shopping for clothes. She seemed to have a lot, but what did he know? "That sounds like a good idea. Don't worry about a budget. Just get her what she needs." He paused. "And whatever she wants."

Michelle looked like she was going to say something, but she didn't. An uncomfortable moment passed as she prepared to leave. "I guess I'll see you tomorrow afternoon, then."

"Any idea what time?"

"Is four okay?"

"Four is fine," he replied, walking her to the front door. "Thank you so much."

"You're welcome." Michelle smiled politely. "I'm looking forward to it."

"Me, too—I mean, I'm sure Nell is."

"I know what you meant."

Esa closed the door, experiencing an odd mixture of relief and apprehension. Clearly, Michelle Beck was competent, but she seemed to have an awful lot of demands and requirements. He should have taken care of business when he had the time. Because now, he had one more thing to worry about: suppose he'd picked the wrong nanny?

6

Michelle couldn't stop thinking about Nell as she rode the
Number Seven Subway out to her dad's place in Woodside.
She hadn't been exaggerating when she'd told Esa she was
looking forward to taking care of the smart, shy, slightly dubious little girl; she was. Michelle knew that it was going to take
Nell some time to trust her. She felt there had already been a
few moments when Nell was on the verge of letting her guard
down. Maybe it was just wishful thinking. The minute Theresa told her about Nell's circumstances, Michelle felt an immediate connection with her. When Michelle's own mother had
died, she still had her dad and brother. As far as she could tell,
the only one Nell had was her clueless uncle, Esa.

Michelle reminded herself to cut him some slack. He'd
suffered a huge loss, too, and it couldn't be easy to be a single
professional athlete, and wake up one day and find yourself
responsible for a little girl. Yet Esa's nonchalant attitude was
making it tough for Michelle to feel sympathetic. It wasn't
hard to figure out what was racing through his mind during
their meeting: *Just make this problem go away. I don't know
how to deal with it, and I don't want to.*

Lost in her thoughts, Michelle almost missed her stop. There were a lot of blanks that still needed filling in. She especially wanted to talk to "Aunt Leslie" to find out all she could about Nell. And, of course, there was everything else: packing, moving, unpacking, getting acclimated, getting Nell acclimated, going over the ground rules with Esa Saari. The next forty-eight hours were going to be pressure filled, but Michelle was ready for it. It was, after all, what she'd signed on for.

A sense of optimism and anticipation gave a bounce to Michelle's step as she walked the seven blocks from the subway stop to her dad's place. She did some of her best thinking while walking through Woodside. A cynic might say that was because there was nothing interesting to see in the neighborhood. Okay, so maybe there weren't any grand, historical buildings here worth preserving. And yeah, most of the houses and apartment buildings looked like they'd seen better days. And unlike nearby Flushing with the National Tennis Center and the old World's Fair grounds, there weren't many parks or interesting public spaces. But Woodside was a good place to have grown up in. It was just a solid, working-class community. No pretensions, just lots of people from all different backgrounds and ways of life quietly living together. Woodside had never been gentrified, and probably never would be. No one had ever accused it of being trendy. But Michelle liked that recent arrivals added some spice to the neighborhood. Now you could get any kind of cuisine you were in the mood for. Indian for lunch? Ethiopian for dinner? A Greek cheese pie for dinner? It was all there, along with the V & V, the best bakery in the *world*.

As she walked up Roosevelt Avenue, Michelle texted her brother, Jamie, making sure he was home and not at the firehouse. Jamie's marriage had blown up seven months earlier. His ex couldn't handle the possibility that when she kissed her husband good-bye before he went off to work each day, it might be the last time she'd ever see him alive. Michelle still felt badly for her brother, but her father's reservoir of sympathy seemed to be running out. He'd been complaining that Jamie wasn't looking too hard for new digs.

When she walked in the door she saw her brother, all six feet two inches of him, stretched out on the couch, his thin legs dangling over the side. Michelle gave him a kiss on the forehead. "When'd you get home?"

"A little while ago." Jamie eyed her suspiciously. "Why'd you text me? What's wrong?"

"Nothing's *wrong*. I just need your help with something. Where's Dad?"

"Shopping, I think. He should be back any minute."

Michelle grabbed that day's *Sentinel* from her brother's chest and started fanning herself, flopping down in her dad's favorite recliner. "Jesus, Jame. Could you turn up the air conditioning a little?"

"Dad likes it low. He gets cold now, remember?"

"He's cheap, you mean."

Jamie grinned. "Yeah, that, too."

Growing up, Michelle's girlfriends never failed to remark on how cute Jamie was, which always made her want to heave. But once she and Jamie were older, she could see the reasons for their infatuation: his velvety chocolate eyes, his sweet smile. Since his mood seemed okay, she decided to act on her dad's nudging and pop the real estate question.

"How's the apartment hunting going?"

"Goin' okay," Jamie said evasively. "You know what it's like. Besides, I don't think I should leave. Someone has to be here to look after Dad."

Michelle stopped fanning herself. "Not this again."

Jamie had gotten it into his head that their father needed "looking after"—*their* father, the toughest son of a bitch to ever wield a Halligan at Engine 32—when he'd retired two years ago, after forty-five of breaking his back. Jamie was delusional: their father was as robust as ever. What pissed Michelle off was Jamie's presumption that if their father did need "taking care of," she should be the one to do it.

"Michelle."

"Jamie. He's not even sixty-five yet. He still goes down to the firehouse and hangs out. He still has his poker night. He still goes to see the Mets and the Islanders. Just because he retired doesn't mean he's turned into some feeble old man overnight."

"I see him slowing down. You don't."

"And you live here, and I don't. What would you like me to do about it?"

Jamie looked to be preparing a comeback, but he let it drop. Good thing, too. Michelle didn't want to point out that she'd been the de facto "caretaker" for both him and their dad after their mom died. There had been times her dad leaned on her heavily, maybe a little bit too much, considering she was a child. Part of the problem was, he didn't know how to deal with a little girl's grief. He tried, but he couldn't. And so Michelle figured out a way to go it alone. She wasn't going to let that happen to Nell.

Jamie hopped up and loped into the kitchen, grabbing from the fridge a container of milk that he drank straight out of. "Why'd you need to talk to me," he shouted.

Michelle joined him in the kitchen. "I need to borrow your truck, if that's okay with you."

"When?"

"Tomorrow."

"What for?"

"I took another job as a live-in. They need me to start tomorrow."

Her brother put the carton back in the fridge. "Isn't that kind of short notice?"

"Yeah. But there are extenuating circumstances." She glanced at the dishwasher. The green light was on, meaning the dishes were done, but no one had emptied it. She fought the urge to do it herself. They were grown men.

"I'm all ears."

Michelle laid it all out for him, from Nell's mother's death to Esa's willingness to let her name her price. It was a pretty sad story. But all her brother had to say when she concluded with, "So, can I borrow your truck?" was, "Esa Saari. What a fuckin' showboat."

"What?"

"The guy's a typical Euro winger: all glory and no guts." Jamie was vehement. "The Blades haven't had a decent digger in five years, maybe ten. Probably since Michael Dante hung up his skates. I can't believe my sister is going to work for a Blade."

Michelle rolled her eyes. "I don't care who he plays for. I'm not taking care of him, I'm taking care of his niece."

"I'll help you move in tomorrow. I wanna see his place."

"No."

"C'mon, Michelle."

"Why? So you can tell the guys down at the house about it?"

"Hell yeah. Why else would I want to see it?"

"You're such a pack of busybodies, I swear to God."

"No shit." He scratched absently at the tattoo of his wife's name on his forearm. "Where's your stuff?"

"Most of it's in storage. There's not much."

Her brother slid into a kitchen chair. "I don't know why you didn't just move back here until your next job. Truth be told, I still can't wrap my mind around why you left that gig with the Karles. Moving out to L.A.? Sounds pretty sweet to me."

"This coming from the guy who's on my case about taking care of our father?"

"I'm just sayin'," Jamie muttered.

"I love you, but you are so talking out your ass," Michelle said affectionately. "What, you think I'd be lazing around the pool all day? I'd be *working*—taking care of the kids, and try-ing to remind the Karles that I'm not the maid. No amount of money is worth the aggravation, trust me. And I told you, I didn't want to be that far away from you and Dad—you know, in case Dad magically went senile overnight."

"Fuck you, Michelle."

"I'm just sayin'," she teased. "So—?"

"Yeah, you can borrow it. But only if you let me help you unload it. I'm serious."

Michelle's shoulders sank. "Fine. But not a word out of you. You have to *swear.*"

"What am I gonna say to him? 'The Islanders will always be the class team of New York no matter how many Cups the Blades win'?"

"That's a start."

Michelle heard the key turning in the front door; her dad walked in, carrying two bags of groceries. He had a big smile on his face as he put them down on the table and gave her a smooch on the cheek. "Hey, kiddo. This is a surprise."

"I know." She gave him a quick once-over: he looked his usual, robust self. Jamie was nuts.

"She's a traitor, Dad," said Jamie.

Michelle rolled her eyes while her father looked at her in confusion.

"She's going to be a live-in nanny for one of the *Blades*." He spat the last word.

Her father looked at her suspiciously. "Yeah?"

"Yeah." Michelle and her father started putting the groceries away.

"Which one?"

"Esa Saari."

Her father glanced at her brother knowingly. "The Finnish prick."

"Jesus, Dad!" Michelle exclaimed, overcome with exasperation. "It's not like my job has anything to do with hockey! I'm taking care of his eight-year-old niece."

"I thought you were taking a long break after working for the Karles."

Michelle stood on tiptoes to put the ketchup in the cabinet next to the fridge, where it had been kept for as long as she could remember. "This just kind of fell into my lap. I couldn't pass it up."

"I still don't know why you left teaching," her father said with a frown, dumping a bag of frozen peas and a box of fish sticks into the freezer. "All that education, and for what?"

"I told you why: the money is better, I don't have to deal with school politics or enforced curriculums, and I'd rather have a deep, lasting relationship with a couple of kids than a shallow relationship with an impossibly sized group of them. Class sizes kept getting bigger and bigger. They still are."

"But you were good at it."

Her father was right: she was as good a teacher as you could be when you were responsible for thirty-one first graders. She knew she was cut out to teach from the way her students responded to her with respect and an eagerness to learn, and from the esteem in which she was held by their parents. But even so, it gnawed at her that she couldn't give each child the time and attention he or she deserved, and she didn't like the way everything in the curriculum was geared toward boosting test scores. She enjoyed being in the classroom, but when it came down to the bottom line, the job wasn't fulfilling her in the way she'd hoped, so she left. A lot of her friends thought she was nuts; how could she walk away from a job with tenure? But for Michelle, happiness trumped job security any day. She knew how fleeting life could be; how many things had her mother wanted to do that she never got to because she died young? Michelle knew she was taking a huge risk when she left teaching, but so far, it had turned out to be worth it.

"You living-in?" her father asked.

"Yeah. And before you say it, I know Saari's single, I know he's a dog, blah blah blah. He's also my employer. Don't worry about your poor, helpless daughter living under the same roof as 'the Finnish prick.' I can take care of myself."

"Yeah? You're like the Mayor of Munchkinland next to him," Jamie said. "If he wanted to—"

"He wouldn't," Michelle snapped. Now she was getting pissed. "I've never had that problem before, and I'm sure I won't have it now. I'm sure if I was working for one of the Islanders you'd think it was the greatest thing on earth."

"Pretty much, yeah," Jamie admitted.

Michelle looked at her father.

"Takin' the Fifth on that one, honey."

"You're both such losers."

"Takes one to know one," her brother retorted, the same call and response they'd had since they were little kids.

"What's the kid's story?" her father asked.

Michelle explained Nell's situation. She could see the connection he was making between her and Nell in his eyes. "Sounds like you're the perfect nanny for her," he said quietly.

Michelle squeezed her dad's shoulder. "I agree."

"Once you get to know her, bring her 'round here some time," her father continued. "Let her get a taste of what a real family's like."

"We'll see. That's putting the cart way before the horse."

The idea appealed to her, though. Nell had never had a father or a sibling; she might enjoy seeing what that was like. And God knew her dad's house was a far cry from Esa Saari's oversized Fortress of Solitude. She'd keep it in mind.

~~∿~~

7

~~∿~~

"Wow."

Michelle agreed with her brother's assessment of her new digs as they unloaded the final boxes of books in her new room. Esa had said she'd have her own TV. He hadn't mentioned it would be a wall mounted, picture window sized marvel of technology. Her brother had to close his mouth to keep from drooling. A little overboard, was Michelle's thought. But she wasn't going to complain.

The room was immense, with high ceilings, pale yellow walls and a gleaming wooden floor that looked like it had never been walked on. Maybe it never had. She had her own desk, two tall dressers, and a double bed topped with an amazingly fluffy comforter. She sat on the edge, bouncing a few times, testing it. Hard as a rock, just the way she liked it. She nuzzled her face in the supersized, goose down pillows. Wonderful. She knew she'd sleep well tonight.

"Will this do?" Esa had asked when he first showed her the room. He seemed uncertain, which Michelle had found momentarily charming. Momentarily.

"It's great," she'd replied. What she really had wanted to

do was exclaim, "Holy shit!" The room she'd had at the Karles was nothing compared to this. In fact, she often wondered if they'd taken one of their old walk-in closets and turned it into her room. But she'd never minded. It had been cozy.

The contrast between the two living spaces was further accentuated by her having her own walk-in closet here. Esa caught her smiling to herself, and he looked at her perplexedly.

"There's no way I could ever fill this closet," she explained. "I don't own enough stuff."

"Maybe that will change over time. Who knows?"

Michelle thought he might be alluding to the salary he'd agreed to pay her, but she gave a little laugh anyway. "Believe me: it's not going to happen."

The final space Esa showed her was the bathroom. Again, it was huge, dominated by a deep, white, claw-foot tub. Maybe it was pathetic, but Michelle had always dreamed of soaking in a tub like that. Everyone seemed to have one on TV or in the movies, whether it fit their decor or not. Now she understood why: a sexy bubble bath in a fiberglass tub just didn't cut it. Esa pointed to the two large shell-shaped sinks that were side by side. "You'll share this bathroom with Nell," he explained, pointing to the door opposite hers. "It links your two rooms." He paused. "Is that okay?"

"As long as my privacy is respected when my doors are locked, I don't think it will be a problem," Michelle answered smoothly. "I can't imagine it being one, not with Nell."

For a moment she let her mind wander back into a vision of herself relaxing in the bath, her head leaning back against the lip of the tub. Then she snapped back to reality.

"Where is Nell?"

Esa grimaced. "In her room. I don't think she likes all this moving . . . too painful, maybe?"

Michelle nodded. *Poor kid. She's been pushed from pillar to post. Well, not anymore.* She steered the conversation toward something more positive. "What did you two end up doing yesterday?"

"Yesterday . . . mmm . . ." Esa rubbed his forehead. "You have to excuse me. All the days feel like they're running together for me."

Michelle smiled kindly. "It's easy to understand how you'd be overwhelmed."

"Such a mild way of putting it!" Esa replied with a good-natured laugh. The sound of it echoing off the tiles seemed to momentarily embarrass him. "Ah, yesterday. We didn't go to the beach. As you pointed out: no bathing suit. We actually spent the afternoon at the planetarium."

"That must have been fun."

"Truthfully? It was boring."

Moron.

"And what did you two do last night?"

"I got a pizza—she loves American pizza, that's one thing I'm learning fast—and we watched *Rio*—you know, the movie with the angry birds?"

"Oh yeah, I know it. The last kids I looked after knew all the lines and songs by heart. It started to drive me a little crazy after a while."

"I think she liked it. I don't know. I had some e-mail I had to deal with, so I worked on my laptop while we sat together on the couch."

Michelle didn't say anything, even though she wanted to point out to Esa that right now, Nell needed his full attention when they did something together, not some half-assed gesture that said, "Here's a pizza and a movie, kid, enjoy yourself." She'd already scolded him about his babysitting faux pas yesterday; she hoped she didn't have to do it again. And again. And again.

After showing her around her new living quarters, Esa introduced himself to Jamie, who suddenly turned from Mr. Trash Talk into Mr. Overwhelmed when confronted with Esa in the flesh. Then Esa disappeared, leaving Jamie looking mildly stunned in his wake.

"You going to be okay here?" he asked, looking uncomfortable all of a sudden.

"What do you think?"

"I think you hit the jackpot."

Michelle made a face. "I *am* going to be working."

"Yeah, looks like a real backbreaking job," her brother teased. He hugged Michelle. "Don't be a stranger."

"I won't. Especially since Dad's about to keel over from malaria."

Jamie's smile disappeared. "Seriously, Michelle."

"Jesus, Jamie, I won't. I'll call you in a few days, okay?"

"I'm pullin' doubles all week. Hopefully it'll be busy." He peered out into the hallway. "Guess I'm not gonna meet the kid, huh?"

"Not today," Michelle said, picturing Nell reading in her room. "But soon. I promise."

"Okay, then." Her brother tousled her hair. "I'm off. Talk to you in a few. And keep an eye on Saari. You can't trust those Finns."

"Right. I'll try to remember that."

* * *

After Jamie left, and she'd put away all her things, Michelle went to talk to Nell. She knocked on the bedroom door. There was zero hesitation in Nell calling out, "Come in!"

She was sitting at her desk in front of her laptop.

"What are you up to?" Michelle asked.

"Working on our list."

"Really? Can I see?"

Michelle came over to the computer, and began reading aloud. " 'Favorite foods: McVitie's biscuits, pizza, crisps, chicken, McDonald's, chocolate chip cookies, brownies.' "

"Wow," said Michelle. Nell was going to be pretty disappointed when she found out she wouldn't be eating junk twenty-four seven.

" 'Things I like to do,' " Michelle continued. " 'Play tennis, go to the cinema, read, write, science, playtime, go to the library.' "

"I can think of loads more, if you like!"

It was weird, hearing such a posh British accent come out of a little girl's mouth. Hermione's voice in *Harry Potter* was different; she was a bit of a snoot. But Nell was shy; it didn't fit together somehow.

Michelle smiled at her. "No, this is great! I like all that stuff, too. And watching TV sometimes."

"Me, too."

"Looks like we're a good match, then."

"Yes." Nell seemed to turn a bit shy as she hit the screen saver on the computer.

"Are you all moved in?" she asked Michelle, not quite looking at her.

"Yup."

She looked a little anxious. "For good?"

"Yes, honey, for good," Michelle promised her. The question killed her. She wanted to scoop Nell up into her arms right now and promise her anything, everything. That she'd be loved, and she finally had an adult in her life she could count on. That even though things seemed to suck right now, they would get better. But that would come.

Michelle perched on the edge of the bed. "I'm surprised you didn't come in to help me move."

"I didn't want to get in the way."

"You wouldn't have. Would you like to see my room now that it has all my stuff in it?"

"Yes!"

"C'mon, then." Michelle started through the door in Nell's room that led into their joined bathroom.

"As you know, this is *our* bathroom," Michelle said, making it sound extremely exclusive. "If anyone else uses it, they'll have to answer to us."

Nell's mouth curled into a small, pleased smile.

Michelle led her past the sinks and claw-foot tub into her own bedroom. "Here it is."

Nell stood transfixed in the doorway, her eyes slowly taking it all in. Eventually, they hit on Michelle's bookcase. She looked at Michelle hopefully. "Can I—?"

"Of course."

Nell practically skipped across the room, her fingers carefully brushing the books' spines as she read the titles to herself. Her hair was a tangled mess. Michelle wondered if she'd even tried to comb it out after she showered. Naturally, her uncle hadn't noticed. Nell could probably chop her hair off and Esa wouldn't see it.

Nell looked up at Michelle with disappointment. "A lot of these are boring old textbooks."

"I used to be a teacher."

"Really?"

"Yup."

Nell considered this a moment, then returned to scouring Michelle's books. "You do have a few good ones in here."

Michelle tried not to laugh. "Like what?"

"*Diary of a Wimpy Kid* . . . and *Marley & Me*."

Michelle decided to stick a toe in the water. "I liked *Marley*, but it was so sad when the dog died in the end," she murmured. "I couldn't stop crying."

Nell swallowed and looked down at the carpet. Her body was as still as a beautiful figurine alone on a shelf. Michelle crouched down beside her.

"Nell," she started gently, "I know about your mom."

"Mum!" Nell cried. "It's *mum*, not MOM!"

"Mum," Michelle corrected. "And I know a little bit about how you're feeling: my mom died when I was a little girl, too. So I just want you to know that if you ever want to talk about it, I'm here."

Nell was stone-faced as she rose. "You have a very nice room."

"Thank you. So do you." She tugged on a lock of Nell's hair. "You still want to do our fingernails tonight, right?"

Nell's face lit up.

"Thought so. How about we see what kind of stuff we have for dinner later—what time do you and your uncle eat dinner?"

Nell shrugged. "Whenever."

Michelle took a deep breath. "Let's go in the kitchen and try to figure out a regular dinnertime for you and me and some other stuff we need to get settled, okay? And then we'll do our nails."

"And toenails! Don't forget!"

"That goes without saying."

A lot of things seemed to go without saying. But not for long.

8

"*Esa Saari? Lord-a-me,* girl, you are one lucky bee-yotch."

Michelle rolled her eyes at her friend, Marcus. The two of them, along with their friend, Hannah, were sitting on "their" bench in Central Park. Marcus worked at a dog walking/training/boarding business called "The Bed and Biscuit" for a woman named Delilah Gould, who was married to another one of the Blades, Jason Mitchell. Hannah was a personal chef working for an outrageously rich couple, the Reynauds, who lived in the San Remo, one of the most expensive and exclusive buildings in New York. Michelle, Marcus, and Hannah had become friends a few years back when they found themselves sharing the same days off.

Michelle took a sip of iced tea. "He's totally clueless."

"And totally smokin'," Marcus added, carefully running a hand over his bald, black pate as if he still had an untamed mane of luxurious hair.

"What's that got to do with anything?" Michelle replied. "Not only has he been letting Nell live on junk food, but he's been letting her stay up as late as she wants, *and* he hadn't enrolled her in school yet. I had to do it. Can you imagine?"

"Kinda," Hannah put in. "I mean, he's a pro athlete and a bachelor, and all of a sudden he's got to take care of his little niece? He must be freaking out."

"Well, I wish he'd freak out more eloquently," Michelle grumbled. "Talking to him is like talking to a wall. He just doesn't want to deal. I could say, 'Esa, I'd like to buy Nell a tiger,' and he'd say 'Fine, do it.' He's clueless about setting up boundaries."

Marcus playfully bumped her shoulder. "Screw boundaries, woman! Tell us about his apartment!"

Michelle related the details to her friends with relish. By the time she got around to describing the kitchen, Hannah was groaning with envy.

"Does he even use it?" she asked.

"Doesn't look like it."

"I hate that," Hannah said gloomily.

"Is the kid cute?" Marcus wanted to know.

"Very. Blond hair, biiigggg blue eyes."

"I think it's written in the orphan handbook that you have to be cute," Marcus declared. "Seriously: have you ever heard of an ugly orphan?"

"What about all those kids in *Oliver Twist*?" Michelle countered.

"They weren't *ugly*. They were *ragamuffins*. There's a difference."

Michelle ignored him. "She's got this adorable British accent. And she's so polite. Smart, too. I really lucked out."

Marcus stared at her long and hard. "Uh-oh. Someone's in love."

Michelle felt self-conscious. "So far it's a great fit, that's all." She broke off a piece of a chocolate chip cookie (which she was now rationing with Nell) and popped it in her mouth. "I told her about my mom."

Marcus perked up. "Did she freak?"

"No, Marcus, she didn't 'freak.'" Sometimes Marcus's penchant for drama got to Michelle. "She didn't really react. But I have a feeling the more she trusts me, the sooner she'll open up."

"Is Saari spending *any* time with her?" Marcus asked.

Michelle hesitated. "A bit. Like I said, he just doesn't know how to deal. But it bugs me; Nell's been through enough. I worry about her feeling abandoned by him, too."

Hannah slurped her mochachino loudly. "Have you mentioned this to him?"

"I'm trying to keep it low-key for now. I've only been there a week and a half. I don't want to get in his face too much."

"I'd want to," Marcus sighed longingly. "I'd want to get in his face all day, every day."

Michelle ignored him.

"Where's Nell now?" Hannah asked. "With Esa?"

Michelle shrugged. "I'm not sure. She mentioned something about going with Esa to see his friends Rory and Erin." She took another sip of tea. "She wasn't very happy about not being with me today. I had to explain to her about days off."

"I wouldn't want any time off if Esa Saari was my boss," Marcus purred. "You have to admit: the guy is stunningly gorgeous."

Michelle smirked. "Oh, now he's 'stunningly gorgeous'? 'Hot' no longer covers it?"

"Well, he is," Marcus insisted. "Don't pretend you didn't notice."

"Of course I noticed he was *good-looking*, but I didn't sit there mesmerized, thinking, 'Oooh, look at Esa Saari, he's gorgeous.'" Actually, the thought had crossed her mind, but so what? Noticing attractive members of the opposite sex was simply human nature.

Hannah leaned across Marcus to better address Michelle. "Is he involved with anyone?"

"I think he's involved with a lot of people," Michelle said dryly. "Nell thought I was one of her uncle's 'girlfriends.'"

Marcus looked at Hannah and snorted. "Why, you want her to set you up with him? Dream on, girlfriend. Unless you suddenly sprout titties, long legs, and cascading blond hair, ain't no way that man would even look your way."

"Why do you always have to be such a bitch?" Hannah snapped. She looked at Michelle apologetically. "I was just curious. I wasn't getting at anything."

"I know."

Marcus's bitchiness was over the top, as usual. Hannah was a good-looking woman: chestnut haired, willowy, nice hazel eyes. Guys were always trying to pick her up. But if Marcus's tabloid expertise was correct, the Finn really wouldn't give Hannah the time of day, since she didn't look like a Barbie doll. Michelle found this pretty pathetic, though somehow not surprising.

Marcus eyed Michelle and Hannah. "Is it me, or are we all boring as sin today?"

"I'm not!" Michelle protested. "I told you all about my new job."

Marcus plucked at his lower lip. "True. A job we better *keep* hearing about."

"As if work isn't already seventy-five percent of what we talk about," replied Michelle.

"Get this," said Hannah. "The douche bags called me at three o'clock in the morning because they wanted me to come over and make them buckwheat pancakes."

Marcus looked horrified. "And you *did* it?"

"I had no choice! I'm their personal chef!"

"Yeah, but that's a shitty thing to do to someone," Michelle said indignantly. "What, they couldn't figure out for themselves how to make pancakes?"

"I would never put up with that shit in a million years," Marcus declared. *"Never."*

Hannah smiled mischievously. "Don't worry: I'm going to write a roman à clef one day and they're going to be so, so sorry." She heaved a heavy sigh. "Rich people are so selfish!"

Michelle laughed loudly. "I'm not sure that's politically correct, Han."

"I don't care. It's true. They seem to forget that the people who work for them have lives of their own."

Michelle was forced to concede. "I know." She couldn't count the number of times the Karles had screwed her over, saying they'd be home by a certain time then turning up hours later. Hell, Esa himself knew her less than an hour before asking her to babysit Nell. Michelle feared that might be a harbinger of behavior to come, and committed to always standing up for herself. She'd laid it all out in the contract. But that didn't mean he'd looked at it.

Marcus nudged both Michelle and Hannah in the ribs gently. "Ladies, looks like our boredom is about to end!

Remember I told you about my new friend? Well, he's coming our way."

Michelle followed Marcus's gaze to a brown-haired man with chiseled features who was coming toward them pushing a baby stroller. The baby was a little girl, about five months old, all decked out in pink, from her sun bonnet down to her sandals. The man was smiling, returning Marcus's wave.

"A manny?" Michelle asked.

"Can't you tell? Look at how that poor child is dressed. She looks like a blob of cotton candy with eyes. If he were the dad, his wife would have laid out clothes for the baby. Clearly David is the one who picked out her clothes. Which is a little worrisome, considering."

"Hey."

David stopped at the bench, extending his hand to both Hannah and Michelle to shake. "I'm David."

"I was just telling Michelle and Hannah all about you," Marcus said, flashing a charming smile.

"Good things, I hope."

"Only good things." Marcus regarded Hannah and Michelle. "Hannah is a personal chef for a nightmare couple, and Michelle is the nanny for a little orphaned girl who's being neglected by her rich uncle."

"Marcus!" Michelle said sharply. She shook her head at David as if to say, *That Marcus—you know what he's like.* "Her uncle is a professional athlete who knows nothing about kids in general, never mind an eight-year-old girl."

"You live in?" David asked.

"Yeah. You?"

"With a baby? Yeah." He looked down at the "blob of cotton candy" in the stroller fondly. "This is Abby."

"She's a cutie," said Hannah.

"She is, but she's starting to teethe, so I'm bracing myself for some tears."

"Sounds like you've done this before," Michelle noted.

"I have."

"How'd you get into it?"

"HEL-LO, other people here," Marcus huffed, waving a hand in front of Michelle's face. "Other people who already know this information."

David appeared not to hear him. "Lost my job in construc-
tion. My brother and sister-in-law needed someone to watch
their baby, and I volunteered to do it. I wound up really loving
it. So here I am."

"Yes, here you are," Marcus said sweetly before turning to
Michelle with a glare. Michelle glared back. Geez! She was
just being friendly with the guy.

"There's a group of nannies and their toddlers who meet
Thursday mornings at the playground at Eighty-third and Riv-
erside," Michelle continued. "You should check it out. Best
gossip in town."

David laughed. "I will. Thanks." He crouched down to
check out Abby. She was drooling. He pulled a cloth out of a
baby bag, and gently wiped her mouth. "Yup. Teething definitely on the way."

There was something sweet about a man tending so carefully to a baby, whether it was his job or not. Michelle was
seeing more and more mannies these days. She wondered how
he was with older kids.

"Well, it was nice meeting you," David said. "I really need
to get home and put her down for her morning nap."

"I hate that expression, 'put her down,'" Marcus murmured to Michelle with a shudder. "It sounds like you're putting a dog to sleep." He turned on a bright smile for David. "It
was lovely seeing you again. Hopefully I—we'll run into you
again soon."

David smiled. "That'd be great." He waved good-bye and
strolled away with Abby.

"Isn't he a doll?" Marcus sighed.

"He does seem sweet," Hannah concurred. "Are you going
to ask him out?"

"Maybe. Maybe not. We'll just have to see how it goes."

9

"*Yo, Saari: you* haven't said dick about the new nanny. What gives?"

Esa was sitting at a table at the Wild Hart pub with the usual Rat Pack of teammates: the Mitchell twins, Rory, David, and Ulfie. Tully Webster had passed on the invite, saying he needed to get home because one of his kids had a bad head cold, and his wife needed him to help out. He stared pointedly at Esa as he said it. Esa stared back until Tully broke eye contact. What the fuck? Esa had thought. As if he wouldn't do anything if Nell were sick.

Esa downed some Guinness. "What do you want to know?"

"Is she hot?"

Jason shook his head. "I knew that was the first question you'd ask, man. You're so predictable."

Esa thought a moment. "I wouldn't say she's hot. She's cute."

"Cute can be hot," Ulf persisted. "What's her name?"

Esa was irritated. He wanted to hang out, not talk about Nell's nanny. "Her name's Michelle, and I haven't really noticed if she's 'cute hot.' I've just been trying to let her do her thing. Stay out of her way."

"I had a dog named Michelle once," Ulf volunteered.

Eric stared at him in disbelief. "You make me feel like poking my own eyes out sometimes, you know that?" He reached for a piece of quesadilla in the center of the table. "Why are you trying to stay out of her way, Saari? Attracted to the help?"

"Not my type," Esa stated flatly, which was true. He liked his women tall, blond, and malleable. None of those words applied to Michelle Beck, particularly "malleable." But it didn't matter. She wasn't there as his girlfriend. All he knew was that the feeling of helplessness and chaos that had been dragging him down before he hired her was gone, and that Nell seemed happy. So the attributes Michelle did have—protective, loyal, affectionate, just to name a few—were definitely what Nell needed.

"I put it the wrong way," he amended. "I'm trying to let her establish a rapport with Nell."

Jason snorted. "You mean you've handed the kid over to her so you don't have to worry about her anymore."

Esa was surprised to find himself getting defensive. *"No."*

"So the nanny is cute," said Ulf, determined to stick to that part of the conversation. "Does she have a boyfriend?"

Esa shrugged. "No idea. I don't ask about her personal life."

"She can't have much of a personal life if she's a live-in nanny," Eric reasoned. "How much time a week does she get off?"

"Uh . . ."

Eric smacked his palm down on the table as his mouth fell open. "You're not even sure, are you? Did you even read the fucking contract?"

"What's to read?" Esa replied cavalierly.

"Dude," said Jason, "don't you think you should talk to her about how erratic your hours can be, with road trips and stuff? What if there's a conflict between that and what's in the contract, asshole? Then what are you going to do?"

"She knows what I do for a living."

"But you were interviewing her, dickwad, not the other way around," said Eric. "Don't you think you need to have an actual *conversation* about it?"

"Yeah. I guess." He vaguely remembered Michelle saying

she needed to talk to him about a few things, but she always seemed to catch him when he was walking out the door. He couldn't remember what those "few things" were. Maybe she hadn't gone that far into detail?

"Speaking of talking to each other about things," Rory murmured to Esa.

"What's that?"

"What the hell was that on Wednesday, you dropping Nell off at our flat in the morning because the nanny was off and you wanted to go to Barneys? What would you have done if Erin and I weren't home? Why couldn't you have brought Nell with you?"

"I didn't want her to get bored," Esa confessed.

"There's something to be said for that," said Eric in his defense. "I mean, who doesn't remember being dragged around on errands with their parents? It IS boring."

"That's no excuse," Rory countered. "We all have to do things we don't want to do. So what if she got bored? A little boredom never killed anyone." He glared at Esa. "Don't hide behind the boredom excuse: you didn't want her with you. For those few hours, you wanted to be free as a bird."

"Go fuck yourself," Esa muttered.

"No, you go fuck yourself," Rory countered. "You better sort *all* of it out, Esa, or you're going to find yourself nanny-less, not to mention friendless, pretty fast."

Esa tried maintaining his scowl, but couldn't. Rory was right. He and Michelle needed to be on the same page when it came to Nell. He had to sit down with her. The idea didn't exactly thrill him, but he knew it had to be done.

"I'll speak with her tomorrow night." He had a dinner date, but he was sure he could switch it so he got home early enough to say good night to Nell, and talk to Michelle. It wouldn't take long.

* * *

"These guys are unbelievable," Michelle marveled as she settled down on her bed with a bowl of chocolate chip ice cream to watch *American Pickers*. The stuff they bought and sold always made her wonder if her dad had any hidden treasures around the apartment.

Nell was safely tucked in bed. She'd balked when Michelle set the new "eight thirty bedtime rule." That was the time she used to send seven-and-a-half-year-old Malina Karle to bed, and within minutes, the girl was asleep. The same turned out to be the case with Nell. She and Nell enjoyed a bit of reading before sleep. They were starting *Harriet the Spy*, which Michelle had adored as a kid. It helped relax Nell, which was good, because she was beginning to get nervous about school.

Michelle had just downed her first spoonful of ice cream when there was a knock at her door. She froze. She knew it couldn't be Nell; Nell usually knocked on the bedroom door between their two bathrooms. Which meant it was Esa.

"Yes?"

"May I speak with you, Michelle?"

"Of course," she replied, as mild ripples of resentment waved up and down her body. "I'll meet you in the kitchen in a minute."

Shit, she thought, putting her ice cream down on the night table. Leave it to Esa Saari to want to talk when it was on her watch. Though technically she was responsible for Nell round-the-clock five days a week, her past experience had been that once her charges' parents were in for the night, they more or less took over. But Esa wasn't always home for the evening, at least not early enough to help tuck Nell into bed, and that pissed Michelle off. It seemed irresponsible, almost neglectful.

Granted, there had been times she'd been awake and she'd heard him come in and check on Nell, but it would have been nice if he was there sometimes when she was awake. He'd told Michelle he'd be home early enough to do so tonight. And he wasn't. Thank God she hadn't said anything about it to Nell and gotten her hopes up.

She slithered out of her sweatpants into a pair of jeans, giving her hair a cursory brush. Her terrycloth slippers were a bit ratty, but oh well. There wasn't much she could do about that.

She joined him in the kitchen, where he had just pulled a bowl of blueberries out of the refrigerator. He took a few spoonfuls, then put it back.

"Those are good."

"They are," Michelle agreed.

"Has Mrs. Guttierez been accommodating with all the foods you've been asking her to buy?"

"Very much. I think she's relieved, actually. She wasn't too happy, either, that—" Michelle halted.

"I was feeding Nell badly?" Esa supplied.

"You were feeding her the way a bachelor uncle would," said Michelle politely. "Which is to say, badly," she couldn't resist adding.

"But no permanent damage done?"

Not on that front, Michelle thought. "Not as far as I can see."

"Good, good."

She thought of Marcus's upgraded description of Esa from "totally smokin' " to "stunningly gorgeous." She'd concede he was "totally smokin' " but "stunningly gorgeous" sounded too much like a description of Angelina Jolie.

"Can I get you a glass of wine?"

Michelle gave him an odd look. "Water's fine."

"Yes, of course." Esa looked sheepish. "I'm an idiot. I meant water, but I was just out to dinner and had some good wine . . . I forgot for a moment the, uh, situation."

Michelle didn't know whether to be flattered, or annoyed. He forgot for a moment the situation . . . did that mean he was simply seeing her as a woman, not a nanny? Why would she care, anyway? Marcus's voice hijacked her brain: *Because he's smokin' hot, dumbass! And being noticed by someone who's smokin' hot is major!*

"It's all right," Michelle assured him.

"Do you mind if I have some wine?"

"No, of course not."

Michelle sat down at the kitchen table, quietly watching as he poured himself a glass of pinot noir and some water for her. She found herself wondering where he'd been out to dinner, and with who. Probably one of those busty blondes Marcus said was always on his arm on the gossip pages. Wasn't like she was going to ask him. That was one of her most important rules: private lives stayed private.

"Here you go." He sat down across from her, handing her her glass. "Are you enjoying working in this kitchen?"

"Yes, very much."

"And Nell—is she enjoying what the two of you eat?"

"You should ask her. Better yet, you should join us sometime."

Esa looked away guiltily. "Mmm. I know." But when he turned his gaze back on Michelle, he sounded annoyed. "I told you I wanted to tuck her in tonight. But she was already in bed when I came home."

"Her bedtime is eight thirty, Esa. Not ten thirty. I explained that to you."

"Couldn't you have made an exception?"

"Maybe, if it were the weekend. But it's not. I want her to stick to this schedule on school nights."

"Of course," Esa mumbled.

"You wanted to talk to me?"

"About my schedule."

"Yes?"

"In case you haven't figured it out by now, I'm not someone with a normal schedule. Not only is it not nine to five, but it changes every week in terms of what nights I play. In a few weeks the team will start taking road trips."

"I know that," Michelle replied easily.

Esa looked puzzled. "Did we talk about this already?"

"Well, I've mentioned it to you a few times, but I guess you forgot," Michelle murmured. "I told you: I need your *actual* schedule."

"I'm so sorry," Esa said, rolling his wineglass between his hands as he avoided her eye.

"You're lucky you've hired someone who knows the deal when it comes to hockey schedules. My brother and father are fans."

Esa looked up with a pleased smile. "Blades fans?"

"Islander fans."

"Your brother didn't mention that when I met him."

"Too starstruck."

Esa clucked his tongue. "Islanders fans . . . that's too bad."

"For the Blades, I hear."

"I don't know who your sources are, but take it from me, they're dead wrong," Esa insisted with a playful smile.

"We'll see."

Michelle took a sip of water, buying herself time to return

to professional mode. Banter, teasing each other a bit . . . it felt weirdly off course, somehow. They didn't know each other long enough for that. She'd reached a point of comfort and ease with Mr. and Mrs. Karle, but that was after living with them for two years. And there was two of them, as well as a live-in housekeeper and cook. It wasn't just her and a bachelor.

"About your schedule?" she prodded.

Esa blinked. "Right." He reached into his blazer pocket and pulled out his iPhone. "We just got it finalized. I'll e-mail you a copy. Actually, you can look at it now, if you like."

A minute later he was leaning over her, one hand on her shoulder, showing her his schedule on the tiny screen. Michelle followed his slim index finger as it ran down the weeks. "See? I need you to be flexible."

She took a deep breath. "Esa, I told you, I understand that." Her eyes scoured the schedule. "This is perfect. It'll help me pick my days off. I do insist one of those days is Friday or Saturday, remember?"

"Of course," he said after a split second. Michelle could tell from his ruminative expression he was thinking about how he was going to juggle dates with various women if he couldn't go out both Friday *and* Saturday.

Michelle expected him to immediately return to his side of the table. She held her breath, acutely aware of his body beside her. Instead, his hand lingered for a moment on her shoulder before he removed it and sat back down. "Thank you, Michelle," he said quietly.

"Hey, that's what you pay me for, right?" she replied amiably, more for her own benefit than his. His hand on her shoulder? She liked it. Not enough to really think about it, though.

"Now I have something I need to talk to you about," Michelle said.

"I know, I know. My running here and there," Esa replied with a hangdog expression.

"You really need to spend more time with her," Michelle admonished softly. "I know your schedule is nuts, but you do have *some* free time." She paused. "She starts school a week from Monday."

Esa once again checked his iPhone, then looked up at

Michelle with what could only be described as a "stunningly gorgeous" smile. "I can take her."

"Oh, she's going to be so thrilled!"

"You're coming too, right?"

Technically, there was no reason for her to go if Esa was taking her.

"That's up to Nell. She might like you all to herself."

"But you're the one who went with Nell to tour the school, met with Nell's teachers, dealt with the paperwork, got Nell all the supplies she needed, including her uniform. Of course you have to be there."

Michelle looked at him inquisitively. "Are you afraid of taking her on your own?"

"Of course I'm not," Esa scoffed. "I just thought it might ease her nerves even more if we were both there."

"I see. I'll talk to her and get back to you. Anything else you want me for?"

For some weird reason, the question didn't sound the way it was meant to, as it just hung there in the air for a few seconds.

"I'm fine." Esa stood. "I'll let you get back to what you were doing. Thank you for accommodating me."

Sounds sexual, said the Marcus in her head, in a formal, Finnish kind of way.

"That's my job."

Now you sound like his escort, honey.

"I have practice early tomorrow, but I'll leave Nell a note on the kitchen table, okay?"

Michelle smiled. "She'll like that."

"Good." Esa took a small sip of wine. "Well, good night."

"Good night," said Michelle, hoping he didn't escort her back to her bedroom. Thankfully, he didn't. She was glad to see her ice cream hadn't melted into a creamy puddle as she hopped atop her bed with the bowl in her lap. It didn't matter, though; she'd lost her appetite.

10

Esa wanted Nell to have the best education money could buy, and judging by the tuition for Philips-Jackson, she was going to have it. The fees were astronomical, but according to Michelle, it was worth it. There were girls from all over the world there, so she wouldn't stick out like a sore thumb. In addition, the academics were tough and Nell was smart. The headmaster had promised Michelle that Nell would be "challenged, but not overwhelmed." Esa had been impressed when Michelle showed him the list of extracurricular activities the school boasted. There would be more than enough for Nell to get involved in if she wanted.

The first day of school arrived, along with Indian summer. It was sunny and hot, steamy as only a day in Manhattan could be. He and Michelle would be walking her to school. Leaving the apartment and hitting the street, Michelle had reached for Nell's hand, but she warned her off with a glare that reminded Esa of his sister. "I'm not a baby, you know."

"Got it," Michelle replied. Esa shot her a look over Nell's head. Michelle just shrugged.

"Are you nervous?" Esa asked his niece. Dumbass. Of course she was.

"Not really," Nell replied nonchalantly.

"Well, that's good. I mean, it's okay to be nervous."

Nell looked at him. "I *know* that."

Esa nodded his head stupidly; at least it felt stupid to him. *See? You can't even connect with her on the simplest level. Even the easiest question sounds forced. You should have said good-bye to her at the apartment. You should have left this to Michelle.*

He wanted to tell her how much she looked like her mother, but at least he was smart enough to know that was a dumb idea. Talk about screwing a kid's head up on the first day of school. He knew it would "take time," but he hoped a day would come when she would ask him questions about Danika and what she was like as a little girl. He hated to admit it, but he didn't want to talk about Danika just so she'd be alive in Nell's head; he wanted to talk about Danika to keep her alive in *his* head.

"You know," said Michelle, looking down at Nell with unabashed affection, "I had to switch schools when I was ten, and on the first day, I puked all over my desk."

Nell looked horrified. "That is sooo gross."

"I know. And soooo embarrassing."

Nell was goggle-eyed. "Did people make fun of you?"

"Yep. They called me Michelle Barf for a while, but then everyone forgot about it and things were fine."

"That's good," Nell replied, looking relieved.

Michelle tugged on her braid. "So don't worry about being nervous today, because you're not the only one who's new to the school. I'll bet you anything there's more than one puker in the bunch, don't you think, Uncle Esa?"

"Of course. And nose pickers, too."

"Eeewwww!"

Esa and Michelle both laughed. The silence that collided against the end of the shared laugh made him feel self-conscious. He wondered: would others dropping their kids off at the school assume he and Michelle were Nell's parents? The thought of it almost made him laugh again.

He heard the twitter of the girls before he saw them. The

six-story, ivy-covered school was set far back from the street, down a brick, tree-lined walkway between two town houses. The closer he, Nell, and Michelle drew to the school's court-yard, the louder the twittering. The endless cacophony of high little voices made everything sound so urgent. Esa fought the urge to take Nell's hand. This had to be tough for her. Thank Christ she had Michelle.

Once in the courtyard, Nell stared down at the ground ner-vously. Michelle was giving the premises a careful once-over. "There are tons of girls who are here for the first time," she told Nell. "Tons."

Nell looked up at her. "How can you tell?"

"I was a teacher once, remember? Trust me, kiddo: I can tell."

Nell braved a small smile.

Michelle nodded in the direction of Nell's backpack. "You got everything?"

"Yeah."

"We'll stay here with you until the bell rings."

Nell looked up at Esa. "Will you stay, too?"

"Of course I will," he said, hating that she needed this reassurance from him.

"Good."

Esa made a point of not looking at Michelle. She didn't seem the "I told you so," type, but Nell's question had to make her feel justified in admonishing him to be a greater presence in Nell's life.

Finally, the school bell rang, and girls started filing in, though some looked reluctant. There were a handful of small ones who started to cry and cling to their mothers, or maybe they were nannies.

Michelle looked down at Nell with an encouraging smile. "You ready to roll?"

Nell nodded nervously.

"I could tell," Michelle stage-whispered, looking at Nell with utmost confidence.

Nell looked a little teary. "And you'll be here when I get out of school?"

"Yup. Standing right here."

Esa could feel what was coming next.

"Will you be here, Uncle Esa?"

"I wish I could be, but I can't. I have a game tonight."

Nell's voice sounded very small to him when she replied, "Oh."

Esa found himself madly scrambling to take away his niece's look of disappointment. "Maybe you and Michelle could come to see me play one night. Would you like that?"

"Mmm . . . maybe."

"Just maybe?"

"It looks sort of boring," Nell confessed, making Michelle laugh.

"Well, you just think about it," said Esa.

Michelle drew Nell into a bear hug. "All right, Missy Miss, you better get inside. Remember: I'll be here when you get out."

Nell nodded bravely before letting Esa hug her—briefly.

"Have a good day!" he and Michelle called out in unison, as Nell, back ramrod straight and shoulders thrown back as if she were off to do battle, marched through the front door of the school. Laughing in unison, now talking in unison. It meant they were on the same page. About Nell.

* * *

Sooooo . . . that's that, Michelle thought as she and Esa stood together awkwardly in the school courtyard.

"I think she'll be all right, don't you?" Esa asked.

"She'll be fine," Michelle assured him. "She's a trooper. As you know. It meant a lot to her that you were here today."

"I'm glad."

Did it mean anything to you? Michelle wondered. She supposed it said something that he'd made the effort; after all, he'd rolled in at two in the morning. She'd been up with insomnia, fretting about Nell's first day. That's how she knew. She didn't know what Esa had been out doing, and she didn't want to know, as long as he didn't break his promise to Nell.

The courtyard was clearing out. Michelle readjusted the sunglasses on her face. She couldn't believe how hot it was. If she stood here in the sun much longer, she was going to stroke out.

"Where are you off to now?" Esa asked.

"Home—I mean, to the apartment—"

Esa smiled, pleased. "Which you will think of as your home, I hope."

"I do, it just felt weird saying it. Anyway, back to the apartment. I wanted to tidy Nell's room a bit, and do our laundry."

"Ah."

"You?" she asked. He'd asked her what she was doing. Why couldn't she ask him? She just hoped his answer wasn't "home." It would be too weird doing stuff around the apartment with him there, too. She'd feel compelled to make conversation with him, just like she was doing now.

Esa looked at his watch. Michelle knew it was expensive; the *New York Times* was always running full-page ads for it. She had no idea what the name was. Until a watch was invented that cooked, cleaned, helped get rid of cellulite, and convinced her brother that their father wasn't always one step away from death's door, she was content with using her phone.

"To the gym. Then to lunch with a friend. Then to Met Gar."

Michelle smiled, unsure of how to respond. "I better run." She started away, but then turned back to him. "What time does your game start tonight?"

"Seven thirty. Why?"

"I'll see if Nell has any interest in watching some of it before she goes to bed. She probably won't. It's not like she'd be watching the Islanders, you know?"

Esa laughed lightly. "If I ever catch you trying to brainwash my niece into liking them, you'll be very sorry."

"I see. Well, we'll see how she does with the Blades. But don't be surprised if she chooses to watch *Good Luck Charlie* instead."

Michelle could tell from the blank expression on Esa's face that he had no idea what she was talking about.

"It's a kid's show. One of her favorites."

Esa nodded. Then, almost shyly: "I should probably, maybe, try to find these things out."

"Might not be a bad idea."

Esa looked uncomfortable, running a hand through his black hair. Michelle noticed it was so black it almost bore shades of blue. If anyone asked her about his hair color, she'd say "Raven."

"Look," he said, glancing around the courtyard as if they were spies in danger of being discovered, "why don't we go back to the apartment, make some coffee, and you can tell me all the things I should know about Nell."

"You're kidding me."

"No. I'm not. Why do you look so surprised?"

"Because that's not part of my job, Esa. If you want a relationship with her, you have to find these things out yourself. By spending time with her."

Esa looked pained. "What little girl would want to spend time with her uncle?"

"A little girl whose mother died in a plane crash?" Michelle hesitated a moment, but then put a reassuring hand on his forearm. "I know this has to be hard on both of you. But it's especially hard on her. Think about it."

"I can't read her. One minute she seems to like me, the next she seems detached. I'm not good—"

"Then get good." Christ, she sounded like some irritable old schoolmarm. Some irritable *ex*-schoolmarm. But his "woe is me" stance didn't fit in with a man who had become a successful professional athlete.

"Those are normal reactions for kids who are grieving. She needs *time*."

"Yes, of course." Esa was looking at her with what looked a helluva lot like admiration. "You're very feisty. Do you know that?"

The compliment threw her off balance, and made her realize that she owed him one. He might be inept at coping with Nell emotionally, but he was making damn sure that she didn't want for anything else. He deserved some kudos, didn't he?

"She's lucky to have you." Michelle's cheeks were getting hot and she didn't know why.

"I'm doing it for Danika," he said evasively.

And yourself, Michelle thought, though she'd never get him to admit it.

"Well, whatever your reason, Nell's lucky."

Ugh. She sounded like some puck bunny, fawning over him, worshiping the ground he walked on.

"I better go," she said briskly. "Like I said, stuff to do . . . see you around."

"Right."

She had almost made it to the street when he called out to her. "Michelle!"

She turned around to the sound of cars crawling up the street behind her. She and Esa stood facing each other for a long, uncomfortable moment, like there was an invisible cord between them that neither could see, but both knew was there.

"Thank you," Esa said, just like the other night.

"You're welcome."

She turned back to the street. She had a feeling that "thank you" was his fallback position. Simple, uncomplicated, impossible to misinterpret unless you had an extremely active imagination. There was something else he wanted to say, but didn't. She was glad.

11

It wasn't Esa's night. From the opening face-off, he'd been off his game. He was skating well, but he just wasn't seeing right. Normally, he could see plays developing and anticipate where to go for open ice, and where his line mates would be. But tonight against Boston, it was like there'd been a fog on the ice. He was reacting rather than anticipating. He'd turned over the puck a couple of times in the first period, and as a result, Coach Dante cut his ice time in the second and third. Dante let Esa know about his displeasure in the locker room and on the bench. Luckily, the rest of the Blades weren't off their games. Thank Christ David Hewson was playing well. He almost single-handedly kept the Blades close, standing on his head and keeping the Blades within one of Boston.

With less than a minute left in the game, Boston iced the puck. Coach Dante pulled Hewson and, looking to add an offensive spark and perhaps jolt him out of his doldrums, tapped Esa on the shoulder, sending him out on the ice as the sixth skater. Boston won the draw, but a big hit by Rory in the corner knocked the puck loose. Jason pounced on the loose puck and sent it up the right-wing boards. Esa picked it up at the top of the circles and, sidestepping a stick check, headed to the slot. Esa thought he saw Eric sneaking in from the left wing and threw a backhand pass across the ice. The Boston center had seen the same thing and intercepted the pass. He quickly flipped the puck to center ice, where it was gathered in by a Boston winger who'd broken up ice behind Eric. Once the winger crossed center ice, he wristed the puck into the empty Blades net. The remaining six seconds were an afterthought. The Blades had lost 4 to 2.

* * *

"*What planet were* you on tonight, dick bag?"

Esa gave Ulf the finger as the two of them, along with Jason, Eric, David, and Rory strolled into Finkel's House of Noodles down on Canal Street. Ulf had been bitching lately about being bored with the Wild Hart, so the rest of the Rat Pack had challenged the Swede to find somewhere else to hang out. And what had the idiot come up with? A combination Jewish deli and Japanese noodle house.

"This is unbelievable," Eric marveled. "You really want to hang out in this shithole, Ulf?"

"I seem to remember someone whose hobby was scouring the city for tacky bars with his brother," said David.

"Yeah, *bars*," Eric retorted. "Not restaurants."

"It got a good review," Ulf insisted.

"Where?" Rory asked.

"*PennySaver*," Jason answered.

Esa was too tired to do anything but shake his head sadly.

Finkel's was empty. Not a soul, apart from the waitress and, Esa assumed, a cook in the kitchen. But you never knew: maybe the waitress was the cook.

The waitress, an egg-shaped Asian woman with a dour expression, doled out their slightly sticky, laminated menus as they seated themselves around the one table in the place large enough to hold them all.

Rory glanced around. "No one's been in here since 1945. I can feel it."

"C'mon, guys." Eric looked at his teammates with condescension. "It's obvious what this place is."

Esa frowned. "What?"

"It's a front. Meth lab in the back. Or the meeting place of some secret society."

Jason ran a hand over his weary face. "See, this is why it's bad that we all watch soaps. Especially you, being married to a soap actress. There are all these wild storylines, and you get them stuck in your brain, and then you start coming out with shit like this . . ." He snorted. "Yeah, bro, there's a meth lab in the back. No, even better: an old-timey opium den. The waitress is a ninja who kidnaps young women and sells them to Middle Eastern sheiks."

"Hey, I wouldn't mess with her," Esa said. "She looks like she could poison your food with a look."

His friends laughed, which cheered him a bit. It was a nice momentary diversion that helped take his mind off how distracted he'd been during the game.

Frickin' Ulf had to be telepathic; no sooner had Esa finished the thought than he was back to, "You still haven't answered my question: what planet were you on tonight?"

"Let it go, you asshole," Esa replied. "I already heard it from Dante. I don't need to hear it from you guys."

"It's Nell, isn't it?" Rory asked. "Nanny or no, you're still worried about her."

"Yeah, I am."

Liar, he thought. You're a goddamn liar. It wasn't Nell that had been poking holes through his concentration on the ice: it was Michelle. He was envious of the way she related to Nell. He could never be that way with Nell, and he knew it. He'd have to force it, the way he had been all along. Michelle had told him it was just a matter of spending more time with Nell, but he wasn't so sure about that.

Then there was the issue of Michelle herself. She was cute. Not his usual type, but cute. Mainly though, he liked her personality. She was tough. She was the one in charge in the house, and knew it. That pissed him off a little, since it was *his* apartment and she was his employee, after all. But the truth of the matter was that if someone wasn't supervising everything, it would all go to hell. They both knew that. He hated to admit it, but he was mildly—*very* mildly—intimidated by her. That was new; he'd never been intimidated by a woman in his life. He kinda liked it. What the fuck was wrong with him?

Rory looked mystified. "Why are you worried? From what you told me, Nell had a smashing start to the school year, and she's adjusting well. That sounds like something to be glad about if you ask me."

"Don't get me wrong, I am glad," said Esa. "But . . . it's just a sense I have . . ."

He shrugged, burying his face in the menu to avoid Rory's stare. Nothing got by that Irish bastard. Nothing. Sooner or later, Rory would embark on playing "Poke the Finn until he snaps." Rory was a champion nudger. He'd get it out of Esa eventually. Not tonight. But when he did, this little hiccup in Esa's equilibrium would have long passed.

* * *

"So, how was school today?"

Esa settled down on the couch beside Nell, whose nose was buried in a book.

She looked up at him. "It was okay."

"Anything interesting happen?"

"Nope."

"C'mon, you've been at school for two weeks now," he prodded gently. "Something interesting must have happened in that time. Tell me one thing."

Nell looked up from her book again, thinking, and looking just like Danika, bringing a dull ache to his chest. Lately, he'd been trying to remember the last thing he said to his sister, and he couldn't. Probably just *"näkemiin,"* good-bye in Finnish. They rarely, if ever, said *"rakastan sinua,"* I love you. They just weren't brought up that way. He wished it had been different. He wished they'd said it more, and he wished he'd spent more time with her.

"Well," said Nell with a deep sigh, as if unloading an immense burden, "we had a science quiz and I got a ninety-two."

"That's great."

"I suppose."

She went back to her book. Esa sat there beside her, feeling hapless, treading water. How should he keep the conversation going? Get more detailed answers out of her? Maybe he'd ask her what the book she was reading was all about. But that might make her feel like she was doing an oral report. Tully Webster was right: he had no idea how the hell to take care of her. Ten minutes passed in torturous silence; at least it felt "torturous" to him. Nell seemed deep in her reading. Esa had a feeling he could set his legs on fire and she wouldn't notice until the last minute. He passed the time answering his e-mail, doing his best to ignore Lou Capesi's barrage telling him he should do such and such charity event. It was only a matter of time before the fat bastard started trapping him after practice.

Esa started getting squirrely. It was eight thirty; shouldn't Michelle be hanging out on the couch with Nell by now? He had important stuff to do. He'd gotten an e-mail from two Victoria's Secret models who were waiting for him right now at the Plaza. His mind flew back to him and Rory walking up that pitiful, backward High Street in Rory's hometown of Ballycraig two summers back. He'd told Rory he was ready for a "real" relationship. He must have been drunk.

Esa was on the verge of inappropriately knocking on Michelle's bedroom door when she appeared in the living room in a lovely sleeveless shirt that showed off toned biceps, and a pair of pencil thin jeans. She was wearing makeup. And a smile.

"How do I look, Nell?"

Nell's face lit up. "Really, really pretty, Michelle."

"Thank you." She came to the couch and kissed Nell's cheek. "Have fun tonight. And if you decide to play your uncle in Wii bowling, don't humiliate him too badly."

Esa felt the synapses in his brain short circuiting. A stroke? All he knew was that Michelle's words weren't making any sense.

He rose from the couch with a strained smile. "Michelle, can I talk to you in the kitchen for a moment?"

She looked at him quizzically. "Sure."

Esa followed her into the kitchen. She was leaving a trail of very delicate perfume in her wake. It was nice. At least his brain could still react properly to that.

"Is everything okay with Nell?" she asked worriedly.

"Everything's fine."

Michelle looked confused. "Then what's up?"

"I was wondering where you were going."

Michelle looked taken aback. "Where I go on my nights off is none of your business, Esa."

"Right, of course, I'm sorry," he backpedaled. He knew she was right; he just couldn't remember the conversation.

"Is there a problem?"

"No, no problem." *Except my night is fucked.* "Do you think you'll be in late?" *Maybe he could tell Didi and Monique to wait for him.*

Michelle tilted her head, looking at him as though he was some sort of enigma she was trying to figure out. "You forgot," she finally said.

"What?"

"You forgot it was my night out. Even though I made that giant calendar for all of us to look at whenever we wanted. You forgot it was my night off. You made other plans."

He couldn't quite meet her eye. "Guilty."

He could tell Michelle was holding back her temper. "When will you understand that it's not all about you anymore?"

"I know, I know."

"Do you?" Michelle asked sharply.

Esa's eyes locked onto hers. "Yes, I do."

The air between them shimmered, intensified. Esa felt like he was in a staring contest.

Michelle broke contact first. "We're on the same side, you know," she said quietly.

"Of course," Esa agreed, but the feeling of his brain misfiring was returning.

Michelle smiled awkwardly. "I should go."

"You look very nice," said Esa. "Date?"

"Maybe. It's—"

"None of my business," Esa finished tersely.

"Bingo."

"Well, whatever it is you're doing, I hope you enjoy your evening. You deserve it. You work very hard."

Michelle blushed. "Thank you."

"Yes, well . . ." Esa glanced around, not sure where to look. This was fucked up; he was acting like some pussy schoolboy who didn't know how to talk to women—looking around, words trailing off, awkward. He was glad Rory wasn't here. His reputation would be ruined.

Even more pathetic was how confused he was feeling. The thought of Michelle going on a date irked him. It didn't make sense. That was a lie. He didn't want it to make sense, because it was laughable.

Once again Michelle was the one who broke the awkwardness. "I've really got to go. I don't want to be late. Don't let Nell scam you into letting her stay up *too* late."

"I won't." He forced a smile. "Have a nice evening."

"You, too."

Esa remained frozen in the kitchen, listening as Michelle and Nell exchanged good-byes. He heard the front door open and close, and then there was no sound but the constant hum of the refrigerator. Nell was still out in the living room, turning pages. Esa pulled out his cell, shaking off the temporary madness of even giving a shit about Michelle's night. He forced himself back to being annoyed about having to turn down a night of fun and frolic. Next time he'd be sure to check the big calendar. But for now, he was screwed.

12

"Michelle?"

Hearing her name tugged Michelle out of her reverie; worse, it embarrassed her. Here she was, in a nice wine and cheese bar with David, the manny, and all she could think about was the displeasure on Esa Saari's "stunningly gorgeous face" earlier in the evening when she'd intimated that she might be out on a date. She shouldn't care. But she did. She liked the way it made her feel, even if it was just momentary: like she was attractive. She hadn't felt that way in a long time, despite the good-looking man sitting across the table from her.

"Sorry. You know what it's like being a nanny: your mind keeps getting pulled back to kid stuff, even when you don't want it to."

David nodded sympathetically. "I hear ya."

Michelle had been surprised when David called and asked her out for a drink. Her first thought had been that he wanted info about Marcus. But as they stayed on the phone chatting a bit, it dawned on her that he was asking her out because he liked *her*. It had nothing to do with Marcus, because David wasn't gay. She accepted his invitation. Now she wondered if it was the right thing to do.

After spending a few hours with him, Michelle could already tell he was one of those guys about whom people said, "He's a total catch." Meaning that in theory, as a single woman who one day hoped to alter that state, Michelle should be feeling like she might have landed the big one. Yet she didn't.

It was fun swapping war stories with him. But in the back of her mind remained the specter of Esa, the way he'd looked at her, and the tightness in his voice when she'd told him it was none of his business what she was up to tonight. Maybe he disliked that she might be out with another man. Michelle liked that.

There was something about Esa's vulnerability where Nell was concerned that tugged at her. Even though he was so damn clueless sometimes it made her want to strangle him, it also made her want to help him, for Nell's sake.

David took a sip of wine, his expression mildly perturbed. "Is everything okay?"

"Yes, of course. Why do you ask?"

"You just seem *really* preoccupied."

"No, it's just . . ." She realized she could get away with a half truth, at least. "I feel guilty about this. Marcus thinks you're gay, you know."

David groaned. "I was wondering about that."

"He's been planning to ask you out. I don't feel it's my place to tell him he's misread you."

David bit into a cracker with cheese. "No, of course not."

God, Michelle thought, he is such a good guy. Not a moron, like Saari. Not a dog, like Saari. Not an egomaniac, like Saari. You should be attracted to David. But you're not. What the hell is wrong with you? Instead you're thinking about a self-centered jerk. Admit it: clueless as Uncle Esa is, he's hot. And there is some kind of sexual tension there. It could be because she held more power in the house than he did. Or it could be the stirrings of a general attraction. Which didn't matter, because it could never, ever be acted on. She could lose her job. Worse, she would lose her self-esteem. Assuming she wasn't imagining things. Which she didn't think she was.

Christ, another rude reverie. Snap out of it. She pinched

her own thigh, hard, and she was back at the wine and cheese table. And there was David, across the table, looking at her with amusement.

Michelle shifted in her seat uncomfortably. "What?"

"You're really, really off somewhere else in your head tonight, aren't you? And it has nothing to do with nanny stuff, or Marcus."

Michelle grimaced guiltily. "I'm sorry."

"Need to talk about it?"

Yeah: I'm developing a crush on the loser I work for.

"No, I'll be fine."

"I have an idea."

"What's that?"

"Let's finish up here, then go hit a movie. Something totally mindless where we can escape for a few hours. Might make you feel better."

"Yes, let's," said Michelle, liking the idea. She wouldn't have to talk. She could let images and sounds just wash over her. Drown out the stupidity. She liked David. And if she spent more time with him, it could wind up being something more. Couldn't it?

* * *

"Excuse me. Who the hell are you?"

Michelle's guts constricted when she returned from the movies to find Nell laughing and playing Wii bowling not with her uncle Esa, but with some towheaded, brick shit house of a man whose biceps were bigger than Nell's head.

"It's Uncle Ulf!" Nell called out distractedly, pumping her fists in the air at the sound of electronic bowling pins going down. "Strike!"

"Way to go!" said "Uncle Ulf." He closed his hand and fist bumped Nell's.

"Uncle Ulf," Michelle said in an overly calm voice as she took off her coat, "I still don't know who you are."

"I'm Esa's teammate." He extended a hand to her as Michelle walked into the living room. "Very nice to meet you."

Michelle barely shook his hand. "Where is Esa?"

"He had some things he had to attend to," Ulf replied vaguely. "I've told him before that I don't mind babysitting, so he called me." He glanced down at Nell affectionately. "We've been having a good time, haven't we?"

Nell nodded fervently.

The back of Michelle's head was about to blow off. "Nell, have you met Uncle Ulf before?"

"Well, no, but, I know he plays hockey with Uncle Esa and he already knows how to play Wii bowling . . ." She looked at him smugly. ". . . even though I'm better."

Ulf narrowed his eyes competitively. "We'll see."

Nell looked so happy Michelle almost felt guilty pointing out that it was way past her bedtime. "Someone's up very late tonight," she teased.

Nell looked stricken. "Am I in trouble?"

"Of course not. It's been kind of a special night, Uncle Ulf being here and all."

"Can we can play one more game?" Ulf implored, sounding like a child himself.

Michelle stared at him, not quite knowing what to make of this. "Actually, Nell's got to get to bed now."

"Pleeease?" Nell begged. "Just one more."

"Nope." Michelle stood firm. "It's time for Uncle Ulf to go, and for you to hit the hay. You're going over to Selma's tomorrow morning to work on your science project, remember?"

Nell's shoulders slumped. "Okay."

Ulf patted Nell's head. "We'll play again soon, I promise."

Nell perked up. "Cool."

"Night, Nell."

"Night, Uncle Ulf."

"I'll be in in a minute to tuck you in, okay, kiddo?" Michelle said to Nell.

"Yup."

Once Michelle was sure Nell was in the bathroom brushing her teeth, she rounded on "Uncle Ulf."

"Where the hell is Esa?"

Ulf squirmed. "Like I said, he had stuff to do."

"Really? Did it involve gin and the use of condoms?"

Ulf looked sheepish. "Well, you know, guys like to help each other out . . ."

"So—what? He called you and said he wanted to get laid, and you came over and he just *left*?"

Ulf winced, putting his hands over his ears. "Your voice is getting squeaky."

Michelle took a deep breath, composing herself. Whenever she was really upset, her voice went up in pitch. Her brother used to call her "Minnie Mouse" when they fought.

"Sorry," Michelle said very deliberately, trying to take it down a peg. "Can you tell me what happened?"

"Nothing 'happened.' Saari called me. I came over, he hung out with me and Nell for a while, and then he split."

At least he didn't just leave her the minute Ulf arrived, Michelle thought. How considerate.

"Where did he tell Nell he was going?"

"Dinner. With a friend."

Idiot. Idiot, idiot, idiot.

"She seemed cool with it," Ulf added.

"Well, that's lucky for Esa, isn't it?"

"He said he wouldn't be gone long," Ulf said, as if this was somehow a point in Esa's favor.

"Nice of him."

Michelle forced another deep breath through her nose. It was wrong of her to take out the rage she was feeling toward the world's crappiest uncle on this Ulf person, who'd clearly enjoyed himself, and whose company Nell had clearly enjoyed as well.

Michelle stretched her neck to one side, then the other. "Look, I'm sorry I sound so angry. I'm just surprised."

"As long as it's not my ass being chewed out, I'm fine." He gave her the once-over. "How was your date?"

"*What*?" Maybe it wasn't wrong to direct some anger at this Swedish hulk after all.

"Esa said you were on a date."

Michelle tightly clasped her hands together in front of her. "Esa's talking out his—I don't know why he would think that."

Ulf wiggled his eyebrows suggestively. "So you're not seeing anyone? Ever been out with a hockey player?"

"It's none of your business, and it's also beside the point. I would never go out socially with one of my employer's friends."

"I'm not Esa's friend. I'm his teammate. The guy's a total douche if you ask me."

"Let's just call it a night, okay?"

Ulf deflated. "Yeah, all right."

"Thanks so much for watching Nell."

"Hey, anytime. The kid's great. A real kick-ass Wii player. I told her next time we hang out, I'll show her a couple of magic tricks."

"Sounds great," said Michelle, hoping he would take the hint to leave as she swung the front door open wide.

"I'm pretty good."

She gritted her teeth. "I have to get Nell to bed now."

Ulf nodded. "Tell Saari to call me tomorrow. I wanna hear about Didi and Monique."

"Yeah, I'll do that," said Michelle, practically shoving him out the door. "Thanks again."

She locked the door, furious. Which was it? He wanted to get closer to Nell, and he understood it wasn't just about him anymore, or he was just paying lip service to that and had no intention of stopping sleeping around? What. A. Jerk. Michelle fumed.

Well, if he thought he was getting away with this one, he had another thing coming.

13

"*Hi! How was* your night with Didi and Monique?"

Michelle hoped the sound of her voice ringing out in the pitch darkness scared the shit out of Esa as he walked through the front door at two a.m. She didn't hear him gasp, but there was a sudden tear in the air that let her know he'd heard her.

She'd been absolutely livid over the "Uncle Ulf" episode. *Livid.* Ulf seemed nice enough, but that wasn't the point. The point was that Esa Saari talked out both sides of his mouth, and it was bullshit. Nell deserved better.

Michelle knew she could have waited until morning to talk to him, but her fury was eating her alive, leaving her unable to sleep. She thought: why not just get it over with? Maybe it wasn't nice to ambush the jerk this way, but she didn't care. It wasn't nice of him to leave Nell on a night he'd promised to spend time with her.

Esa flipped the light on, walking slowly toward the living room, smiling like a handsome, clearly buzzed jackass.

"Aw, Michelle. You didn't have to wait up for me."

"I didn't think this could wait."

He threw himself down on the couch next to her. "How was your night?"

"It was fine. Yours?"

Esa smiled slyly. "Memorable."

"I'll bet." God, what a *jerk*. "What happened to hanging out with Nell?" she asked. "What about that conversation we had where you claimed to realize life wasn't just about you anymore?"

"I couldn't get out of this appointment."

"Bullshit, Esa. How hard is it to pick up the phone and tell Dodo and Mickey or whatever their names are that you have to take a rain check?"

"You don't understand."

"No, you don't understand."

Esa snorted. "I understand one thing."

"What's that?"

"I'm tired of you telling me what I'm doing wrong."

Michelle's mouth fell open. "How—"

Esa crushed his mouth to hers. Michelle struggled, but her attempt was halfhearted. The jolt of it, the way he'd lunged at her like an animal, was so thrilling that for a few stunned seconds Michelle's indignation disappeared. But when it returned it was stronger than ever. She shoved him away.

"How dare you?" she sputtered.

"It was the only way I could think of to get you to shut up for a minute."

Liar, she thought. *I should quit on the spot. That would teach him a lesson.*

Esa collected himself. "I'm sorry. That was inappropriate."

"Very."

"But don't you think waiting up to ambush me is inappropriate as well?"

Michelle knotted her hands in her lap. "I was furious, Esa. I'm still furious. About the message your actions sent to Nell."

"You could have been furious at me in the morning."

"I couldn't sleep," Michelle shot back. "And I wanted to talk to you about it before you saw Nell."

"Can I ask you something?"

"What?" Minnie Mouse was threatening to overtake her vocal chords. Michelle had to be careful.

Esa looked amused, which pissed her off. He thought this was a big joke?

"Do you always sound like a schoolteacher?"

"I don't always sound like a schoolteacher."

"You do when you talk to me. Do this, don't do that—"

"Because you don't pay attention!" Michelle reddened, realizing that she sounded *exactly* like a schoolteacher. Well, whose fault is that? "You say one thing, then do another. You say you want to get closer to Nell, but then when there's an evening planned for you two to spend together, you hand her off to your friend."

"I didn't know tonight was one of my nights with Nell."

"Because you don't pay attention," Michelle repeated gently. "If you'd checked the calendar—if you'd checked with me—you would have known that. But you didn't. How am I supposed to interpret that?"

"That I'm busy?"

"No, that you don't give a damn. You don't want to look at the calendar, or talk to me about schedules, because that makes it too *real*."

"Makes what too real?"

"The fact that Nell is here *for good*. That you're not going to wake up one day to find it's all been a bad dream and you can just carry on being who you were—who you are: someone with no responsibilities!"

"You don't know what the hell you're talking about," Esa snapped.

Michelle changed the subject. "You owe Nell an apology. She was excited about spending tonight with you."

Esa looked ashamed. "I'll apologize to her in the morning. And again, I apologize to you, for, you know—"

"Never happened," was Michelle's curt response.

Esa nodded, though Michelle swore that he looked insulted for a split second. *Oh, right, the great Esa Saari. Any woman he kisses should feel grateful. Jerk.*

Michelle turned her full attention to him. The fight in him, if you could call it that, was fading. Now he just looked like a man who was damn tired. But that didn't mean she was going to let Golden Boy off the hook.

"You asked me a few things," she said. "Since I'm such a bossy schoolteacher, mind if I *tell* you a few things?"

Esa revived a little with an amused smile that infuriated Michelle. "Go on."

Michelle rose. "I will make your life miserable if that's what it takes to make you give Nell all the love and attention she deserves from you. I swear to God, if you keep letting that kid down, I will kick your ass so hard you won't be able to sit for a week."

"I could fire you for talking like that to me. You realize that, don't you?"

"Go ahead," Michelle replied without hesitation. "Fire me." He thought he could play the power card with her?

"Of course I don't want to fire you," Esa murmured. "It's just that I've always chafed when it came to people telling me what to do."

"That must make for some hard times for your coach."

"It has in the past, not anymore."

"Just to keep you in the loop, Nell is going to her friend Selma's house tomorrow to work on a science project. She's staying there for lunch, and then, if it's all right with you, I thought I'd take her to meet my brother and dad. She said she'd like to see where I grew up. I thought it might be fun for her to be around a family. I'll have her back whenever you want, and then you can go out and do whatever it is you do."

"Michelle."

She closed her eyes, steeling herself for another hassle. "What?"

"Why don't I spend tomorrow night with Nell since I fucked up so badly tonight? You can do . . . whatever it is *you* do. It seems only fair."

"Deal."

*   *   *

After Michelle had dropped Nell off at her friend Selma's house, she had a few hours free to spend with Marcus and Hannah in the park. Unable to stop herself, she told them about Esa kissing her.

Marcus's eyes, normally bleary even at this late hour of the morning, sparked to life. "My, my."

"It didn't mean anything," said Michelle, shrugging it off.

He looked at her down the length of his nose. "Then why did you tell us about it?"

"Because it was just so weird."

"Weird how?" Hannah pressed, sucking down some Red Bull. "Good weird or bad weird?"

"Bad weird. He was tipsy."

"Which means he had no inhibitions, which means he was doing something he wanted to do," said Sherlock Holmes, aka Marcus.

"Men will lunge at a tree trunk when they're drunk, Marcus. As you know, this is a gorgeous man who bags models on a regular basis. I doubt it was something he 'wanted to do.' "

"How long did it last?" Hannah asked.

"I don't know!"

"Tongues?" Marcus demanded.

"No." Michelle was getting warm just talking about it. She shouldn't have told them. But it had plagued her the rest of the night. It wasn't a drunken sloppy kiss, it was skilled. If it had been drunken and sloppy, she would have pushed him away right away. But she didn't. And if she found the idea of him kissing her so awful, she would have pushed him off then, too. But again—she didn't. Soooo . . .

"It just disturbs me," she went on, "because there's an employer/employee boundary—"

"Oh, shut up, Michelle." Marcus looked bored. "He kissed you. It affected you. Now what?"

"We agreed it never happened."

"Good idea," said Hannah.

"I know. But it's still going to be awkward."

"You didn't see him this morning?" Marcus asked.

"Briefly. He came into the kitchen, grabbed some coffee, told Nell he had something fun planned for tonight, promised her he wouldn't be 'a dick' and let her down, and left to go practice. I wish he wouldn't say things to her like 'dick.' I did scowl at him on that one."

"And what was her reaction? Not to the word 'dick'—to

her suddenly magnanimous uncle promising her a night of fun?" Marcus continued sourly.

"She told him she'd rather be with me tonight," Michelle said, feeling slightly guilty. "Not in a mean way. Just—straightforward."

Hannah looked philosophical. "Well, it's his own fault."

Marcus tapped his lower lip. "So where does this leave our little Michelle?"

"In charge."

"What if he tries to lock lips again?"

Michelle snorted. "He won't."

"But what if he does?"

"Then I'll say, 'I'll quit if you do that again,' and that'll be the end of it. I mean, it is harassment."

"You'd never quit," said Hannah. "You'd never leave Nell."

"Even if her uncle makes working there impossible?" Michelle countered.

"Let's wait and see what your definition of 'impossible' turns out to be," Marcus said with a purr.

"As always, you are the biggest jerk on the planet," said Michelle.

"And damn proud of it."

* * *

"This is a lot different than the Tube."

Nell's face was alight with curiosity as she sat with Michelle on the subway. She seemed to have had a great morning. When Michelle picked her up from Selma's she was grinning. Selma's mother remarked on what "a lovely, polite little girl" Nell was, mentioning that she'd heard whisperings of a sleepover at some point. Michelle had no problem with that.

She looked down at Nell. Her eyes were scouring every inch of the subway car. "How's it different?"

Nell crinkled her nose. "Dirtier, I think."

Michelle laughed. "You're probably right."

She was glad her dad had come up with the idea to take Nell to meet them. Nell had no siblings, and had never known her dad. And lately, she'd shown a lot of interest in Michelle's childhood. Michelle sensed it wouldn't be long before they'd be talking about their mothers.

They were walking from the train station through Michelle's old neighborhood when Nell looked up at her and asked, "Were you poor when you were little?"

The question caught Michelle completely off guard. The answer was no, but seen through Nell's eyes, she could understand how she could think that. Nell had grown up in one of the most exclusive areas of London, and now she lived in an exclusive part of Manhattan. Another reason bringing her out to her dad's was a smart move: she'd get to see that not everyone in the world moved in the privileged bubble of the wealthy.

"I wasn't poor," Michelle answered breezily. "Just regular."

Nell nodded, but Michelle wasn't sure if she completely understood.

Michelle felt Nell tense when they boarded the elevator up to her father's apartment. "Don't be nervous," Michelle whispered in her ear. "My dad's a big ole teddy bear and my brother is kind of a doofus. Do you have a slang word for that in British?"

"Wally," Nell supplied with a giggle. "He's a wally."

Michelle opened the apartment door, greeted by a familiar scene: her brother was watching TV. She could hear her dad moving around in the kitchen.

At least her brother sat up when Michelle and Nell entered, his trademark boyish smile sliding into place. "Hey, you must be Nell. I'm Jamie." He held out a hand for her to shake. Nell hesitated, then shook his hand, if you could call it that. They barely skimmed palms.

He leaned forward toward Nell, rolling his eyes. "Michelle boring you to death yet?"

Nell looked at Michelle uncertainly.

"He's teasing. But you can answer him any way you want, Nell."

"Michelle is never boring!"

"Just give her time."

Her brother gestured at the TV. "You guys ever watch *Swamp People*? It's fu—awesome. These guys wrestle alligators and shit."

"He cursed," Nell whispered to Michelle.

"Yes, I know," Michelle said, "but he's not going to curse again, are you, Jamie?"

"Try not to. Sorry, Nell." He smiled encouragingly. "You wanna watch gators with me?"

"They scare me." Nell moved closer to Michelle.

"Me, too," said Michelle.

"Yeah? So what do you two like to watch?"

"*The Simpsons*," Nell answered happily. "And sometimes I watch *American Pickers* with Michelle."

Jamie nodded approvingly.

Nell was giving Jamie a careful once-over, which made Michelle happy to see. It meant she was interested, slowly shedding her feelings of being intimidated. "You're a fireman, right?"

"Yep. Our dad was, too. Speaking of which"—he looked at Michelle pointedly— "Dad's blood pressure is really high."

"It's always been high, Jamie."

"I'm just sayin'," Jamie sniffed.

"Can I see the firehouse sometime?" Nell asked shyly.

"Sure. It's got a pole you can slide down. You'll love it."

"Sweet," said Nell. Michelle stifled a laugh. Hearing Nell use American slang in her upper-class accent was amusing.

"What? I have to wait in here forever to meet Nell?" Michelle's father called out from the kitchen.

"SOB's as impatient as ever," Jamie muttered.

"Why would he change now?"

Michelle tussled Nell's hair. "Wanna meet my dad?"

Nell looked a little nervous. "Okay."

Michelle squeezed Nell's shoulder reassuringly. She sniffed the air. "I think he's baking some cookies."

"'Cause that's really good for his health, too," Jamie said under his breath.

"You need to stop fixating on Dad's health," Michelle said quietly. "It's driving him nuts, and it's starting to drive me nuts, too. So can it."

Michelle brought Nell through to the kitchen. She was right: a plate of chocolate chip cookies sat on the counter.

"Hey, there's the little girl I've been hearing so much about." Michelle's dad slipped off his oven mitts, extending a hand to Nell. "Ed Beck." He glanced at the stove behind him. "You like chocolate chip cookies?"

"*A lot*," said Nell.

"Whaddaya say we have a few with some milk?"

Nell nodded avidly.

He pulled out a kitchen chair for her. "Here, have a seat."

Michelle looked at her father. "Sure, don't pull one out for me or anything."

"Guests get the best," her father teased as he joined Nell and Michelle at the table, splaying his hands in front of him. "So, Nell. How's life treatin' ya?"

"Dad," Michelle said under her breath.

Nell seemed to entertain the question seriously. "Pretty well."

"Glad to hear it. You like school?"

"I guess," Nell mumbled.

"Everyone hates school at the beginning of the year. Then by the time you break for summer, you'll be sad." He jerked his head in Michelle's direction. "I bet by now you're finding out she's a pretty good cook, huh?"

Nell smiled.

"Gets it from her mom."

For a split second, it seemed the wrong thing to say. But Michelle's father, thank God, just rolled on. "Gets her crankiness from me."

"Michelle's not cranky!" Nell protested.

"Yeah? Wake her up real early in the morning and see what happens." Now he clasped his hands together before him, folding them on the table as if he were interviewing Nell. It was hilarious.

"Now, Nell, if you don't mind me asking, what are your long-range plans?"

Instead of looking mystified, Nell really seemed to be enjoying this.

"Well," she said very solemnly, "I'd like to go to university one day."

"For what?"

Nell blushed a little. "For English. I want to be a writer."

"A terrific choice." Michelle's dad reached behind him for the plate of cookies, placing it in the center of the table. "Here's the thing, kid," he said, biting into one. "College can sometimes wind up being a big waste of time. Look at Michelle here: four years, and for what? You want to wind up like her, smart as hell but all alone? Take it from me: skip college, get married, and have a family. You'll be a helluva lot happier."

Nell looked confused.

"He's *joking*," Michelle assured her, which of course, he wasn't. He might have said it in a jesting way, but there was no mistaking the subtext. Her dad, after some convincing, had started out proud she'd gone to college, but that faded fast when she opted for being a nanny. "How are you gonna meet men?" he lamented over and over. As if that was what mattered.

"She's a bit young to be thinking about stuff like that, Dad," Michelle said.

"Never too young to dream about your future if you ask me. Now," he said, looking around the table with a big smile, "who wants milk?"

14

"It's okay, Nell! Don't be afraid."

Esa stood in the apartment doorway of his teammate Jason and his wife, Delilah. He thought it might be fun if Nell came over and met Stanley, Jason's big, black Newfie, as well as the couples' three other dogs (though Jason was always quick to point out they were *Delilah's* dogs first): Sherman, an aging golden retriever; Shiloh, a cairn terrier who was too "yippy" for Jason's liking; and Belle, an old, white, half-blind mutt whom Jason pretended to find annoying. Nell hadn't grown up with any pets, and Esa had noticed that her eyes always followed people who were walking their dogs down the street. Going over to Jason's was the perfect solution: Nell would get to meet cool dogs and he could hang out with Jason.

It was impossible to open the door at Jason's and not find Stanley already there, standing behind his human companion in all his goofy, slobbering majesty, his big brown eyes always on the lookout for love and affection. But Esa had forgotten that not everyone was used to seeing an animal that big. At least Delilah had finally trained Stan, and now the dog knew not to knock his master down in a frantic effort to get to

the new person and smother them in gooey dog kisses. Nell
spontaneously reached for Esa's hand, which made him feel
good, till he realized that the reason was that she was afraid,
not that she had any new wish to be close to him.

"That's Stanley," said Esa. "He's the surprise I was telling
you about! Have you even seen a dog that big?"

"No," Nell whispered, pressing herself against his side.
Esa looked at Jason.

"Looks like a giant teddy bear, right?" said Jason, trying to
coax her inside. "Well, guess what? He acts like one, too. C'mon
in, pet his head if you want. His fur is really fuzzy and warm."

Still grasping Esa's hand, Nell slowly moved forward and
tentatively reached her hand out, giving Stanley a few light
strokes that barely touched his head. She smiled and dropped
Esa's hand. "It IS fluffy!" She resumed petting his head slowly,
relaxing by degrees as she came to see Stanley was basking
in it.

"He loves it," she said to Jason.

"Yup. He does. He'll let you do that for hours. And scratch
his belly. He's a total love ho—mebody."

"Can I play with him?" Nell asked Jason hopefully.

"Hhmm. Well, it's kind of hard to run around in here with
Stan, he's really big. But if you don't mind just petting him
and stuff . . ."

"That would be fine," Nell said eagerly.

"Okay, but I have to tell you something first: he drools a
lot. So if it's gonna freak you out to get dog schmoo on you,
it's okay if you don't want to hang with him. Lots of people
don't like the schmoo."

Nell pondered this. "I think I'll be all right with the schmoo."

"You sure?" Esa double-checked.

"Just give her the drool rag," a female voice called out.
Seconds later, Delilah came in from the kitchen, smiling. Esa
liked Delilah. She seemed a little scatterbrained and eccen-
tric, but you could tell right away that she had a big heart,
especially if you had four paws and a cold nose. Esa couldn't
imagine a more boring occupation than dealing with dogs,
though apparently, Delilah was very good at it.

Delilah picked a rag up off the dog-hair-covered couch and
handed it to Nell with a smile. "Hi, I'm Delilah."

"I'm Nell."

"You're going to play with Stan, huh?" Nell nodded shyly. "Well, don't let him push you around. He'll hound you for treats if you let him."

"Which means it's okay to give him a few," said Jason with a wink, pointing to a small plastic jar filled with dog bones on one of the shelves.

"We have three other dogs, too, if you want to meet them," Delilah continued.

"Babe," Jason said to Delilah quietly, "you know you can't get Stan's hopes up this way. He's expecting to play with Nell *now*. If you make him wait while you take Nell to meet Sher, Shi, and Belle first, he's going to feel really dissed."

Delilah turned to Esa with a smile. "Have you met my husband, the Newf whisperer?"

Jason opened his mouth to protest but Delilah got in there with a kiss first. "You're right, you're right," she soothed him. "She can meet them after she plays with Stanley." She smiled down at Nell. "We can have a snack later, okay? You don't want Stanley gobbling them up."

Esa looked at Jason. "I thought you said Stanley had been trained."

"He is. He doesn't knock people down anymore and stuff. But that's as far as it goes. I mean, I had to leave a little trace of rebellion in his soul, you know?"

Esa suddenly remembered a fun fact about Stanley he could share with Nell. "Stanley is the Blades' mascot. If the team makes it into the playoffs, we always have Stanley at home games to bring us luck."

Jason rubbed Stanley's chin. "Been slacking off a bit in that department, eh, boy?"

"Not his fault."

"No. Lately, it's been yours."

"Screw you," Esa mouthed. If Jason was starting on him this early in the season, then it was going to make for a very long, bumpy ride.

"Ready to get down with Stan the Man?" Jason asked.

Nell smiled shyly as Esa helped her off with her coat, and she eagerly settled on the living room floor with Stanley, who immediately rolled on his back and wanted a belly rub.

"Such a whore," Jason sighed under his breath.

Delilah put on her coat. "I've got to run out for some Greenies and check up on how things are going over at the kennel." She regarded Esa. "She's adorable," she said quietly. "How's she doing?"

I have no fucking idea because I'm an asshole, Esa thought. "She's adjusting pretty well."

"Good. After what she's been through . . ."

"I know." *Does anyone care what I've been through?* He wondered what Jason had told Delilah, what his version of things was.

Delilah said her good-byes to Esa, Jason, and Nell, and left. Esa was happy to see that although Nell still seemed slightly hesitant to "play" with Stanley, she was smiling, and he imagined that the dog's shameless "pawing" of her would soon break down all her defenses.

"Brew?" Jason offered.

"Uh . . ." Esa hesitated. It had to be okay to have one beer while his niece played. It wasn't like he was going to get drunk. "Yeah, sure."

"Hey, Nell." Jason handed her a big hair brush clotted with black hair. "You can brush him if you want. He *loves* it."

"Can I put gel in his hair?" Nell asked eagerly.

Esa cleared his throat. "Nell, I—"

Jason looked pained for a moment, then shrugged and said, "Yeah, sure, what the hell." He disappeared, returning with a tube of hair gel that he handed to Nell. "Here you go. We'll be hanging out in the den, watching the big TV. Come get me if he tries to eat it."

"What was all that bullshit a minute ago about letting Stanley keep some of his rebelliousness?" Esa asked, following his teammate into the den. "How's he going to do that if he winds up with a pointed head?"

"Ah, a little gel won't kill him. It's not like I'm going to let him go out in public or anything."

Esa nodded, checking out the room as Jason opened the mini fridge and tossed him a bottle of Heineken. Biggest flat-screen he'd ever seen, killer sound system . . .

"Nice man cave."

"Man and woman cave," Jason corrected with a frown. "If

you think that TV is just for my viewing pleasure, you've got your head further up your ass than I thought. Delilah commandeers the set for animal shows. I swear to God, if I have to watch another episode of *Meercat Manor*, I'm gonna blow my fuckin' brains out."

"So go do something else."

Jason looked down as he cracked open his brew. "Well, you know . . ."

"Yeah, I do know: you like to watch TV with your wife, you pussy."

"Fuck you, Saari."

They clinked their beer bottles together as they flopped down on the couch. Jason tilted his head in the direction of the living room. "How's it goin'?"

"It's going fine."

"Nell is cool. I'm impressed that she didn't cry when she met Stanley. A lot of little kids are freaked out by his size; they think he's a baby bear."

"She's pretty fearless," Esa said with a surprising touch of pride in his voice.

"I hear Ulfie sat for you last night."

"Let me guess: he called you first thing this morning to tell you about it."

"He said the nanny was hot, dude."

"As if he'd ever have a chance with her," Esa said contemptuously, pissed off at the Swede's observation about Michelle. It was sleazy. Cheap. Esa took a slug of his beer. "Yeah, last night was a cluster fuck. I didn't realize it was 'my night' to stay in. And then when I did, the nanny was on her way out. And there were these two Victoria's Secret models . . ." He thought about last night's threesome, but rather than feeling the usual flush of erotic pleasure course through him, he felt kind of grubby. "So I asked Ulfie to cover for me. I was pretty sure I'd get in before the nanny."

"But you didn't."

"No."

"Hey, maybe she was off having hot sex, too. You never know." Jason took a slug of beer. "Well, hot or not, Ulfie said she's kind of a bitch."

"She's not a bitch," Esa shot back. "She's just very structured and protective of Nell. Which is what Nell needs right now, I guess."

"So Nell likes her."

"Loves her. And she loves Nell. She told me she'd make my life hell if I did anything to hurt Nell."

"Whoa. Major lioness behavior."

"I know." Esa poured more beer down his throat. "She was actually waiting up for me in the dark so she could tear me a new one. Almost gave me a heart attack."

Jason laughed.

"That's fucked up, though, right?" Esa checked. "To wait up to ambush your boss?"

"I don't know. If she's as protective of Nell as you say she is, and she knew you were off screwing those two models, maybe she thought you had it coming to you. Waiting for you in the dark is hilarious. I like her."

"Yeah, you would. Anyway, like I said, she ripped me to shreds. Told me Nell had been looking forward to spending the evening with me, and my keeping my previous plans with the twins and having Ulf babysit was kinda low." Esa looked at his friend. "Do you think it was low?"

Jason shrugged. "I guess if you disappointed Nell, it is pretty bad."

"Does she seem traumatized to you? One little slipup, and the woman makes me feel like the biggest loser of all time."

"Dude, you're paying *her*. Who cares what she thinks as long as she does her job?"

Esa tilted his head back and took a long slug from the beer.

"Holy shit. You like the nanny."

Esa slowly swallowed the beer in his mouth before fixing Jason with a contemptuous stare. "Don't be a moron, Jason. It's because I'm paying her that it pisses me off she's making me feel bad. Who the hell does she think she is?"

Jason broke into his trademark smirk. "Are you asking me, or are you asking yourself? If you're asking yourself, it's because she's gotten under your skin."

"Fuck off."

"No, you fuck off."

You fuck off because you hit the nail on the head. She *had* gotten under his skin. Kind of. He'd kissed her to shut her up, but it was bound up in a momentary flash of desire that had nothing to do with his drinking earlier in the evening. The kiss had stunned him. It had obviously stunned Michelle, too—but only after the fact. For the few brief seconds their lips were pressed together, she'd responded eagerly. He was used to that with women, but somehow this felt one degree different. He'd been trying not to give it too much thought.

Jason's smirk was still intact. "What's your nanny up to tonight? Hot date?"

"No idea."

"If she's as smokin' as Ulf says, I'm sure she's got a boyfriend."

Esa eyed him warily. "Probably."

"Probably just a matter of time 'til you meet the guy." Jason looked intent on making Esa suffer as he took a long, slow sip of beer. "What's your policy on her having her boyfriend stay overnight?"

"We don't have one, but it's unlikely it's something she'd want to do. It would send the wrong message to Nell."

"Yeah, but the guy could sneak out before Nell wakes up."

"Will you just shut the hell up about the nanny?" Esa said angrily.

"Touchy."

"Eat me, Mitchell." He picked up the remote. "Anything good on TV?"

"Good tactic, change the subject. ESPN Classic has the final game of the 1994 Stanley Cup Playoffs, when the Blades kicked major, major ass. Didn't win, but Jesus, if you ever want to get inspired watching a team who played their guts out, this is it."

"Sure, why not?" Esa replied woodenly. Watching some of the old timers when they were in their prime might be inspirational; plus he knew Temu Tekkanen was on the opposing team that year, and had laid to rest any lingering prejudices that Finnish players were pussies.

Jason set up the game on TV. He was right; it was outstanding. But it did little to block out the niggling voice in his head that kept asking: What *was* Michelle doing tonight? And who was she doing it with?

15

"*Do you mind* if I join you ladies for breakfast?"

Michelle couldn't hide her pleasure when she saw how happy Nell looked upon hearing Esa's request. This would be twice in twenty-four hours that he'd spent time with her. If Nell's endless chatter about the big black Newf, Stanley, was anything to go on, she'd had a good time last night with her uncle. It boded well.

"What do you think, Nell?" Michelle asked. "Should we let him eat breakfast with us?"

Nell tapped her chin with her index finger as if pondering the fate of Western civilization. "I guess so."

Esa sat down. "Well, thank you."

"I've been hearing a lot about a certain dog named Stanley," said Michelle, biting into one of the scones she'd made for Nell.

Nell looked at Esa imploringly. "I want a dog!"

Esa glanced at Michelle uneasily. "I don't think that's a very good idea right now. A dog is a big responsibility."

"Okay," said Nell, looking unhappy but momentarily appeased.

Esa regarded Michelle. "Mind if I have a cup of coffee?"

"Of course you can. There are scones, too, as you can see."

"Just like the ones I used to have at home!" Nell chirped.

Michelle wondered if it bothered Esa that his niece still referred to London as "home." He gave no indication of it, though even if it did, it wasn't like he was going to correct her.

Esa poured himself some coffee and returned to the table, nodding his head approvingly as he bit into his scone. "Very good."

"Thank you."

"The coffee is good as well."

"Thank you again."

"I take my coffee very seriously."

"As do I."

Esa cracked a small smile. Maybe relaxation was on its way after all.

Meanwhile, Nell was devouring her scone. "You better slow down, lady, or you're going to get sick," Michelle chided.

"My sis—your mum used to do the same thing," Esa told Nell. "She loved muffins and all those sorts of things, the sweeter the better."

"I know that," Nell replied curtly. She slid out of her chair, addressing Michelle. "May I be excused?"

This was one of those moments when it was Esa's call, not hers. When silence ensued, Michelle gave him a small, discreet kick under the table.

"Of course you can be excused," said Esa, "but I need to tell you something first." He took a deep breath. "I didn't mean to upset you, Nell."

"Okay." Nell's voice was flat as she walked out of the kitchen. Esa looked so hapless that Michelle actually felt sorry for him.

"What did I do? One minute, she's so happy to have me at breakfast. The next, she wants to run away from me. I thought she'd be happy to hear something about her mother . . ."

"She's still grieving, Esa." Michelle fought the impulse to put her hand over his. "Her emotions are all over the place. She might have interpreted what you said as an insinuation that she's forgotten things about her mom."

"If anything it would be the other way around," Esa muttered. "I've probably forgotten things she could tell me."

"Maybe you could tell her that. That you need her help when it comes to Danika. It might help her feel close to you."

"Why do you know all these things?"

"All what things?"

"All these psychological things."

"I've worked with kids for a long time. I read up on the subject of children and grief when I learned about Nell's situation. And my mother died when I was a little older than she is now. I know what it's like to be left to deal with that on your own."

"Oh." Esa looked uncomfortable. "But your father and brother . . ."

"My dad did the best he could, but he was too wrapped up in his own grief to really help me with mine, and my brother was just a kid himself. At any rate, I was emotionally stranded."

"Is that one of the reasons you took the job? Because you didn't want the same to happen to Nell?"

"Yes."

"She's lucky you're her nanny," Esa said softly.

Michelle looked down at her lap. "I'm glad you think so." *Can't peer down forever. Eventually you're going to have to look up at him.* She forced her head up, feeling awkward. If Esa felt the same way, he wasn't showing it. His face was completely devoid of emotion. Poker face.

"Tomorrow is your day off." He looked proud. "See, I checked the calendar."

Michelle raised her coffee cup to him. "Commendable."

Esa looked studiedly casual. "Any plans?"

Michelle smiled tightly. "That's–"

"None of my business," Esa finished for her politely. "Of course."

"Esa." Michelle felt like she was being a bitch, even though she wasn't. "I'm not trying to be deliberately secretive. I just think it's wiser if our personal lives are kept separate."

"I agree, to a certain extent," Esa replied carefully. "But there is an issue having to do with your personal life that we failed to discuss when you started as Nell's nanny."

"What's that?"

"If you want to bring someone home to sleep with."

It was true: they hadn't talked about it. But his blunt way of putting it shocked her. "That's something you don't need to worry about," Michelle replied evenly. "I would never do that."

"But you live here," Esa continued, a slight undertone of challenge in his voice. "I'm sure there will be times—"

"First of all, I don't have a boyfriend," Michelle retorted. "And it would send the wrong message to Nell."

"Ah." A weirdly satisfied expression crossed his face, as if he'd gotten hold of some forbidden information. Which he had: Esa now knew she didn't have a boyfriend. Not that he'd have any reason to care, but still. Michelle hated the feeling of being at some kind of disadvantage. She had no right to ask what next came out of her mouth, but she couldn't help herself.

"And what about you? Will you be bringing women home?"

Esa smiled enigmatically. "Now we're getting into my business."

"The way you just got into mine." Michelle sipped her coffee. "This is the part where you remind me you're my boss, right?"

"I was a prick when I said that. Drunk, too. But if I may ask: were you this forward with your former employers?"

"It was a completely different situation."

"I see."

"You still haven't answered my question. Boss."

Esa shrugged. "I don't know what I'll be doing, though I'm sure you're going to tell me what *you* think I should be doing."

Michelle took a bite of her scone, suddenly dry in her mouth. "I wouldn't presume."

Esa laughed. "You presume often, usually to my benefit, I must admit. So tell me your thoughts."

"I think that if you're going to do that"—an image of him sweeping some, giggling, Amazonian blonde up into his arms and carrying her into his bedroom flashed before her—"I think you should set an alarm clock, and have the woman out of here before Nell gets up. Otherwise, she'll be confused."

"Because it will send the wrong message," Esa said wryly, echoing her words of a moment before.

"Yes." Was he mocking her?

"And what message is that, exactly?"

"That one-night stands are okay."

"Why do you assume any woman I'd have over would be a one-night stand? Maybe it would be a girlfriend."

"Maybe it would."

"But you wouldn't do it," Esa reiterated.

"No."

"Hhmm."

Michelle dabbed at her mouth with her napkin. "Have we resolved the issue to your satisfaction?"

"I suppose." Esa broke off a piece of scone. "Do you think Nell is ready to come see me play?" he asked, putting each of his fingers in his mouth one by one to suck off the crumbs.

Michelle felt a sharp quickening go through her that wasn't supposed to happen. "Yeah. I think she might like it."

"I have a game tonight . . ."

"That's perfect." Michelle loved the idea of going to a Blades game and being able to tease her brother and dad about it afterward, especially if the Blades won.

"I'll arrange for you two to be in one of the skyboxes, then."

Michelle felt uncomfortable. "Isn't there a green room where friends and family watch the game?"

Esa looked pleasantly perplexed. "How do you know about that?"

Michelle rolled her eyes. "How many times do I have to tell you? I know about hockey. I thought the skyboxes were for VIPs and stuff."

"You and Nell are VIPs," he pointed out easily.

"Oh." Michelle looked uncomfortable.

"What's up?"

"I really think she'd rather be with everyone else."

"Fair enough. I would love it if you could bring her early and you two could watch me warm up. Maybe she'd like that?"

"I think she would." It was almost sweet, the way he'd framed it as a question.

Michelle remembered going to games with her brother, how they always had to get there early to watch the players warm up. One time Darius Kasparaitus had flipped a puck over the Plexiglas to him and Jamie acted like he'd been tossed a diamond. He probably still had the puck somewhere.

"We're settled, then: green room for my niece and her very protective, outspoken nanny."

Michelle smiled. "That almost sounds like a compliment."

"It almost is." Esa drained his coffee cup, though he didn't move. In fact, he seemed glued to the chair. "I guess I'll go talk to Nell."

That it was more a question than a statement belied his anxiety. Michelle didn't like the way he was starting to make her feel: one minute she thought he was the world's most selfish, arrogant jerk, and the next she found herself moved by his vulnerability. This would be one of those moments.

"No time like the present."

Esa appeared dismayed. "Right."

"It's a good thing you're doing, Esa."

* * *

Esa rapped lightly on Nell's door, then stuck his head inside. "Okay if I come in?"

Nell, engrossed at her computer, shrugged diffidently.

Esa hesitated. Close the door, because it was a private talk? Leave it open? Did it matter? He left it open just a sliver and walked over to her desk, peering over her shoulder with interest.

"What're you looking at?"

Nell shrugged and hit the screensaver. It was a picture of a polar bear on an ice floe.

"I remember you liked the bears from the zoo," he said lamely.

Silence. Why did there have to be silence?

He stood up to full height, surprised to find himself nervous. "Nell, I wanted to apologize again for upsetting you in the kitchen. Obviously, I wouldn't have mentioned Dan—your mum—if I thought it would distress you."

Nell remained stock-still, staring hard at the polar bear.

"I just thought that maybe it would make you feel good if . . ."

The walls of his throat began closing.

"I thought—if you heard you shared . . ."

He closed his eyes against the tears that threatened. He couldn't do it; he couldn't talk to his niece at length about his sister without breaking down.

"I have a home game tonight. Do you and Michelle want to go?"

Nell slowly turned to look up at him. "Okay."

He managed a small smile. "Good. It'll be nice to have you there cheering me on. And Michelle knows a lot about hockey, so—"

"How come you don't go out with Michelle?"

Esa furrowed his brows in confusion. "What?"

"How come you don't go on dates with Michelle? She's nice."

Fuck. "I'm her boss, Nell."

"So?"

Esa felt flustered. "That's not what people do. Bosses don't go out with the people who work for them."

"Why not?"

"Because they don't."

"Well, if you ask me, that's stupid."

"Yes, well, I guess it is." Esa tugged on the end of one of her ponytails, the way he'd seen Michelle do, pleased when she didn't jerk her head away. "I'm glad you two are coming to the game." He took a step back. "So, uh, that's it. See you later."

Nell nodded and Esa, shaken, headed for the door. Okay, so there hadn't been some big heart-to-heart. He wanted there to be, but he couldn't do it, he was too afraid. At least he'd apologized, and she'd accepted. That had to count for something.

As for Nell's questions about Michelle, even he couldn't figure that out.

"Going over to Rory Brady's for a bit," he called out to Michelle in the kitchen. Rory was good with kids; Erin, too. They'd be able to help him out here. At any rate, there was no way he wanted to be alone with thoughts of his sister dancing through his head. He snatched his jacket and headed out the door.

16

"*Well, if it* isn't the famous Mr. Esa Saari, come to grace us with his presence."

Erin's grin helped lighten Esa's mood as she ushered him into her and Rory's apartment. Esa had called ahead to make sure his friend was home. Rory made it clear ages ago that he hated when people showed up at his door unannounced, even if it was his best mate on the hockey team.

"Go on and park yourself," said Erin, rising up on tiptoes to kiss his cheek as she gestured at the couch. She rubbed her shoulders briskly. "It's starting to get a bit chilly out there."

Erin was right: Fall was tapping New York on the shoulder, reminding the city to get ready. Personally, Esa liked the fall and winter. It was kind of hard to grow up in Finland and not like it.

"How's it going?" Esa asked her. When Erin and Rory had first moved to Manhattan two years ago, Erin, an art history major, had gotten an internship at the Guggenheim Museum. The internship led to a job as an archivist.

"Still loving it. That's not to say there aren't some days that find me at my wit's end—my boss is a real arsehole—but overall, no complaints."

"That's good. Speaking of assholes, where's your husband?"

"Just getting off the phone with his Gran. She's not doing so well."

Esa sat down on the couch. "What's up?"

"She's always prided herself on being healthy as a horse, but she's got a cough she just can't shake and is dead tired all the time. The stubborn thing won't go to the local doctor."

Rory walked in to the living room, shaking his head. "Jesus wept."

"How is she?" Erin asked worriedly.

"Stubborn as a cow, as always. She still won't see Dr. Laurie."

"Maybe she's afraid of finding out what's wrong," Erin suggested quietly.

"Oh, I'm sure that's it," Rory agreed. "Or she thinks she can heal herself with the power of prayer. What a load of bollocks."

"How did you leave things with her?"

"I told her I was sending Dr. Laurie 'round, but I wouldn't tell her when. She was livid but I don't care."

"She'll get over it."

"'Course she will." He put his arm around Erin and drew her in for a kiss before acknowledging Esa. "What about you, you Finnish prick? Anything exciting going on with your relatives?"

"In a manner of speaking."

"'In a manner of speaking'?" Rory mocked. "Since when do you talk like that?" He narrowed his eyes accusingly. "Are you hooked on that feckin' *Downton Abbey* like everyone else in the world?"

"You leave *Downton* alone!" Erin protested. "It's wonderful, isn't it, Esa?"

"I don't watch it. The nanny does, though. I think."

"Then what's this 'In a manner of speaking' crap?" Rory ribbed.

Esa suddenly felt weary, almost punchy. Maybe he shouldn't have come. "I don't know. Maybe that last hit I took scrambled my brains more than I thought. At any rate, I'm not in the mood to spar with you."

Erin and Rory exchanged glances. "I'll go get us some coffee, shall I?" Erin offered. "Okay with you, Esa?"

"Yeah. Great." It was ironic: he should be tanked up on the

stuff. God knows he'd slugged down enough at breakfast. Instead, he felt completely drained. If he could, he'd cab it back home, crawl into bed, and sleep until he had to be at Met Gar.

"What's up, mate?" Rory asked as Erin disappeared into the kitchen.

"I don't know." Misery wrapped itself around Esa like a cloak. "Actually, I do know."

"Go on."

He hesitated. "It's Nell."

"Yeah?"

"I don't know how . . ." He couldn't believe how quickly a knot started forming in the center of his chest.

Rory waited.

"I don't know how to deal with the emotional side of things."

"What do you mean?"

"This morning at breakfast, I mentioned a similarity between Nell and my sister to her, and instead of being pleased, she ran off to her room. I didn't mean to upset her, and I told her that. But the nanny saw it as a chance for me to maybe bond with her. Let her know that it's hard for me to talk about Danika as well. That maybe we could help each other."

"And—?"

Esa began choking up. "I couldn't do it. I don't know how I even managed to mention it at the breakfast table. But when I finally went to talk to Nell, I came close to breaking down."

Rory sat beside him, putting a hand on his shoulder. "Would that be so bad?"

"Yeah, it would be bad!" Esa snapped, shoving his friend's hand away. "I'm the adult! I should be strong!"

He looked away toward the window, clenching his jaw hard. His eyes were still giving him a hard time, too: burning, threatening to spill hot tears. Fucking figures, he thought.

"It's okay to cry, you know," said Rory.

"I know that," Esa retorted.

"I'm just sayin' there's no shame in it. Irish men cry all the time."

"That's because you're all a pack of over-the-top drunks."

"Oh, and the Finns are a bunch of teetotalers."

Esa swallowed and turned back to his friend. "She's my sister's kid, Rory. I want to give her the world. I want to put her in a plastic bubble so she never has to feel any pain again. But I don't . . ." He cradled his head in his hands.

He heard Erin tiptoe into the living room and put down two cups of coffee on the coffee table. "Should I go?" Esa heard her ask Rory quietly.

Esa looked up at her. "Don't be silly. I came here to see both of you."

"Right, then." Erin settled down on the small futon opposite the couch, tucking her feet beneath her. She looked expectantly at Esa, then Rory, then back to Esa.

"I brought my sister up to Nell this morning, and rather than being happy about it, it upset her."

"Go on."

"Unfortunately, it upset me, too. Not that I'd show it." Esa groped for the right words. "I want to be closer to her. But the bond we share is too painful for either of us to talk about."

Erin nodded in understanding.

"When we do talk, I don't know the right and wrong things to say to her. I don't seem to ask the right questions."

"Maybe the nanny could help," Rory offered.

Esa laughed ruefully. "Oh, yeah, she'll help all right— after she tears me a new one. She thinks part of the problem is that I don't spend enough time with my niece."

"Do you?" Erin asked.

"Look, I do what I can, all right?" Esa replied defensively.

"Do you?" Erin repeated. "If you want my opinion, you've got a chicken-and-egg situation here: you don't spend enough time with her because you're not sure what to say. And the reason you're not sure what to say is because you don't spend enough time with her."

Esa looked to Rory for his opinion. "I think she might be right, Esa."

Esa took the pads of his thumbs and pressed them against his closed eyelids. "I just want things to be simple. Why can't things be simple?"

"Where did you get the idea life was simple?" Rory asked.

"Mine *was*. For a long time." He pulled his thumbs from his lids, giving his eyes a moment to refocus. "Now there's Nell and the nanny and—"

"What about the nanny?" Erin wanted to know. "Isn't she good with Nell?"

"She's great with Nell." He paused. "That's the problem."

"Why's that?" Rory asked.

"Nell seems to think the nanny and I—"

"Say no more," Rory interjected.

"It just shows her craving for family," Erin reiterated. "Spend more time with her and she won't be making noises about you and the nanny."

"I don't know about that."

* * *

"The kid in the building?"

Esa looked up from lacing his skates to Eric Mitchell, standing beside him as he fastened the tiny gold crucifix around his neck. He and Jason: these crosses were the brothers' good luck talismans. Some guys had rituals, some talismans. Some had both. Esa was a ritual man himself, always slipping his left arm into his jersey before his right. Left first because it was the side closest to the heart, the organ that all passion and energy came from.

"Yup, Nell's here." He was thrilled she decided to come. She'd get to see what he actually did when he was working, what a cool job he had. Maybe he'd finally impress her in some way.

"We gonna meet her?" Coach Dante asked, walking by and overhearing the conversation.

"I guess." Esa hadn't really thought about it.

"Whaddaya mean 'I guess'? She'll be in the green room with everyone else, right?"

"Yeah."

"She's a nice kid," said Jason Mitchell, putting his cross on. "Saari brought her over the other night to play with Stan. She liked him, drool and all."

"She liked him so much she wants a dog," Esa muttered.

"So, get her a dog," said Jason.

"Really?" His friend's cavalier attitude pissed Esa off. "And who's gonna wind up taking care of the dog? I'm sure that's not in Michelle's contract."

"Now she's 'Michelle,' not 'the nanny,' " Eric taunted.

"What do you think I call her at home?" Esa snapped.
"'Nanny'?"

"Whatever. Why can't she take care of the dog? Just pay her more."

"It's not part of her job description."

David Hewson snorted his way into the conversation. "Since when did you become Mr. By The Book?"

"Since I learned Michelle is a ball buster," Esa offered. The description was extreme, but it was the only way he was going to get these assholes off his back. "I need shit to go as smoothly as possible."

"So we'll get to meet her tonight, too," said Eric.

"Obviously."

"Wait'll you see how hot she is," said Ulf, jumping in as well.

Rory, who, in Esa's opinion, had taken way too long to enter the conversation and help him out, finally dove in. "Is that all you care about? How hot someone is?"

"Dude, he's too fucking stupid to care about anything else," said Eric. "His head is like a beach ball: gigantic with nothing inside but air."

"That's not the only thing about me that's gigantic," Ulf snapped back. "This bullshit about me being stupid is getting boring, you douche bags."

"Yeah?" said Barry Fontaine, chiming in from across the locker room. "Well, maybe if you contributed something besides tits and ass to a conversation, it would stop."

"Someone had to take over for Eric," Ulf replied with a smirk.

"Whoa!" said Jason, fist bumping Esa. "Score one for Mr. Potato Head."

"But she is hot," Ulf added, unable to stop himself.

Shut the fuck up, Esa thought, knowing that if he said it out loud, the ribbing would go on, this time at his expense. The last thing he needed was having his brain clogged up with this bullshit.

Michael Dante clapped his hands twice, loudly. "C'mon, you biddies! Enough gossip. Finish suiting up and get your asses out on the ice to warm up. Today's word of the day is 'devastation.' I want these bastards completely devastated by the end of the game. I want them clutching their water bottles like little girls holding their dollies as they blink back tears and worry about playing us again. Destruction and devastation. Do it."

17

"Delilah! Where's Stanley?"

Michelle smiled happily as Nell raced across the green room to the woman Michelle assumed was Jason Mitchell's wife. Nell was certainly losing her inhibitions fast, which was fine with Michelle. It made her glad to see Nell so animated. It also gave her a minute to take in their surroundings. She wished she could discreetly take pictures with her phone to show her dad and brother afterward, but that would be tacky. Actually, she wouldn't have a hard time remembering it: gigantic, wall mounted TVs, plush couches, tables of food with everything from muffins and juice to fresh salads and desserts. A far cry from sitting in the nosebleed seats at Nassau Coliseum, gobbling down hotdogs until her stomach ached. The memory made her nostalgic.

There were a few other women there, some with kids. Michelle intended to introduce herself, but first and foremost, she wanted to keep an eye on Nell. She walked over to the small woman with the wildly curly hair Nell was chattering with and extended her hand.

"Hi, I'm Michelle Beck, Nell's nanny."

"Delilah Gould."

"She and Uncle Jason are the ones with the Newf," Nell explained excitedly. "I really want one," she told Delilah.

"They're a lot of work," Delilah said, echoing Esa's exact words.

"I'd take care of him," Nell insisted.

Michelle smoothed the top of Nell's hair. "It's your uncle you have to convince, you know. And so far, his answer has been 'No.'"

"Mong," Nell muttered unhappily under her breath.

Michelle hadn't heard exactly what she'd said, but she knew it wasn't good. "Excuse me, what did you just say?"

Nell looked embarrassed. "Nothing."

Michelle smiled politely at Delilah. "Can you excuse us a minute?"

"Of course." Delilah moved on.

"Nell, tell me what you said."

"I called Uncle Esa a 'mong,'" Nell admitted reluctantly.

"What's a 'mong'?"

Nell looked down at the carpet sheepishly. "It's kind of a slang for—you know, 'mongoloid.'"

"I see." Michelle took a deep breath. She was actually glad to have to seriously reprimand Nell, because it was proof she was beginning to feel comfortable acting like a real kid. She was letting her guard down.

"First of all, we don't call people names. And that's a very rude name, and very, very offensive. We also don't call our uncle names. We clear?"

Nell looked up at Michelle. "I'm sorry."

"I accept your apology. Just don't do it again."

"I won't." Nell furrowed her brows worriedly. "Are you going to tell Uncle Esa?"

"No. Why should I? You and I settled it ourselves, right?"

"Right," Nell replied, looking relieved.

"I do want to add one thing, though: if I find out you're talking that way in school about anyone else, I will have to tell your uncle. Okay?"

"I'd never! I swear!"

"Let's keep it that way, all right?"

"Okay." Nell's gaze was drawn to the long tables of food. "Can I get something to eat?"

"Sure. We didn't really have much of a dinner, did we, coming down here so early to watch warm-ups. Hey: did you enjoy that?"

Nell's eyes widened. "Uncle Esa can skate really fast!"

"Oh, that's nothing! Wait until you watch him in the game. Sometimes it's hard to even keep track of him!"

"Wow," Nell whispered to herself. She trotted off to the food table. A few seconds earlier, out of the corner of her eye, Michelle had seen Theresa enter the room. She started toward her, but Theresa was already on her way over, a huge smile on her pretty face.

"Hey." Theresa hugged her. "I was hoping you and—Nell?"—Michelle nodded—"would turn up at one of the games." She tilted her head in Nell's direction. "Beautiful girl."

"I know."

"Looks nothing like Esa."

"I know that, too."

Theresa laughed. "How's it going?"

Michelle lit up from the inside out. "Really well. Nell and I get along. She's a dream to take care of."

"Has she talked much about what happened?"

"Not really, but it's coming, I can feel it. She trusts me more and more every day."

"And how are things going with Esa?"

"Oh, fine," Michelle assured her. "He's inept when it comes to Nell, but he's getting better."

"He hasn't tried sneaking any women into the apartment?"

"Nope," Michelle said nonchalantly, even though the thought ruffled her.

"Interesting," Theresa murmured.

"I think he knows I'd kick his ass if he did," Michelle explained.

Theresa raised her eyebrows, impressed. "Taming the wild tiger."

"For his niece's sake."

"Uh-huh." Theresa leaned in to her. "You're blushing a little, you know."

Michelle knew she was, which only made it worse. "I'd be lying if I said he wasn't attractive. But that's irrelevant. He's my boss, and there are very strict rules about that sort of thing. In fact, it's in the contract. And there's a Nanny's Code of Ethics."

"And what if Mr. Suave wanted to break those rules?"

"Oh, please," Michelle scoffed. "That's one thing I never have to worry about. He knows it would result in my leaving, and he would never do that to Nell."

"Good to hear."

Michelle glanced around uncomfortably. "I feel a bit like a fish out of water."

She felt like a dope asking the next question, but she couldn't help it as she gestured discreetly at a gorgeous, stately blonde who was pacing in a corner of the room, talking a mile a minute into her cell phone. "Is that Monica Geary from *The Wild and the Free*?"

"Yup. She's married to Eric Mitchell."

Michelle nodded vaguely. "I think I remember reading that somewhere."

"She's a doll. Do you watch the show?"

"Not for years. I used to watch it with my mom after school. Back then Monica was the town's rebellious teenager who turned out to be one of the Romanovs."

"Well, the current storyline is hilarious: her character has been transported back in time and she's an Aztec princess. You should see the headdress they make her wear."

"Ah, so you're a fan."

"Not me! Michael!" Theresa exclaimed as she flipped her hair over her shoulder. "All the players are addicted to soaps."

Michelle filed this info away. Could come in handy for future tormenting-of-Esa purposes.

"I might be wrong," a delicate, black-haired woman with an Irish accent said to Michelle as she joined the conversation, "but judging from the way your eyes keep going to that little blond girl, I'm going to deduce you're Esa's nanny."

"I am. Michelle Beck."

"Erin Brady. Pleased to meet you."

Theresa glanced behind her longingly at the buffet tables.

"Would you two mind if I ditched you for some food? I'm freakin' starving."

"No, don't be silly, go," Erin urged her.

Theresa gave Michelle another quick hug. "Don't be a stranger."

"I won't." Michelle watched Theresa walk away, looking back at Erin with a sigh. "I'd kill for that body."

Erin chuckled. "You and me both, sister. Hard to believe she's birthed three kids."

"I guess it's all genetics," Michelle said with resignation.

"Jesus on a bike, don't say that," Erin replied, putting a hand to her throat. "If that's true then they'll be buryin' me in me ma's Spanx." The two of them laughed.

Michelle glanced over at the buffet table to see how Nell was doing. She was talking to Delilah. She looked happy.

"She's lovely," Erin said, as if reading Michelle's thoughts about her charge.

"She is," Michelle said proudly.

"Esa was 'round our place this morning," said Erin. "He's all tied up in knots about talking to her."

Michelle hid her disappointment. She hadn't wanted to pry, but when Esa was in Nell's room all of a minute and a half before calling out that he was heading to Rory's, Michelle figured he and Nell hadn't exactly "connected."

"It's hard for him," said Michelle. "I don't think he's hard-wired to talk about his emotions."

"Not many men are," said Erin wryly.

"I'm encouraging him as much as I can to spend time with Nell, but in the end, I can't do it for him."

"I know." Erin paused for a long moment, looking guilty. "I probably shouldn't tell you this, but I'm going to anyway. In the interest of Nell."

Michelle tried not to jump all over this with inappropriate eagerness. "What is it?"

"His sister. He's afraid of talking to Nell at length about his sister. He knows it's the bond they share, but he's worried about breaking down crying and looking weak, since he thinks it's his job to look strong all the time." Erin shook her head in bemusement. "Amazing, the way they're such fat-heads. Anyway, I just thought you should know. It's not just

Nell who's fragile right now; he is, too. Mind you, *I* told him he's got to look things square in the eye for Nell's sake, but for all I know, it went in one ear and out the other."

"Probably," Michelle said quietly, while inside, compassion for Esa was sprouting like a seedling pushing up through frozen, cracked earth. Her job was Nell, and she'd assumed that Esa couldn't connect with his niece because he was a single, womanizing hockey player who knew jack about little girls. She thought he was upset at having this child thrust upon him, precipitating seismic changes in lifestyle. All that was true. But it never occurred to Michelle that Esa might still be grieving, too. Not that that excused his actions; but it did help explain them.

"Thanks for telling me," said Michelle. "It's a valuable piece of the puzzle for me to have."

Erin looked satisfied. "I thought it might be."

*   *   *

Maybe Nell was his personal good luck charm. Esa's game had been coming around, but tonight it was like the puck was finding him. He'd set up Rory for the first goal of the game, saucering a perfect pass to him on a two-on-one break. In the second period he'd anticipated Eric Mitchell pinching, and broke back to cover the point, putting him in position to back check and break up a three-on-two shorthanded rush. Even though he hadn't scored, Coach Dante had been double shifting him, chirping in his ear on the bench that this was the kind of play they expected from him; that they knew he was capable of.

As time was running down in the third, the Blades were clinging to a one goal lead. Despite their great play, they hadn't been able to get any breathing room since the Phoenix goalie was standing on his head. With less than two minutes left in the game, David Hewson went to clear the puck, and accidentally shot it into the crowd for a delay of game penalty. Desperate to tie it up, Phoenix pulled their goalie, turning it into a six on four power play. Showing his growing confidence in Esa, Dante sent him out on the ice alongside Rory to kill off the penalty. Inspired, Esa skated from the top of the circles to the point and back again, preventing a clear shot at the goal.

With less than twenty seconds left, a quick point-to-point pass freed a Phoenix player up for a one timer. In a burst of speed Esa dove skates first into the shooting lane.

Crack! The puck hit off Esa's skate and rebounded out of the zone. The buzzer sounded and the Met Gar crowd roared its approval, but Esa couldn't hear it. His mind was clouded with pain. He felt like someone had taken a sledgehammer to his ankle.

* * *

"He's okay, Nell. I promise."

Nell was gulping down huge mouthfuls of air as Esa crumpled to his knees on the ice. Michelle thought she'd only been half paying attention. She seemed restless and at times, downright bored. Michelle had anticipated that might be the case, which was why she'd brought Nell's game-loaded iPhone along. But Nell had been surreptitiously watching—and listening— all along. And when she heard the words "Saari is down," her small body became rigid, and she began hyperventilating.

"Uncle Esa—Uncle Esa—" she gasped, looking wildly at Michelle. "He's hurt—he's—he's hurt—he's—"

"Nell, look at me." Michelle put her hands on Michelle's shoulders and looked her deeply in the eye. "Slow down. I want you to take one long, slow, breath for me." Nell screwed her eyes shut, concentrating hard as she did what Michelle asked. "Good, good. Again." Nell did it again. "Good. Now keep doing that, and listen to me.

"I've watched a lot of hockey games with my dad and my brother, okay? It looks like what happened is that your uncle went to block a shot from the other team, and the puck hit him hard in the ankle. Now that hurts a lot, but it's probably not that serious."

Nell's eyes filled. "But you don't know. It could be bad. It could be."

"As soon as we can, we'll go find out what happened."

Nell's lower lip quivered. "Can I see him?"

Michelle hugged Nell to her. "I don't know if you can see him right away, but if you can't, we'll wait for him at home." She hugged her tighter. "It's going to be all right. You'll see."

"Paskapuhe!"

Sitting in the trainers' room with his elephant-sized left ankle immersed in an ice whirlpool, Esa knew what Dr. Linderman was going to prescribe. Even so, when he heard the words, he couldn't help but react. Okay: his left ankle had blown up and every single way the trainer manipulated it sent a burning crack of pain through his body. But all he needed was to ice it and he'd be as good as new. Instead, Linderman wanted him to sit out the next three games. *Three games.* That meant he'd be off the ice for a week.

Linderman looked tired. "Esa, I have no idea what you just said, but I can guess. You have a deep bone bruise. We're going to keep icing it, put you in a walking boot, and give you lots of therapy. But if you're going to be healthy long-term, you need to stay off the ice for a week." Linderman sounded like he'd said this to hundreds of players over the years, which he probably had. But it rubbed Esa the wrong way; it sounded patronizing.

"Look, Doctor, I appreciate your caution," Esa said gratefully. "But—"

"Saari, just shut up and take your medicine like a good boy," Head Trainer Kris Taggart interrupted.

"I don't see why you just can't tape it," Esa protested. As if missing three games wasn't bad enough, the walking boot was going to require him to hobble around.

"Do you want it to heal or not?"

Esa threw Taggart a dirty look, but he knew the trainer was right: he had no choice but to deal with it.

"Fine," Esa muttered miserably.

"Do what you're told and you should be ready to play in the game against Philly. Obviously, you need to keep off it as much as possible."

"I'm not a fucking idiot, Kris."

"No, just a Finnish idiot."

"Hey: I'm going to have the walking boot on," said Esa, thinking he might have found a loophole. "Doesn't that mean I can walk around?"

"The boot is to keep your ankle immobile. Walking in it is still going to put pressure on your ankle. *Elevation*, remember?"

"*Nussia*," Esa muttered. This couldn't have come at a worse time. He couldn't stand being injured. It made him feel weak, which was the last thing he needed right now. He was still waiting to hear from his agent about the meeting with Kidco's brass.

Kris patted him on the shoulder. "I know it sucks, man. But at least it's early in the season, and at least it's not worse." He tilted his head in the direction of the TV mounted high on the wall. "You wanna watch the postgame show?"

Esa, whose left leg was going numb in the ice whirlpool, frowned. "Yeah, I guess so."

Kris and Dr. Linderman left him to his misery.

* * *

"*Good news: it's* just a bruise."

Relief spread across Nell's face as Theresa put down her iPhone, relaying the news about Esa to them. Michelle wasn't Esa's wife, or even his girlfriend; she had no pull finding out what had happened to him. But as the coach's wife, Theresa did.

"It's nothing to worry about, sweetie," Theresa assured Nell. "He's just got to rest his foot for a week or so and he'll be as good as new."

Nell still looked dubious. "He won't be crippled or anything?"

Theresa's gaze sought Michelle's. Of course Nell jumped right to the worst-case scenario. How could it be otherwise, based on her past history?

"Nope."

"So he won't limp like the Hunchback of Notre Dame?"

"Nope."

Michelle pictured it and pressed her lips together to curtail a smile, especially when she saw how disappointed Nell looked. It would be exciting to have an Uncle Quasimodo.

"I told you everything was okay," said Michelle.

"Can I see him now?"

Michelle looked to Theresa; she had no idea. Theresa made a sad face. "I'm sorry, honey, but you can't just yet. The players stay in the locker room for a while after the game."

Nell looked crestfallen.

"I have an idea," said Michelle. "We'll go home now and wait for him. We can make popcorn and everything!"

Nell's eyes lit up. "Yeah, let's do that."

"Sounds like a plan." Michelle turned to Theresa. "Thanks so much for your help."

"Oh, please," said Theresa, waving her hand in the air dismissively. "It was nothing. I'm glad I could help." She put her hands on her knees and bent forward so her face was level with Nell's. "It was really nice meeting you."

"You, too," Nell said shyly.

"Can I give you a hug?"

"Certainly," said Nell.

Theresa threw Michelle a look of amusement and hugged Nell lightly before moving on to embrace Michelle as well. "Poor kid," Theresa murmured in her ear. "God forbid Esa ever does get seriously injured."

"I know."

Michelle didn't want to think about it. She couldn't afford to.

* * *

"You're gonna be out for three fuckin' games? That sucks, especially since you've finally got your head out of your ass on the ice."

Esa, sitting on a bench in the Blades locker room postgame, knew he could count on Jason Mitchell to give voice to what he himself was thinking.

"Nice walking boot," Ulf noted. "I've had to wear those a couple of times. It's not too bad."

"That's good to know."

"You should wear one on your head, Torkelson," said David Hewson with a snort. "Maybe it'll stabilize your brain."

Ulf gave him the finger as he buttoned up his shirt. "Guys, I have a new bar for us to try tonight."

Rory groaned. "What's wrong with the Wild Hart? We've been going there for years. The patrons don't hassle us. And, if I may point out, since the owners are related to my missus, there are lots of nights we drink for free."

"True," Jason noted. He regarded Ulf with a smirk. "Why do you want to check out another bar? Think you've got a better chance of bagging some tail?"

"Maybe," Ulf said defensively.

Esa sighed. "Tell us about this place."

"It's called Nipsy's—"

"Whoa, hold it right there," David cut in. "I'm not going for a beer at a place called Nipsy's. It sounds like a bad comedy club."

"I wouldn't even name a dog Nipsy," said Esa.

"Bret Sauvages on the Flyers told me it was great," said Ulfie.

"And you trust that Quebecker?" asked Eric. "He's about as smart as you. He's shit compared to you on the ice, though, I'll give you that, Ulfie."

"I vote for the Hart," said David.

Everyone agreed and turned to Esa for his acquiescence. It dawned on him, sitting there with his friends, that he had no desire to go to the Hart, or any other bar. He wanted to head home to see Nell. It felt like the right thing to do, especially if he was sincere about breaking down the emotional wall between them.

He decided honesty was the best policy. "Guys, I'm gonna pass," said Esa. "I want to go home and see if Nell enjoyed the game."

At the mention of Nell's name, Ulf's face brightened. "I hope she did and comes see us play again."

Esa hauled himself up to a standing position. "I'll see you guys later."

"I'll give you a ring tomorrow," said Rory. "Maybe we can figure out a time I can pop 'round."

"Sounds good," said Esa, faking enthusiasm as best he could. He just wanted to get home, rest his ankle, and try to connect with Nell. That was more than enough for one night. He couldn't think beyond that.

19

"*Hello, ladies.*"

The sight of Esa on crutches jarred Michelle.

Nell bounded off the couch and ran to him, throwing her arms around his waist, which made him rock unsteadily on his feet. Michelle read Esa's face: surprise, then pleasure. He hugged Nell back, his expression uncomfortable but determined. Michelle had been worried that he might go out after the game with his teammates, and Nell, anxious and disappointed, would fall asleep before he got home. But here he was, actually looking like it was where he wanted to be.

Nell released him, staring at his walking boot.

"Pretty ugly, huh?" Esa offered.

"It looks like an astronaut boot." She gnawed on the tip of her index finger nervously. "Does your ankle hurt badly?"

Esa considered the question. "Not right now."

Nell leaned forward, studying the walking boot more intently. "Can I touch it?"

"Sure."

"How come you have to wear it?"

"It helps keep my ankle from wobbling around."

"In other words, it stabilizes it," said Nell.

"Yeah. Exactly."

"Is it all swollen?"

"It was, but I soaked it in an icy whirlpool and the swelling has gone down. Now it's just black and blue."

"You're not going to be paralyzed or anything, right?" Nell asked apprehensively.

Esa glanced at Michelle with concern before turning his attention back to his niece. "Of course I'm not." It dawned on Michelle that this might be his first realization of how frightened Nell was of anything happening to him.

"Let's go sit down," Esa suggested.

Nell was hopping around merrily as she led him to the couch where Michelle sat. "We were waiting for you," Nell explained. "We made popcorn and everything."

Esa smiled, easing himself down on the couch before lifting his left foot and putting it up on the coffee table. Michelle felt badly for him: it wasn't hard to see how much he hated this. The only reason she cared was her fear that his resentment might manifest in curtness, casting a dark cloud over the house.

Nell plunked herself down in the space between Michelle and Esa, happy as a sprite as she helped herself to some popcorn. The three of them sitting there felt uncomfortably domestic to Michelle. She moved over an inch or two, away from Nell and Esa, creating more space.

"Did you enjoy the game?" Esa asked.

Michelle wasn't sure if he was asking her, Nell, or both of them.

"Um . . ." Nell began, looking at Michelle.

"You can tell him the truth."

"It was kinda boring," Nell admitted.

"I'm sorry," Esa replied ruefully.

"But we liked the warm-up. Right, Nell?" Michelle prompted.

Nell nodded.

"Did you like being in the green room with everyone?" Esa asked, reaching for reassurance.

Michelle felt an unwanted ripple of tenderness toward Esa flutter through her. He was trying so hard.

"Yes. Delilah was there. And Erin, too." Nell's smile faded a tiny bit. "But no Stanley."

"Stanley only comes when the team is in the playoffs," Esa explained.

"Will you be in the playoffs?" asked Nell.

"I don't know." A cloud passed over Esa's face, his expression unmistakably miserable. Rationally, Michelle knew that Nell was old enough to understand that adults could feel glum, too. But the little girl seemed to take her uncle's change of mood personally; she nodded solemnly, then moved to nestle herself against Michelle, settling in the crook of her arm.

Since there was no ignoring the looming presence of his injury, Michelle thought it might be best to talk about it. "How long are you going to be laid up for?"

Esa frowned as he grabbed a handful of popcorn. "A week."

Nell brightened immediately. "Michelle can take care of you like she takes care of me!"

Michelle blanched. "No, sweetie, it doesn't work that way. Your uncle doesn't need anyone to take care of him; he's a grown-up."

"But you can't walk about much, can you, Uncle Esa? You're going to need help, right? And Michelle—"

"I'll be fine," Esa said brusquely.

Nell looked stung. "I'm sorry," she said, snuggling deeper into the crook of Michelle's arm.

"No need to be sorry," Esa said.

Tell her you're sorry, you moron.

Esa ran his hand over his face with a weary sigh. "I'm sorry if I sound cranky. I'm just in a bad mood because my ankle hurts."

Jumped the gun on that one, Beck. Give the guy time to finish a sentence, for chrissakes.

"Okay," Nell said quietly.

For a few seconds, the TV was the only sound in the room. Despite Esa's assurance that his ankle was the source of his crankiness, Nell remained in firm retreat against Michelle. Michelle rubbed her shoulder reassuringly. When Nell looked up at her, Michelle gave her a wink that made Nell crack a sad, little smile.

Nell's withdrawal, though not major, killed Michelle. It

was painful to see that Nell's initial reaction was to blame herself for Esa's short burst of temper. But that was something grieving kids did: they blamed themselves for everything, including their parent's death.

Esa was mindlessly grabbing for big handfuls of popcorn as he stared numbly at the TV. It was almost as if he wasn't even aware of Michelle and Nell's presence. But then Nell shifted position against Michelle, and her movement appeared to stir the recognition that he wasn't alone.

"Tired?" he asked Nell.

She just shrugged.

"Well, I am," Michelle declared with a yawn.

Nell immediately changed her tune. "Me, too."

She scrambled off the couch. "Can you and Michelle both tuck me in?" Nell asked Esa.

Michelle couldn't recall ever feeling more put on the spot. "Honey, your uncle has to rest his foot."

"But it's a short walk," Nell pointed out.

Esa looked awkward. "I guess, if it's what you really want—"

"It is."

Nell skipped ahead to her bedroom, leaving Michelle and Esa to follow.

"Are you in pain?" Michelle asked him lamely as he lifted his foot off the coffee table and moved slowly toward her, more to fill the awkward silence than anything else.

"What do you think?"

"Whoa. Remind me never to ask you how you're doing again." Michelle upped her pace a bit so she didn't have to actually walk *into* the bedroom alongside him. Michelle just hoped Nell didn't say anything about her and Esa going out. Talk about awkward. But if the issue came up, she—they'd—just have to deal with it.

* * *

"Michelle. Can I talk to you a minute?"

Michelle slowed her pace as she and Esa left Nell's bedroom. She'd said "Good night" to him, and was heading for her own room, more exhausted than she realized. She'd had a feeling this was going to happen.

"What's up?"

"Can we maybe sit on the couch?"

"So this is going to take awhile."

"Probably not, but I've got to keep off my ankle, remember?"

"Right." Feeling guilty, Michelle followed him as he walked with a hitch to the couch.

They sat down in tandem. Michelle picked up her half-empty glass of soda and took a drink. She was suddenly thirsty, filled once again with sympathy for him that she didn't want to have, as she looked at him sitting there, the shine in his ice blue eyes temporarily snuffed out. "You don't have to apologize," she said.

Esa looked taken aback. "What?"

"You want to apologize to me for your being such a jerk when I asked you how your ankle felt. And I'm telling you, I understand."

"Thank you," Esa said humbly. He reached for the remote, turning off the TV. The silence was loud as a gong. "I feel like I have to apologize to you a lot. That I'm a jerk a lot."

"You are," Michelle confirmed.

"I'm sorry for that, too."

A small flicker of life returned to his eyes. It took Michelle a moment to read it; it was heartfelt sincerity.

"Apology accepted," she told him.

Esa slicked back his hair with a sigh. "I know it's going to be a cluster fuck, having me around the house for a week. I'll try to keep out of the way as much as possible."

"Don't be silly," Michelle assured him, even though it was something she was worried about. It would be so weird with him here more than usual. Would she be obligated to talk to him? Would he want to know where she was going when she went out during the day?

"Nell is probably going to love it," she pointed out to him, trying to convince him as much as herself. "You'll be here when she gets home from school, and you'll be here for dinner every night. I'll enjoy it, too," she said, trying to cheer him up. "You can give me a break and help her with her homework."

"Only if you want her to fail," said Esa, grimacing slightly as he leaned forward for some popcorn. "I was done with school by the time I was fifteen."

"That doesn't matter. She'll just be happy to have you here."

Esa regarded Michelle with curiosity. "Why did she want to know if I was going to be paralyzed?"

"She freaked out when she saw you were hurt."

"Shit," Esa replied, looking guilty.

"Look, it makes sense. Luckily, Theresa was able to get the lowdown from Michael pretty fast. She wanted to see you right away."

"But she's okay now?"

"I think so," Michelle said carefully. She and Esa put their hands into the bowl of popcorn at the same time, the tips of their fingers brushing. There was a tiny electric charge before each of them quickly withdrew. Employer and employee, right? No wonder it felt weird.

"Do you think we—I—should look into therapy for her?"

Michelle answered honestly. "I don't know."

"But what do you think?" Esa's gaze was steady, his voice surprisingly plaintive. "You know her better than I do."

"You should wait and see. She's *just* starting to really trust me and share things. Having a stranger ask her questions might not be a good thing."

"I didn't think of that." Depression once again overtook his striking features. Michelle wasn't sure what to do. Her instinct was to tell him how great it was that he came home tonight right after the game, but she didn't want to sound like a cheerleader, or worse, like a teacher encouraging a student. *Good for you, Esa! You're starting to get it! I'm going to put a gold star next to your name!*

"I'm kind of beat," Michelle said, a subtle (or maybe not so subtle) hint that she wanted to wrap things up. She couldn't think of anything else they had to talk about.

"Me, too. But if you don't mind, I just need to ask your advice on one more thing."

"Sure." She had to admit she liked him wanting her advice. It meant that he realized she was the day in, day out, central stabilizing presence in Nell's life. Assuming that was what the advice was about. She couldn't imagine it would be about anything else.

"I know tomorrow is your day off. Do you have any

suggestions for things I can do with Nell? I'm going to be pretty much housebound."

"Movies. She likes chess."

Esa scowled. "She plays chess?"

"She's been trying to teach me. I'm pretty hopeless."

"I think she might have to settle for checkers."

"She'll probably want to go off on her own and read for a while. She likes Wii 'Just Dance' and bowling, though obviously you can't participate in either." Michelle paused. "She likes Barbies."

"All of that is helpful. Thanks."

Michelle looked at him, trying to ignore how attractive his vulnerability made him. She shouldn't do it. She knew she shouldn't do it. But she couldn't help herself.

"Look, I can change my schedule around if it makes things easier for you while you have to keep off your feet."

"You don't have to do that."

"I know that. But I feel sorry for you."

"I never thought I'd hear those words coming out of your mouth."

"Neither did I."

They laughed in unison. Michelle glanced away, wanting to move, but couldn't. It was as if the charged hush buzzing through the living room was pinning her to the couch. Esa leaned in close and Michelle, against her better judgment, surrendered to the gentle skim of his lips over hers. This was wrong, and it was bad. But it was also wonderful, the way his mouth was pressing against hers a little more fully now, a little more insistently. Stop being stupid, she reprimanded herself as her heart beat fiercely in her chest. Do not go down this road.

Much to her surprise, they both pulled away at the same time. "I know what you're going to say: that wasn't smart," said Esa with a small, rueful smile.

"No, it wasn't," Michelle agreed, her pulse still twittering. "But in this case, you're not the only one to blame. I mean, I did respond," she admitted reluctantly.

"You did. Very nicely, I might add."

Blushing, Michelle covered her face with her hands. "Now you're embarrassing me."

"I'm sorry."

Goddamn, why did he have to be so good-looking? It would be so much easier to say what now needed to be said if he weren't quite so handsome, or such a good kisser. If he weren't her boss. She reminded herself of all the things he was: arrogant, a womanizer, a man terrified of his own feelings and emotions.

Michelle took her hands from her face. "Look." She wanted to extricate herself from this as soon as possible. She wasn't good at this, whatever "this" was, exactly, and she never had been. "I don't have any problem putting this down to your current situation."

Esa knit his brows together, puzzled. "What do you mean?"

"You're upset and I'm the only woman who's here—"

"You value your attractiveness so little?" Esa cut in.

The heat in Michelle's cheeks deepened. "No, it's just that you and I both know I'm not your type."

Esa shook his head. "Unbelievable."

"What?"

"You telling me how *I* feel."

"Look," Michelle said again. She had a habit of always starting sentences with "Look" when she knew she had to reason with someone whose views or opinions were different from hers. "You and I both know that whatever the reason for that kiss, it's irrelevant. We can't play house, Esa. We're just going to have to ignore the pink elephant in the room. Either that, or I'm going to have to—"

"Don't even say it." He sounded so angry Michelle was taken aback. "I would never do that to Nell, and neither would you."

Shame forced Michelle's eyes down again. "I know."

"All right." Esa wiped the salt on his fingers off on the front of his jeans. "So we're going to pretend this didn't happen."

Michelle nodded.

"I just wanted to make sure I'm clear on this." He grabbed Nell's soda and took a slug. "You don't have to help me out tomorrow if it's a hassle for you. Seriously."

"It's not a hassle," Michelle assured him. "I already told you: I feel sorry for you."

"Perhaps I should play the pity card more often with the ladies," Esa said sardonically. "It seems to have its rewards."

Michelle opened her mouth, closed it, and quickly erased what she wanted to say to him which was: once an asshole, always an asshole.

She stood. "I'm really tired."

"As am I."

"I guess I'll see you tomorrow, then."

"Yes. Good night, Michelle."

"Good night, Esa."

She heard him flip the TV back on as she headed for her room. She knew she was going to lie awake all night, dissecting, replaying, second-guessing herself. She should have listened to her original instinct about working for him when she was thinking about taking the job. But always, always, it came back to Nell for her. And from here on out, that needed to be her sole focus.

20

"How's it going, Esa?"

Esa thought the answer was pretty self-evident as he sat down gingerly in his agent's office. It was going badly. It was going like shit. It wasn't going at all.

Esa gestured at his left leg. "Bone bruise on my left ankle. I'm out for a week."

Russell seemed unfazed. "Minor injury. Happens to everyone."

"Yeah, I know that, Russ, but no athlete likes to be out, especially for a week. I'm going to miss three goddamn games."

"You have my sympathy."

Esa frowned. "Thanks."

Russell planted his palms on the desk in front of him, leaning forward in his chair. "I talked to Kidco management. Unsurprisingly, they have no interest in contract talks sooner rather than later. They want to see how the season goes."

"I figured." Typical, Esa thought disgustedly. Team management always played it this way with players whose contracts were running out. Why had he thought they'd treat him any differently? "Good, not great." He'd heard that was Kidco's

current assessment of him. They said they'd paid for "great."
There was every possibility that if "great" Esa didn't make a
triumphant return, he was going to find himself with a crappy
contract offer, if any.

Russell leaned back in his chair. "We do have another option."

"Yeah, I know: talk to other teams, create some competition."

"That'll definitely put a fire under their asses," Russell
pointed out. "The thing is: are you willing to seriously entertain offers? I doubt it'll come to that, but I need to know."

Esa frowned. "I don't really have much of a choice, do I?"

"Not unless you want to take the gamble of seeing what
happens with Blades management."

"Nussia." Right then, his ankle began to throb. Psychoso-
matic. Unbelievable. He rubbed his chin, the gristle there
bristling against his fingers. He'd woken up late and hadn't
had a chance to shave.

"Yeah, I'll entertain other offers," he told Russell miserably.

"Okay. I'll put some feelers out, but I don't think you have to
worry about that: they'll all be champing at the bit to get you."

"Glad you think so." Two years ago, Esa's response would
have been an unabashed, "No kidding." Now he was doubting
his market value.

"C'mon, Esa. How long have I been in this goddamn business? No worries, okay?"

"Right." He wished his agent's words chased off some of his
gloom, but they didn't. Perhaps he'd feel better about using this
trump card if he wasn't sitting here in a walking boot. And of
course, there was Nell. What if he did have to accept an offer
somewhere else, and they had to move? That meant uprooting
her—again. Maybe Michelle would move with them, he mused.
Keep on being Nell's nanny. As if that was going to happen.
Although you never knew; she *was* pretty dedicated to Nell.

He wrapped things up with Russell, but rather than hail a
cab right away, he sat down on one of the benches in the
marble-pillared lobby. He knew he should go home and rest
his leg. But it was Monday, and Michelle would probably be
there, doing whatever nanny tasks she did during the day.

He was really grateful to her for being willing to shift her
schedule around to help him and his bum ankle out. It hadn't
been too weird when they'd hung out on Saturday, because

Nell had been there to focus on. But he could imagine how awkward it was going to be for the next few days around the apartment with just the two of them there: there'd be some big-time avoidance going on.

He thought about the kiss. It had felt inevitable somehow, the most natural thing in the world. Her statement that he'd only kissed her because he was upset and she happened to be there had shocked him. She was so confident of herself in every other area; how could she dismiss her own attractiveness?

Granted, she was right that she wasn't his "type," but more and more, his type was starting to grate on him. He loved sleeping with gorgeous women, and being photographed with them rocked. But the conversation wasn't exactly riveting. And once you stripped away the fucking and ego boost, there wasn't much there. Michelle was smart and funny; he could actually talk with her. She was a good person, too. He had no idea if the women he dated were good people; conversation never got that deep. For all he knew, they went home and smacked their folks around or poked neighborhood dogs with sticks.

He shifted his weight uncomfortably, his eyes following a young, red-haired woman in a business suit walking by. Good-looking women always turned his head. Always would, probably.

Michelle was in that category now: good-looking.

He hated to admit that he was starting to like her—as in, *like* her like her, as that douchebag Swede Ulfie would put it. He couldn't remember the last time he'd actually felt that way. Obviously he was shallow. Or maybe guarded was a more accurate term. Real relationships meant vulnerability, and if there was one thing in his life he despised, it was being vulnerable. It opened you up to all kinds of complications, which was the last thing he needed right now.

Michelle was right: great as the kiss was, it couldn't lead to anything, and there was no use pretending otherwise.

He decided he'd go to Met Gar for a bit, ice his ankle in the whirlpool. See if he could get treatment from a trainer. The faster he healed, the better. Maybe he'd be able to make practice on Thursday. Not only that, but the more time out of the apartment, the better.

21

"What a nice surprise."

Michelle rolled her eyes at her father's teasing, kissing him on his whiskery cheek as she entered his apartment. Once a week, usually on one of her weekend days off, she headed out to Queens to see her dad. Today, however, she'd checked if it was okay to visit him on a weekday after she'd gotten Nell off to school. She wanted to be out of the apartment as much as possible while Esa was laid up. Thankfully, her dad was home. So here she was, Monday morning, complete with a bag of his favorite crullers from V & V.

He rattled the wax paper bag Michelle handed to him. "My favorite, I hope."

"Have you ever known me to bring you any different?"

"You know what? I haven't. C'mon, follow me into the kitchen."

Same old words, same old routine, and she liked that. There was comfort in it, especially when her life had taken quite the unexpected turn on Friday night.

"How's it going?" her father asked, putting up the water for coffee.

"Same old, same old."

Her dad glanced at her over his shoulder. "You look tired."

"Taking care of a kid is tiring!" Michelle said, even though her weariness had nothing to do with Nell and everything to do with sleeping like hell since the kiss. "You of all people should know that."

"You were no problem. Your brother on the other hand . . ."

Michelle laughed. "He sleeping?"

"No. Morning shift, thank God. You know what it's like when someone is pulling doubles night after night: it's like living with a vampire."

"I remember."

Her dad finished at the sink, giving a small series of coughs as he moved to the coffeemaker on the blue linoleum countertop opposite. That was Jamie's latest fixation: their father's cough. Michelle pointed out that he'd been coughing since they were kids. But Jamie insisted it had gotten worse, even though Michelle was there every week and it sounded the same to her.

"How's the kiddo doing?"

Michelle broke into a big smile at her favorite topic. "She's doing great."

"That's good to hear."

"She's thriving in school, she's coming out of her shell more . . ."

"When are you going to bring her over again? I could use a little girl to spoil."

"Let me see what my schedule is like in the next week, and I'll get back to you."

"My, that sounds very official," said Michelle's father, moving to the fridge to pull out the can of coffee.

"Well, you know, her uncle's schedule changes from week to week, which means my schedule does, too."

"Uncle Esa." The disdain in her father's voice made Michelle bristle."I saw he got injured Friday night. Can't say I'm sorry."

"It's not nice to wish injury on someone."

"I wasn't wishing injury on him, Michelle. I was just saying that the fact he's injured doesn't make me sad." Her father narrowed his eyes accusingly. "Why? It makes you sad?"

"Of course it does, for Nell's sake," Michelle replied evenly.

"We were at the game when it happened and she completely wigged out."

"Poor kid."

"Exactly."

"You should let me and Jamie bring her to an Islanders game one night so she can see how real hockey is played."

"Yeah, that'd be great," Michelle deadpanned. "She pretends to watch a team that hasn't been in the playoffs in a decade. You'll stuff her full of franks until she feels sick and then bring her home to me, where she'll spend half the night throwing up."

"You *are* her nanny," her father admonished playfully. "And don't forget, we had the greatest four-year run in history."

"You're a pip, Dad, seriously."

The coffee machine gurgled into action and her dad sat down at the table, covering his mouth as he gave another cough. He looked at Michelle defensively. "Before you even start, allow me to tell you, you never get the smoke out of your lungs. But try telling that to Jamie: every time I so much as clear my throat, he gives me 'the look'—you know, his 'Go to the doctor, I'm worried you're gonna drop dead' look."

"He's just looking out for you."

"I'm sixty-four years old, Michelle. I've been taking care of myself for a long time. Plus he's a goddamn firefighter himself. Just wait until he's been on a crew for forty-five years. He's gonna sound the same way."

"I know."

"If he keeps this up, he's going to get a swift kick up his ass and two weeks' notice from me."

"*Ouch*," Michelle said with a wince.

"Maybe you could tell him what I said."

"Tell him yourself!"

"He'll listen if it comes from you."

Michelle snorted. "Oh, right. As if he's ever listened to anything I've said."

"There's always a first time."

"Dad, you know Jamie doesn't listen to anyone, except his captain."

"Well, he better start," her father warned.

They made small talk for a while: the weather, her dad's

very active social life, Nell, and eventually Esa. There was no avoiding it: she did work for him. And live with him. And kiss him. *Shit.*

"Tell me about the injured Finn," said her father, dunking a cruller in his mug of coffee. He'd been doing that for as long as Michelle remembered, dunking his crullers. It used to drive her mom nuts, especially when he'd let them break off into the coffee and then when he was done with his drink, he'd spoon out the mush from the bottom of the mug and eat it.

Michelle sipped her coffee. "What about him?"

"Is he getting on any better with the kid?"

"Her name's Nell, remember? And yes, he's getting better."

"Still bedding those models?"

A frosty shiver crept up Michelle's spine. "I wouldn't know. He certainly doesn't bring them home, if that's what you're asking."

"Big of him." Her father shook his head disapprovingly. "Those rich, single athletes are all the same: they just want T and A. They don't even care if the T is real anymore. It's all about size."

"No offense, Dad, but I really don't want to get into whether my employer can spot a pair of silicone boobs at five hundred feet. And PS, you're starting to sound like Jamie, who thinks he's the world expert on everything."

"I read. I know what I'm talking about."

Michelle put her palms up in a gesture of surrender. "Okay, whatever you say." She knew better than to belabor the point, especially since it could lead directly to her dad going into protective mode, wanting to know if Esa had ever zeroed in on her boobs, which she was pretty sure he hadn't, because she didn't have much of a bust to speak of.

Unfortunately, she was too late: her father was peering at her across the table suspiciously. "He ever give you the eye?"

Good old Dad, going straight for the jugular today.

"Do I look like a model to you?"

"You look better than a model, sweetie. That's what worries me."

"Dad, you don't have to worry, all right?" Which was true.

"Well, just remember: if he gives you any problems, Jamie and I can take care of him."

"I appreciate that, but trust me, I know how to handle him. Plus I have a feeling I might get fired if my dad and brother roughed up my boss."

"Didn't think of that."

"Clearly. Now pass me one of those crullers and fill me in on some neighborhood gossip, because I'm way out of the loop."

* * *

Esa had been worried a week off would cause him to get rusty; that pouring all his concentration into avoiding Michelle, rather than visualizing his ankle healing quickly, would lead to his playing like shit when he hit the ice again. But he was wrong: From the moment the game started, he picked up where he left off. It was as if there was a magnetic attraction between him and the puck. Halfway through the first period, he'd broken a scoreless tie with Philly by deflecting a shot from the point. Though they'd never admit it, he could tell by the fist bumps, as he skated by the bench after scoring, that his teammates were relieved that his injury hadn't set him back.

He'd played okay through the second, but in the third period he'd kicked it up a notch. Up by a goal, the Blades were preparing for another nail-biter as a tight checking third period continued. With eight minutes left and Philly a man up and pressing for the equalizer, Esa found himself and Rory out on the ice killing off the penalty. He was starting to love playing shorthanded. He had skated out to press the right point when out of the corner of his eye, he saw Philly's left defenseman break toward the slot. Taking a step to his left, Esa thrust his stick out at what turned out to be the perfect moment. He broke up the pass and the puck skittered out toward center ice.

Knowing he had at least a stride on the Philly defense, Esa rushed to pick up the loose puck. Speeding down the left wing, he sensed Rory breaking down the right wing, with a Philly defenseman in close pursuit. When he crossed the blue line, Esa pointedly looked to his right while still managing to keep one eye on the Philly goaltender. Seeing the goalie's legs subtly move in preparation for shifting to his left, Esa snapped a wrister toward the five hole as he reached the top of the circles. The lamp flashed and the horn blasted.

22

"*Saari, you Finnish* bastard! You can skate, but you can't hide."

Esa's heart sank as Lou Capesi's voice thundered behind him as he walked out of the locker room with Rory after the game. Capesi had been on his ass relentlessly lately about Blades' charity events. He'd done a few his first year and had hated it, especially the auctions in which he had to kiss the highest bidder. There was one woman who created a vacuum seal between their two mouths. If that wasn't enough, she was like an octopus, her arms like tentacles that wouldn't let him go. She sure as hell got her money's worth.

Rory looked amused as they slowed. "I can guess what this is about."

Esa frowned. "Yeah, me, too."

"I'll wait for you in the green room."

"You're going to abandon me in my hour of need?"

"Hey, I don't want him to rope me into anything! I've done more than my fair share!"

"Yeah, and you love it, you attention whore."

"Have fun."

Esa gave Rory the finger as his friend passed Lou with a big, cheery smile before disappearing into the green room. Esa halted, waiting for the team's rotund head of PR to catch up with him.

Not surprisingly, Lou was panting slightly. "Good game tonight."

"Thanks. What's up, Lou?"

"Don't 'What's up, Lou' me. You know what's up. It's time for you to contribute some of your precious off-ice time to doing some PR just like everyone else."

"I'm still trying to get all my ducks in a row with Nell," Esa answered evasively.

Lou's face softened. "How's the kid doin'?"

"Good. She likes school." He paused. "She loves the nanny."

"Thank God for that. You get along with her?"

"Yeah. She's nice and she's great at her job. I'd still be in way over my head without her."

"I was talking about the kid, not the nanny. But it sounds like the nanny's got your ducks covered."

Esa shot Lou a dirty look. "I mean personal stuff."

"Yeah right."

Esa knew he was trapped. "What do you want me to do?"

"The Kids on Skates charity event? Where we provide free sticks and skates to kids and you guys give them free lessons? You know about it?"

"This is my third year on the team. What do you think?"

"Then you know it's a great charity. Some of these kids would never get to play hockey otherwise. Players who've done it in the past have had fun."

"Yeah, I know," Esa admitted. Rory had participated last year (of course), and Ulfie and the Mitchell twins had been involved since the charity was established six years ago.

Lou dug into one of the front pockets of his pants, pulling out a handful of salty almonds that he threw into his mouth. "You're doing it," he garbled. "End of story." He reached into his pocket again. "Besides, it'll reflect favorably on you, if you catch my drift."

"Oh, that's just great." Esa laughed bitterly. "It's not enough that I have to prove to them I'm worth signing again. Now I have to show them I'm a humanitarian as well."

"All part of the game, my friend." Lou chomped down on more almonds. "I mean, you and I both know you're a heartless prick, but management doesn't have to know that."

"Fuck you, Lou."

"So it's pretty much an all-day deal," Lou continued as if he hadn't heard. "Ten thirty to four thirty, three sessions. I have to check whether it's a Saturday or a Sunday—not that it matters, because like I said, you're doing it."

"Jesus Christ." Esa was getting restless as Lou repeated himself. All he wanted was to get the hell out of here so he could get Rory and they could head out to the Hart to meet everyone else. "I'm not Ulfie," he told Lou. "I understood you the first time you told me I had no choice."

"Just making sure."

"Let me know the date as soon as you can so I can talk to the nanny and work out the scheduling."

"Does your nanny have a name, Saari?" Lou mocked. "Or do you just call her 'nanny'?"

"Michelle. Her name is Michelle." Esa shifted his gym bag to his other shoulder. "Can we wrap this up now?"

Lou seemed oblivious to his impatience. Either that, or he was ignoring it. "I've got one other charity event that I want you to think about."

"What?" Esa asked sharply.

"The one where women bid on a kiss from you."

Esa shook his head vehemently. "No fuckin' way. I'm never doing that again. I still have nightmares about it."

Lou scowled at him. "It brings in a lot of money."

"I don't care. Ask Ulfie to do it. I'd rather break my own legs."

"Prima donna asshole," Lou muttered.

"What was that?" Esa asked, zipping up his jacket.

"Nothing. All right, get outta here. Enjoy the rest of your night."

"Yeah, you, too."

Esa started down the hall, leaving Lou behind to scribble furiously on a battered old clipboard that was probably older than Esa was. He resented Lou dropping that little comment about him earning brownie points with management if he did more PR. He knew it was no secret that there wasn't any

movement on them making him an offer yet, but the thought
that anything apart from his performance on the ice might be
factored in really pissed him off. A thought hit him: maybe
Lou was bullshitting him just to get him to do the event, in
which case Lou was an even bigger jerk than he thought. No,
he liked Lou. All the guys did, even though he was a huge
pain in the ass. But that was his job, right?

He didn't want to let Lou know, but he would have committed to the charity event anyway, out of a growing sense of
awareness where kids and money were concerned. He'd never
wanted for anything, and God knows, Nell certainly didn't.
But he knew there were a lot of kids who didn't have much. If
he could make them happy for a day, then it was worth it.

Jesus, who was the guy thinking these things? Before Nell
came to stay, this guy didn't exist. Then again, before Nell
came to stay, a lot of things didn't exist.

*   *   *

"Ugh, I hate fractions!"

Frustrated, Nell threw her pencil down on the kitchen table
and squeezed her eyes shut, near tears. Michelle couldn't blame
her: she'd hated learning fractions, too. It didn't help that her
third grade teacher, Mrs. Engler, hated teaching math. The short-
tempered woman played a large role in shaping exactly the kind
of teacher Michelle vowed she'd never become.

"I hated them, too," Michelle offered, drawing her chair
closer to Nell. She was trying to help, but the tougher the
problems, the more upset Nell became. Patience was not her
strong suit. Luckily, it was Michelle's.

"You've only got two more to go, and then you're done
with your homework for the day."

"I suppose." Nell picked up her pencils, painstakingly drawing small squiggles on one corner of her handout. "My mum
used to help me with maths sometimes."

Michelle blinked, taking a deep breath. This was the last
context in which she expected Nell to start mentioning her
mother. It was a very good sign.

"Really?" Michelle asked with interest.

Nell didn't look at her; she just kept doodling on the page.
"Did your mum help you?"

"Yup."

A small smile came to Nell's face as she peered up at Michelle through her bangs, which definitely needed a trim. "Was she good at it?"

"Nope." Michelle laughed. "But she tried."

"My mum was sort of good at it."

"That must've been helpful."

Nell shrugged. "It was. I guess."

"Why don't you see if you can figure out the next problem on your own and I'll start dinner."

"Chili?" Nell asked hopefully.

"That's tomorrow night. Tonight we're having spaghetti."

"I'll accept that."

"Well, la-di-da, Miss Saari!"

Nell giggled as she wiggled her skinny butt on the kitchen chair, trying to get more comfortable before tackling the dreaded math problem in front of her.

Michelle was elated as she started to gather the ingredients to make sauce. She wished she could tell Nell how much it meant to her that she'd shared something about her mother. Yes, she'd shut down a little toward the end ("I guess" being a classic deflection), but the fact that she'd opened up in the first place was major. She'd have to tell Esa. Maybe she'd e-mail him.

It had been a week since "the incident" as she now referred to the kiss in her mind. And if there was an award given for "Best Job of Minimizing Contact by Two People," she and Esa would have won it, no contest. It had been more awkward than she'd anticipated, despite the three of them spending a good chunk of time together the day after he hurt his ankle. Actually, it had been excruciating for her, pretending in front of Nell for a prolonged period of time. She had no idea how it had been for Esa.

*   *   *

"How's it going?" she asked Nell a few minutes later as she assembled the fresh spices and vegetables on the kitchen island. This was one of the things about nannying that teaching didn't give her: she could nourish her charges not just intellectually, but nutritionally.

"I'm stupid," Nell lamented.

"You're not stupid. You're impatient. Take your time."

Nell turned in her chair to look at her. "Maybe Uncle Esa could help me."

"Maybe."

"Does he have a game today?"

"Nope."

"Then where is he?"

Nell had started wanting to know where Esa was every minute of every day when he wasn't practicing or playing a game.

"I don't know."

Nell nibbled on the tip of the pencil's eraser. "Can I ring him?"

"Sure. Use your own phone, though, okay? I don't want him thinking I'm calling him."

Nell looked puzzled. "Why?"

"I only need to call him if there's an emergency, and this isn't. I don't want to worry him if he sees my number come up," Michelle explained. *Plus, I don't want it flashing through his mind for even a millisecond that I might be calling him for some other reason.*

"Okay," Nell said easily, sliding out of her chair and heading toward her bedroom. Michelle grabbed a tomato and started dicing it. She hadn't been cutting more than a minute before Nell reappeared with a huge smile on her face.

"Guess what?"

"What?"

"Uncle Esa is going to have dinner with us tonight, and then after that he's going to help me with my maths homework."

"That's good," said Michelle, forcing a smile. "Did he say where he is?"

"I didn't ask him. But he said he'd be home in a bit." A bit? What the hell did that mean? Fifteen minutes? Half an hour? Two hours?

Michelle sliced the tomato in front of her to ribbons. "Nell, can you call him back and tell him dinner will be ready in about an hour?"

Nell sighed heavily as if put upon. "All right."

Michelle lifted her eyes from her task. "Something wrong?"

"No," Nell mumbled.

"Good." Michelle grabbed another tomato, cutting more slowly. "You really liked it last week when he ate dinner with us a lot, didn't you?"

"Yeah, except I think it's very rude to text during dinner."

"So do I. Maybe if you ask him not to, he won't."

Michelle knew part of the reason he did it was to avoid making conversation with her. But it also meant he didn't talk as much as he could have with Nell.

"All right, I'm going to call him," said Nell, sliding off her chair again.

"An hour," Michelle reminded her as she started out of the kitchen.

"I KNOW!"

Another nice, cozy dinner for three, Michelle thought ruefully. It was the last thing she wanted. But if it meant Esa spent more time with Nell, then she'd grin and bear it.

23

"Something smells good."

Michelle ignored the small uptick in her pulse as Esa strolled into the kitchen. His timing was impeccable: Nell was just setting the last fork down on the table, and she herself had just finished tossing the pasta. All that was left was to grab the salt and pepper shakers and they could sit down.

Nell looked up at her uncle, smiling.

"We're having spaghetti," she announced.

"Smells good," Esa said to Michelle. He sounded like a bad actor who'd been directed to sound "casual," but couldn't do it.

"Thank you."

Now that her pulse had stopped its ascent, Michelle realized how uncomfortable she was. Him walking into the kitchen saying "Smells good" . . . Nell's setting the table . . . her making dinner . . . the only thing missing was her pecking Esa on the cheek and asking, "How was your day, honey?" If he'd been wearing a tie, he'd have walked in loosening it.

Esa approached the island in the center of the kitchen where Michelle was standing. "Anything I can do?"

"Nope, everything's taken care of. Thanks for asking, though." She carried the bowl of pasta over to the table, then remembered something. "Actually, if you don't mind bringing the salt and pepper shakers over . . ."

"No problem."

"You forgot the cheese, Michelle!" Nell rolled her eyes, slithering out of her seat to fetch the bowl of parmesan cheese on the counter.

"I love spaghetti," she informed Esa as she sat back down, her eyes watching Michelle as she filled her pasta bowl.

"I didn't know that," said Esa.

"I know," said Nell. It was a simple statement of fact, nothing pointed or guilt inducing behind it. Which almost made it worse, in Michelle's estimation.

Done serving Nell, she instinctively reached for Esa's plate next, same as last week. God. Damn. She knew it came from years of serving her father and brother, but she didn't. *He probably thinks I am the maid. Or the housekeeper.* But Esa put his hand out to stop her, same as he had last week.

"No, no, I can serve myself."

"Sorry," Michelle mumbled, feeling like a jerk. She was the one who kept screwing up, not him.

"Selma's family says grace before dinner," said Nell.

"So you've said," said Michelle.

"Maybe we should," Nell suggested tentatively.

Esa laughed curtly. "I don't think so."

Nell looked apprehensive. "How come?"

"Do you believe in God?" asked Esa.

Michelle shot him a withering look. Did he really intend getting into a theological discussion with an eight-year-old? It never failed: every time she thought he was finally smartening up, he did or said something that set the process back.

"I don't know," said Nell with uncertainty. "Do you?" Her eyes were scouring his face, trying to discern whether she'd said the right thing or not.

"I don't know, either," Esa admitted. "So maybe until we figure that out, we shouldn't say grace."

Nell pondered this. "I get it," she finally said. "We're hypocrites if we say it."

"Exactly," said Esa. He glanced at Michelle, looking pleased, as if he somehow deserved credit for Nell's powers of reason. Or maybe he was proud of how smart she was.

"Do you believe in God, Michelle?"

Michelle had been hoping to dodge that particular bullet, but it was too juicy a topic for a kid to let go of so easily. Cowardly as it might be, she was going to take the easy way out, and hedge her bets.

"I don't know, Nell."

"No one knows anything around here!"

They all laughed, moving on to small talk about their day, chat that Michelle facilitated for Nell's sake because Esa was still so inept at it. It was also a way of controlling the flow of conversation, ensuring it centered on Nell. Not that her own day had been chock filled with excitement, but she really wasn't comfortable with Esa knowing any of its details, and she imagined he felt the same way about his.

But it was dumb for her to think they could avoid direct interaction forever. Esa cracked first.

"I know we—you—haven't worked out the schedule for a couple of weeks from now, but I was wondering, if it's possible, for you to work on Saturday of that weekend. I have a charity event I have to do."

"Oh, what's that?" Michelle asked. She was genuinely interested.

"A thing called 'Kids on Skates.' The Blades organization provides free sticks and skates to poor kids and we teach them how to skate—or at least, give them a little fun on the ice."

"Sounds great. I don't think it'll be a problem."

"I don't know how to skate!" Nell said with a pout.

"Oh." Judging by the blank look on Esa's face, this had never crossed his mind.

"I want to learn."

"Uh . . . okay." Esa considered this. "How about this: if it's okay with Michelle, maybe she could drop you off at Met Gar after the event, and I could give you a skating lesson. Does that sound good?"

"Very good! Except for one thing."

Esa eyed Nell wearily. "What's that?"

"Can Michelle stay while I have my lesson?" She looked excitedly to Michelle. "Can you? *Pleeasse*?"

"Nell, your uncle probably wants to spend a little time alone with you," said Michelle, proud of being able to extricate herself from a potentially awkward situation so quickly.

"No, it's all right," said Esa.

Coward.

Nell shook Michelle's forearm. "So can you? *Pleeeeeasse*?"

"Let me think about it, okay?"

"Okay," said Nell, lips pressing together in disappointment as she twirled some spaghetti on to her fork.

"Can you skate?" Esa asked Michelle, his tone a tiny bit too smug for her liking.

"*Yes,* though it's been awhile." Skating was like riding a bike: you never forgot how to do it. So what if she still had vivid memories of Jamie calling her a "total spaz" as she fell on her ass repeatedly out on the ice? She'd gotten the hang of it eventually.

Nell looked thrilled. "You have to come, then! It'll be so much fun!"

"I said I'd think about it, sweetie, and I promise I will. Cross my heart."

*   *   *

"*Congrats, Saari: you* don't suck with kids."

Esa accepted Lou's backhanded compliment with a smile as he sat down on the Blades bench. "Kids on Skates" had just wound down, and it had been a huge success. Esa was surprised by how much he'd enjoyed it, despite occasional verbal abuse from Rory, who couldn't resist reminding him that he was a "prima donna arsehole."

The kids had been great. Some of them were naturals: a few minutes of instruction and they were whizzing down the ice. Others made Esa glad helmets were mandatory for children. He felt kind of bad for them: he could see how desperate they were to master just the basics, and how envious they were of those who were having no problem. It gave him pause, because he'd been a natural from the time he could skate. When he was a kid, he'd never stopped to think that kids who had a tough time might feel bad about themselves. All he'd done was mock them. God, what a little bastard he was.

There were a few "disciplinary cases," as Eric Mitchell

called them—kids who didn't realize hockey sticks were meant to stay on the ice, not be wielded like swords—but overall, the kids were extremely well behaved. Esa got a kick out of half of them being girls. He wondered: would Nell have any interest in playing hockey once she learned to skate? If she was anything like her mother, the answer was no. But maybe her father was an athlete. You never knew.

Rory skated over and sat on the bench beside him, reaching for a towel from the folded stack. "Some tough little fuckers with potential out there," he said, mopping his face.

"I know," said Esa.

"You looked to be enjoying yourself."

Esa cracked open a bottle of Gatorade. "I was."

"I was just congratulating him on not sucking with kids," said Lou.

"Nice way of putting it," said Rory.

"Wha? You want me to tell him he's Mr. Rogers?"

"I have no idea who that is, Lou. I'm from Ireland, remember?"

"Oh yeah. I'm sorry. About you being from Ireland, I mean."

"Go chase yourself, you fat fuck," Rory replied, patting down his neck. He glanced at Esa. "C'mon, let's head to the locker room."

"No, I've got a date." Esa took a long drink of Gatorade. It hit the spot perfectly. Sometimes he thought he could live on this stuff. "Michelle is bringing Nell down. She wants to learn how to skate."

"The kid's coming?" Lou looked delighted. "I've got to stick around!"

"I don't want people watching her and making her self-conscious."

Lou looked crestfallen. "I guess I get it." He hitched his pants up. "Can I at least say hello to her?"

"Jesus Christ, Lou, I'm not that much of a prick."

"You say that a lot, you know," Rory noted.

Esa patted Rory's shoulder. "I appreciate that. You're a true pal."

"Just thought I'd give you something to chew on."

"I've got enough to chew on, believe me."

Rory looked thoughtful. "You know what? I believe you do."

"Look, can you do me a favor?"

Rory pushed a tangled lock of hair off his forehead. "What's that?"

"Can you make sure the guys get the hell out of here? The last thing I need is for them to stick around to get a look at Michelle, like some pack of twelve-year-old boys."

"Ashamed of your friends, are you?"

"Shit, yeah."

Rory laughed. "No problem." He shot Esa a devilish look. "I believe she already knows Ulfie."

Esa gave him a long, dirty look.

"And Nell does know Jason," Rory continued.

"Cut the shit and just get them out of here. Michelle and Nell will be here any minute."

"All right, then." Rory rose. "I'm off to run interference. Let me know how it goes, yeah? With *Nell*, of course."

Esa threw him another dirty look before saying, "Bite me."

"Seriously, it's a good thing you're doing, Esa, teaching Nell to skate. It's important."

"Yeah." Esa was getting a little bit tired of everything he did with Nell being assigned such importance. Couldn't he just be teaching his niece to skate?

"I agree with Bono one hundred and ten percent," Lou chimed in.

"I think you better shut up, Lou, before he spears you like a meatball," said Esa.

The theme from *The Godfather* suddenly started playing, and Lou pulled his iPhone from his jacket pocket.

"Fuck a doodle fuck," he grumbled with a frown. "I can't stick around to say hi. I got a text from the missus. She wants me home pronto: my brother and his wife showed up three hours early for dinner, and she hates my sister-in-law like poison. I gotta hoof it."

"Three hours early?" asked Esa.

"My brother's a goddamn food mooch," Lou complained. "His wife doesn't cook. My wife does. She's probably been plying him with food since the minute he walked in the door. And he's been loving it, let me tell you. Another time, I guess. Tell the kid I said hello."

"Have you forgotten her name, Lou?" asked Esa innocently.

"No, I haven't forgotten her name," Lou retorted with a scowl. "I just like calling her 'the kid.' You got a problem with that, Saari?"

"No problem at all. I was just double-checking." Esa paused. "So tell me her name."

"It's Nell. Oh, and Saari? *Va fangool!*"

Esa looked at Rory questioningly. "He just told you to have intimate relations with yourself."

"Ah."

Muttering under his breath, Lou waddled away from the bench and down the carpeted ramp into the bowels of the arena.

"Guess I better be off as well," said Rory. "Hold back the wolf pack."

"I appreciate it."

"Yeah, well, you better. I'll see you at practice tomorrow morning."

"Yup."

Following Lou's lead, Esa decided to see if he'd gotten any messages, but then he remembered his phone was in his locker with his street clothes. Well, if Michelle really needed to reach him for something, she knew where he was.

Body jumping with nervous energy, he climbed over the boards onto the ice, and began to skate.

24

Michelle felt some of her anxiety melt away as Esa, who'd been circling the ice like some kind of high-speed dervish, slowed and skated over to the Blades' bench where she and Nell now sat. It had been weird, having a special pass to get into Met Gar, followed by a security guard escorting them to the ice. Nell loved it; it was all very cloak-and-dagger to her. Michelle thought about Jamie and her father, and what their reaction would be to this "private" skating lesson. Jamie would jeer first and think later, calling Esa a big show-off. Her dad would think it was great that Esa was going to teach Nell to skate.

"Hi, Uncle Esa!"

Nell's excited voice bounced off the walls of the complex. Perhaps it was because it was empty, but the space felt huge to Michelle, so huge that she couldn't imagine how it was possible all these seats were filled game after game. The ice, though slightly scored from the afternoon's activities, reminded Michelle of a smooth white bolt of silk. It was almost soothing.

"Hello, Nell."

Esa smiled warmly at Nell, extending the look to Michelle as well. "How was your afternoon?" Michelle asked politely.

Esa looked thoughtful. "I think it went well."

"You think? You mean you're not one hundred percent sure that you were great? Please don't tell me you're learning humility at this late age."

Esa looked pleasantly mystified by what she'd said, then refocused on Nell. "What did you two do today?"

"We went shopping. We got the thick socks you told us we needed for skating, and Michelle got some new knickers."

"I see."

"That's what we call panties at home," Nell explained. "Knickers."

"Yes, I know that," Esa murmured, slowly training his eyes on Michelle.

Oh, if he thought it was going to be Flirtation Day, he was wrong. Trying to ignore the way her body had responded with tingles when their eyes met, Michelle made her gaze go dead until he was forced to look away.

"So." Esa climbed over the boards to join Nell and Michelle on the Blades bench. "First, skates." He pulled two cardboard boxes out from under the bench, handing one to each of them. Michelle looked at him quizzically, her gaze coming back to life. She'd been under the impression they'd be renting skates. Esa smiled enigmatically, gesturing for her to open the box. Inside was a pair of classic white ice skates, the sheen on the blades so high you could see a piece of your reflection.

Nell, who'd received the same skates in her size, held them up by the laces, transfixed as they dangled in front of her eyes. "Look at them. They're so lovely."

"They are," Michelle agreed. She held hers up in front of Esa's face. "How did you know my shoe size?"

"We all leave our shoes by the door, remember?"

"Right." She'd hoped there might have been a clandestine element to it. She had an image of him furtively creeping into her room, holding his breath as he slowly turned the knob of her closet door, hoping it didn't squeak. Sad proof she needed some excitement in her life.

Esa dropped his gloves, clapping his hands twice. "Now, socks on."

"You're very bossy," said Nell.

Michelle looked down at her lap, fighting a laugh. Sometimes, it was bad that kids blurted out the first thing that came to their minds. This wasn't one of those times.

"Okay, now skates."

Esa moved to kneel down in front of Nell but she scooched out of range. "I can do it myself," she insisted.

"They need to be laced up tight or you can hurt your ankle," he explained.

"I still can do it myself," said Nell. She wasn't budging.

Esa looked frustrated. Michelle held her breath; for a split second, it looked like Esa might snap at Nell, but he seemed to get hold of himself. "All right, let me put Michelle's skates on first so you can see how it's done."

Panic crashed through Michelle as Esa knelt before her like some kind of hockey Prince Charming and reached for her left foot. Her eyes shot to the scoreboard, the empty chairs across the arena, anywhere but down at him. Yet she was overwhelmed with a sense of futility. Surely she wasn't the only one who felt the titanic surge in energy between them as he gently cupped her heel and slowly slid her foot into the skate. How could something so mundane feel so intimate? Michelle finally made herself look down at him, intuition telling her that he was feeling the energy, too, maybe even relishing it. He was lacing up her skates painstakingly slow, almost as if he didn't want it to end. "How does that feel?" Esa asked, raising his head to look at her when he was finally done. "Nice and tight?"

Michelle's heart shot up into her throat. "Um . . . yeah."

"Good."

She considered him a moment. There was no guile in his ice blue eyes. He was oblivious—to her anxiety, to his double entendre, to all of it. Thank God.

As casually as she could, Michelle plucked up her right skate before Esa could get to it. "I think I can handle this on my own," she said with a self-confident smile before turning to Nell. "Let your uncle do your skates. He ties them up nice and tight: you won't have to worry about hurting your ankle."

"All right." Nell glumly surrendered her right foot to Esa.

When he was finished lacing Nell up, and had made sure everyone's skates were tight enough, Esa scooped up two helmets, handing one to his niece and one to Michelle.

"I don't want to wear this!" Nell protested. "I'll look like a mong."

Michelle responded instantly with a sharp, swift glance. "We talked about that, remember?"

Esa looked lost for a moment, but didn't follow up. Michelle donned her helmet. It felt awkward. It was, however, preferable to getting a concussion.

"Okay, we're ready."

The three of them walked out on to the ice. Somewhere in those few seconds before getting laced up and leaving the bench, Nell's enthusiasm went into hibernation. She took two tiny, choppy steps, then pressed herself up against the boards. Michelle was right there with her, though she was trying to make it look like she just wanted to be with Nell. In reality, she was scared shitless. There was no way this was like remembering to ride a bike.

Esa skated a small figure eight in front of them. "Who wants to learn first?" he asked with a big grin.

Michelle glared at him. "I already told you: I know how to skate."

"Oh, right. I forgot. Then that leaves you, Nell." Esa took his terrified-looking niece by the hands. "Keep your ankles and knees nice and locked. I'm just going to pull you around, very slowly."

"Okay."

Michelle watched as Esa began to slowly pull Nell around the ice. She looked terrified at first, but after a few turns she started to relax, and even smile. Esa was nodding with encouragement. Since he was preoccupied with Nell, Michelle figured now was the perfect time to give herself a refresher course in skating.

The technique was simple. In fact, she could still hear her brother's voice in her head: push off with one foot, glide. Push off with the other foot, glide. Repeat. And that's it.

Michelle dropped her hand from where she'd been steadying herself against the wall, and as gingerly as she could, she pushed off against the ice with the blade on her right foot, which suddenly felt wobbly, but she didn't fall. She repeated the process with the left. Then right. Then left. She started to smile. So what if her strides were kid-sized? She was skating.

Until she wasn't, sitting on her butt on the ice like a big mortified baby as Esa, holding Nell's hand, skated over to her.

"Are you all right?"

"I'm *fine*," Michelle said tersely, slowly getting up. "Just a little rusty."

Esa offered his hand to help her up, looking amused. "Just a little?"

Michelle glowered at him. "You'd better not start making fun of me."

"Or what?"

"You two just go and skate," Michelle insisted. "I'll catch up."

"Really?"

"Just watch me."

"Can the three of us skate together?" Nell asked, looking back and forth between Esa and Michelle. "After I learn?"

"Well . . ." There was a hint of the mischievous in Esa's voice as he flicked a long, damp lock of hair off his forehead like some beautiful black stallion. "You'll have to ask Michelle. She's the one who's rusty."

"Of course the three of us can skate," said Michelle. "Like I said, you just skate with your uncle and I'll catch up to you in a bit, and then we'll all skate around together a few times. Okay?"

* * *

"Michelle, look at me!"

Michelle smiled weakly and waved to Nell as the little girl whizzed back and forth across the blue line. She had the Saari blood, all right: it had taken her all of ten minutes to get the hang of skating. Esa had hopped back on the Blades bench and was chugging Gatorade. Michelle was on all fours trying to get up gracefully from the ice. For the life of her, she couldn't figure out why the hell she kept falling, unless it was the universe's way of punishing her for her hubris. Two steps forward, one step back; or, in her case, five glides forward, one tumble to the ice. The first time it happened she saw Esa instinctually move to help her, but she gave him such a dirty look he just laughed and carried on with Nell. The thing was, it kept happening, and he kept laughing, and that pissed her off.

She'd just gotten herself upright (Christ, she was going to be a mess of pain tomorrow) when Esa hopped off the bench and skated over to her.

"Why don't you let me help you? I can fix this in five minutes."

"I'll bet."

Esa folded his arms across his chest. "Are you enjoying falling?"

Michelle could feel her cheeks turning red, that awful heat spreading across her face that she couldn't control. She hated it.

"You've been lucky so far: you haven't gone sprawling and knocked any teeth out. That would make a very exciting end to the day, I must confess."

"You're a jerk," Michelle muttered.

"I'm a jerk?" Esa chortled. "You have a pro hockey player at your disposal to help you skate and you insist on falling down, just to prove—what?"

"I'm not trying to prove anything."

"Then stop trying to knock your own teeth out and let me help you."

Michelle knew he was right, which was why she glowered at him again.

"You're taking uneven strides, so you have no rhythm. You're taking a long stride with your right leg, then a small stride with your left leg. Also, you're pushing very hard with your right skate, and you're digging the front of it into the ice. That's why you're falling."

"Anything else?" Michelle asked dryly. He had to be thinking she was a total moron.

"It's the unevenness you have to work on. You seem to drag the left foot a slight bit . . . like . . . um . . ." He looked around the arena, snapping his finger. "What's his name . . ."

"Igor?" Michelle supplied coldly.

Esa brightened. "Yes, that's who I was thinking of."

"Thanks. You're bolstering my confidence by leaps and bounds here, Esa."

"I'm sorry." He tilted his head in Nell's direction. "You have no choice but to do it for her. You promised her the three of us would skate together."

"I know what I said. You don't need to remind me."

"Then let's do it."

Esa came behind her, gently placing his hands around Michelle's waist. His hands felt huge gathered there, her skin suddenly warming.

"I don't see why you have to—"

Esa huffed in exasperation. "Because I'm going to *guide* you. You're going to skate in time with me, do you see? And then, when I think you've got it, I'll let you go and you'll skate on your own. And if you're fine on your own, then we can skate with Nell. Make sense?"

"Yes." Michelle contemplated apologizing for looking like a fusspot, but decided to just let it go.

"Good. Let's start."

Determined to keep mortification at bay, Michelle started slow. Push . . . glide. Push . . . glide. She was concentrating hard on making sure her strides were the same length, and that she wasn't gouging the ice with her skate. "Good," Esa murmured, his voice encouraging and low. Whenever Michelle glanced up at him for confirmation that she was doing all right, she received an encouraging smile that was so sexy it made her want to fly down the ice to get away from him.

There came a point when Esa let his hands drop from her waist, and she started skating on her own. She'd been concentrating so fiercely that she didn't notice he'd stopped supporting her until his left hand reached out to hold hers. The jolt of realization that he hadn't been supporting her nearly caused her to tumble, but she caught herself in time.

"You okay?" Esa asked.

She took his hand. "Fine."

"See what a good teacher I am?" he boasted. "You're skating beautifully."

"Maybe you just had an exceptional pupil."

"Maybe," Esa murmured with a boyish smile.

"Actually, I think you must be a good teacher: Nell seemed to pick it up right away."

"Genetics might have helped a *little* bit."

"A little."

Maybe it was because he wanted to make sure Michelle had her sea legs first, but Esa didn't skate straight over to Nell.

Instead, his hand remained clasped around hers as they continued skating the perimeter of the rink in a leisurely fashion. Michelle was enjoying it: the magic feeling of gliding across a surface as flawless as a pane of glass, the small chill in the air, the mini boost to her confidence that came from having not tripped or sprawled when he'd let her go. But most of all, she was enjoying holding hands with Esa and skating with him. She'd never skated with a guy before, and it was fun. *Fun. Right. Use the word you really mean, Michelle: romantic.*

It *was* romantic, the warmth of his hand suffusing hers, the sense of two striding as one as they glided around and around . . . Very romantic, which was why it was time she gave herself a good kick in the ass and made herself remember who she was and why she was here.

"I think it's time we skated with Nell, don't you?" she said. "She's been very patient."

Esa, who appeared to have been daydreaming, nodded. "Yes, she has." He looked as though he were trying to bring the world back into focus as his fingers slowly unfurled from around hers. Michelle wondered what he saw when he looked at her. *You value your attractiveness so little?* Why did she have to think about that now?

Side by side but not holding hands, they skated toward the blue line, where Nell was still buzzing back and forth. "Nell," Michelle called out when they were close enough for her to hear, "I think I can skate well enough not to embarrass you and your uncle here, so if you still want the three of us to skate together, now's your chance."

Esa took Nell's hand. "Are you sure you still want to do this?"

"Yes! Of course!" Her face fell. "Why? You don't want to?"

"No, nothing like that. I was just trying to tease you."

"Oh." Nell considered this, and so did Michelle. Nell had a sense of humor, and so did Esa. But his efforts to connect with her through teasing were hit or miss. All roads led to the same thing: he needed to get to know her better. Then he'd have a sense of what would fly, and what wouldn't.

Nell reached for Michelle's hand, smiling up at her as she did. "Are you ready, Michelle? I think you are."

"Oh, you do, huh?"

"Yes. I was watching your skating lesson a bit and I think you're doing very well."

"Then what are we waiting for?"

It felt to Michelle as if the whole world was holding its breath and watching as she, Nell, and Esa lined up, and at Esa's count of three, pushed off on their right skates. There were a few wobbly seconds at the beginning before they got in sync, but then they were off, gliding down the shimmering carpet of ice, nice and slow. Michelle stole a surreptitious glance at Esa: on the outside he was the confident, cool uncle, but the hope in his eyes gave him away; she could see how important it was to him that Nell was having a good time. Michelle wished she could point out that he had nothing to worry about: skating between them with Esa holding her left hand and Michelle holding her right, she looked *ecstatic*.

She looked up at Michelle with a big, happy grin. "Isn't this lovely, Michelle?"

Michelle grinned back. "It is." It was.

Nell nodded to herself, as if Michelle had just confirmed something. Nell looked at her uncle, asking him the same question. "It's great!" Esa replied with unabashed enthusiasm. Nell's entire body seemed to light up.

"I bet if anyone came in right now and saw us, they'd think we were a proper family!" she said giddily.

Thawap! Michelle felt as if she'd just been hit in the chest with a little girl-sized snowball. She instinctively turned her head, watching as Esa's gaze slowly traveled to meet hers. What should I say? his eyes seemed to be asking. That *was* what he wanted to know, wasn't it? The gaze continued and she broke eye contact, fearful that if she kept staring into his eyes much longer, she'd stumble and fall. Fearful of that, and more.

~⁓~

25

~⁓~

"I enjoyed today very much."

Michelle, standing at the sink scouring some large pots that couldn't fit in the dishwasher, smiled warmly as she looked over her shoulder at Esa as he strolled into the kitchen.

"Me, too."

"I'm glad."

It had been a tiring day, but a happy one for Nell and her uncle. Nell was starting to warm up to Esa a little. He still couldn't broach the subject of her mother with her—and sometimes, Michelle got the sense that he didn't want to. She liked to think it was enough for now that Nell was beginning to open up to him. Bonding with her uncle on their shared loss would come eventually.

Esa came and stood by the sink, lifting a pot out of the drying rack. "I can dry." His eyes traveled around the kitchen. "Where do you keep the dishtowels?"

Michelle lifted a hand from the soapy water, pointing out the lower drawer where the dishtowels were folded. "Knock yourself out."

Esa fetched himself a towel and began drying the pot. "I think Nell really enjoyed herself. Don't you?"

"C'mon, Esa. You know she did."

"Did she say anything when you tucked her in?"

Michelle concentrated hard on scrubbing the saucepan in her hand. "No. But she really didn't have to, did she? She was high as a kite all day." She did mention being a "proper family" again, but Michelle saw no reason to go there, not when they were having a nice relaxing conversation.

"She really does have natural skating ability," Esa enthused. "Is there a girl's ice hockey team at her school? Maybe it's something she'd want to do."

"Maybe." Michelle began rinsing off a pot. "You should ask her."

She felt a bit dowdy standing there with her dishwashing gloves on, but her mom had always worn them, and had always advised her to wear them since she was a little girl. "You can always tell a woman's age by her hands," her mom had said. Weird that she was thinking about that now.

"Esa."

"Mmm?"

"I just had an idea."

Esa looked dubious. "What's that?"

"I thought what you did with Nell today was great. But another thing that might help bring you two closer is if you tuck her in more often on nights when you're home."

"I do tuck her in!"

Michelle hesitated. "Sometimes. And sometimes she goes off to bed on her own."

Esa hesitated. "Don't you think she's too big to be tucked in?"

"*No*," Michelle said, shocked. "She's a little girl! Why on earth would you think that?"

"It just feels—"

"Uncomfortable?"

"Mmm."

"Might I remind you it's not about you?"

Esa laughed lightly. "Ah, the Beck slap on the wrist. It's been awhile. I've missed it."

Michelle forced her attention back to the soapy water as a tiny jag of arousal went through her. Esa was silent as he finished drying the pot in his hands, quietly placing it on the counter. Michelle knew what was going to happen next, and she knew she should leave the kitchen now. But she didn't. And so, when Esa slid up behind her, wrapping his arms around her waist and pulling her to him, she leaned back against him, eyes closing as she felt the heat of his lips upon her neck, provocative.

"Michelle?"

"I know. I know what you're going to say." As gingerly as she could, she took her hands from the soapy water and peeled the rubber gloves off, putting her arms over his.

"Tell me, then," he murmured in her ear. Michelle moaned, trying not to let herself become so overwhelmed so easily, so quickly.

"You're going to tell me," she said weakly, eyes rolling up in her head as he lightly nipped her earlobe, "that this is inevitable and it's useless to fight it."

"Correct." He pulled her tighter to him, his rising hard-on pressing into her ass. "And you're going to tell me this isn't a good idea."

"It's not."

Esa's laugh was low and seductive. "Haven't you figured out by now that I'm a bad man?"

Michelle couldn't speak.

His mouth was pressed to the shell of her ear again, his hips pushing ever so slightly against her. "I want you, Michelle. Why don't you tell me what you want?"

It was too much. Michelle turned in his embrace, and taking his face in her hands, dragged his mouth to hers, her whole body straining against his. Esa gave a wicked little laugh and then his tongue was in her mouth, sinking deep, swirling, demanding a response. She answered him, heat charging through her. If he was bad, then she was worse, because she knew this was wrong, but she was going to do it anyway.

Esa ended the kiss, the unapologetic lust in those hooded, ice blue eyes of his enough to make her woozy. Taking her by the hand, he led her through the vast living room to the other side of the apartment where the bedrooms were. All she wanted to do was get him out of those clothes and ride what she had no doubt was that magnificent cock of his.

He ushered her into his bedroom, kicking the door closed behind them and locking it. Michelle barely had time to catch her breath before Esa had her pressed up against the wall and was crushing his mouth down on hers, rough and demanding. Michelle arched against him, heat pumping through her. Esa groaned, and a small thrill of triumph played through Michelle, knowing that using her body this way turned him on. But she wanted him tighter against her; she wanted to be able to feel him throbbing through his jeans. She lifted one leg and, running it smoothly, silkily up the outside of his thigh, wrapped it around his hip, pulling him closer.

Esa gave a low animal growl as he bit her neck. Michelle inhaled sharply, giving herself over to the tiny bursts of pain he was inflicting on her. Her mind was so fogged she couldn't decide whether she wanted to have this torture continue, or to beg him to fuck her right now.

Esa made the decision for her. Tearing his mouth from her neck, he pushed the leg she had wrapped around his hips down, falling to his knees in front of her. Oh, God, the torture was going to continue. She could feel the pulse beat between her legs as his impatient fingers worked the zipper of her jeans as he pulled them down over her hips.

"Black lace panties," he murmured approvingly, glancing up at her. "Are these a pair of those new knickers you bought earlier today?"

Michelle laughed.

"I'm guessing you wanted this to happen," said Esa, his tongue flicking out to lick her between the legs. Michelle gasped, hands instinctually reaching for his shoulders. "You're so wet," he whispered as he continued to lap at her. "I think we better do something about that."

Michelle shuddered as he hooked his thumbs over the top of her panties and yanked them down. She kicked her panties and jeans away, her nails digging into his shoulders with anticipation. Her breath held as Esa took the pad of his thumb and slowly began rubbing her clit. "Is this all right?"

Michelle could only nod as her nails dug even deeper, her legs beginning to tremble.

"How about this?" he continued in a low voice, slipping two fingers inside her as his thumb continued to play. Michelle began pumping her hips against him in rhythm to his fingers. Christ, she was close. He had to know. He did know: plunging a third finger inside her, his voice was deep and authoritative as he commanded her to come for him.

She came hard, her orgasm thundering through her body, her cries of pleasure coming from deep within. She was filled with such joy that she began laughing, looking down at Esa.

"Wow."

"That's all you can say?" Esa replied in amusement. " 'Wow'? You're a teacher. Tell me what my grade is."

"Definitely an A plus."

"I think that might be the only one I've ever gotten in my life, though I'd like to try for another."

The ache inside Michelle returned full force as Esa started unbuttoning her shirt. He looked pleasantly surprised when the shirt opened to reveal a black bra with lacy-edged cups.

"Michelle. Never in a million years would I have suspected this is what you'd be wearing under your everyday clothing."

"Really?" Michelle asked, gazing back at him hungrily as she slid the bra straps down her shoulders. "What did you think? I wore granny panties and a training bra?"

Esa laughed. "I'm not sure what I thought." His eyes widened with appreciation as she tossed her bra aside. Michelle couldn't believe how uninhibited she felt. This was not the way she usually was in the bedroom. Not that she was boring or unresponsive, but there was something about the way Esa made her feel when he looked at her, like she was the sexiest woman on earth, that gave her permission to be bad.

"You're beautiful," he marveled. He reached out, fingertips brushing her nipples. Nice, but not naughty.

Michelle stilled his hand. "That's not what I want."

Esa's eyes flashed with desire.

"What I want," Michelle purred, reaching down to stroke his erection through his jeans, "is for you to take off your clothes, take me over to the bed, suck my tits until I'm close to losing it, and then come inside me hard."

Esa looked at her in wonder as he sucked in a ragged breath. "Jesus, who *are* you?"

"I'm the nanny."

This time his laugh was low, bordering on a growl as he

whipped his long-sleeved T-shirt off over his head and hastily
undid his jeans, shoving them, along with his boxer briefs, down
his hips, and kicking them clear when they hit the floor. His
body was as Michelle knew it would be: rock hard, cut, muscular, sculpted, his dick as big as she expected it would be. The
ache inside her intensified.

Esa scooped her up in his arms, dropping her on the bed.
Climbing atop her, he braced his weight on his forearms, and
lowering his head, he began flicking his tongue against her
right breast, then her left. And all the while, his large, hard
erection was pressing against her. There was no way Michelle
could resist moving her hips against him to increase the friction. Esa growled, his mouth moving on to suck her tits, hard.
The aching inside her was turning into desperation. Panting,
she grabbed his face in her hands, kissing him hungrily.

"Fuck me," she whimpered. "Please."

Sitting back and kneeling between Michelle's splayed
thighs, Esa reached over and pulled a condom out of his night
table drawer. He tore the package open with his teeth, then
sheathed himself before putting a hand on each of her thighs.
"Open your legs for me, Michelle."

Groaning with need, Michelle accommodated him, but he
wasn't quite done yet. His gaze hazy with lust, his hands slid
up to her knees and he pushed them up, hard. "I want to go
deep," he said. Michelle, so aroused she felt close to delirious,
could only nod.

She lifted her head off the pillow, watching as he slowly
pushed his way deep inside her, then slowly pulled out again.
Slow and deep again, then out. Michelle let out a strangulated
noise as she put her head back on the pillow, shuddering at the
sensation of how he filled her.

"This okay?" he asked hoarsely, coming forward so they
were face-to-face.

Michelle shook her head vehemently. "No. No. I want it
harder." She pulled her knees up a fraction higher, locking her
ankles around his upper back.

"Fuck," Esa whispered as he thrust into her with more
force, giving her what she wanted. Michelle gasped, her hands
gripping his shoulders as she rocked against him.

Esa threw his head back and continued thrusting, hard and

fast, as Michelle felt the waves of sensation rapidly building inside her. She was trembling uncontrollably now, frantic for release.

"I'm close," she panted. "I'm so close . . ."

Esa started slamming into her, again and again and again, faster and faster until Michelle felt herself begin to shatter, her orgasm screaming through her. She lost herself in it, reveling in every hot pulse of pleasure. Esa tensed, giving himself over to a few final deep thrusts, his body shuddering against Michelle's as she held him tight. Both of them finished now, he put his sweaty forehead to hers, then kissed it. An unexpected wave of tenderness for him swept through her, catching her completely off guard. It scared her, so much so that she pushed it out of her mind. They'd taken care of the sexual tension between them. That was all that mattered.

26

Spooning with Esa in his sumptuous king-sized bed in the afterglow, Michelle wondered what it would be like to spend the entire night with him. It was impossible, of course, because of Nell, and because—well, it just was.

Thinking back on their lovemaking threatened to arouse Michelle all over again, which embarrassed her. She couldn't believe how shameless she'd been with him. She'd shocked herself. Perhaps deep down, she wanted to show him she wasn't some buttoned-down prude. But more likely, it was the knowledge that this was her one chance to go for it with this incredibly sexy man as they finally chose to sate the sexual tension between them. Now they could get on with their lives.

Every time Michelle found herself drifting off, she'd force herself awake. Finally, she reached behind her, giving his thigh a gentle shake. "Esa? We—"

Esa's hand tightened around her waist as he kissed her shoulder. "Not yet, Michelle," he requested in a weary voice. "Let's just try to enjoy this for a couple of minutes more."

Michelle felt stung as she glanced back over her shoulder at him. "What are you talking about?"

"C'mon. You know what I'm talking about," he said gently. "You want to discuss what just happened. You're going to say it was a mistake, and then you're going to tell me it can never happen again. All I'm asking for is that we relax for a few minutes more before we go through this song and dance again."

" 'Go through this song and dance'?"

Offended, Michelle sat up, drawing the sheet to her chest, trying to ignore how gorgeous he looked right now, his thick black hair all askew, his gaze drowsy. It seemed unfair that someone so striking should be such a jerk.

Esa groaned, propping himself up on one elbow as he rested his head in the palm of his hand. "I'm sorry. That was a bad choice of words. But you know I'm right: you're going to tell me this was a mistake."

"Am I that predictable?"

"In a word, yes."

Michelle gave him a dirty look. "I don't think it was a mistake," she said carefully. "I think it was an itch we both needed to scratch. And now that it has—"

"It can never happen again. Right?"

Michelle's mouth fell open in indignation. "You're such a jerk!"

"Tell me what you were going to say, then."

"What I was going to say was . . ." Words began tangling in her mouth as she began growing flustered. ". . . is that you—okay *maybe* I was going to say something along those lines."

Esa laughed.

"You seem to forget there's a little girl living in the house."

"I haven't forgotten that at all, actually."

Michelle was confused. "What are you saying?"

"I see no reason why it can't happen again, and I see no reason why, if it does, Nell can't know."

Michelle stared at him like he was crazy. "Are you *kidding* me?"

Esa rolled onto his back with a sigh. "Go on. Explain it all to me. I'm all ears."

"Let's say it did happen again. You don't think it would confuse the hell out of Nell? She's already got this fantasy about the three of us being a family. I don't think her knowing we're sleeping together, if we ever do sleep together again, would be healthy. It would give her unrealistic expectations, and that's not fair. And, as I told you in an earlier conversation, I don't want to send her the message that sleeping with your boss is okay."

Esa rubbed his hands over his face. "Okay, so we'll hide it from her."

"Esa." Michelle was growing frustrated. "Do you really think this is going to happen again? Seriously?"

"Do you really think it's not?" he countered. "We're attracted to each other. We live under the same roof. What do you think?"

Michelle was silent.

"Ah." A look of satisfaction overtook his face. "Miss Rational finally admits defeat."

Michelle searched hard for the right words. "I really need to think about this. I don't usually do this sort of thing, you know."

Esa looked unfazed as he reached out, lazily running his index finger back and forth across her knee. "It wouldn't matter to me if you had. We enjoyed each other. That's all that counts."

"Even so, it's important to me that you know I'm not some kind of slut, like you. Which is another reason that I'm not really sure about all this, especially the part about it happening again."

Esa looked flirtatious as he laced his fingers behind his head. "You're saying you don't want to share me, is that it?"

Egotistical bastard. "No, that's not what I'm saying at all." Michelle paused. "I guess what I'm saying is I don't want to be in a relationship with you."

"I don't want a relationship with you, either," Esa quickly retorted. "So what's the problem?"

"*Nell,*" Michelle hurled back, trying to ignore the sting of his words. "If we're not in a relationship, it doesn't look very good to just be fuck buddies, does it?"

"No, I suppose it doesn't," Esa grumbled.

Selfish jerk, Michelle thought again. "The other reason I'm reluctant to let this happen again is that I have no desire to become your in-house concubine. The thought is demeaning."

"I don't have concubines."

"Your ever-changing gallery of women, whatever you want to call it," Michelle said testily.

Esa ran his thumb back and forth across his lower lip thoughtfully. "I guess I can understand that."

"Good."

Esa eyed her quizzically. "So—?"

"So—?"

"Let me make sure I'm getting things straight." He looked at her pointedly. "We're not going to rule out the fact it might happen again, even though, according to you, that's highly doubtful," he said dubiously.

Michelle felt like the tangled vines of her own words were twisting around. "Right."

"And we don't want a relationship with one another."

"God, no."

"And it's not going to be a 'thing.' "

"Right."

"So basically, what we're doing is just going back to the way things were: coexisting in a state of sexual tension."

"You sound like an attorney with a Finnish accent laying out a case."

"That's kind of how I feel, Michelle."

"I . . ." Michelle suddenly felt like her mind was trapped in a revolving door, going round and round. The way Esa just laid it all out did make it sound, in a way, like she wanted to pretend it never happened.

"I told you: I'm just confused," she admitted, touching his face.

Esa's look softened. "I know."

"I want to do the right thing by Nell." And I also stepped over a big line here in terms of professional conduct, Michelle thought to herself.

"How about this." Esa sat up, putting his arm around her shoulder. Michelle loved his scent: sex and sweat and man. "We just go with the flow. See what happens."

Michelle hesitated. "All right," she said, even though she wasn't a "go with the flow" person.

"It's settled, then." Esa closed his eyes with a sigh, his head leaning back against the headboard. "This is nice. Peaceful."

Michelle lifted her head to look at him. With his eyes closed, he actually looked vulnerable. "It's not peaceful with the others?"

"Not really," said Esa. It was clear he wasn't going to supply her with details.

She brushed a stray lock of hair behind his ear. "I should go."

Esa opened his eyes, picking up his watch from his night table. "It's not even midnight yet. You could set an alarm to make sure you're up before Nell."

"I know." Michelle suddenly felt awkward. "I'd just feel better if I were back in my own bed. I'm a light sleeper, and sometimes, when Nell gets up in the middle of the night to pee or get a glass of water, she peeks in on me to make sure I'm there. She needs to know I'm there, Esa."

He kissed the top of her head, then turned her face toward his. "I think I told you this already, but just in case I forgot, in the heat of the moment, you're very beautiful."

A lump formed in Michelle's throat. "Well, so are you."

"When a man compliments you, you should say 'Thank you.'"

"Thank you," Michelle forced herself to whisper. Her heart desperately wanted to believe he'd never said this to anyone else. But she wasn't a fool: he probably said it to every woman he'd ever slept with. The only difference was, the others were beautiful and knew it.

He kissed her, with concentration, with tenderness. "Thank you," he murmured when he pulled away. "For a wonderful day and night."

"My pleasure."

Harsh reality intruded as Michelle slid out of bed and began collecting her clothing. "You have practice early tomorrow morning, right?"

"Yes, but I'm back by ten, and then you have the day and night off?"

Michelle nodded. "Don't forget to set out Nell's uniform tomorrow night before school Monday. And—"

"*Michelle.*"

"I know, I know." When in doubt, deflect. She came around to his side of the bed and kissed him. "Sleep well."

"You, too."

"Minx," he added sexily as she headed for the bedroom door.

Heat trilled through Michelle's body as she headed quietly to her private bathroom, her clothing a bundle in her arms. It might wake Nell up if she ran a bath. She was better off taking a quick shower. Maybe the hot, steamy water beating down on her would make her drowsy, and she'd fall asleep fast. That way, she'd be able to put off going over their encounter until tomorrow. She doubted it, though. Her good-girl brain had already kicked into high gear, demanding she answer one simple question: what the hell have you done?

27

Strapping himself into his seat for the flight out to L.A., Esa started thinking about Michelle. Again.

The team was on an extended road trip. Up until now, he'd been a big fan of road trips: there was always a new selection of gorgeous women to sleep with. The next morning, he was on his way and didn't have to worry about seeing them again. The only thing he had to give any serious thought to was playing. Yet here he was, the team's charter pulling away from the gate, and he couldn't stop thinking about Michelle.

It had been three nights since they'd slept together. She'd been different than he'd expected, which maybe wasn't fair. He didn't think she'd be uptight, but he wasn't expecting a "fuck me hard" type, either. Just thinking about that nearly gave him a hard-on. The shock only added to the pleasure of finally having her.

Did that make him sound like a pig? She'd agreed the tension between them had been growing. It was unavoidable. So it wasn't like he'd used her, or objectified her. It was like . . . something.

He glanced over at Ulfie, who was already asleep. Esa was

glad: he really wasn't in the mood to talk right now. He had no doubt that when Ulfie woke up, somewhere over the Midwest, he'd be unable to avoid conversation. His own ruminations about his personal life would have run the course by then. Not that he'd discuss this latest development with Torkelson.

Sex with Michelle felt different. He'd slept with lots of women in his life. Apart from playing hockey, what on earth was better than sex? Nothing. But with Michelle it felt like more than two bodies colliding. Not all the sexual encounters he'd had over the years were one-night stands; he'd had a string of serious girlfriends, even a fiancée or two mixed in the bunch. But even during the encounters that had an emotional component to them, he felt that he was outside himself, watching.

It was a detachment thing. An ego thing. He'd find himself thinking, *I'm going to show this woman how great I am in bed. I want to watch her come because it'll confirm my own prowess to me.* He always made sure his partners had a good time, but not because that's what lovers did for one another. He did it because he wanted them to tell him how great he was afterward. And they always did.

But he was in his body the entire time he was with Michelle. He was aware of every sensation she triggered in his body. He'd wanted to please her: not for the usual reasons, but because giving her pleasure made him happy. He closed his eyes as the wheels of the plane started rolling faster down the tarmac.

What the fuck was wrong with him?

* * *

The screams were piercing enough to jolt Michelle from a heavy sleep it had taken hours to achieve. It took a few heart pounding, disorientating seconds before she realized they were coming from Nell.

Michelle flew into Nell's room, the serene, pearl glow of the nightlight guiding her to Nell's bed where she sat and gently shook her out of her nightmare. Nell's eyes jolted open with a gasp; she, too, took a few seconds to figure out her bearings. Then she began to cry.

"Uncle Esa's dead!" she wailed.

"He's fine, honey. It was just a nightmare." Michelle gathered Nell up in her arms, rocking her. "It was just a bad dream."

"He died in a plane crash like mummy," Nell sobbed. "Mummy died after she'd been away for three days and Uncle Esa's been away for three days and he's on a plane and now . . ."

Michelle hugged her harder. "It was a nightmare, Nell. Just because your mom died after being away for three days doesn't mean the same thing is going to happen to your uncle."

Michelle continued rocking her. She'd had a bad feeling this might happen. Nell had been anxious when the team had flown south for a few days, but she'd dealt with it. But this was different. For her, a week was a very long time for Esa to be away, and so far away, too.

Nell looked up at her with a tearstained face, her lower lip quivering. "What if the plane he takes back home crashes?"

"It won't, honey." Michelle picked up Nell's iPhone from the night table and checked the time: three a.m., which meant it was midnight in California. "Would you like to call him?"

"He's probably sleeping."

"That's okay. I'm sure he won't mind. The last thing in the world he'd ever want is for you to be upset and worried."

"But we text."

Michelle smiled sadly. "I know." Esa was so awful and awkward on the phone that texting had proved to be the best way for him and Nell to communicate when they were apart. However, in this case, there was no way it would suffice.

"I don't know," coaxed Michelle, "I have the feeling you might feel a million times better if you heard his voice."

"No, I'm all right now," Nell insisted after a long pause. My ass, Michelle thought. It broke her heart sometimes, the way Nell sometimes denied she was a little girl and instead acted like a little adult who had to be strong. Maybe it was the way she was raised, or a way of protecting herself; a survival tactic she'd learned in the year after her mom's death. "Nell." Michelle wiped away the wetness on her cheeks. "It's all right to need reassurance after a nightmare like that, especially from your uncle."

"I don't want him to think I'm a baby," Nell said quietly.

"He would *never* think that. Ever." Michelle picked up the phone. "Let's call him."

Nell shook her head no. "I'm okay."

"You're sure?"

"Yes."

Michelle put the phone down. "All right." She kissed Nell's forehead. "Can I get you a glass of water?"

"No, I'm okay. Honest, Michelle."

"Well, if you need me, you just wake me. Try to get back to sleep." She gave Nell a kiss and tucked her back in, glad she was able to console her. She didn't know what Nell's year with Leslie had been like, but she was going to call Leslie tomorrow and ask her some questions, big ones that Esa should have asked when Nell came to live with him.

Michelle slipped back into bed, trying not to think about Esa. Though he was out of the apartment more often than he was in it, she missed him. In the three days between when they'd had sex and he'd left for his road trip, things had felt weird. The sexual tension was worse than before. Or maybe she was just imagining it. For someone who prided herself on being in control, the only time she felt like she wasn't floundering was when she was taking care of Nell. She turned onto her back, couldn't get comfortable, and shifted back onto her stomach. She should have pushed harder for Nell to talk to Esa. Too late. She'd tell Esa about Nell's nightmare when he got home. For now, she'd just keep doing what she did best: loving Nell, and keeping her safe, happy, and secure.

28

The last thing Esa expected to see when he walked into his kitchen at six-thirty a.m. following a red-eye flight back from L.A. was Michelle at the table sipping coffee, her head bent low over a crossword puzzle. Obviously she was waiting for him. Despite his exhaustion, he felt desire creep through him; maybe Michelle had changed her mind and had decided they should just go for it.

"Hey," he said, determined to keep it casual. "Surprised to find you awake."

Michelle folded the newspaper closed. "I have a lot on my mind."

She looked pensive. Not a "go for it" expression. Esa fought the urge to stand behind her and rub her shoulders. She probably wouldn't let him. He'd have to settle for conversation.

"How was your flight?"

"Fine."

Michelle smiled faintly. "Good."

Esa felt an uneasy tug in his gut. "Michelle, is everything all right with Nell?"

"Yes and no." She quickly tucked a strand of hair that had

come loose from her ponytail behind her ear. "Look, you know I normally wouldn't hit you with something the minute you walked in the door, but today's my day off, and I thought you should know before Nell wakes up."

"Right," Esa said with a tight smile. Jackass. He hadn't checked the calendar while he was out west; his focus had been solely on the ice.

"The good news is that she had a great week at school," Michelle said proudly. "She got high grades on her language arts and math tests, and she was named Student of the Week, which made her very happy."

Esa sat down opposite her, bracing himself. "Now tell me the bad."

"She had a horrible nightmare about you dying in a plane crash. It took me several minutes to calm her down and assure her you were okay. I kept urging her to call you, but she wouldn't. Every night this week, she's been doing everything she can to stall going to bed." Michelle hesitated, then her hand crept to his. "You're going to have to talk to her."

Esa nodded, filling with sadness. Every time he thought he had it beat—thought he and Nell had it beat—something would happen that would set things back. He felt like he kept rolling a rock up a mountain, only to have it roll back down again.

"I called Leslie," Michelle continued.

Esa pulled his hand away. "*What? Why?*"

"Because I thought it would be good to know what Nell was like last year after your sister died. She said Nell was a little trooper."

Esa looked distressed. "Of course she was. Just like my sister. Danika hated showing weakness."

"Sounds like a family trait."

"Yes, it is," Esa admitted without any hesitation. "Finns are very stoic. We pride ourselves on being tough and not complaining. We fought off the Soviets on our own for fifty years. Some people say we're cold and unemotional." He decided to issue a challenge. "Tell me: have you found that to be true?"

"I don't think right now is the time or place to talk about what happened between us," Michelle said softly.

"Of course." His exhaustion was making a rapid return. "Did Leslie say anything else?"

"Just that she tried to get Nell to talk about Danika, but she didn't want to, even though she's known Leslie all her life. She sounded really nice. Very open, relaxed."

"She is." He rubbed his eyes. "I'm sure Nell would have opened up to Leslie eventually," he said curtly.

"Are you?"

"Yes."

"You sound angry."

"Not angry. Perplexed. It mystifies me why she couldn't get a nanny for Nell if she was traveling so much. Wouldn't that have been better than uprooting her and sending her to me?" Michelle looked shocked, but Esa forged ahead before she could say anything. "I know what you're thinking: that I'm saying this because I resent having Nell. But it's not true. I love Nell. And I'm glad she's here. Really. But I've been thinking about this a lot lately. And the more I do, the more I realize Leslie wasn't as good to Nell as she could have been."

Michelle regarded him uneasily. "Actually, she was, Esa."

Shit. What was she going to hit him with now, before the sun was even up? He waited.

"Her giving Nell to you had nothing to do with her career. It had to do with her personal life." Michelle hesitated. "She got engaged to a man who doesn't like children. He pretty much ignored Nell whenever he was over at Leslie's. Or he would act like her presence was a huge imposition."

Esa felt a thundering behind his eyes. "What?"

"To her credit, Leslie didn't want Nell growing up in that kind of atmosphere."

"She could have dumped this asshole!"

"People can't help who they fall in love with." Michelle looked down at the table. "That's what I've heard, anyway."

Esa felt warmth spreading through him as he momentarily forgot about the Leslie/Nell situation. What Michelle had just said about not being able to control who you fall for should not have been affecting him this way, and it shouldn't have prompted her to look away, either. Esa thought she was pretty delusional in thinking their going to bed again *might* happen.

It *definitely* was going to happen. Not right now, not today, but it was.

He tugged his wandering mind back to the Leslie situation. "Why didn't she tell me all this?"

"Because she knew you'd want to go to London and punch the guy's lights out. You know, the way you do right now?"

Esa shook his head in anger. "The idea of anyone being mean to Nell . . ."

"I know."

Quiet settled over them like a veil. Michelle, the woman who was always in control, looked distraught. If I went around the table and held her in my arms, he thought, would she push me away? There was only one way to find out.

He went to her, stroked her cheek, wrapped his arms around her neck from behind. "I missed you," he confessed.

Michelle seemed to hold her breath. Then she rose, turning to him.

"I kind of missed you, too."

Esa couldn't help but smile. " 'Kind of'?"

Michelle looked troubled. "Esa, this is just too—"

"Yes, weird, I know. So let's keep it simple so your head doesn't explode." He drew her into his arms. She was stiff at first, but gradually she loosened up, wrapping her arms around his neck. Her body was warm, her scent soft and innocent, and he found himself going very still. He wanted to make that innocence disappear, right here, right now. Take her on the table, or up against the counter, her legs wrapped around his hips while he pumped in and out of that tight, wet pussy.

Michelle gently pushed him away after a few seconds. "That's as much simple as I can handle right now." She looked up at him apologetically. "Okay?"

"Yes, of course." He was lying. His longing for her wasn't flagging one bit, and he thought: I'm used to just taking what I want and getting it, and I want you. But he'd told her he'd keep it simple, and he had to follow through. The only way to do that was to get out of the kitchen as fast as he could, so those plump, inviting lips of hers weren't right in front of him.

"I'm really beat," he said.

Michelle nodded. "Me, too."

"Nell will be up in a few hours?"

Michelle, who Esa knew truly did think of Nell first, looked accommodating after a thoughtful pause. "I can leave later today so you can get some sleep. Say noon?"

"Thanks, Michelle," said Esa as a wave of gratitude washed over him. "I really appreciate it."

"It's important you're not dragging your ass all day—for Nell's sake."

"Right."

"Good night, Esa."

"You mean 'Good morning.' I'll talk to Nell first thing tomorrow—I mean, later today. I promise."

"Good."

Esa watched her leave, her tiny body receding away from him through the kitchen doorway, then through the living room, until finally she was out of sight. He heard her bedroom door open then close quietly. Finally, he was left with the continuing gallop of his own heartbeat. Simple had always been his MO when it came to women. Now, not one but two women were bringing disorder to his carefully controlled life, and he wasn't kicking against it the way he might have just a few short months ago. Was that good or bad?

29

"*What are we* doing today?"

Nell's voice was laced with impatience as she threw herself down onto the couch beside Esa. He understood: she'd been awake since eight, waiting for him to get up, and he'd only just now, at eleven thirty, stumbled out of bed to grab a cup of coffee. Michelle left the moment he woke. He hadn't slept as well as he'd hoped.

"I don't know yet," he said honestly. "Let me have some breakfast, and we can think about it."

Nell frowned. "All right."

"Tell me about school this past week. Michelle said you did well on your exams."

"Tests. They call them tests here. Yes, I did well. Because they were BOR-ING. They were very easy."

Esa looked down into his coffee cup so Nell didn't catch his painful smile. She sounded like Danika, who always made school sound like a breeze. Esa was never sure whether she really did glide through every subject, or whether she just said it to make him feel like a dolt. The only thing he glided through was the ice.

"She said you were Student of the Week."

"It's just an honorary title. You don't get a cash prize or anything." She looked disappointed.

"That kinda sucks."

"Uncle Esa! You shouldn't say 'sucks'! It's not nice."

"You're right."

She kept glancing at him sideways as he sipped his coffee. "I'm going to miss Michelle today."

Esa broke into a smile. "I bet."

"Are you going to miss Michelle today?" Nell asked, watching his face carefully.

Esa scratched the whiskers on his chin. "I guess. I mean, it was fun when we went ice skating."

"Maybe we can do more things together," Nell suggested.

"Maybe," Esa said noncommittally. Nell looked disappointed again, but there was nothing he could do about it. He wasn't going to refuel her fantasies about the three of them becoming a family.

Nell settled back against the couch, seemingly fascinated with her left braid. She undid it, then started rebraiding it again. Esa had been slightly dismayed that when he'd gotten up she hadn't greeted him with a big hug the way she had the night he'd come home with the walking boot on his foot, especially knowing that she'd had a meltdown about his plane crashing. He took a long gulp of coffee to fortify himself. He was going to get the plane crash issue out of the way so it wasn't hanging over them all day.

"Hey. I need to talk to you about something, Nell."

Nell kept braiding her hair. "What?"

"Could you maybe stop doing that for a minute and look at me? This is kind of important." Christ, he sounded like a wuss. But he felt as if asking her directly—"Please stop doing that"—would sound like an order, even though it was just a request.

Nell flipped her half-finished braid over her shoulder and looked at him with mild alarm—exactly the thing he didn't want. "Am I in some kind of trouble?"

"No, of course not. Michelle told me you were very anxious about me being away last week," he began.

Nell's eyes darted away.

"She said you had a really, really bad nightmare."

Nell took the end of her right braid and started chewing on it distractedly as if she didn't really hear him.

"Nell." Esa was surprised by how quickly he found himself becoming shaky inside. "Being worried about me when I'm not here is okay, and so is having bad dreams. It makes sense, after what happened with your mum." He gently removed her braid from her mouth. "Nothing's going to happen to me. Not on a plane, or anywhere else."

"You don't know that for sure," Nell insisted, sitting on her hands. "Anything could happen anytime. Anything."

That's not true, Esa wanted to say. But it was. He wasn't sure how to respond.

"You're right: I don't know for sure," he eventually admitted. "But I'd say the odds of something happening to me are pretty slim, especially my being in a plane crash. Plane crashes are pretty rare."

Esa could imagine what she was thinking: then how come mum died in one? He often thought the same thing. But Nell was just a kid; of course she'd think that. He hated that she was so young and had already figured out that life could be terrifyingly random. Innocent people died in plane crashes.

"You should have called me after the nightmare. It wouldn't have bothered me. In fact, it would have made me feel like a good uncle to make you feel better."

Nell looked down at her lap, swinging her feet. "I didn't want you to think I was a baby."

"I would never think you were a baby. In fact, sometimes I think you're more grown-up than me."

Esa felt off the hook when he saw Nell holding back a small smile.

"You want to laugh. I can see it."

Nell adamantly shook her head. "No."

"You're fibbing, but I'm going to let it go for now."

"Can I go?"

"Not yet." The words he wanted to say next were simple, yet he found himself struggling to get them out because he probably should take his own advice. "It's okay to cry anytime you feel sad or scared, you know."

Nell's ghost smile transformed itself into a scowl. "That's what Michelle says."

"Michelle's right."

"If you died, would I live with Michelle?"

Esa felt as if someone had just kicked him in the stomach. "Nell," Esa replied in a reassuring voice, "I'm not going to die anytime soon."

"But if you did."

"If I did, then yes, you would live with Michelle."

"Do you promise?"

"I promise."

"Good," said Nell, relieved.

"So we agree: if I'm away and you want to talk to me, you're going to call me, right?"

Nell nodded.

"Do *you* promise?"

This time Nell did smile.

"Would you like to have your friend, uh, Emma come over?"

"Selma," Nell corrected, looking somewhat indignant. "That's her name. And she's at her dad's this weekend."

"Sorry." God, what a loser. One name to keep straight and he couldn't even do that. The mistake made him look like he didn't pay attention to her life. But he did. He tried. He just had so much other shit going on.

"Do you have any other ideas?" Esa asked hopefully, draining his coffee cup. "Any movies you want to see? Bookstore?"

Nell looked sullen as she shook her head no. "I know!" she burst out suddenly.

"What?" said Esa, catching the wave of her enthusiasm.

"Can we have Uncle Ulf over for lunch and play Twister?"

Esa blinked. Wow, for an eight-year-old, Nell really had a highly developed sense of humor.

"Can we?"

She wasn't kidding. Her gaze was imploring.

"Nell, he's probably busy. Besides, I don't get why you like him so much."

"He's fun," Nell said simply. "Maybe Jason and Delilah could come, too. And Rory and Erin."

He angled his body toward the arm of the couch for a

moment so she wouldn't see the grim expression on his face. Twister with his teammates. Yeah, that'd be fun. Not. He wished he could tell her that bachelor uncles didn't play Twister. Bachelor uncles spent the day with their nieces and then maybe they watched a movie together after ordering in pizza for dinner. Eventually the niece gets tired and goes to bed, and the bachelor uncle calls one of his female mainstays to set up a date for the first night Michelle is back and can watch Nell, because Michelle doesn't want him, and what is he supposed to do, be a monk? Unfortunately, the bachelor uncle wasn't going to get what he wanted. Nor should he, Esa realized.

He turned back to Nell, forcing a smile. "Sure. Why not? Why don't we have them for dinner instead of lunch?" *That way Ulf will get the hell out of here quicker.*

Nell was off the couch in a flash, clapping. "Yippee!"

"Listen: you have to be prepared for some of them not being available. It's Saturday and lots of couples go out on Saturday nights."

Nell wasn't in the least bit fazed. "So what if Uncle Ulf is the only one who comes? It'll still be fun!"

Fun but painful, Esa thought, *because I'll be hitting myself in the head with a hammer.*

"Uh . . . yeah."

"We can just hang out today and I can make some signs for the Twister party!"

Her enthusiasm was making him feel like a total shit.

Esa nodded his head slowly. "Sounds good."

Nell went skipping toward her room, then came rushing back just as Esa was rising from the couch.

"Uncle Esa?"

"Mmm?"

Nell's fingers twirled nervously around one of her braids. "I really like you a lot," she said faintly.

Esa's heart stopped. Say *it.* Say the more advanced, emotional version that would put to rest once and for all any worries she might have about being uprooted again. But he couldn't do it yet. He feared overwhelming both of them. So he returned the same exact sentiment. "I really like you a lot, too, Nell," he replied with a big, loving smile.

It was all she needed to hear. Looking happy, Nell scurried back to her room. Esa was left with a sense of wonder that was both terrifying and gratifying. This was not the way he imagined his life playing out. He was supposed to have been granted a certain type of freedom that was increasingly beginning to strike him as pathetic and hollow. He went to get another cup of coffee and an aspirin. Twister . . . Ulfie . . . he was going to need it.

30

The scent of cigar smoke hit Michelle full in the face as she walked into her father's apartment. Though the kitchen was at the back, the gag-inducing aroma was everywhere. Michelle could already smell it in her hair. She'd have to take a shower when she got home.

She had wanted to spend some time with her friends, but it wasn't fated. Marcus was dog sitting for a wealthy, high-strung couple who forbade him from having anyone stop by their apartment. "The money's too good to pass up, honey," he'd told Michelle over the phone with a sigh. "Trust me when I tell you I'd much rather be with you than this quivering min pin, who weighs less than my iPad." Hannah was in Wood-stock for the weekend, cooking for her employers and their ten "best friends." "Who has ten best friends?" Hannah complained to Michelle. Two of the guests were vegetarians, one was vegan, one ate gluten-free only, one was on Atkins, and another followed the Caveman Diet. Michelle felt guilty laughing, but she couldn't help it.

Michelle hadn't had a chance to see her dad last week and felt guilty about it. But her dad seemed okay with it. Actually, a little too okay, and now she understood why: he was hitting the stogies again.

She cut a trail through the noxious cloud of smoke to find him sitting at the kitchen table playing Spades with his best friend Micky Dolan, whom Michelle had known her whole life. Her dad and "Uncle Micky" graduated the fire academy at the same time, had been assigned to the same house, and retired together. Michelle loved Uncle Micky. He had taught her magic tricks when she was little, and used to bring her presents: a CD here, a bottle of nail polish there. He could be a bit of a blowhard at times, but his wife, Aunt Reenie, kept him in check, though not where his weight was concerned: he'd blown up like a house since the last time Michelle had seen him, his blue eyes sunk deep into his pudgy face like two raisins.

"Hey, look who it is." Micky struggled to stand but Michelle waved him back down.

"How've you been, Uncle Micky? I haven't seen you in a while."

"Screw him," said her father. "I get a kiss first."

Michelle gave her dad a kiss, followed by a stern look. "Dad, you're not supposed to be smoking, remember?"

"I've got Febreze, don't worry."

"*Dad.*" She was beginning to understand her brother's mounting frustration with him. "I'm not talking about the smoke, and you know it. I'm talking about the smok*ing*. I could have sworn you were told to cut it out years ago." She looked back and forth between her uncle and her dad. "What is it with you guys? I swear to God, almost every firefighter I know smokes. It doesn't make sense."

"Sure it does," said her uncle, reaching across the table for one of her dad's famous chocolate chip cookies. "We spent more than forty years breathing in toxic shit. We're immune to it."

"Over the years our lungs have become flame retardant," her father added with a chuckle.

Michelle frowned. "Right." She went to the fridge, popping open a can of diet soda. She tried not to keep much at Esa's because she didn't want Nell drinking it. But she was used to eating and drinking chemical junk; she'd grown up eating it after her mother died.

She groaned aloud, unaware that she'd done so. Her dad twisted in his seat. "You okay?"

"Yeah. I just forgot how fake these could taste. I haven't had one in a while," she fibbed.

"Pour it down the sink," her father suggested, turning back to his friend.

"I can't do that. It's wasteful."

"Then drink it," said her uncle. He glanced up at her over the fanned cards he held in his hands. "You probably drink fancy stuff now, huh? Bottled water that costs six bucks?" He smirked. "I'll stick with New York City tap water, thank you very much. It hasn't done me any harm."

"Shut up," said her father. "It's not up to her if that fuck-face Finn wants to spend his money on all that stuff."

"Dad." Michelle's heartbeat lurched as she feared the pink climbing her neck to her face might give her away. "He's not a fuck-face, all right? He's really doing well with Nell."

"Yeah, great, he's Uncle of the Year," her father groused.

"He's trying. Very hard."

A significant look passed between her father and uncle.

"What?" asked Michelle. "What was that for?"

"You seem to be softening up on Esa Saari," her dad noted.

Michelle grabbed a cookie, biting down hard. "I live with the man! I see how hard he's trying."

"So he's a good boss?" asked her uncle.

"Very good."

"Has he tried any funny stuff?"

"No," Michelle mumbled through her chewing, washing the cookie down with a sip of soda. *Good one. Lie to your beloved uncle, too, while you're at it. You're on a roll; why the hell not?*

"He bring any models home?" her uncle continued with a wolfish smile.

"I just told you, he's trying really hard to be a good uncle," Michelle retorted. The idea of Esa sneaking models in and out hurt like a hard pinch to the back of her arm. She'd kill him if he did that, even though she had no right to.

"We'll see how good an uncle he is if he's got to drag that kid across the country or halfway around the world," said her father.

Michelle felt as if everything started happening in slow mo: the blink of her eyes, her intake of breath, the involuntary furrow of her brows . . . "What are you talking about?"

Her father, half jesting, pointed a finger at her in admonishment. "This is why you should check out the sports pages sometimes, Michelle, especially since your boss is a professional athlete."

"I don't understand," she replied, the words feeling thick in her mouth.

"Saari's contract with the Blades runs out at the end of the season. There's some talk they might not renew it. He'd be a free agent. The *Sentinel* says Dallas wants him badly. L.A. is interested, too. The *Post* says his agent is entertaining offers from the Russian league."

"But—why?" Michelle blurted. "Why wouldn't the Blades resign him?"

"It's all about the Benjamins. They paid a shitload of money for him," said her uncle, "and they're thinking he ain't re-signing for as much." He narrowed his eyes quizzically at her. "If you ask me, you seem to be getting a little upset over this."

"He's just never mentioned it to me. That's all."

"Makes sense," said her dad with a shrug. "Most guys in his position just ignore the rumors, keep their heads down, and play their guts out, which is what the Finnish fuck seems to be doing." Her father flashed her a reassuring smile. "Don't worry, honey: it's doubtful you're gonna be out of a job."

"I know." Michelle gulped down half the can of soda, bubbles tickling her nose. It wasn't herself she was worried about.

31

"God, Erin, would you please spin so I can get this Swede's ass out of my face?"

It was down to Esa and Ulf on the Twister mat. After telling Nell not to be disappointed if Ulfie was the only one who showed, Erin and Rory jumped at the invite, thrilling Esa. It would have been excruciating if it were just him, Nell, and Ulfie, especially if they had watched one of the episodes of *Are You Smarter Than a 5th Grader?* that Nell had tivo'd and Ulfie lost.

"Erin!"

"Don't get your knickers in a twist, Esa, for God's sake."

Esa tensed, listening for the sound of the spinner. It was just winding down when another sound caught his attention, that of a lock turning in a door, followed by a woman's voice, surprised, as if she walked in on something she shouldn't have.

"Oh."

Esa snapped his head up to look at Michelle. Her lips were pressed together lightly, her eyes looking at everyone but him. He could see that she was dying to laugh, which only made his frustration at having Ulfie's fat ass in his face worse.

Nell ran to Michelle, her energy as fresh as it was two hours earlier when the evening had began. "We're playing Twister!"

Michelle's eyes drifted to the Twister mat. "So I see." This time she did look at Esa. Yeah, he was definitely right: the wicked little crinkles in the corners of her eyes, the casual press of her lips? She would howl with laughter at him if she could. He scowled at her, but she didn't seem to take any notice. Did she think he liked being in this stupid contorted position, the mossy aroma of Ulf's socks wafting up to choke him?

"I'm sorry to interrupt," Michelle said to the room at large.

"You're not!" Ulf insisted.

"He's right," said Esa. "We're about to wrap this up. *Now*, as a matter of fact. Right, Erin?" His neck was beginning to hurt from holding his head up.

"Esa wants it over and done with because he's afraid Ulf is going to fart in his face," Rory explained to Michelle.

"My classy husband," Erin said with a long-suffering sigh. She gave Michelle a small hug. "How are you? You're lookin' great."

"Things are going pretty well. You?"

"Same for me as well, pretty much. Work has been a bit of a pain, they're—"

"CALL IT, ERIN!" Esa roared. His ankle was beginning to twinge with pain.

Huffing dramatically, Erin spun the Twister wheel again. "Right foot, red!" she shouted. "Will that do?"

As if synchronized, Esa and Ulfie each slid their right foot to the same circle. *Crap.* This meant Erin would have to decide who had gotten there first, Esa or Ulf, and the goddamn game would go on even longer.

"Well?" Ulf asked Erin. Esa noticed his opponent's legs were beginning to quiver. Despite being in superb physical condition, all the weird positions they'd been contorting themselves into were beginning to take a toll on both of them. If the game didn't end soon, Esa was going to call it. There was no way he was going to risk an injury playing this game.

"Ulf was there first."

"Thanks for that, Erin," said Esa sarcastically as his eyes scanned the friggin' Twister board for an open circle of red that wouldn't require him twisting himself like some kind of yogi. He finally found one. It required he do a minor split, but worrying about it proved to be futile, since he fell on his ass before he even had time to execute the move.

"You lose!" Nell sang out.

"Yep," said Esa, thrilled at losing his balance.

"Guess your smooth move makes me the winner, Saari," said Ulf, gloating.

Esa pushed himself onto his hands and knees. "Congratulations."

"I think we should play one more game and include Michelle this time," said Ulf.

Esa slowly stood up, waiting to see what Michelle's reaction would be. It was a weary smile. "Thank you for the invite, but I can't. I'm going to bed now."

Ulf looked horrified. "What's this bed talk? It's early!"

What. The. Fuck? Esa thought. He caught Rory's eye: his friend looked perplexed, confirmation that his own feelings of bewilderment weren't out of line. He felt bad for Michelle: she looked put on the spot, especially with Nell clinging to her and looking up at her hopefully. "Please, Michelle? Just one?"

Michelle playfully tugged on the end of Nell's nose. "Nope. I will some other time, I promise. But right now, I'm dead on my feet."

"C'mon," Ulf urged.

"She said no," said Esa sharply. "Leave her alone."

Ulfie chuckled low, muttering something to himself in Swedish. *Prick.*

The mood in the room had gone from goofy to awkward to tense in under two minutes. Esa wasn't sure how to fix it. Then he thought: Why do I need to fix it? Torkelson's the one who wouldn't take no for an answer. If anyone should be trying to paddle back to shore, it's Ulf.

Finally, Nell broke the quiet.

"We've got some pizza left over if you're hungry, Michelle," said Nell.

"I'm fine, honey. Thanks." She glanced around the room

again. "I'm just going to grab a glass of water and then I really do have to go to bed. Good night, everyone."

* * *

"Michelle?"

Michelle turned from the fridge where she'd just grabbed herself a nice, cold bottle of Aquafina to find Ulf Torkelson hovering in the kitchen doorway, regarding her tentatively. She'd been surprised to come home to a game of Twister in progress, especially when she saw Esa and Ulf on the mat. Esa Saari playing Twister? He really was trying to do his best for Nell. As for Ulf, Michelle didn't know him at all, apart from their brief exchange at the babysitting debacle. All she knew was that Nell adored him.

"Hi, Ulf," Michelle replied, twisting the top off the bottle and tossing it in the trash.

He took two shy steps toward her. It was incongruous, this giant man looking so uncertain.

"There's something I need to ask you."

"Okay."

He sounded very serious—so serious Michelle felt her insides lurch with panic. Her first thought was: Esa had told his teammates he'd slept with her. No. Knowing Esa, it was probably more along the lines of, "I finally fucked the nanny." Ulf was creeping in to the kitchen to tell her what a ho Esa was, that a nice girl like her should steer clear of a guy like Esa.

Ulf took a deep breath, closing the distance between them. God, he was huge. There was something about him that reminded Michelle of Shrek. He was a giant, blond Shrek.

"Michelle, I was wondering if you would like to go out to dinner with me?"

Oh, shit. This was ten times worse than him telling her Esa had been boasting.

"I know we don't know each other—"

At all, Michelle thought.

"—but you seem really nice, and I'm very decent, if I do say so myself. Both of my ex-wives would attest to that."

"Two ex-wives?"

Ulf shook his head sadly. "Two tales of heartbreak and

woe, of a good man's nature being taken advantage of. I can tell you all about it over dinner. Do you like fish?"

"Ulf, I'm really flattered that you're asking me out," said Michelle diplomatically. "But I'm not interested in seeing anyone right now."

"Why not?"

He reminded Michelle of a child whose curiosity, whether appropriate or not, wouldn't be sated. In fact, he reminded her a bit of Nell. No wonder they got along. "I just have a lot of other things going on right now," she said with a gentle smile.

One of which was the man who'd just strolled into the kitchen. "Hey," Esa said. "What's up, you guys?"

"None of your business," said Ulf.

Esa's demeanor quickly changed from casual to challenging. "Really."

"Yes."

"That's interesting."

Ulf was glaring. "Actually, it's not."

Having completed the task she'd come into the kitchen for, Michelle decided it was time to leave. Tension between the two men was rumbling like distant thunder and she didn't want to be here when the first deafening clap sounded. Nor did she want the anger roiling inside her to manifest itself on her face. What the hell was Esa doing?

"I'm beat, guys. Good night."

Both men looked dumbfounded as she walked past them. It was an emotion she shared, except she wasn't showing it. She knew this subject was far from closed.

32

Esa Saari, Master of Coolness, King of Self-Control, was losing it. When Ulf followed Michelle into the kitchen, his guts had turned like screws on a rack. He knew the Swede had the hots for Michelle. And even though he and Michelle weren't a couple, it still bugged the shit out of him to imagine Ulfie asking her out. Unable to help himself, he'd entered the kitchen, trying to play it cool. He hadn't expected Ulfie to be so hostile, so fast. Something was up.

"So, Torkelson," said Esa, sauntering over to the fridge, more to give himself something to do than anything else. "Michelle's gone, so . . ."

"None of your business, Saari."

Esa yanked the refrigerator door open. "Were you bothering her?"

" 'Bothering.' What the fuck does that mean?"

Esa ducked his head deep in the fridge, the better to hide his gritted teeth. "Asking her out."

"I told you, Finn: it's none of your business." There was a long pause. "Unless you have the hots for her and you can't stand any other man talking to her," Ulf taunted.

Esa pulled his head out of the fridge, slamming the door shut hard. "For once in your life, could you not be a moron? Michelle works for me."

"Yeah? So? Doesn't mean you don't want to fuck her."

Esa was on him so fast it wasn't funny, shoving him hard. "Don't talk about her that way, like she's some cheap piece of ass."

Ulf shoved back, glaring. "Since when did you ever meet a woman you didn't want to screw, Saari?"

I did—I—we—oh, shit, the words, those words . . .

"Michelle works for me, you jerk. I care about her. Which is why I came in here: I wanted to make sure you weren't harassing her."

"No, you wanted to make sure I wasn't asking her out, because you were worried she'd say yes."

"Yes, I was worried," Esa replied, aiming to sound like Michelle's protective big brother. "Because you're a pig. And if she'd said yes, then I'm sorry, my friend, I'd have to tell her the truth about you."

Ulf looked smug as he cracked his knuckles. "But you'd never know if she said yes to me, would you? Because you two keep your private lives private."

Having his own words thrown back in his face—that was what he'd told his teammates—caused a flicker of unease in Esa. He and Michelle were going with the flow, right? Keeping it simple. His definition. So did that mean they were both free to do what they wanted? If Michelle suddenly lost her mind and decided to go out with Ulf, he had no say in the matter, just like she had no say if he wanted to hook up with that hot little hotel heiress on the West Coast who'd been e-mailing him.

"Yeah, you know, I guess you're right," Esa finally said dismissively. "Just know that I would kick your fat Swedish ass if she got involved with you and things didn't turn out well. Nell adores her. The last thing I need is a nanny who's an emotional mess and can't take care of my niece properly."

Esa was proud to have thought that up on the spot, making it about Nell. No one could argue with the logic of what he'd just said. If Ulf had even a handful of brain cells, he'd back off, and he'd shut his mouth about Esa having the hots for

Michelle. He doubted that was going to happen, considering the way he and all his teammates lived to rag on each other.

"You get it now, you asshole?" Esa asked sarcastically.

Ulf gave him the finger and turned away. "Whatever."

"Yup, whatever." Esa headed back out to the living room. Mission accomplished.

*   *   *

"You slept with him? Oh. My. Sweet. God."

Marcus's hand flew to his throat in shock as if he were on a soap opera when Michelle finally spilled the news. They were sitting in the Starbucks on Ninety-third and Broadway, the weather having turned too cold for them to meet outside. Despite Marcus's performance, none of the other patrons looked up. They must all be New Yorkers. Michelle punched Marcus on the shoulder anyway. It was just the two of them. Hannah was at a torte-making seminar at the Culinary Institute of America. Michelle had wanted to get input from both of them, but she simply couldn't hold it in any longer.

She told Marcus about how tension between them had been building. "How delish," he'd commented with a shudder. Next she went into elaborate detail about the skating outing with Nell. "How nuclear family," Marcus had noted dryly. When she got to the part about them giving in to their desires, that's when he'd squealed, "You slept with him? Oh my sweet God!" Michelle wished the table was large enough for her to crawl under.

"Oh my sweet God is right." Michelle felt forlorn as she stirred her latte. It felt good to finally confide to her friend what happened. But somehow, in telling it out loud, the enormity of it struck her for the first time.

"Was he good?" Marcus asked in a stage whisper.

Michelle blushed. "I don't kiss and tell."

"That blush means he was better than good."

Michelle brought the steaming coffee mug to her mouth, quickly tearing it away when the burning liquid scalded her lips. "It's been very confusing. And distressing."

"I'm listening."

"Well, for starters, he's my boss. I've breached professional ethics."

Marcus rolled his eyes. "He's gorgeous and single. You've only ever worked for married couples with kids before. I don't really think it's a breach."

"It's never a good idea to sleep with your boss, Marcus," Michelle countered.

Marcus frowned. "How do you think half the romantic relationships in this city get started? Anyway, go on."

Michelle put her hands around the coffee cup. Jesus. Even that was too hot. She pulled them away. "Then there's the fact I don't usually do this kind of stuff. I'm not a casual sex kind of person. And this was definitely casual."

"How do you know?" Marcus asked, digging into the whipped cream atop his café mocha.

"Because we agreed it was. Neither of us wants a relationship." Michelle broke off a little piece of lemon bar. "But we kind of agreed . . . not to define it . . . like . . . just to keep it simple and go with the flow . . ."

Marcus clucked his tongue. "I hate that expression. It's such bullshit. And for someone with a master's in education, you sound remarkably incoherent."

"I feel remarkably incoherent."

"Go on," he urged again.

"I hate that I'm attracted to him. I hate guys like him, who think they own the world and can have any woman they want."

Marcus helped himself to a piece of her lemon bar. "Well, considering you're not a fool, you must see something in him."

Michelle was silent. That was it. Marcus hit the nail on the head.

"Look." Marcus took a big gulp of his drink, dabbing at his whipped cream moustache with a folded paper napkin. "You don't do casual, therefore you can't do 'go with the flow.'" Marcus peered at her quizzically. "Are you sure you don't want a relationship with him?"

"Absolutely." The idea made Michelle want to laugh as she again tested her latte. "I doubt he's capable of one. But at the same time, this weird thing happened on Saturday night." She told him about the incident with Ulf in the kitchen, the way Esa had casually strolled in and the two of them had clashed like two rams within seconds.

"You're both full of shit with this 'go with the flow.' Why else would he walk into the kitchen and defend his turf?"

"Mmm."

"You need to talk to him."

Michelle groaned. "I know. Thank God there's more to talk about than this. In fact, there's something he's been withholding from me that I'm really pissed about." She told Marcus about Esa's contract woes.

"Major sin of omission," Marcus declared.

"Tell me about it."

"Michelle, what do you want to happen?"

"I want to turn back time." Michelle shook her head, remorseful. "I can't believe I went there. He said all along that I'm so predictable, that I'd say our sleeping together was a mistake. And I denied it. But I think maybe he's right about me: I can't go with the flow." She took a careful sip of coffee. "The tension will be awful. It is awful. It's always there, waiting to happen again. Worse than it was before."

"You're a big girl. If it gets too unbearable, you can always find another job."

Michelle was appalled. "And leave Nell? Are you crazy?"

"Then you're just going to have to suck it up, dearie."

"I hate that you're so brutally honest." She braved a sip of her drink. It finally went down smooth and warm.

"True friends do that for one another." Marcus leaned across the table in classic gossip mode. "Now. Let me tell you about this photographer I met while babysitting that min pin for that psychotic stockbroker couple. He lives in their building, and he was in the lobby with his mastiff, Tyrian . . ."

* * *

One of the advantages of spending so much time in the company of women, Esa mused, was the ability to occasionally read the unspoken correctly. He'd surprised Michelle and Nell by having dinner with them, when he'd originally planned to meet his agent. He thought Michelle would be happy. Instead, though she was pleasant enough toward him, he was being kept at arm's length. Maybe she was just having a bad day, but he doubted it. He knew when he was the source of a woman's displeasure. The only reason he could think of was the incident in the kitchen with Ulfie, but that didn't make sense. If anything, she should have been flattered by his behavior. Well, he knew how to get a woman to talk to him.

Once they'd closed Nell's bedroom door after putting her to bed together, he snaked his arms around Michelle from behind, drawing her close. "What's bothering you?" he whispered, planting the merest whisper of a kiss on her neck. "Why were you so tense during dinner?"

He felt her melt against him just for a moment as he went for another kiss, but then she eased herself away from him.

"I'm upset with you," she said.

I knew it had to do with me, Esa thought. "Why?"

"When did you plan to tell me the Blades might not renew your contract?"

Esa felt like someone had just put one of those huge gongs next to his ear and struck it, hard.

"We need to talk about this," Michelle continued.

Christ, he hated those six fucking words, he really did. They'd dominated his life since he'd gotten custody of Nell.

"Yeah, I guess we do," he said, massaging the base of his skull with three fingers. He walked into the living room and sat down on the couch. Michelle followed suit, sitting where she used to sit when she'd first moved in and things were strictly professional. Great. He guessed they'd be taking it a lot slower than he'd planned.

"Well?" she asked.

"Where did you hear this?"

"My dad. Apparently I'm the last one in the city to know about this. When did you plan to say something?"

"When it looked as if it might actually happen. I don't know if that's the case yet."

Michelle looked perturbed. "And when will you know?"

"I don't know," Esa said tersely. "All I can do is play hard and hope Kidco makes an offer that could serve as the basis of negotiations. Meanwhile, my agent has to reach out to other teams to insure I've got a job next year and to put some pressure on Kidco. Anything else?"

"Yes, a lot. Have you thought about what would happen if you had to move? How it would affect Nell?"

Esa was growing angry. "You know what? No, I haven't.

Because I can't. I have to focus on upping my game to make sure that the Blades want to re-sign me, and that other teams want to sign me if Kidco doesn't. I can't worry about something that might not happen. And if it does happen, then we'll deal with it."

"We? You just assume I'd come with you?"

The gong sounded again. "You wouldn't? You'd leave Nell?"

Michelle looked pained. "Esa, I don't know. All I know is that I think you should have mentioned this to me."

"When? When I interviewed you for the job? Would you not have taken it if I'd told you?"

"I don't know."

Esa's fingers returned to the base of his skull, massaging, digging in deep. "So now you know. I've got enough pressure on me without worrying about you freaking out on Nell's behalf about something that might not even happen." He felt like a castaway on the shore, watching simplicity slip further and further away like an unmoored boat. "This whole thing is too complicated to me." He looked at her. She was beautiful, so sexy in part because she didn't realize it, but he had to show self-control. It was the only way.

To his surprise, Michelle seemed to be reading his mind. "'Go with the flow' doesn't work for me," she said in a complete non sequitur.

Esa felt panic. "Well, a relationship doesn't work for me."

"I'm not asking you for one."

"Good," Esa said quietly. "I hope we can go back to being friends. I enjoy spending time with you and Nell."

"Of course. It would be silly to go all the way back to the formality that existed in the beginning before we knew each other. And impossible, I think."

"Yes." It would be impossible, he thought, even unthinkable.

Michelle rose with a relieved sigh. "I'm glad we talked."

"Me, too." The pain at the base of his skull wasn't abating. Instead, it was slowly crawling up the back of his head. "I need to ask you something."

"What's that?"

"Did Ulfie ask you out?"

"Yes, and I said no. Was that what worried you when you came in the kitchen all macho?"

"Yes. No. I don't know. It just bugged me that he was asking you at all."

Michelle smiled at him sadly. "Believe it or not, that makes me feel better about our 'mistake.' It lets me know that it wasn't just a physical thing for you."

"Of course it wasn't," Esa murmured, closing his eyes. Christ, his head was really beginning to throb. "I care about you, Michelle."

"I care about you, too, Esa."

"Everyone's happy, then."

"I'm going to go watch TV in my room. Good night."

"Good night."

He leaned his head back against the ledge of the sofa, staring up at the ceiling. It saddened him to think he'd never hold her again, or move inside her. But he was willing to sacrifice that in order to return to the simplicity of caring about two things: hockey and Nell. That was one more than he'd ever cared about before and it was probably the limit of his capacity. Why he'd ever thought he could do more was beyond him. He wasn't that kind of man, and never would be.

33

"Are you mad at me?"

Nell's question couldn't have surprised Michelle any more than if the little girl had snuck up behind her and shouted "Boo!"

It was Sunday morning and they were in the kitchen baking banana nut muffins. Nell was standing on a stepladder at the counter beside Michelle, slowly stirring the batter. Her voice had been timid.

Michelle stilled her hand. "Why on earth would you think that, sweetie?"

Nell glanced away. "I don't know."

"Yes, you do. You wouldn't have asked if you didn't know. Don't get all bashful on me. I thought we could talk about everything. Why would you think I'm mad at you?"

"Because things feel weird," Nell confessed reluctantly.

"Weird how?"

"I don't know. Sort of nervous."

"Hhmm." Michelle smoothed Nell's long hair, trailing down her back. "I'll have to think about that. But I promise, I'm not mad at you."

"Is Uncle Esa mad at me?"

"Of course not, honey."

Nell looked relieved, but Michelle felt awful. Kids were perceptive; things *had* been awkward. It was two weeks since she and Esa had agreed that sleeping together was a mistake. And despite their intention to remain friends, when the three of them were together things felt mildly strained.

Perhaps it would be better to go back to the way things were in the very beginning, with him spending more time on his own with Nell. It wasn't like he was still clueless about how to interact with her, and by now he knew he didn't have to "do" things with Nell all the time. As far as she could tell, he no longer needed Michelle's help finessing things.

It would make things easier on Michelle, too. She felt like she was flip-flopping like a politician: One second she knew they'd done the right thing; the next she'd look at that thick black hair she'd run her fingers through, and those blue eyes that flashed with wild desire for her, and she'd think she was an idiot not to sleep with him again. Heat would speed through her body as she pictured them doing it in every room of the house in every position imaginable. Her fickleness was more irritating than confusing. Everyone knew forbidden fruit was attractive, so it wasn't hard to figure out why she wanted him now that sex was off the table.

Looking at Nell as her little charge concentrated on stirring the batter, Michelle knew Marcus had been right when he'd told her to just "suck it up" when it came to her, Esa, and Nell spending time together. She and Esa couldn't completely reverse course. It was impossible. They were simply going to have to work harder at overcoming whatever discomfort they felt. Period.

* * *

"You're thinking too much, sexy. Let me fix this."

Esa smiled languidly as the puck bunny he'd picked up after the game against Tampa quickly unzipped his jeans and yanked them, along with his briefs, roughly down his hips. He kicked the jeans away, watching as she slid down his body until she was kneeling in front of him, a naughty look on her face. She flicked her tongue across his low belly for a moment, then took one hand and cupped his balls, starting to stroke and caress them. Esa closed his eyes, groaning. *Yeah,* he thought. *That's it. This is gonna do it.*

He hadn't planned on bringing anyone back to his hotel room after the game, but then he thought, why not? He loved sex with beautiful women, and this woman was gorgeous: long legs up to her neck, dirty blond hair cascading down her back, ripe breasts straining against a tight white T-shirt. The minute she'd caught his eye in the bar and lifted a drink as if to toast him, he knew he wanted to tap that sweet ass. Why shouldn't he? That's who he was. That's what he did.

Except right now, he couldn't seem to do it.

The mutual groping had turned him on. He'd always loved the feel of a woman's body against his, the little moans he could get them to make just by nipping at their neck. The way they arched into him always made him hard as a rock, his cock already twitching, yearning. But this time, something happened that had never happened before: his hard-on disappeared. He ground against her in a vain effort to revive it, but nothing helped. That's when she chided him for thinking too much and fell to her knees in front of him.

She was rubbing him between the legs now with one hand, the other going for the tip of his penis, her thumb slowly going round in circles. The sensation was pleasant, but his dick still wasn't responding.

"Let's try this," the woman whispered. As best she could, the woman began to suck his limp cock, stopping every once in awhile to swirl her tongue around the tip. Nothing. Nada. And the harder she tried, the more tense he became, which guaranteed he'd never get it up. Finally, he gently put his hands on her shoulders, indicating she should stop.

"Hey." He put his index finger under her chin, tilting her head up so she was looking at him. "I appreciate the effort, but I don't think it's going to happen tonight."

"But I want to fuck you."

Mortification shot through Esa as he helped the woman to her feet. "I'd like to fuck you, too, but I guess I'm more tired than I thought." He suddenly felt like a jerk standing there with no pants, and quickly put his briefs on. The woman, meanwhile, wouldn't give up. She took his face in her hands and kissed him hard before murmuring in his ear, "There's always tomorrow morning."

"Actually, there isn't. I have a plane to catch."

The woman huffed in frustration. "I don't believe this. I've been planning this for ages and now—"

"I'm sorry." All Esa wanted was to get her the hell out of his room. "Sometimes these things happen." Christ, he sounded lame.

The woman crossed her arms across her chest. "The least you could do is get me off." She flicked her tongue against his ear. "I'm so, so wet, Esa."

Esa's hand curled around one of her wrists as he gently began tugging her toward the door. "I can't. I'm sorry. I just—can't."

Her jaw dropped in outrage. "Selfish prick. And a limp dick to boot, I might add."

Esa opened the door. "Sorry."

"I'm going to tell everyone about this," she threatened, jerking her wrist from his grasp as she stormed into the silent hallway. "I'm going to post it on every hockey forum there is."

"Okay, you do that. Good night," said Esa, suddenly feeling as if he'd been awake for three days straight. He closed the door, making sure to lock it behind him.

"*Kirottu*," he murmured, sitting down on the edge of the bed. He scrubbed his hands over his face, then made his hands into fists, pressing his knuckles hard into his eyes sockets. The skin of his hands felt cool, the pressure welcome. He knew what was going on.

Now he just had to figure out what to do about it.

$\sim\!\!e$

34

$\sim\!\!e$

"Michelle, wake up."

Michelle felt a gentle jostling of her shoulder. Sleep . . . dark room . . . jostle . . . Nell! Her eyes flew open as she bolted upright, swinging her legs over the side of her bed.

"Michelle."

It was Esa quietly saying her name in the darkness, his hand staying her shoulder. Michelle blinked, her eyes straining to adjust, not only to the darkness but to his sitting on the edge of her bed. "What's wrong with Nell?" she asked frantically.

"Calm down. It's nothing."

"Then what are you doing in my room at"—Michelle picked up her iPhone from her nightstand— "two thirty in the morning?"

"I don't think we made a mistake sleeping together. I want a relationship."

Michelle thrust her head forward, squinting at him. "What? You're drunk. Get out."

He leaned over and turned on the bedside lamp. "No, listen to me."

"No." Michelle swung her feet back up onto the bed and under the covers. She needed this drunken asshole Finn like she needed a hole in the head. He was probably just horny and wanted sex. Well, he wasn't going to get it.

"*Michelle.* Hear me out. Please."

"Can I hear you out in the morning? When you're sober?" Anger thundered across his chiseled face. "I'm not drunk."

"Then why are you here?"

" I'm here to talk about you and me. And I'm not leaving."

Judging by the stubborn set of his jaw, Michelle knew there was no dissuading him. Self-conscious, she ran a hand through the rat's nest that was her hair, and tried not to think about the stretched out Islanders T-shirt she was using as a nightgown. Not very attractive. Then again, she hadn't been expecting one of the most handsome men in New York to creep into her room in the middle of the night. "This better be good."

Michelle waited and waited, Michelle thought, thinking of the language in the books she used to teach first graders to read. After what seemed like forever, Esa still hadn't said a word. For someone who had to tell her something so urgent and refused to leave, he was certainly taking his time.

"Hello? Esa?"

"I'm not great at expressing my emotions. I think you know that."

"I do, at least where Nell is concerned."

"Well, it's an all-round problem." His eyes pinned hers so hard she couldn't look away if she wanted to. "I haven't been able to stop thinking about you."

"Okay," Michelle said cautiously.

"I took a woman back to my hotel room when we were in Tampa."

Michelle scowled at him. "Didn't have to share that."

"You're wrong. I couldn't perform. I made the woman leave. I couldn't stay turned on because it wasn't you."

"Okay," Michelle repeated, more guarded this time. She couldn't deny it: the fact he couldn't get it up *was* extremely flattering. It made her feel powerful. They'd only been together once; if this was the effect she'd had on him, then maybe she was sexier than she'd thought.

Esa took her hand, his fingers twining through hers firmly.

"I know we both said we didn't want a relationship. I think we were both lying. Out of fear."

"That's blunt."

"I am blunt. You know that."

"Yes, I do." The tightness with which he was holding her hand, mixed with his unwavering gaze and the soft lighting in the room, made her lower her guard. Slightly. She wasn't entirely willing to surrender her wariness yet.

Esa grimaced as if in pain, but Michelle realized he was simply struggling to find the right words. "I've never had a *real* relationship." His eyes searched hers. "What about you?"

Michelle's guard went back up. "What about me what?"

"You know what." He sounded irritated. "Have you ever had a real relationship?"

"No," admitted Michelle reluctantly. She didn't like where this was going.

"How come?"

Michelle looked down at the quilt covering her legs. The answer wasn't something she needed to ponder. She'd figured it out years ago. She just hated thinking about it, because whenever she did, tears soon followed, and the irrationality of her feelings made her feel silly.

She slowly looked up at Esa. "Because," she said quietly, "I've always been afraid of them dying on me."

Michelle had never told that to anyone. Admitting it didn't make her feel better. It made her feel like that lost little girl who'd wandered from room to room after her mother died, convinced that if she wished hard enough, she'd find her. She put the focus back on Esa.

"What about you?"

Esa laughed dryly. "You know why. Because I'm a shallow playboy."

"But you've been engaged."

"More out of a sense of obligation than anything else. Neither relationship lasted long. I felt trapped right away."

"Oh, and you wouldn't feel that way with me eventually?"

"Maybe you'd be the one to feel that way." He edged closer to her on the bed. "Look, I'm not going to lie: the idea of something real scares me to death. But continuing down the path I was on scares me worse, especially when I realize it wouldn't include you.

"I'm not saying it will be easy. I'll need to get the hang of it. All I'm asking is that you think about giving it a shot."

"And Nell?"

"I've given a lot of thought to that." Esa ran his thumb over the top of her hand. "I think it would be healthy for her to experience what it's like to be part of a family."

"Your original argument." Michelle paused. "We're not her parents, Esa," she murmured softly.

"No, but we're the closest she has, at least you are. And I think I could get there eventually. I'm trying." Their fingers still entwined, he brought her hand to his mouth, kissing it gently. "I'm as shocked by what I'm saying as you are."

"That's good to hear," she said, meaning it.

"So you'll think about it?"

"Of course."

Esa smiled, looking more like a man who was simply happy, not a sexy lady killer known to bed every good-looking woman who turned his head. Ironically, this made him even more attractive. He planted a lingering kiss on her mouth, then rose, looking reluctant to do so. "I guess I'll head off to bed, then." He paused as sexual tension whispered its way into the room.

"Good night," Michelle said, determined to ignore it.

"Good night."

"Esa?"

He'd barely reached the door when Michelle called out his name.

He turned. "Mmm?"

"Yes."

*   *   *

With an unmistakably smoldering look in his eye, Esa sauntered back to her bed, and sat down. His mouth was warm as he pressed it against Michelle's, sending a flurry of fireworks through her body before he'd even slipped his tongue between her lips. When he pulled away to look at her face, Michelle was surprised to see a small smile of amusement playing across his lips.

"You gave your answer awfully fast," said Esa.

"I'm a nanny. We're known for efficiency."

Esa laughed as his hands moved slowly to caress her shoulder, giving her goose bumps. It was going to be slow this time, just the way she wanted it. He laid her back, gently positioning himself on top of her, supporting his weight on his elbows. Michelle fought to breathe normally as his mouth again sought hers, his tongue giving her lips a caress before he nipped at her lower lip, sending a lightning bolt that shot all the way down to her toes. She wrapped her arms around him, the heat in her body hissing to life like tiny solar flares as their kissing turned frenzied. Maybe it wouldn't be so slow after all, and maybe she didn't care. As long as it culminated with this handsome man coming inside her, nothing else really mattered.

Esa rocked ever so slightly against her, making her gasp. It already felt damn good. But him on top felt too constraining right now. She gently rolled him off her so they were lying side by side, and put her hands on his hips, pressing her lips to his forehead. His skin was burning, fevered. A lock of his dark black hair fell over his forehead in disarray, and the way he flipped his head back to get it off his face electrified Michelle, the pure unconscious sexiness of it.

Michelle's palms ran up his body from his hip to his shoulder, her hands gripping them, feeling the broad hard muscles beneath. Esa was watching, clearly enjoying it when her attention shifted from his shoulders to the tough, hard muscles of his abs. Michelle leaned forward, flicking her tongue against one of his nipples through the tight material of his white T-shirt. She looked up at him. It only took one second of being held in thrall by Esa's blue eyes for Michelle to feel totally and completely immersed in desire for him. He slowly sat up, and the next sound she heard was his T-shirt hitting the floor. Then he lay back down beside her, the pads of his thumbs tracing lazy circles around her nipples through the frayed cotton of her T-shirt. Michelle raised herself, tearing the T-shirt off. Now she was just in her panties. Esa groaned before gently pushing her onto her back, his head bent in concentration as he began tonguing her nipples. Michelle could feel every inch of her body responding as it should: nerves on fire, pussy getting wet. His mouth was sliding all over her now, his lips and tongue playing her like a delicate instrument. She began to groan, turned on by the fact that he seemed to be enjoying it just as much as she was. He slid her panties down, tossing them off the end of the bed as he drew her legs apart. Michelle was quivering with anticipation, and when it finally came, when he finally put his tongue to her and started exploring her, teasing, circling, delving, she thought: so this is what madness feels like. Michelle spread her legs wider, each dive and flick of his tongue making her feel as though she were going to burst out of her skin. Close to coming, she began shaking uncontrollably; Esa took the cue as his tongue madly flicked at her, circling round and round. Michelle cried out, succumbing to the hot pulses of pleasure overtaking her body, and Esa crawled back up her body, holding her as her breathing and pulse began their slow descent back down to normal.

"We're not done, you know," she murmured, rubbing her naked body back against the hard-on she could feel straining through his jeans. Chuckling, she flipped them so she was now the one in the dominant position. She pushed his legs apart, kneeling in the V created so she could easily undo his jeans. Esa lifted himself slightly so she could yank off his jeans and his briefs at the same time, tossing them to the growing pile of clothing beside the bed.

Hands on Esa's thighs, hair falling across one side of her face like a curtain, Michelle sat back on her heels, smiling at him seductively as she kissed the dark curling hair on his belly. Esa moaned, and Michelle paused, more to look at his body than anything else. So hot. So perfect. The heat coming from his skin made her throat clog with lust, but she drove the feeling away as she slowly ran her tongue from the base of his cock to its head, her tongue slowly spreading the glistening drop of fluid she found there.

"Oh, Christ," Esa groaned. "That feels so. Fucking. Good."

"That," Michelle said, with a wicked little chuckle, "is nothing."

She circled her tongue around the sensitive head a few times, then curled her hand around him, beginning to stroke gently. Esa's hips arched up off the bed, and Michelle squeezed just a little, enough to entice, eliciting such a sexy groan from him that she was tempted to abandon her enterprise altogether, and just climb atop him and fuck him. But that wasn't what she wanted. She felt him begin to lose control as she wrapped her lips around the head of his cock and began moving her head up and down, mouth sucking hard, tongue swirling wildly over the tip when she pulled back before taking him deep again. Esa's moans grew deeper the longer Michelle prolonged the torture. She turned up the tempo by degrees, surprised to find how exciting it was to her to explore and taste him, especially when he begged, "Please," in a hoarse voice, and his hands clutched at her quilt, his feet planted firmly on the bed so he could thrust deeper into her mouth.

Michelle smiled to herself; it was time for her final act of magic. And so, with a wet, hot, enthusiasm she knew would push him over the edge, her mouth moved up and down his dick with wild enthusiasm until finally, they were both rocked by the shudders of his body.

35

"Wow. That was . . . uskomaton."

"I can guess what that means," Michelle chuckled as Esa pulled back the quilt and slipped into bed beside her, drawing her near. The way he was smiling at her, so affectionately, as if it were the most natural thing in the world that they should be lying together like this, lulled her into a sense of safety. There was no way you could be held tightly by a man this strong and muscular and not feel safe. The soft light of the night table lamp cast shadows across his cheekbones and the high gloss of his hair. How could someone so unmistakably male be so beautiful at the same time? Not handsome, beautiful. Gorgeous. Hot. Michelle got the feeling there weren't enough adjectives to describe him. Not only that, but if she kept thinking about it, her hunger for him was going to make an inconvenient reappearance.

Esa pulled back, kissing her shoulder. "I love having sex with you." He paused. "And more," he added awkwardly.

Michelle felt an odd swooping inside her. Was he professing love? That was impossible. Her mouth felt dry as she asked, "I'm not sure what you mean."

"Spending time with you," he managed. "And Nell. Just—things. Real things. Things, like I told you earlier, that scare me."

Michelle cupped his cheek. "What scares you?"

"That I don't know who I am. It's never been who I am. It's never been what I wanted."

"Looks like Nell changed that."

"Not just Nell," he whispered with a languid kiss. When he finished he pulled back just enough that Michelle was able to see the anguished look on his face. "You're going to have to help me. I don't know how to do this."

"Don't you remember what I told you? Neither do I."

"Yes, you did tell me that." He looked determined. "I want to be the best there is."

Michelle whistled low. "Okay, time out. Stop right there. This isn't sports, Esa. You're not competing to be 'the best.' Just be you."

"I can compete against myself," he pointed out. "To be the best boyfriend and uncle."

"Please don't. Just be you."

Esa looked befuddled as he shrugged. "Okay."

"In all your macho, arrogant wonder," Michelle teased.

"And am I permitted to ask you to continue as *you* are?"

"Well, that depends," Michelle returned nonchalantly. "If it's complimentary, of course. If not, then keep it to yourself."

"Mmm," said Esa, running his thumb slowly over her bottom lip, "of course it's complimentary. Keep loving Nell the way you do while still keeping her on—what's the expression—'the straight and narrow.' Whatever it is you're doing with her, you're doing it right, Michelle."

"It's not just me," Michelle said softly.

"No." Esa refused to accept it. "It is. One day I'll be there, but I'm not yet. Let's not pretend."

Michelle just nodded. She didn't agree with him. She thought Esa was doing pretty well for someone whose original feelings were resentment and inconvenience. He wasn't completely comfortable yet with Nell, but that wouldn't happen until he felt at home with this new version of himself he claimed not to recognize. Michelle wasn't going to get all schoolmarmy and push him. He'd figure it out. She hoped.

Esa yawned and stretched his arms above his head, then

settled back down, Michelle cuddling in the crook of his arm. "So, Nell," he said. "Am I sleeping in here tonight?"

"Sure," Michelle said quietly. "I think this is where you should sleep every night. This is where she's used to me being." She paused.

"You can stay until six. Then you can go back into your room and I'll wake Nell at six thirty."

"But—"

"I don't want to hit her with too many things at once, Esa."

"All right," he grumbled. "Do we tell her about us? She'll be able to tell."

"I can just mention it casually when I walk her to school in the morning. I'll tell her the truth: that we're dating." She snuggled closer to him. "Or maybe I won't even have to mention it. She'll just see it for what it is, and it'll be fine."

"And if she comes to ask me any questions, I'll send her to you."

"Esa!"

"I was joking!"

"Half joking."

"All right, half joking," he admitted, kissing the top of her head. "To make things easier, I'll just sleep in my own room tonight. We can figure out logistics after Nell knows."

"Okay."

Michelle felt a pang of regret as Esa climbed out of bed, slipping his jeans back on. So what if Nell's alarm went off and she came into the room and he was there? But she couldn't. Not yet, at least.

Michelle Beck and Esa Saari. She nearly succumbed to a barking laugh. Getting involved with someone like him was the most uncharacteristic thing she'd ever done in her life, and that wasn't even taking into account that he was her boss.

"Good night, beautiful Michelle." Esa leaned over, his mouth tenderly skimming hers before turning out the night table lamp. "I'm sorry for waking you up."

"Quite all right," said Michelle, grinning. "Some things just can't wait."

36

"*No hat on* your head, no chocolate kisses."

Nell scowled at Henry, the doorman, but did as she was told, yanking her black beret down over her ears. It had become a tradition that when Nell left home for school, Henry, thin as a straw with a face like hewn rock, would give her a couple of chocolate kisses ("Real American candy"), and ask her about her previous school day. It was bitter cold, surprising for early December. Michelle was glad he made the chocolate contingent on the hat.

Henry nodded approvingly. "That's what I like to see. You don't want your ears falling off from the cold."

Nell rolled her eyes. "Your ears can't fall off from the cold, Henry, unless you get frostbite." Her eyes lit up. "And when that happens they turn all black! It's soooo gross!"

Henry looked appropriately horrified. "It sounds it."

"It *is*." Nell looked gleeful. "Sometimes they have to amputate!"

"I'd rather have them fall off."

"Me, too."

Henry regarded Michelle warmly. "How are things with you?"

"Great." *I'm sleeping with Esa, who I know you hate, because you think he's a lousy tipper at Christmas.* "You?"

Henry grinned, giving Michelle the thumbs-up. "Couldn't be better." He'd obviously resolved a few thorny issues with his girlfriend.

"That's what we want to hear." Michelle fastened the top button of her peacoat, turning up the collar before slipping her gloves on. "All right, Henry, we're off."

"Have a good day, ladies."

"Bye, Henry." Nell pushed through the front door.

"She seems good these days," Henry noted to Michelle when Nell moved out of hearing range. "Chipper. Seems to have adjusted."

Michelle smiled proudly. "She's doing really well."

"Thanks to you."

"Her uncle, too. He's doing his best."

"Yeah. I'm sure he is," Henry agreed reluctantly. "I can't imagine what it must be like to have no responsibilities and then BAM! Here's this kid on your doorstop—a girl, no less."

"Exactly," Michelle murmured with a polite smile. "Have a good day, Henry."

She and Nell began the walk to school. Nell's expression was unmistakably cross.

"Okay, you've got my attention," Michelle said lightly. "What's wrong?"

"How come I have to wear a hat when it's cold and you don't?"

Michelle whipped out her own beret from her coat pocket. "Foiled."

Nell's shoulders sank.

"I don't see why you don't like your beret. I see lots of girls at your school wearing them."

"I just don't like hats!" Nell kicked at a small crumpled napkin some litterer had left on the sidewalk. "My mum hated them, too. She never made me wear one. Ever."

"Well, I am, so deal with it."

"You're so mean sometimes, Michelle!"

"I know," Michelle teased. "Very mean. The meanest."

Nell blew out a puff of frustration, but she didn't reply. Michelle knew just the way to turn her mood around.

"I've got some great news. I think you'll really like it."

"Is it about a new computer?" Nell asked eagerly.

"Nell, you don't need a new computer! We've been over this."

"Is it about getting an iPad?"

Michelle couldn't hide her shock. *"What?"*

"Everyone in my school has one," Nell insisted. "Except me."

Michelle frowned dubiously, pulling her coat collar even closer to her neck to ward off the unseasonably cold breeze flowing up the avenue. "I'm sure you're exaggerating."

"I'm not!"

"Well, an iPad is something you need to talk to your Uncle about. Maybe as a Christmas present. C'mon," Michelle urged, surprised by how eager she was for Nell to guess the surprise. "I know you can get it. I'll give you a hint: it's something you've asked about a few times. Something you've dreamed about."

"Hhmm," said Nell, tapping her lips thoughtfully. Suddenly she gasped. "Are you and Uncle Esa getting married?"

"What? God, no!"

Nell's face fell, leaving Michelle cursing herself for the vehemence of her knee-jerk reaction. "That's something people do when they've been together for a really long time, but I still think what I have to say will make you happy," Michelle said, backpedaling. "The news I wanted to tell you was that your uncle and I are seeing each other."

"Like he's your boyfriend now?"

"Yes."

Nell was practically skipping down the road. "Does this mean we're a family now?"

Michelle hated putting a dent in her joy, but felt she had to before Nell started to let her imagination run away with her. "Not exactly. Your uncle is your uncle and I'm your nanny."

"But I can pretend! And then when you do get married we'll be a proper family!"

Michelle smiled weakly. "Right."

She could go round and round with Nell: We're not going

to get married. But you might. That's not likely, honey. But you don't know. Round and round, and there would be no point to it, except to diminish Nell's happiness. Just let her have it for now, Michelle told herself. There would be time enough later to adjust explanations depending on how things played out.

"I didn't want to go to school today, but now I do!" Nell declared.

"I know you're not a fan of Mondays."

"But this is a special one! Will Uncle Esa be home when I get back from school?"

"Actually, sweetie, he won't. He has a game tonight."

"Oh well." Nell looked disappointed for a moment, but it didn't last long. "I feel really, really happy! Do you feel happy?"

Warmth zipped through Michelle's body. "I do, sweetie. I really do."

* * *

San Jose was getting to every loose puck, winning every battle. At first, Esa thought it was just him, that he was having an off night. But as Coach Dante rolled the lines and the defense pairings changed, it became obvious everyone was out of sync. They were getting outskated, outhit, and outhustled. Every pass they made was just a little off, either out of reach or forcing the recipient to break stride, slow down, and lose all momentum. They had no puck possession time, repeatedly being whistled for offsides or icing. It was only thanks to a couple of posts that they got out of the first period only down by two goals.

In the locker room Coach Dante played cheerleader, telling them they'd weathered the storm and were ready to get back in the game. He took to the white board, which he rarely ever used, to sketch out what San Jose was doing to throw off their break outs. He circled the locker room, patting players on the shoulder, or tousling their hair, telling them all that it didn't matter how you started; it mattered how you finished. Esa could feel some energy and enthusiasm bubble up in the team. Rory started singing some unintelligible Gaelic war song and the rest of them laughed. Clearly everyone felt like they'd get things back on track. They took to the ice for the second period, convinced they'd be able to come back and take charge.

They were wrong. Only two minutes into the period, Eric misplayed a San Jose dump in, resulting in a turnover. To keep it from turning into a scoring chance, he pulled down the San Jose winger who had broken toward the slot. Coach Dante encouraged Esa and Rory, who he sent out to kill the penalty, to turn it around. They almost did. Esa won a battle along the half boards and got behind a pinching defenseman. Racing up the left wing with the puck, he had two steps on the other San Jose point man. Rory flew up the right wing, turning it into a two on one. When Esa got to the top of the circles, he snapped a wrister that beat the San Jose netminder . . . and clanged off the crossbar. The puck rebounded past Rory and was scooped up by a back-checking San Jose winger. With both Esa and Rory trapped, San Jose came up ice on what turned into a four on two. A slap shot was redirected by a winger and found the back of the Blades net. Just like that they went from almost getting back into it to being down by three. The building and the team deflated. They played the rest of the second period as if skating in mud. The only reason they didn't give up any more goals was that they were so boring they probably put the San Jose players to sleep.

In the locker room after the second period, Coach Dante the cheerleader was gone, replaced by Coach Dante the psychopath. Screaming at them all for their lack of focus, their lack of passion, their lack of brains, and their lack of balls, he reamed them all out both individually and collectively. They sat in silence as their beloved coach, known for his unfailing effort when he himself was a player, told them they weren't fit to wear the Blades sweater. He ended by telling them to go out and try to recover from how they'd embarrassed themselves.

They did play better in the third. Ulfie threw a bone-crunching open-ice check that got the crowd back in the game and gave some life to the bench. Eric Mitchell partially atoned for his earlier giveaways by making a nice pass to his brother, who cut to the side of the net. Jason put away a one-timer to finally get the Blades on the board, making it three to one. But

San Jose was content to dump the puck in and sit back and play the trap. When San Jose got a delay of game penalty with three minutes left, Coach Dante pulled the goalie and, desperate for more offense, put Esa on the point for the six-on-four power play. With time running out, Esa one timed a slapper which was blocked by a San Jose forward. The puck headed toward center ice, where it was gathered in by another San Jose player who, once he crossed the red line, nonchalantly shot the puck into the empty Blades net. The remaining minute went quickly, with most of the action being in the stands, as the few remaining Blades faithful filed out of Met Gar.

* * *

"I'd say let's get shit faced, but I don't think it would make us feel any better."

The glum truth of Eric Mitchell's statement barely elicited grunts of agreement from Esa and his teammates. The game against San Jose was over and they were at the Wild Hart. Esa hoped the warm pub atmosphere—the taste of the Guinness, the comforting sight of the regulars on their bar stools, the jukebox that hadn't been updated in at least thirty years— might offer some comfort. He was wrong. If he and his teammates had been smart they'd have just gone home. But stupidly, almost like robots who were programmed and couldn't do anything else, they'd gone to the traditional watering hole. The regular patrons at the Hart left the Blades alone, win or lose. But tonight there were a few Blades fans who'd decided they needed to convey their dismay on a more personal level, and had made the trip uptown to the Hart.

They were respectful, up to the point. What pissed Esa off was the way they recited a laundry list of what the team had done wrong, followed by descriptions of the plays they should have made. Sometimes it felt like every fan in New York thought he should be a commentator on *Hockey Night in Canada* alongside Don Cherry. The Blades thanked their critics through gritted teeth. Once the rabid fans realized they weren't going to get anything other than robotic responses from the players, they left.

"We have to have at least one round," Ulf announced, breaking the silence.

"He's right," said Rory. "We can't park our arses here and just boo-hoo without ordering something. Especially since—"

" 'The owner's my wife's uncle,' " the Mitchell twins recited in unison.

"Fuck off," said Rory. "It's true. I can't afford to look bad."

"I don't know, you looked pretty bad on the ice tonight if you ask me," said Eric.

Rory's entire body sank with wariness. "Don't start, Mitchell. We all sucked. We're all culpable for what happened, yourself included. So allow me to repeat myself: fuck off."

Rory's uncle-in-law swung by the table, his expression grim. "Drinks are on the house."

"You don't have to do that," said Eric.

"No, I don't," Joe O'Brien agreed dryly. "But it's clear as day you fellas are hurtin', so just accept it as an old man's gesture to try to cheer you a bit."

"You're not old, Mr. O.," said Jason.

"People who lie go to hell, Jason Mitchell. You just remember that." Joe looked around the table. "You boys want any food?"

"Only if that's on the house, too," Rory joked.

Joe wagged his index finger at him affectionately. "Now that's pushing it, son."

All of them said they were weren't hungry. One brew and out. No one wanted to linger.

There was no clinking of glasses when they got their beer, because there was nothing to toast. All they shared at this moment was a collective sense of misery. And then it got personal.

"I guess that effort won't help you win a new contract from your next team, Finn," Ulf blurted, as he finished his beer and slammed the mug on the table.

Eric Mitchell stared at him. "That's out of line, Ulfie. The game is the game and business is business."

Never one to take a hint, Ulf didn't back down. "C'mon. You mean you guys haven't been reading how Esa is out shopping himself around for next year? It doesn't piss you all off?"

David Hewson answered at once. "No, it doesn't piss me off. The only leverage any of us have in negotiating with management is the threat of signing someplace else. The minute we slow down or underperform, they'll cut our ass or ship us off to Columbus for a bag of pucks and a player to be named later."

"Esa's playing as hard as ever," added Rory. "If he sucks, he sucks honestly, just like the rest of us." That brought some laughter and helped cut the sudden tension.

"The last thing I want to do is leave here," Esa announced, staring into his beer. "Nell is just getting settled and I don't want to uproot her. She's been through too much already." A brooding silence settled over the table. "I need my agent to push for the best deal I can get because it's not just about me anymore. It's about Nell now, too."

The silence grew uncomfortable. It was finally broken by the sound of sniffling. Ulf lifted his head: there were tears running down his cheeks. "I'm an asshole," he said simply. "You know I love Nell. I'm sorry."

Esa stood up, walked around the table to where Ulf was sitting, and planted a kiss on top of the bowling-ball-sized head.

"Time to go," said Eric Mitchell. "These two need to get a room."

37

"*I know you're* awake. I can feel the waves of Finnish glumness even in the darkness."

Michelle's words cracked some of the gloominess Esa was indeed feeling. Christmas was less than two weeks away, and for five days, he'd deliberately been playing phone tag with his parents. But he knew he couldn't hide forever.

He reached out, taking her small hand in his, always a comfort. "What are you doing awake?"

"Your glumness. It woke me up. I could *feel* it."

Esa laughed lightly, turning on his side so he was facing her. He loved being in bed with her, especially since they were being more open about it, Esa not always heading off to his room before Nell awakened. Michelle still struggled with having broken the "Nanny's Code of Ethics"; she fretted about sending the "right message." Every time she worried, Esa reminded her that they were demonstrating to Nell what a functioning family unit looked like. "Could look like," Michelle was always careful to point out. They'd had to make adjustments—he could no longer sleep in the nude, for example, and he had had to sacrifice his bed for Michelle's—but it seemed minor. And though he still felt sometimes as if he'd slipped into another man's skin, it was preferable to the life he'd been leading. He hadn't realized how dead he'd been inside, even before Danika's passing. Blankness was the perfect way to avoid vulnerability, an empty chalkboard where he decided what was written upon it. Hiding behind a stereotype. Fucking and running was so much safer than sticking around. He wasn't going to lie: a lot of the time he was scared witless. But better that than wake up one day a pathetic old man with a facelift and bad dye job, clutching a pint-sized bottle of Viagra in his veiny hand and coming on to women half his age. Guilt tapped at his heart as he thought about the burning resentment he'd felt toward Nell when she'd first moved in. He hated that there were things he still couldn't say to her, no matter how hard he tried. He told himself it would come with time. But then again, he *was* Finnish.

Michelle snaked a hand out from beneath the covers, brushing her knuckles along his jawline. "What's going on?"

"It's my parents. They want Nell and me to come over for Christmas. It's the last thing I want to do. It'll be joyless. They keep leaving messages and I haven't been returning their calls."

"We've also been avoiding the subject of the holidays, you know. Nell's assuming it's going to be the three of us here."

"What have you told her?"

"That things were up in the air with your schedule. But I think the uncertainty of it stresses her out a little, Esa."

"I know, I know." How good he was at pushing away things he didn't want to think about. "I really don't want to go to Finland."

"You can't blame them for wanting to see her, Esa," said Michelle softly.

"Can't I?" Esa retorted. "They barely visited Danika. Now all of a sudden they want to spend time with Nell?"

"You could have them here. Show them where you work, where Nell goes to school—"

"No way." The thought brought an unwanted rush of blood to Esa's head. "I don't want Nell feeling uncomfortable in her own home. Shit, *I* don't want to feel uncomfortable in my own home."

"They could stay at a hotel," Michelle suggested. Esa knew she was trying to be helpful, but she didn't know his parents. He didn't want them infecting the life he'd built for himself in any way, shape, or form.

"It wouldn't be good enough. They'd criticize New York. They'd hate the apartment. They'd inspect Nell's room and say she was spoiled."

"They sound delightful," Michelle deadpanned.

Esa rolled onto his back, groaning. "There has to be a way out of this."

It was a long, long time before Michelle rolled on top of him, her chin resting on her palms as she gazed at him. "Got it."

"What?"

"Meet them in London. They've at least been there before, right? Plus it'll give Nell a chance to see Leslie."

Esa bit the tip of her nose. "You're so smart."

"I know."

"You'll love it."

Michelle lifted her head slightly. "Love what?"

"London. You'll be with us. You *are* Nell's nanny."

Michelle's lips parted slightly, but no sound came out.

"Michelle?"

"Esa, I'm spending Christmas with my father and brother."

"Fuck."

Michelle kissed his shoulder, her expression guilty. "I'm really sorry."

"No, no, don't be sorry. There's a simple solution: you fly to London to join us the day after Christmas."

"Brilliant!" She grinned at him. "Like you said, I *am* Nell's nanny, after all."

"It's only for a few days because I have to get back, but like you said, Nell can see Leslie, and it does help me control the interactions with my folks."

"London," Michelle marveled.

The stressful sound of the blood whooshing in Esa's ears was receding, thanks to Michelle's unabashed amazement over travel.

"I still wish you could be there for Christmas Day itself," said Esa, his gloom returning for a sudden encore. "The thought of having Christmas dinner in a hotel restaurant—or any restaurant at all—is so depressing . . . Christ. Well, I guess it's better than being stuck in their house watching my mother cook reindeer and listening to my father recite boring old stories."

"Maybe you could all go over to see Leslie together," Michelle suggested, sounding upbeat.

"My parents hate Leslie for giving Nell to me and not them." He knew he was painting a completely horrible picture of his parents. Perhaps that was because they were miserable people. Unhappy was a better word. They were unhappy.

"I think you'll agree it's better if you and I are with Nell when she goes to Leslie's," Esa continued. "No way am I dropping her off there on her own with that fuck-face fiancé of Leslie's there."

"Good point." The bedroom was dark, but not so dark he couldn't see the slow smile spreading across Michelle's face. "You love her so much."

"Of course I do," Esa murmured, tensing. He knew what Michelle wanted him to say next—that she was waiting to see if he would really go there, and it was sending the torrents of blood straight back to his head, the pressure on his skull intense. But she didn't push. Instead, she pulled closer to him, her head resting on the pillow beside his.

"I hate the thought of you dreading Christmas."

"I always have."

"That's sad, Esa."

Esa stared up at the ceiling. "I know. Every year, the same present: new skates. Every year, just the four of us. I remember some of my friends' families would go hiking or sledding. But we never did. My father was always worried I would break my leg and 'ruin my future.'" Esa snorted. "As if I didn't do those things with my friends behind his back." He chuckled softly. "Danika knew. She used to blackmail me: 'Give me your allowance or I'll tell Mom and Dad you went sledding with Kai.' It was one of the few things we shared, that joke." His throat tightened, a prelude to tears. What the hell was wrong with him, with this stupid, fabricated sentimentality? He squeezed his eyes shut, focusing all his energy on driving away unwanted emotions.

"Esa?" Michelle whispered.

He pulled her tight to him, not wanting to use words. He hoped to Christ she didn't say something like, "You know you can talk to me." For some reason, it would make it worse.

But she didn't. And in the ensuing silence, he came up with an idea. A wonderful idea that would make both him and Nell happy.

"What if Nell and I spend Christmas Eve and Christmas Day here with you? And then the day after, the three of us fly to London to meet my folks?"

"But your parents—"

"As long as they get to see Nell, that'll be all that matters," Esa cut in. "Trust me. My family has tons of relatives they can spend Christmas with. There's no way they can kick up much of a fuss when I tell them I don't have that much time off."

"I guess that could work," Michelle said slowly. "Are you sure?"

"I'm sure. I don't want to dread Christmas this year, Michelle. I want it to be wonderful, especially for Nell. And you know what? It's going to be."

38

"*When are they* going to be here, Michelle? When, when?"

If Michelle didn't know better, she'd be worried: she'd never seen Nell this impatient or hyperactive. Then again, she'd never seen Nell on Christmas Day. She asked Esa about it, since he had spent at least a few Christmases with his niece, but he was pretty clueless. "I was usually hungover on Christmas morning," he admitted sheepishly. "Too much glogg the night before."

She was glad Esa didn't dread Christmas this year. Esa's parents weren't thrilled when they heard his plan, but there wasn't much they could do in the face of his bluntness: he told them that there were people in New York Nell was close to, and he thought it important she spend the day with them. London was a good place for them to meet so that Nell could see Leslie. To offset their disappointment he'd booked everyone into Claridge's, one of the top hotels in London.

Michelle put a hand on Nell's shoulder to still her, guiding her away from the door. "They'll be here soon, I promise." They were due in half an hour, which, knowing her dad, meant the front desk should be buzzing them right . . . about . . . now.

"They're here!" Nell exclaimed.

Michelle had Henry send them up.

Michelle's anxiety surprised her. She hadn't gone out of her way to tell her dad and Jamie about her and Esa, but she wasn't going to hide it, either. She wanted today to be simple and happy.

She opened the door to the sight of her dad standing there without her brother. There was no need to ask if Jamie was okay, because she knew right away what the deal was.

"Hyraa joulua!" Nell said to him excitedly. "That's Finnish for 'Merry Christmas!'"

"No kidding," said Michelle's dad, leaning over to give her a kiss. "Merry Christmas, kiddo."

"Michelle and I made gingerbread!"

Michelle rolled her eyes affectionately. "Nell, let's let my dad in the door, okay?"

"Where's Jamie?" she asked her dad sweetly, taking his coat as he came inside.

Her father wouldn't meet her eyes. "Took one of the shifts down at the house. He needs the money."

"Mmm."

"Michelle."

"It's okay, Dad, I get it."

Her hands trembled slightly as she hung up her father's coat. Her brother was such an asshole, giving her such a hard time when she'd told him she wouldn't be over on Christmas Eve, accusing her of abandoning the family, even though she'd pointed out to him that their dad's apartment would be packed with relatives, and that she'd be seeing him on Christmas Day. He tried to talk her into bringing Nell over both days—without Esa. So what if the Finnish prick spends the holidays alone, he'd sneered. She'd come so dangerously close to telling him she was falling in love with that Finnish prick. And then there was his usual bullshit about their father and his worsening cough, ghoulishly intimating that their dad was on death's door and that this Christmas might be his last. "Well, then he'll be spending it here with me, you, Nell, and Esa Saari," she'd said. She'd stood her ground with Jamie. Now she was being punished for it.

Nell was still wound up like any little kid on Christmas. "Where's Jamie?" she asked Michelle's dad.

"Down at the firehouse, kiddo. He had to work. But . . ." her dad said to Nell as if sharing a big secret while he reached into the paper shopping bag he carried, "he did tell me to give you this." He handed Nell a perfectly square little present. Nell rounded on Michelle. "Can I open it now?"

"In a minute," Michelle promised. "C'mon, Dad, follow me into the living room."

"Where's Saari?" he asked, taking the room in.

Nell actually frowned at him. "His name is Esa," she corrected politely. "Saari is his last name."

Michelle's dad looked taken aback, but he got the message.

"In answer to your question, I think he's finishing up in the shower. You *are* half an hour early," Michelle pointed out.

"So shoot me."

Nell looked at Michelle worriedly. "It's just American slang, honey. He doesn't really want me to shoot him."

"Good."

Nell bounded on to the couch, pointing at the tall, beautiful fir tree in the corner. "That's our Christmas tree. I picked it out."

Michelle's dad looked impressed.

"And I picked out most of the decorations. Michelle helped, though. Right, Michelle?"

"Yup."

"What, the Finn had no decorations?" Michelle's father asked her under his breath. "The guy's never had a tree before?"

"Dad," Michelle said very quietly with a hint of warning in her voice, "his name is not 'the Finn.' Or 'Saari.' It's Esa, okay? If you slip again, you're going to upset Nell."

Her father saluted her. "Gotcha, Chief." He sat down on the couch beside Nell, pointing at the unwrapped gifts surrounding the tree. "Looks like Santa was good to someone."

"It's Father Christmas. And Santa isn't real."

"Sure he is."

"You're mad."

Nell's eyes were glued to the shopping bag on the floor next to Michelle's dad. Michelle got the feeling she was trying to will gifts out of the bag and onto her lap. She bumped her father's shoulder, tilting her head in Nell's direction.

"Whatcha looking at, kiddo?"

"Nothing."

Michelle's dad reached into the bag. "Maybe this would interest you?" He passed a gift to Nell.

"Thank you," Nell said shyly.

Michelle's dad rattled the shopping bag. "I've got your present in here," he told her. "And Sa—Esa's."

Michelle was touched. "You didn't have to get him a present."

"Guests should never show up empty-handed, right?"

"Can I open these now?" Nell asked Michelle.

"Let the kid open them," her father said before Michelle had a chance to answer.

"As if I was going to say no!" She smiled at Nell indulgently. "Go ahead."

Nell went for her dad's gift first, delicately opening the wrapping paper. No wild tearing here; it was as if she wanted to save it for next year.

Nell gasped when the present finally revealed itself. "It's a new Barbie! Thank you, Mr. Beck!"

"Hey, I thought we had an agreement: I call you Nell, you call me Ed."

Nell blushed. "Thank you, Ed."

"Enjoy it, kiddo."

Nell carefully folded the wrapping paper, put it on the coffee table, and opened Jamie's present, which she'd been clutching tightly ever since Michelle's dad had handed it to her at the door. It was a Magic 8 Ball. She slowly turned the box over in her hands, eventually looking at Michelle in confusion.

"You ask it questions, and it gives you answers. It's fun."

"Okay."

"We'll play it after dinner, if you'd like."

* * *

"Hello, nice to meet you. I'm Esa."

"I'm Ed."

Tumult went through Michelle as Esa shook hands with

her dad. The situation suddenly felt charged. What if they rubbed each other the wrong way?

"Where's your brother?" Esa asked Michelle.

"He took a shift at the firehouse," she replied. "He gets double pay plus overtime."

"That's too bad. I was looking forward to seeing him."

"Got you a little something," Michelle's dad said to Esa, whose eyes shot to Michelle's questioningly. She shrugged. She was as much in the dark as he was. The impish look on her dad's face as he handed Esa his gift worried her. Her father and Uncle Micky had been known around the firehouse for their off-color gifts. If he'd bought Esa a book of dirty jokes or one of those pens with a woman on it in a bikini that disappears when you turn it upside down, she'd kill herself.

Michelle found it hard to gauge Esa's reaction when he opened her dad's gift and held it against him: it was an Islanders jersey with his name on it. But as a slow smile spread across his face that turned into an appreciative laugh, Michelle's worries abated. Things would probably go well today. It might even be a blessing her brother wasn't here.

39

"My turn!"

Michelle's father had a childlike grin on his face as he handed the Magic 8 Ball over to Nell. Dinner had gone well: she'd outdone herself in the cooking department, and Esa and her dad seemed to get along just fine. Even so, Michelle could see when Esa stopped actually enjoying her dad's needling and started pretending to enjoy it. It was all in the tightness of his smile. Her dad, thankfully, remained oblivious.

The thing that mattered most was that Nell was having a wonderful time. She'd been thrilled when Michelle had produced traditional British Christmas crackers. They tore them apart and everyone, including Esa, who wasn't known as someone who liked to look ridiculous, wore the paper crowns they found inside. A feeling as soothing as sinking down in a warm bath suffused Michelle when, at one point, she'd glanced around the dinner table. The word that came to mind was "family." This was her family. And right now, her family was playing with Nell's Magic 8 Ball waiting for their food to settle a bit before dessert.

They'd been having a blast passing the ball around, their

questions ranging from the mundane ("Will it rain tomorrow?") to the outlandish ("Are Chihuahuas really tiny aliens?"). Nell loved it. Which is why she had one arm outstretched, fingers wiggling impatiently at Nell's dad, who was cradling the ball.

"Wait a minute, kiddo," he said. "I think if you're over sixty you're allowed to go two times in a row."

"I think not, Ed," Nell said primly, making the adults laugh as she took the ball from him.

Nell closed her eyes, her hands cupped around the black plastic ball as if it were cradling something sacred. "Will Michelle and Uncle Esa get married?" she intoned, shaking the ball hard. She opened her eyes. "It says 'Yes'!" She looked at Esa and Michelle excitedly. "It does!"

"It's just a game," Esa reminded her with an indulgent smile.

"But it *could* happen," Nell insisted. "I'm going to ask again!"

Michelle contemplated stilling her hand and telling her she was being silly, but that would look suspicious. It *was* just a game.

Nell closed her eyes, asked the same question again, shook the ball vigorously, and opened her eyes. "It says 'Without a doubt'!" she squealed. "You two *are* getting married! I knew it!"

"Nellie." Michelle's dad's voice was gentle. "It's just a game, kiddo. It's not based on anything real."

"Yes, it is! Uncle Esa and Michelle are going out and they could fall in love and get married, so it could happen!"

Michelle wasn't sure how to characterize the silence that ensued. "Awkward" and "uncomfortable" seemed a little too flimsy. Maybe uneasy? No, no. no. She was beating around the bush. The word was *embarrassing*.

"I didn't know Michelle and Uncle Esa were going out!" Michelle's dad said to Nell with a false brightness that made Michelle want to cringe.

Nell nodded seriously. "Oh, yes."

Michelle's father's eyebrows shot up, looking like twin mountain peaks. "Well, that's interesting. Michelle didn't say anything to me—and I'm her dad!"

Nell looked at Michelle quizzically. "How come you didn't say anything to your dad, Michelle?"

"Because I didn't want to make a big announcement," Michelle explained to Nell—and her father.

"Telling your own *father* you're dating someone isn't making a big announcement," he insisted, "unless it's something you're ashamed of."

Nell wrinkled her nose in confusion. "But why would Michelle—"

"She wouldn't be," Michelle cut in softly. She went to fix her eyes on her dad, but his gaze was already locked on Esa.

"What about you? You have anything to say?"

"Me?" Esa replied coolly. "No." He playfully snatched the ball from Nell. "My turn!"

*   *   *

After playing with the Magic 8 Ball, Michelle had thought for sure her father would tell Nell that dinner had made his belly rumble and he couldn't stay for dessert. That had always been one of his favorite ways of escaping an uncomfortable situation. But instead he'd stayed, which could mean only one thing: he wanted to talk to Michelle. She supposed it was necessary, if only to fill in some of the blanks. But she wasn't looking forward to it.

"Do you want to talk to him together?" Esa offered after they'd put Nell to bed. They were standing in the hallway outside her bedroom. Michelle's dad was in the living room watching *Sports Center*.

"That obvious, huh?" Michelle hadn't said a word to him about her father wanting to talk.

"Yeah."

"You know what? I think I'll talk to him on my own," Michelle decided aloud. "I'm an adult, for God's sake. It's not like we're two fourteen-year-olds who were caught screwing around in the basement."

Esa wrapped his arms around her. "Well, I'm here if you need me." He kissed her mouth softly. "Today was wonderful. Nell was so happy."

"I know."

"I was happy, too," he said.

"Even though my dad wouldn't shut up about the Islanders?"

"Even with that." Esa looked down at her, his expression so serene it almost brought tears to her eyes. "Were you happy today, Michelle?"

Michelle leaned her forehead against his chest for a moment, laughing softly. "Well, my day isn't quite over yet." She looked back up at him. "But so far? Yes, very happy."

"Here's hoping it stays that way."

* * *

"You know I don't beat around the bush."

"I know that, Dad."

"Never have, never will."

"True."

"So when I tell you that I'm shocked, I'm not joking. What the *hell* is going on here? Are you crazy? You could destroy your reputation!"

"Dad." Michelle sat next to her father on the couch, her feet tucked beneath her. She was close enough to see the needle-fine network of red lines on his cheeks, and just how dark those black arcs beneath his eyes were. He looked tired, but she'd thought that even as a little girl. True to his word, he had cut right to the chase.

Michelle reached for his hand. "I'm not going to destroy my reputation. But since that's the first thing you mentioned, let's talk about that first."

Her father shook her hand off angrily. "Michelle, you're not a goddamn teacher trying to reassure some overwrought kid!"

"Wrong. That's *exactly* who I am, because I have to be. I don't want to get into some stupid, unnecessary argument with you when you don't even know what's going on."

Her father looked insulted. "Who said anything about arguing?"

"Gee, Dad, I don't know. Maybe I thought something like that could happen because you told me you were shocked, asked me if I was crazy, and informed me I could destroy my reputation, all in the space of thirty seconds?"

Her father looked peevish as he hoisted himself forward to pour himself a glass of whiskey. "Well, what the hell am I supposed to think?"

"What were you thinking before Nell spilled the beans? Probably that Esa was a really nice guy, and that it was great that Nell seemed so happy and well-adjusted, right? *Right*?"

Her father's expression turned resentful. "Yeah, but—"

"No buts. That's the thing: no buts. Esa *is* a really nice guy. Nell *is* happy and well-adjusted."

"He's also your boss. I seem to remember a very dedicated nanny who took her Code of Ethics very seriously. What happened?"

"Look. You know me. Do you think this is something I would ever have courted in a work situation? *Ever*?"

Her father took a long, slow, sip from his whiskey. "He seduced you, didn't he?"

"Oh my God. No, he did not seduce me." She reached for one of the small gingerbread cookies on the plate on the coffee table and tore off its head with her teeth. "Do you realize how insulting it is to me when you say that? It makes me sound like I'm some helpless little girlie who's been overcome by the big bad hockey player—"

"With a reputation for fucking everything that moves," her father finished sharply.

Michelle hit right back. "I'm not everything that moves."

"Oh, so you're special. Did he tell you that?"

"Goddammit, Dad," Michelle cursed as she snapped off the gingerbread man's left leg. "Will you stop for a minute and let me talk?"

"Be my guest."

"I'm the last person who ever thought she'd be in a situation like this. I'm sure every nanny who has ever gotten involved with her employer has said that. But I don't care about those other nannies; I care about me and Esa and Nell.

"Of course we tried to avoid this! The only way to really do that would have been for me to stop being Nell's nanny, but considering how much that kid's been through, that seemed like a bad idea. Believe me, the last man on earth I ever saw myself getting involved with is Esa Saari, okay?"

Her father threw his hands up. "That's what I don't understand! You know what he is, but you get with him anyway?"

"I know what he *was*." Michelle leaned forward, elbows on knees, cradling her forehead on an open palm. She suddenly felt incredibly tired. It had been a long day, and it was catching up with her: the cooking, the playing with toys, the worries about her father not liking Esa, and now this. *This*—which was all her fault. Because in trying to avoid making "a big announcement," she'd instead created a tangled ball of confusion, mistrust, and suspicion that her father was going to kick Esa's way. She should have said something to her dad on the telephone before he came over. "Look, just so you know . . ." Something like that. But would he have come over if she had?

Michelle slowly lifted her head. Her father was looking at her expectantly.

"I'm not asking you to try to understand something even I don't understand, okay? All I ask is that you give me some credit here. I'm not a stupid woman, nor am I naive or gullible or easily taken in. So when I tell you that Esa and I are having a relationship, and it's good, and that the two of us with Nell feel like a real family, all I'm asking is that you accept what I'm saying is true. You don't have to like it, but please accept it. Because the relationship isn't going away."

Her father shook his head, incredulous. "This isn't my Michelle."

Michelle made a fist, punching her thigh. "Dad, it is! You just refuse to believe it because the situation is so unconventional."

Her father snorted. "I'll say."

Indignation stabbed at Michelle like an adrenalin needle to the heart. "Excuse me?"

"Honey, have you stopped to think what kind of message you're sending Nell, the two of you sleeping together?"

"I know you won't believe it, but *yes*. The message she's getting is honesty. Creeping back and forth in the night is crazy; it makes it seem like what we're doing is something to be ashamed of, when it isn't. Seeing the two of us together also makes her feel that much more secure." Michelle paused, picturing Nell asleep in bed right now. "It makes her feel like she's part of a family," she finished softly.

Her father grimaced. "Except the three of you aren't a family, Michelle. He could fire you. He could break up with you and tell you he's looking for another nanny and that he never wants you to see Nell again."

"He would never do that!"

"That's not the point."

"That *is* the point!" The apartment seemed to gasp in silence at the sound of Michelle's raised voice. She hoped it wasn't loud enough for Esa to hear. The worst thing that could happen right now would be for him and her father to get into some sort of "discussion." Both were stubborn men who backed down only if forced. She'd be cleaning blood off the walls and floors for days.

"That *is* the point," Michelle repeated, a little less vehemently. "He would never hurt Nell."

"Four months ago he didn't give a shit about the kid. Now you're nominating him for Uncle of the Year?"

Michelle slipped her hands beneath her legs so her father couldn't see her balling them into tight fists. "He's trying, Dad."

"I don't care about him. I care about *you*. What happens to *you*."

"Which brings us back to the fact that I'm a big girl and I can take care of myself."

Her father heaved a deep sigh. "All right, all right, I get it. I just . . ." He shook his head sadly.

Michelle stood. "You just what?"

"I'm just disappointed with you, okay? Now that the shock's worn off, I'm disappointed."

"Disappointed," Michelle repeated blankly. She licked her lips. "That's a little harsh, isn't it?"

"I don't know. Is it?"

Her pain began recombining itself with anger. "Creating a loving, safe home for a little girl who's been through a huge trauma is the work of someone you'd call a 'disappointment'? Interesting. I'm just glad Nell has someone to help her navigate all this, Dad. I didn't. I'm sorry you feel disappointed in me, but I'm not going to apologize for the way things have evolved."

Her father pushed himself up off the couch. "I should take off."

"That sounds like a good idea." She forced herself toward the kitchen. "Let me at least make up some leftovers for you."

"No, no, don't worry, I'm fine," he called after her.

"Okay. If you say so."

Michelle changed tact and walked toward the front hall, her dad following suit. She felt like they were in the concluding moments of some depressing Arthur Miller play as she helped her father put on his coat. There was such sadness here, but there was also an overwhelming sense of impotent rage, at least on her part.

"Have you got everything?" she checked.

"Yep. All good." There was an awkward pause as Michelle opened the apartment door. "Thanks for having me for Christmas, kiddo. Thank Esa, too."

"Of course."

"When do the three of you get back from London? Friday?"

"Yeah. Around seven."

"You'll call me when you get back?"

"No, Dad, you'll never hear from me again." Being a wiseass helped ease some of the pressure in her chest.

Her father leaned in for a quick hug. "Love you, 'chelle."

"Love you, too, Dad," she managed. She started walking with him out into the hall but he told her she didn't have to, he was fine, he was capable of going down to the street and hailing a cab himself. Michelle took the hint, read the subtext. *Love you, 'chelle, but I really don't like you right now.* No, worse than that. *I'm disappointed in you.*

He'd never said that to her before. It hurt more than she could have imagined. She felt a white hissing behind her eyes as tears tried to push themselves free, but she refused to cry. She hadn't done anything wrong.

40

"*We've been here* for an hour and a half. If I were a betting woman, I'd say we're not going to get out of here for at least another two hours."

Michelle heard Esa's groan as they followed Nell to another carefully staged grouping of plush, stuffed animals. They were on the ground floor of Hamleys, London's largest toy store. When Michelle had read that it was two hundred and fifty years old, with seven floors, she thought: who would want to miss that? The answer was: no one. It was mobbed. Every family in London, tourist or native, seemed to be here, and together they'd melded into one chattering, heaving mass of slowly dissipating goodwill. The smart, sane reaction would have been to turn around at once and leave at the sight of wall-to-wall kids and their parents. But Esa had made the mistake of telling Nell, long before they hit the store, that she could have any stuffed animal she liked; Nell wasn't going anywhere. It was insane to be buying Nell another present— they'd celebrated Christmas two days ago—but Michelle understood the impulse: they were having dinner with Esa's parents tonight. Esa was simply letting her pick out a reward ahead of time.

Her phone vibrated in the pocket of her jeans. She let the call go to voice mail; she didn't want to be one of those obnoxious people who talked on their phone no matter where, no matter what. But then it rang again. When she pulled the phone from her pocket and saw who the caller was, she knew she had to take it.

* * *

"*Just take a* slow, deep breath, okay?"

Michelle knew Esa was trying to be helpful, but she didn't want to take a slow, deep breath. She wanted to wail in fear at the top of her lungs that her father was going to die, and it was going to happen when she was in a plane somewhere over the Atlantic Ocean.

Still, she did as he asked, more for Nell's sake than anything else. Her poor girl looked petrified.

"Better?"

Michelle nodded.

They were in Michelle's hotel room, waiting for a car to pick her up to take her back to Heathrow. Nell sat frozen in place at the room's ornate desk, never taking her eyes off Michelle, watching, waiting. "C'mere." Michelle pat the empty space beside her on the bed. It looked for a minute as if Nell wasn't going to move—or worse, *couldn't*—but then she clambered up beside Michelle, who put her arm around her.

"I know you're worried about my dad," said Michelle with a slight quaver in her voice. "And I am, too. But he's gonna be okay." She knew Nell, so she braced herself for what was coming.

"But what if he isn't?" she asked, her eyes filling with tears.

"If he isn't," Michelle answered, pausing to compose herself, "we'll worry about it then. But right now, we have to believe he's going to be okay."

Nell burrowed close to Michelle, wrapping her arms around her waist, resting her head against her chest. "I don't see why we can't all go back to New York. I don't see why Uncle Esa and I have to stay."

"I don't, either," said Esa. Nell's head shot up, eyes full of hope. "Sorry, Nell," he apologized glumly. "Dumb joke."

Michelle felt guilty; she knew the last thing he wanted to do was have dinner with his folks tonight without her there. But neither of them had a choice: he couldn't leave, and she sure as hell couldn't stay. Her father had suffered a heart attack. It was even possible he was being prepped right now for his surgery. Triple bypass. Michelle was overcome with images of him: smoking cigarettes and cigars, eating cookies, and all those endless trays of goddamn lasagna they made down at the firehouse. *Goddamnit.*

"Michelle?"

She looked down at Nell, her image clear and bright, then wavy, then finally blurry as she realized she'd started to cry. "Oh." Michelle swiped at her eyes. "Sorry, sweetie."

"You're afraid he's going to die," Nell whispered. "I know you are."

"I'm not afraid he's going to die, Nell," Michelle lied calmly. "I just wish I was there right now."

"Me, too."

Michelle hugged her tighter. "Plus, I have *crazy brain* right now. My brain is bouncing all over the place."

"Maybe Zak can make you feel better."

Michelle smiled. "Maybe."

"I'll go get him."

Nell scrambled off the bed to fetch the oversized, stuffed polar bear she'd chosen at Hamley's, leaving Michelle and Esa alone for a moment.

"God, I wish I was going to be there to see you get that thing through customs," Michelle sniffled.

"We'll ship it ahead. I really think we should go back with you. Nell's not going to care about a thing, now that you're not here."

"That's not true. She was really looking forward to seeing Leslie."

"I dunno . . ."

"You just want to avoid seeing your parents," Michelle accused playfully.

"That's not true!"

"Yes, it is!"

"No, it *isn't*."

Michelle closed her eyes as the mattress dipped from the weight of Esa sitting beside her. "I want to go back because I want to be there with you," he said softly, taking her in his arms.

Michelle buried her face in his neck, and began to cry. "I'm so afraid he's going to die, Esa."

"I know." He began rocking her gently. "But he's a tough old bastard, eh? You've said so yourself."

"Yeah, but sometimes it's hard not to jump immediately to the worst thing, you know?"

"Because of your mom?"

"I hadn't even thought of that, but it makes sense." She swiped away a tear with the back of her palm. "He's never taken care of himself." She lifted her head, meeting Esa's eyes. "You don't want to know how many firefighters die of heart attacks, both on the job and after they've retired," she said bitterly. "They all think they're goddamn immortal." She rested her head on Esa's shoulder. "Christ, I can't believe I have to sit through a six hour plane flight before even getting a cab to get to the hospital."

"Are you sure you don't want us to come back with you? My parents can see Nell at Easter. This is more important."

"I'll be fine." She lifted her head again, studying Esa's face. She and her brother used to play a game where they'd stare at each other for ten seconds, then start drawing furiously. The one who drew the best picture from memory was the winner, and the winner was nearly always Michelle, because she had an eye for detail. Were she to draw Esa right now, she'd sketch his blue eyes, and razor sharp cheekbones, but she'd also sketch the tiny, nearly invisible freckle touching the top left of his lip. She'd draw the small white scar across the bridge of his nose that made her think of pince-nez, and she'd draw the slight droop of his right eyelid, which happened when he was tired. But most of all, she'd try to capture the way he was gazing at her: with a passionate intensity that wasn't in the least bit sexual. He's in love with me, she realized.

She broke eye contact, shaking her head with a small smile. Too much all at once.

"Michelle? Are you okay?"

"I'm fine," she repeated. Out of nowhere, tears threatened again, and she laughed. "Actually, I'm a mess. One minute I want to cry my eyes out, the next I could just laugh . . . I think I've finally lost it, Esa."

"It's a reaction to stress."

"I know," Michelle agreed sadly, squeezing his hand. "I remember at my mom's wake, going to use the ladies room at the funeral home. I opened the door, and there in the lounge area were three of my mom's friends laughing so hard there were tears running down their faces. I remember feeling just *furious*: how dare they laugh when my mother was dead?

"Now I realize they were just trying to cope. You need to be able to let go in these types of situations or you lose your mind."

"All the more reason for me and Nell to come back with you," Esa insisted.

"Why's that?"

Esa frowned. "Who's going to help you cope? Your brother? The one who suddenly had to work on Christmas Day? C'mon, Michelle. I'm not stupid."

"No, you're not," Michelle agreed. "And it's starting to become inconvenient."

Esa laughed, helping to lighten her mood. Light was where she wanted to try to keep it. That meant trying to steer off the topic of her brother.

"Where's Zak?" Michelle called out to Nell. "My brain is getting pretty bouncy out here!"

"Coming!"

Nell appeared, her body almost obscured by the giant stuffed animal. She released him on the other side of the bed next to Michelle with a small pant. "He weighs a ton!"

"Well, he's a polar bear," Esa pointed out.

"A facsimile of one, you mean." Nell manipulated one of the bear's paws so it slowly stroked Michelle's arm. "See, he's trying to make you feel better. Is it helping?"

Michelle smiled. "It is. Thanks."

"You can take him back to New York with you, if you'd like. Maybe your dad would like to have him in hospital with him!"

"I'm sure he'd love it, Nell, but I doubt the nurses would let him keep it. Hospital rooms are very small."

"Oh."

Zak's paw continued stroking Michelle's arm. "Can I visit your dad in hospital?" Nell asked very quietly.

"Of course," Michelle whispered, eyes flooding. One look at Esa and the next thing she knew she was practically doubled over on the bed, laughing, or maybe it was crying, she couldn't tell. Zak's paw on her forearm stopped moving, and Nell's eyes were big as twin planets. "It's okay," Michelle assured her, trying to get hold of herself after a series of false starts. "Don't look so worried. Sometimes people laugh a lot when they have crazy brain and they're worried, and then they feel silly about being worried and don't know what to think. That's what's happening."

Nell looked thoughtful. "If anything did happen to your dad, you'd still have me, and Uncle Esa."

"That's right," Michelle agreed, feeling pain trying to punch its way out from deep inside her. "And Zak. But I'm pretty sure things are going to be fine."

*　*　*

Michelle was more wired than ever as she walked into New York Hospital Queens. Thanks to a nice tailwind, the flight from New York to London had taken five hours rather than six. She'd thought that perhaps her mind would stop racing on the flight home, but no such luck. Instead, she kept checking her phone, doing a blow-by-blow account in her head of what was probably going on with her dad: He's probably being prepped for surgery now. He's probably in surgery now. He should be out of surgery now, unless there were complications. She hated that she hadn't been there to talk to the doctors before and after the surgery was done, but she was sure Jamie would fill her in, or if not him, then Uncle Micky. Jamie sounded like he didn't know whether he was coming or going when he'd phoned her in London, which wasn't surprising. Michelle was just glad her brother hadn't been pulling a shift when her dad started having chest pains. If her father had been home on his own, he'd have dismissed it as a pulled muscle and lit a cigar. The thought of what might have happened made Michelle nauseous.

Jamie was waiting for her outside the Intensive Care Unit,

flipping impatiently through a well-thumbed copy of *People* magazine. As soon as he spotted her, the magazine was carelessly tossed aside and he was on his feet.

She hugged her brother, but he was stiff in her arms, a sure sign he was distressed. "How's he doing?"

"Good."

"Where's Uncle Micky?" It was seven, early evening. Michelle was surprised he wasn't there.

"I told him we had some family stuff to discuss, so he took off."

Michelle sat down in one of the chairs, bracing herself. "Family stuff." That sounded ominous. Her first thought was morbid and melodramatic: her father was on life support. She pulled herself back to the brink of the rational: there'd been a complication that needed to be dealt with. He was seriously incapacitated.

"Can you at least tell me how the surgery went?"

Jamie rubbed absently at the two day's worth of stubble on his chin. "Yeah, of course. He did good."

"What exactly does that mean?"

"There were no complications, Michelle. If he'd ignored the chest pain, he'd probably be dead."

"God," Michelle whispered.

"So they did the triple bypass. Obviously he's got to do a total lifestyle makeover: eating better, more exercise. He's got to stop smoking the cigars."

"Yeah, what the hell was that all about?"

"I don't know. Thinking he was immortal or something. It was stupid."

"You couldn't talk to him?"

"You couldn't?"

"You live with him, Jamie."

"You should have checked in on him more, Michelle," he retorted.

Jamie was tremendously stressed, so she let the barb pass. "What else?" she coaxed.

"He's been lying about going for checkups. That's why that cough kept getting worse." Jamie glared at her. "You know, the one you said didn't exist?"

Michelle's hands tightened around the arms of the chair. "Let's not do this. We're both tired and overwrought."

Jamie tapped his chest. "I was there with him when it happened, Michelle, and you weren't. So I get to make certain observations."

"Fine," Michelle said tersely. "Observe away."

"To put it bluntly, this is your fault."

Michelle nearly lunged at him. "What?"

"You know what. He goes to Saari's for Christmas and a day later he has a friggin' heart attack? He was really upset about what's going on. It's not a coincidence."

Michelle waited until a group of nurses passing by were well out of earshot before raising her voice to her brother. "How dare you blame me for this? Dad was a time bomb."

"That went off after he found out you were playing house with the biggest dickwad in the NHL."

"This is not my fault, Jamie!"

"Yeah, it is, and you know it is. If Saari were here right now, I'd punch his face in."

"You're talking out of your ass. As usual."

Jamie's face broke out into an obnoxious smirk. "You think you're helping Nell? You're not. Because when he dumps you, that kid is going to be a basket case."

Michelle laughed bitterly. "I love the way you and Dad assume he's going to dump me. Am I really that dull and plain?"

"He's using you, you idiot! He doesn't know how to connect with Nell on his own; he needs you to teach him. Once he figures it out, he'll end the relationship. And there you'll be, taking care of Nell and feeling like shit about yourself as he goes back to the whoring jerk he really is."

"Did Dad tell you this?"

"Yeah, and it kills him—so much he had a heart attack, driving himself crazy over it."

Michelle stiffened. "That's not true. Neither of you know him. And as I pointed out to Dad, he was really getting along fine with Esa until he found out about us. Then, all of a sudden, he changed his mind!"

"Uh, yeah," replied Jamie, as if the reason were obvious. "Wouldn't you, if someone was using your kid?"

"You really think he'd do that to Nell?" Michelle paused, trying to wrap her mind around what her brother was saying. "The logic of this is so twisted, it doesn't even make sense."

"What happened to all that shit you've always spouted about being a professional?"

Michelle clamped a palm to her forehead, counting to five in her head. "I went over all this with Dad. Stuff happens. Did I know it was going to happen? No. Did I want it to happen? Hell, no. But it did, and I'm happy. Why can't the two of you just be happy for me?"

"Because he's a dick, Michelle, and speaking for myself, if you expect me to be happy about the situation that caused Dad to have a heart attack, then you're nuts."

Michelle wished she could slap her brother. "This was the 'family stuff' you wanted to talk to me about? Attacking me for no good reason? Trying to make me feel guilty over something I had nothing to do with?"

"Keep telling yourself that. In the meantime, I have to ask you a favor."

Michelle looked up at the ceiling, laughing mirthlessly. "You're unbelievable." She looked back at him. *"What?"*

"Don't you fuckin' dare upset him and talk about London. I'm serious."

"And if he brings it up?"

"He won't. Trust me."

Michelle's body felt leaden as she pushed herself up from the chair. "Fine. Whatever. Can I see him now?"

Jamie shrugged. "Go ahead. I have to go home and try to get some sleep. I'm pulling another overnight."

Michelle nodded curtly. What she had to say next wouldn't come easy, but she knew it was the right thing to do. "I'm glad you were here, Jamie."

"Yeah, me, too." He leaned over and kissed her cheek, the action seeming to soften his attitude toward her somewhat. "He's probably asleep. Why don't you just peek in on him and then go home and crash?"

"Maybe I'll do that."

Michelle waited until he disappeared around the corner before she burst into tears. Maybe her brother was right about her relationship with Esa causing her father's heart attack, but he was still a jerk for hitting her between the eyes with it before she'd even seen their dad. What did it accomplish, apart from upsetting her more than she already was? It was a typical Jamie move. She put it down to stress. The only other reason she could think of for his cruelty would be his wanting to punish her, but that seemed pretty petty in light of what was going on. It was stress, definitely. She glanced at the swinging doors of the Intensive Care Unit, nausea creeping through her system. She didn't want to see her dad with tubes in his nose, IVs, and hooked up to a heart rate monitor. He was a firefighter, for chrissakes. He was invincible, despite her always reminding him that that wasn't the case. She wasn't sure she could handle it. But she had no choice.

41

"I'm nervous."

Nell's confession troubled Esa. The two of them were sitting in the lobby of Claridge's waiting for his parents to come downstairs for dinner. They'd made plans for six thirty, which meant that his parents would arrive *exactly* on time.

He wished Michelle was here. Not just because he missed her, but because if anyone could thaw his parents, it would be her, and if they approved of Michelle, then they'd have to give him credit for picking a great nanny for Nell.

She'd called him as soon as she got back to the apartment. It was three in the morning in London, but he didn't care: he wanted to hear how her dad was doing. He'd never say it, but his opinion of her dad had dropped considerably in the span of just a few days. Funny how buddy-buddy he was until he found out things were romantic. Who the hell was he to judge? It also pissed him off that he'd marred Christmas for Michelle. Esa had a feeling that Michelle had painted what her dad had said to her when they talked in broad strokes, that if she told Esa the nitty-gritty of their conversation, his reaction wouldn't be pretty.

Michelle had sounded drained and distraught on the phone. Drained he understood; distraught was more puzzling, especially since she'd told him her dad had done really well. It had to be shock; then it dawned on him there might be some grief mixed in there as well. Her dad was alive, but the family had just had a huge reminder of his mortality. And mortality, as he knew from Danika's abrupt death, could suck big-time.

He tugged on the end of Nell's ponytail, the way he'd seen Michelle do. "Don't be nervous."

"But I don't really know them. And mum always said they were mean."

It took Esa a few seconds before he figured out how to respond. "Well, they won't be mean to you. And if they are, we'll leave."

"I wish Michelle was here."

"Me, too."

Mention of Michelle cheered Nell. "Can I tell them we're like a family now?"

Esa puffed up his cheeks and blew out a breath. "Unfortunately, the answer is no. They wouldn't understand."

Nell scowled. "Why?"

"Mmm . . . remember how, for a long time, you kept asking me why I didn't go out with Michelle, and I said I couldn't, because I was her boss?" Nell nodded. "Well, that's what they'll think. That I shouldn't be going out with Michelle because I'm her boss."

Nell studied her thumb, worrying her cuticle. "So is it bad that you and Michelle are going out?"

Fuck. "No, it's not bad, it's different. And a lot of people don't understand or like things that are different. I don't know why. But your grandparents are those kind of people."

"Oh," said Nell, clearly disappointed.

Esa felt bad. "I'm sorry, but that's the truth."

He checked his watch. Tee minus one minute. He was glad the issue of him and Michelle had come up before dinner. He could just imagine their reactions to Nell's cheery, happy news: the stares, the mouths pressed into thin, disapproving lines. How had he and Danika ever gotten out of that house without being totally fucked up? Oh, wait, they hadn't: Danika had no interest in a relationship and had been raising Nell

in a manner directly opposite to their parents. And up until
now, he'd only felt alive when he was king of the ice and all
sexual conquests. That had to say something.

"Is this them?"

Esa's eyes slid from the love seat where they were sitting to
the bank of elevators across the immense, ornate lobby. He
always felt a small, unnerving jolt when he saw his father,
because the resemblance between them was so strong. Esa
had a feeling that this was what he'd look like in twenty-five
years or so, graying at the temples, his eyes no longer curious
but resigned, three or four stripes of worry across his forehead. Yet his father was still a handsome man.

Seeing his mother gave him an unexpected jolt as well, but
for a different reason. He hadn't seen her since Danika's
funeral. He'd forgotten how much his sister looked like her.
He cast an uneasy sideway glance at Nell, wondering if she
saw her grandmother's resemblance to her mum as well. Her
face was anxious.

Esa and Nell stood, Nell taking his hand. They walked to
the center of the lobby to meet his parents. There was an
awkward moment as Esa tried to figure out protocol. Was he
supposed to hug his parents hello? Wait for them to hug him?
Would they hug Nell?

"*Hyraa joulua*," Nell said to them politely.

A tiny, almost infinitesimal smile lifted the corner of her
grandmother's lips. "*Hyraa joulua*," she returned, equally
polite. Esa felt a small part of his heart harden against her.
Why couldn't she have commended Nell for saying "Merry
Christmas" in Finnish?

"*Hyraa joulaa*," Esa said to his mother, kissing her lightly
on both cheeks. His mother said the same, as did his father,
who shook his hand.

"You're looking well," he said to Esa in Finnish.

"As is Nell," his mother remarked in their native tongue.
"Perhaps your sister didn't make a mistake."

"Nell doesn't speak Finnish, remember?" Esa pointed out.
"English only tonight."

"Don't you think maybe she should learn?" his mother
suggested. "I'm hoping that she might start spending summers with us."

About as likely as an asteroid hitting the earth, Esa thought. "Her school doesn't teach Finnish. English only, okay?"

His mother finally acquiesced. "All right," she said in English. "You made reservations?"

Esa rolled his eyes. "Of course." He smiled at Nell, who had moved a little closer to him. "We're hungry, right?"

Nell nodded, smiling up at him bravely. He wished he could say aloud: I know this is hard for you. You hardly know them. But even without Michelle here, it will be all right, I promise.

They were seated in a very formal dining room. It was early yet, so the only other people having dinner were an elderly couple, sipping soup, who looked displeased to see a child enter the room. Esa gave them a prolonged, nasty stare until they looked away.

A very solicitous waiter was soon at their table, handing out menus. "Can I get anyone a drink?"

Nell leaned over and whispered to Esa, "Can I have a Coke?"

"Of course," he whispered back.

"A Coke, please," Nell said to the waiter politely.

Esa stared down his mother's disapproval. Both his parents ordered glasses of chardonnay. He didn't have anything, because it made life easier. His mother would use even one drink against him. He didn't want to give her ammunition.

What happened next felt more like an interview or an interrogation than a conversation as his mother bombarded Nell with questions. Do you like New York? Do you enjoy school? What subjects are they teaching you? Do you miss London? Do you like living with your uncle Esa? Esa interjected a few times, trying to steer the conversation in a more casual direction, but his mother always circled back to Nell. Being Nell, she was unfailingly polite, but there was no mistaking her increasing anxiety.

"Mum, don't you think you've bombarded her with enough questions?" Esa said, trying to keep the tone light.

"I'm just making sure my granddaughter is doing well," she returned pointedly.

"I am," said Nell.

Esa looked down at the table, suppressing a smile. Way to go. That was pure Danika.

His mother's smile was strained. "One more question, Nell," she said, trying to sound friendly.

"Okay."

"Do you like living with your uncle more than you liked living with Leslie?"

You bitch, Esa thought, putting a kid on the spot like that. Nell's bravado melted; now she was looking at him haplessly, the same way she had when she'd first come to him, as if she wasn't sure how to answer.

"It's okay," Esa murmured. "You can always tell the truth."

"I like living with Uncle Esa more, I think, because Aunt Leslie traveled a lot, and Michelle, my nanny, is always home with me."

"Satisfied?" Esa asked his mother in Finnish.

Nell asked to be excused to use the restroom.

"What the hell are you doing?" Esa snapped at his mother. "Asking her something like that? She's a little girl!"

"I want to make sure she's happy."

"Happy, or well cared for?" Esa shot back. "Because as you can see, she's both."

His mother was silent for a while. Eventually, she gave a small nod of approval, nothing more. Typical.

Esa looked at his father. "Do you want to weigh in on this?"

"Nell seems happy," he concurred.

"Not that you'd know about happy children," Esa said in a stage whisper.

"What's that?" his father asked sharply.

"You heard me."

"What's going on with the Blades re-signing you?" his father asked, ignoring the barb.

Esa had successfully put the issue out of his mind for a few days, but he knew it would be back as soon as he and Nell returned to New York. He knew management was going to drag it out as long as they could, they always did, but he could have done without the additional pressure. His teammates had already mentioned it was starting to creep into the back of their minds.

He took a sip of water. "They'll drag it out until the last minute."

His father nodded. "Not unusual."

"No."

"You're still valuable to them," his father continued. "All you have to do—"

"I know what I have to do," Esa cut in, retreating immediately into guilt. His father had never really stopped "coaching" him. He couldn't help it, couldn't let it go. Esa knew his father just wanted him to succeed, but it was hard sometimes, because it often seemed that his father was assuming some kind of lack of intelligence on his part.

"Don't worry, Dad, okay?" he reassured him. "I have one of the top agents in the business. He's not going to let me fall on my face."

His father nodded, placated for now. As for his mother, she'd been studying him as if he were a specimen under a microscope.

"I've been wondering if you've really changed. It must be so. I'm sure the nanny must have a hand in it. No nanny worth her salt would let you carry on the way you were and have a little girl in your care."

"That's right." Esa smiled to himself. Michelle was head of the household, not him. In the beginning, it had made him furious. Now, he saw it was necessary for Nell's well-being. It hadn't been an easy pill to swallow, but he'd known he had to do it, and he had, only to discover it wasn't that emasculating. Maybe because when it came to the sexual side of things, *he* still ruled.

"Where's this nanny Nell loves so much?" her mother asked.

"She had to rush back to New York. Her father had a heart attack."

"Are you taking Nell to see Leslie?"

"It's up to Nell. I think there's part of her that doesn't want to. She feels betrayed and angry at being handed off to me. And I think she feels it would somehow be disloyal to Michelle, which we've both told her is silly. She and Leslie talk on the phone a lot, but when push comes to shove, now that Nell lives in Manhattan, I don't know if she wants to go back to where she used to live."

His mother lifted an eyebrow, pursing her lips in surprise. "Very psychologically astute. That's also something new."

"That's not me; that's Michelle. She used to be a teacher. She knows a lot about kids."

Her mother straightened her silverware, not looking at him. "Does Nell ever talk about Danika?"

His sister, the ghost at the table. Esa was surprised his mother had brought her up at all. It was such a painful, emotional subject, and his family didn't do emotions particularly well. He wanted to ask, "Do you miss her?" but he knew the reaction he'd get: silence, as if the answer were either self-evident or none of his business. If she were feeling generous, or expansive, he might get a curt, "Yes, of course," and then the topic would be closed.

"She's said a few things to Michelle. Michelle also lost her mother at a young age, so it's easier for Nell to open up to her about it. They share that bond."

"Mmm." There was a long pause, then his mother looked up. "Perhaps our only grandchild can spend a few weeks with us in Finland this summer?" she asked coolly.

Esa deflected. "Let's talk about it in the spring."

His mother frowned but didn't argue, at least for now.

Out of the corner of his eye, Esa spotted Nell emerging from the ladies room. "Let's try to enjoy the rest of dinner, okay? For Nell's sake."

42

"I can't live here full time right now. I have to help take care of my dad."

Michelle waited until Esa and Nell had been back from London a few days before discussing this new development with Esa. She'd been dreading it, because she knew he'd give her the look she was getting right now: confusion. He'd looked bewildered by her tepid reaction to the big hug and kiss he gave her when he returned. But then his expression turned worried and he said, "You look so exhausted." It made Michelle feel guilty. Granted, she was emotionally drained from the situation with her father, but that was only a small part of why she wasn't greeting him like a woman thrilled with her lover's return.

She'd had to wall off her emotions when Nell saw her and practically jumped into her arms. Nell was so excited she launched into a rapid-fire description of what Michelle had missed by leaving London early. She became anxious when she asked about Michelle's dad, but Michelle assured her that he was fine, and that Nell could visit as soon as he was up to it.

Luckily, Nell was itchy to get to one of the myriad books she'd bought in London. She said her good-byes and headed off to her room to curl up on her bed to read.

Michelle sat down on the couch, tucking her legs beneath her, then changed her mind. Tucking them under her was her "hanging out" pose. It was the way she sat when the three of them watched TV or movies together, and she worried that sitting that way now made it look like she was settling in for the night when she wasn't. Esa was observant, his gaze quizzical as he sat beside her. Michelle looked away, squinting her eyes as if she were trying to see if the plants in the window were in need of watering. It gave her a few seconds to compose herself. The last thing she wanted was to kick off the conversation by crying.

"Tell me what's going on."

Michelle turned back to Esa, guilt shoving at her insides like a bully. "It's like I said. My dad will be home in a few days, and he needs me to help take care of him."

Esa's brows knit together in complete and utter confusion. "Michelle—"

"On the mornings you have to be at practice early, I swear I will be here to get Nell off to school," she promised. "And on the days you have home games and have to leave early for Met Gar, I'll pick her up from school. I'll try to be here as much as I can. But I can't live in. Not right now."

Esa pressed his lips together. "I still don't understand."

"What don't you understand?"

"Your brother lives with your father, right?"

"My brother has a job, Esa."

"So do you."

She resisted the urge to say, "So when it suits you, I'm just an employee," and instead said, "He's going to help out as much as he can by trying to get as many shifts as he can, to make as much money as he can. That'll be his way of helping my dad. My father's insurance coverage is laughable. He's already been in the hospital for three days, and they're keeping him for at least three more because he's developed a bad cold. Tomorrow he starts having to pay out of pocket."

Esa shook his head disdainfully. "Insane. This country needs socialized medicine, like in Finland."

"I know it's insane. But these are the same bastards who tried to deny health care coverage to firefighters who got cancer after nine eleven," Michelle said bitterly, thinking about two good friends of her brother's, survivors of the Twin Towers, who had died from cancer before they were forty.

"Anyway," she continued, "my dad really doesn't have the money, but my brother and I can help defray the costs. I have some money saved, so that'll help as well."

Esa reached for Michelle's hand and squeezed it. She knew from the look of compassion spreading across his face what he was thinking.

"No," she said.

"You don't even know what I was thinking!"

"Yes, I do. And the answer is no. No help from you. It has to come from me. I owe him." She longed to twine her fingers through his, hold on tight, but she wouldn't let herself. She gently slid her hand out from under his.

His voice was steady. "You owe him how?"

Try as she might, Michelle couldn't hold back tears. "You and I caused his heart attack. He was fine and then he found out about us, and—"

She looked down at her lap, screwing her eyes shut tight.

"You've got to be kidding me." Esa sounded angry. "He said this to you?"

"No—"

"Who, then? Your fucking brother, trying to make you feel guilty?"

"I do feel guilty," Michelle whispered. "That's the whole point!"

"Oh my God." Esa covered his face with his hands for a moment. "I can't believe I'm hearing this. How often have you told me your father never took care of himself?"

"Look at the timing, Esa. He was extremely upset when he walked out of here Christmas night. Finding out about us put him over the edge."

"You're exhausted and overwrought right now, and it's making you irrational. Something terrible has happened to your father, and you can't bear to blame him, so you're blaming us. And your shit of a brother is fanning the flames."

Michelle scowled at him. "You're not helping."

Esa looked frustrated. "What do you expect me to do, Michelle? Listen to you talk this craziness and just accept it?"

"You could try to be more supportive."

"How can I support something ridiculous?"

"Because I'm asking you to!" She swallowed. "For me."

"Fine," Esa said, exasperated. "For you. Anything else?"

"I can't see you anymore," Michelle whispered. "It'll stress him out, and it'll stress me out, worrying about trying to take care of him, Nell, and balance a relationship with you. I can't."

"I don't fucking believe this. I really don't." Esa stood up then, and began to pace. Michelle could have sworn his lips were moving, that he was talking to himself, trying to figure things out. Finally, he planted himself right in front of her. "So you think we can go back to the way things were? Employer and employee. Sexual tension. Look, but don't touch. You think that can work?"

"It's just the way it has to be right now."

Esa shook his head, incredulous. "I find this amazing, that you, the strongest woman I know, is letting someone else dictate how she lives her life."

Michelle glared at him. "He's my father, Esa. And if that's the way it has to be for him to get better, then I'll do it."

"Right. Let's follow this through. Let's assume he gets better. Then what? We resume a relationship?"

"I don't know. I haven't thought that far ahead."

Esa frowned. "Don't delude yourself. You and I both know it won't happen. Your father and brother will convince you it'll set off another heart attack."

Michelle felt as if someone had put burning coals to both her cheeks. "That's not true."

Esa snorted derisively. "Yes, it is." His gaze traveled down the white hallway leading to the bedrooms. "Have you thought about the impact all of this will have on Nell? I don't think so."

"That's not fair." Michelle's hands knotted tightly in her lap. "I'm going to explain it to her so she knows I'm not in any way abandoning her, and I'm going to make it clear to her that I'll be back living here full-time as soon as I can. I'm not disappearing from her life, Esa. You know that."

"Just turning it upside down."

"That's not fair."

"It is fair," Esa said adamantly. "You and I coordinating schedules, Nell's schedule—you're assuming it will all go like clockwork. What happens if it doesn't? What are we—excuse me, I—what am I going to do then? Bring in a sitter she doesn't know? Have a cab pick her up at school and bring her to Met Gar when I have a game, so she can sleep in a sky box until the game is over? What about away games?"

"I'll make sure Jamie doesn't take shifts those nights."

Esa sat back down, cradling his head in his hands. "This is crazy. You're complicating things that don't need to be complicated. If you would just let me help out, there would be no need for all this. Things could stay as they are."

"No, they couldn't!" Michele said angrily. "My father just had a *heart attack*! He had triple bypass! Did you ever think there's a part of me that wants to take care of him until he's back on his feet because he's the only parent I have left? Can you understand *that*?"

Esa was silent for a long time. "Yes, believe it or not." Another long silence. "I think it's better if we consider the romantic part of our relationship over for good. Reconciliation is unlikely, because your father and brother will work on you." He sat down and ran his knuckles across her cheek gently. "I don't want to do it. I know it will be hard when both of us are here, but we're grown-ups, we've dealt with it before. I think as long as Nell sees we're still friends, she'll be all right."

"Yes, I think she'll be all right." Michelle's mind was a Tilt-A-Whirl. "I'm going to go talk to her."

"We could do it together if you'd like."

"I think I'd like to do it on my own. Us doing it together might complicate things."

"Things are already complicated," Esa said coldly.

Michelle ignored both his comment and the chilliness in his voice as she hugged her arms tightly around her own waist, rocking a little. She hadn't anticipated this conversation hurting as much as it did.

Esa rose. "One more thing, before you talk to Nell."

"Of course."

He came to her, unwrapping her arms as delicately as one might unwrap a fragile gift. The right thing to do would be to

pull away, but Michelle let him take her in his arms for the last
time. "I'm here for you," he murmured, his gaze melting into
hers, bearing a promise. "You know that. Whatever you need,
all you have to do is ask." Michelle was silent. "I'm not talking about money, although if you change your mind and need
that, you know it's not a problem. I mean emotional support."

Michelle sensed he was struggling. "I know I'm not the
most verbal man, that I have a hard time expressing my feelings. But you're important to me, Michelle. More important
than anyone else. You know what I'm saying, yes?"

Michelle closed her eyes, resting her forehead against his
chest. She wasn't sure she could bear to look at him, not now
when he'd just declared what she hadn't realized she'd been
longing to hear, not now when she chose to end the sweetness
between them.

Yet painful as it was, she didn't resist when he put an index
finger beneath her chin, tilting her face up to look at his.

"Thank you," he whispered.

"For what?" Michelle felt her heart beginning to splinter.

"The time we spent together." He looked pained. "It's just
so ridiculous that—"

Finally, the perfect excuse to ease out of his arms. "Don't,"
she begged. "Please."

"I'm sorry." He glanced at his watch. Michelle knew it was
more to give himself something to do in the face of this awkwardness than anything else. "Go on and talk to Nell."

* * *

"You'll be coming back to live here all the time though, right?"

Nell's need for assurance didn't surprise Michelle in the
least. Given Nell's history, she knew that no matter how carefully she laid out all the facts, Nell would still have a deep-
rooted fear of abandonment.

"Of course I will."

A tiny part of Michelle wished her answer could be, "No,
honey, I can't." Esa was right: how, exactly, were they going to
go back to a platonic relationship? The more she thought
about it, the more she realized it was delusional to think they
could just turn back time. There would be all kinds of tension,

and Nell would pick up on it in a heartbeat. "Maybe your dad could get better here. It's bigger. We do have a bigger telly."

"I think he'd probably like to recuperate in his apartment, sweetie."

"But have you asked him?"

"Nell," Michelle said in a mildly chiding voice.

"I *know*." She stretched out on her back, looking up at the ceiling. "But what if something happens and you can't come back?"

"Nothing is going to happen," Michelle assured her. "He got the surgery he needed, and now all he has to do is follow his doctor's orders and he'll be back to his old self in no time."

"Michelle?"

"Mmm?"

"Do you think he'd mind if I pretended he was my grand-father? Most people have two, and I don't like the one I have very much."

Michelle had to clear her throat to keep from laughing. "I think he'd like that a lot." She tugged on Nell's ponytail, not-ing how much she needed a trim. "Why don't you like the other one, if you don't mind me asking?"

"Dull," Nell answered in a leaden voice. She added, "And he doesn't smile much. There's no way he would play Magic 8 Ball."

"Well, that's his loss." Michelle made a mental note to ask Esa about the dinner with his folks, then realized that maybe he wouldn't be so free about sharing information now that things were over. "What did he and your grandmother give you for Christmas?"

Nell rolled her eyes. "Knee socks."

"That is sort of dull."

"I told you," Nell replied as if it were self-evident. She looked at Michelle hopefully. "Are you going to be here tonight?"

Good question. She could: her dad was still in the hospital. And Esa still wasn't 100 percent comfortable with Nell on his own. Michelle was his security blanket.

She decided it would be better for her not to be there tonight. She did have a few things she wanted to sort out at her father's apartment. It would give Esa a chance to sort out what they'd just discussed. Her, too.

"No, sweetie, I'm not. I'll be here tomorrow night, though."

"Good," Nell declared. She bounced back up, sitting cross-legged. "Maybe we could get pizza, then."

"Maybe."

"Maybe we could get some tonight!"

"That's up to your uncle."

"I like it better when it's you, me, and him."

Michelle smiled sadly. "I know you do."

The corner of Nell's lips tilted up into the tiniest shadow of a smile as she shyly ran an index finger up and down Michelle's arm. "Are you two going to get married?"

Michelle flushed, clicking her tongue affectionately. "Now that's a silly question! Why would you think that?"

"Because isn't that what people do when they're in love?"

"We're not in love, honey."

"Yes, you are," Nell insisted.

Michelle's body suddenly felt so heavy she feared she might just tip over off Nell's bed like an upright bag of sand. "People can go out with each other and not be in love," she explained, fighting not to sound strained and weary.

Nell went into mulling mode, which meant she'd grabbed her right braid and had started nibbling on the end of it. "But then they fall in love eventually, right?"

Michelle gently removed the braid from Nell's mouth. "Not always," she said. "Sometimes they break up."

Nell flopped back on the bed. "I don't understand this one bit!"

"You will one day."

Nell resumed studying the ceiling. Michelle remembered herself doing the same thing as a little girl, the ceiling seeming like a big blank canvas where she could project what was in her mind and try to make some sense of it. But with each passing second of Nell's silent staring, Michelle felt more weary. Finally, Nell turned to look at her. "Do you think you *could* fall in love?" she wanted to know. "If you started to really, really, really, really, really like each other?"

Michelle knew it was hedging a bit, but she replied expansively, "I think for people to fall in love you'd have to add at least a hundred more 'reallys'!"

"But it *could* happen," Michelle heard Nell murmur insistently to herself.

Michelle slapped the tops of her thighs lightly and stood up. "You should go talk to your uncle about pizza. As for me, I'm going to put someone's wash up." She teased Nell with a grave expression. "And I expect someone to put it in the dryer tonight so I can fold it tomorrow." She kissed Nell on the cheek. "Have fun tonight. I'll see you tomorrow."

43

He's going to drop it for the trailing defenseman. Esa was having one of those games where he could sense what everyone on the ice was going to do seconds before they did it. When the Hartford winger made the drop pass Esa had seen coming; he was the one who was there to intercept it at the Blades blue line. Without turning, Esa backhanded the puck off the boards where it was gathered in by Rory, who was just where Esa knew he'd be. As Rory rushed up the left wing, Esa broke up the ice. The Hartford defenseman stood up to make a play on Rory, who chipped the puck deeper. Esa reached the puck before the Hartford center, who'd been marking him all the way up the ice. Rather than send the puck behind the net, Esa spun right and crossed to the top of the circle. He could see the Hartford goaltender starting to move off the right post, anticipating Esa would keep skating to the slot. Instead, Esa snapped the puck high and inside the post the goalie had just vacated. The red light flashed. The crowd rose to its feet with a roar that overpowered the blare of the horn. Hats began hitting the ice.

The team was all smiles as Esa skated past them, exchanging fist bumps with his teammates before he hopped over the boards and assumed his place on the bench. As the clean-up crew swept the hats into a pile and loaded them into a container, Esa felt someone rubbing the back of his neck. Michael Dante leaned over and whispered in his ear. "Great fucking play. I'd say you just sent a message to Kidco."

* * *

"You doin' steroids?" Eric Mitchell asked Esa as he smiled and lifted his glass to toast him. Esa, the Mitchell boys, David, and Ulfie all laughed and took long drinks of their beers. They were at their usual table at the Hart, celebrating a 6-0 demolition of Hartford, and Esa's first hat trick in the NHL.

The team had been on fire, peaking just as the final seatings for the playoffs were being determined. Esa's productivity of late had driven a commentator on ESPN to nickname him "Lazarus." His agent wouldn't guarantee anything, but he was confident Kidco would soon be making him an offer.

"Yeah, right," said Esa. "If I was doing steroids my arms wouldn't still be toothpicks and my balls wouldn't still be so big." That got a big laugh from his friends, particularly Ulfie who insisted on buying the next round to the amazement of the others, who'd never seen the Swede reach into his pocket unprompted.

Esa was thrilled with his play of late, and wondered if it was the universe's way of compensating for how things were going at home. He and Michelle tried hard for Nell's sake to keep up appearances, but Nell was astute: she silently took note of every move they made (or didn't make). Michelle sometimes used to be there on "Nell/Esa nights"; now she was always at her father's on those nights. Nell didn't say anything. She just watched them. Sometimes he felt: we're all going backward, and it frightened him.

Torture didn't even begin to describe the situation, at least for him. In the beginning, he couldn't refrain from touching her; a small squeeze of her shoulder when he passed her sitting at the kitchen table on his way to the fridge, a smoothing of her unruly hair. Michelle would always freeze, and then later, when they were alone, she would tell him to cut it out. She was trying to look tough as she stood there in front of

him, and he worked hard to keep from laughing because the
difference in their sizes made the scene comical. But there
was nothing funny about her determination to make sure certain boundary lines weren't crossed. Unfortunately, all that
did was make Esa want to throw her down on the floor and
fuck her brains out. Which he had no right to even think; he
was the one who'd said "Consider the romantic part of our
relationship over for good." Michelle's adherence to boundaries was her protecting herself.

A detached cordiality whenever they were alone was the
only way he could survive. Cordiality and a safe physical distance. Often the whole situation pissed him off, because it was
stupid, and the boundaries were those he himself had created.
What made him even more pissed off was that Michelle didn't
seem unhappy with the way things were.

"I did steroids once, back in Sweden," said Ulf, running a
gnarled hand through his growing blond hair. His goal was to
look more like his Viking ancestors.

Rory eyed him dubiously. "Just once?" he asked, hoisting a
pint glass to his lips. "From your brain damage I'd have
thought you spent years on the shit."

Esa hadn't talked that much to Rory about the situation
with Michelle, because Rory could be such a windbag. Esa
loved him, but the Irishman could take a simple situation and
turn it into a drama with more twists and turns than a test road.
Halfway through their one and only conversation about he and
Michelle, Esa's eyes had rolled back into his head. At least
Erin had been more to the point: "If it's meant to be, it'll be."
Succinct, but not much fucking help. No one else on the team
had really known he and Michelle had been together, which
was how he'd wanted it to be. Funny, how he used to put his
personal life out there for all to see. But that was before Nell.

Nell had a week off for spring break coming up soon.
Unfortunately, it coincided with him being on the West Coast,
and he and Michelle had a couple of scheduling issues to work
through. *Had* to work through.

"Christ," said Rory, tossing a bemused look Esa's way,
"what're you looking like such a misery guts for? We not kissing your arse enough?"

"Screw you, Brady." Esa sucked down some of his Russian

imperial stout. "No, I'm just trying to work out Nell's vacation time. She's got spring break the same week we're on the West Coast, and Michelle has some other stuff planned so she can't be with her full-time."

Ulfie shrugged. "So? Bring her with us."

Jason slowly turned his head to peer at Ulf. "The longer your hair grows, the dumber you get."

Ulf rolled past the insult. "Listen to me, you assholes. It might be fun for her. When we practice early, she can come along, or she can sleep in. All we do during the day is pretty much hang out anyway. We can take her to matinees or museums or whatever."

Esa listened with interest. "And what about when we *play*?"

"She sits with Lou. They get along, right?"

Esa nodded slowly. "Lou really likes her." He remembered Lou saying something in the very beginning about not dumping Nell on him, but that was because he'd done it unexpectedly.

"Bingo, problem solved," concluded Ulf, giving Jason the finger.

"Yeah, but she finds hockey boring sometimes," said Esa.

"She won't if she's sitting with Lou," said Eric, warming to the idea. "He'll let her eat all the crap she wants. And she can bring a book if she gets bored. Or her iPad. Didn't you say you got her an iPad for Christmas?"

Esa rolled this over in his mind, finally arriving at, "There's no way Michelle is going to go for it. No way."

"Sure she will," said Eric, who always seemed to have a plan. "Tell her it's a way for you two to bond."

"Hmm."

"I think it could be cool," said Jason. "She'll be like our mascot. She'll love it. There are enough of us to keep an eye on her at all times to make sure she doesn't get into trouble. It'll be like she has this cool pack of uncles looking out for her."

"Nell doesn't get in trouble," said Esa. "She's eight, a bookworm, and extremely well behaved."

"So, it will be a piece of cake, then," said Ulf.

Esa took another sip of his brew, thoughts flying through him. "What will the media make of it?"

David finally piped up. "This is PR gold, my friend; an uncle bringing his little orphaned niece on the road with him?

PTI will be talking about how great you are, and Gumbel will probably profile the two of you for *Real Sports*. Lou's gonna kiss your feet for this."

Esa grunted. What David said was true: Lou could get some human interest pieces out of this. Taking Nell on the road was pretty unique. And it really could help them bond. There was only one real obstacle he had to overcome. It was tiny, beautiful, and as protective of Nell as a lioness of her cubs.

"I can't believe you pack of morons convinced me," he told his teammates. "I'll talk to Michelle."

*   *   *

"*No, no, no,* no. You're not bringing Nell to the West Coast with you," Michelle said as Esa followed her around the kitchen while she put away dishes. She glanced up at him as she crouched down to put a colander in a cabinet below the counter. "Have I mentioned the answer is no?"

Michelle knew men were capable of coming up with some dumbass ideas sometimes, but this took the cake. Bring Nell on the road with him? Was he out of his mind? Yes, there were some scheduling hitches that needed to be worked out over spring break. Michelle figured that if she couldn't get Delilah or Marcus to watch Nell for a little while on those days she had to bring her dad to the doctor and cardiac rehab, she'd ask Jamie to work his shifts around it. That way, Nell would already be at her dad's apartment when she got back, and she could sleep over. It was too bad Nell's friend Selma was going to be away with her family in the Caicos Islands; Selma's mom adored Nell, and Michelle was pretty certain she wouldn't have minded Nell staying over for a few days. She'd figure something out. She always did.

"You're reacting viscerally. You need to hear me out," said Esa, taking a plate from her hand as she strained on tippy toes to put it back on a high shelf.

"No, I don't."

"Yes, you do, because when it comes down to it, she's my niece and I can do as I please."

Instant stress headache. "So why even have this conversation, then, if you're going to do want you want, anyway?" *Which, by the way, nice to see you're back to being a douchebag.*

"Because your understanding and approval in this matter is important to me," Esa said quietly.

Michelle's fingers loosened around the butter knife in her hand. "I appreciate that." She slid it into the cutlery drawer, dazzled by the shine of the silverware. You could never accuse Mrs. Guittierez of slacking off when it came to her polishing duties, that was for sure.

"Should I make some coffee?" Esa asked.

"Chamomile tea'll be fine for me, thanks. I'm trying not to drink coffee anymore after six p.m. It keeps me up."

"All the worrying about your father," Esa deduced.

"Yeah."

"How's he doing?" Esa asked politely.

"Well," Michelle answered. His doctors had all remarked on how fast he'd recuperated. Michelle knew that deep down, he really didn't need her there anymore, but he wanted her there. He enjoyed the attention, and her brother still brought up the timing between Christmas and their father's heart attack whenever he could, just to ensure she stayed guilty—as if she needed his help with that.

"Is he taking care of himself?" Esa's voice remained polite.

"Yes. My brother and I have been helping him revamp his diet, and he's been going to the cardiac rehab center, gradually building up his strength."

"If he's doing so well, then . . .?" The end of the question hung in the air.

"Soon," Michelle snapped.

"I hope so." Esa looked back over his shoulder at her on his way to make the coffee and put up the electric kettle. "Nell misses having you live here full-time very, very much."

* * *

Mugs in hand, they sat down at the kitchen table. One of the things Michelle had figured out over the past three months was that it made things much easier if she and Esa didn't sit together on the couch. They sat together with Nell, because Michelle would never *completely* change direction and not spend time with them; plus, it would confuse and upset Nell too much. But in situations like this, when they were on their own and things needed to be discussed, the kitchen table was better.

Michelle opened the conversation. "So. This insane idea of yours of bringing Nell on your road trip."

"It's not insane at all." Esa coolly sipped his coffee. That's definitely one of the irksome things about him, thought Michelle, who'd been compiling a list in her head. He looked cool even when he did mundane things like sip coffee. King Cool.

"So—?"

Esa's eyebrows knit together in an annoyed V. "You're smirking, Michelle, which means you're not going to take one word I'm saying seriously."

"I *am*. Cross my heart."

Esa remained skeptical. "First, it'll give us a chance to bond."

"What, over postgame brewskies?"

Esa stared at her.

"Sorry," Michelle muttered, ducking her head sheepishly. "Go on."

"She'll think it's cool, going on the road with me."

"Uh-huh."

"It'll be like being surrounded by a cool pack of uncles."

"And what's she supposed to do when her uncles are practicing or actually *playing*?"

"Lou Capesi said he'd watch her. They get along well."

Michelle stared at him, hard, lifting her mug to her lips. "Are you lying?"

"No! This has all been carefully thought and planned out."

Michelle frowned. "Go on."

"As you know, we don't do much during the day. We watch TV, rest."

"Oh, that'll thrill her." She pictured Nell alone in a hotel room while various Blades were passed out in their hotel rooms, snoring. Actually, as long as Nell had a book in hand, she had no problem being alone. But Michelle doubted she'd like it very much when she was supposed to be on a special trip.

"We can take turns taking her to the movies, or museums, or shopping," continued Esa. "Or she can just hang out with us. You know how much she loves Ulfie. God knows why. We can bring games: chess, things like that. She'll have her laptop with her. She can Skype with you and with Selma."

"Hmm."

"Is that all you can say? 'Hmm'?"

Michelle rubbed at her left eye, which was throbbing a little, she was so tired.

"I'm not going to lie, Esa: I have serious misgivings about this."

"Yes, I can see that. What do you think is going to happen?"

Michelle tried to ignore the pain taking slow bites from the back of her head. "You let her go off with Ulf and he loses her. Or you lose her. Or someone tries to steal her. Or something."

"Michelle." Esa's voice was so soft she had to look away, the tenderness in it now creating pain in her heart. "She's going to have a pack of bodyguards who like to hit people with sticks. I know how to take care of her. You know that. We'll have adjoining hotel rooms like we did in London. I'll tuck her in every night."

"What, at eleven o'clock? What if she doesn't want to go to the game with Lou?"

"She will. Trust me."

"I don't like that evil little smile you're trying to suppress."

"I'm not trying to suppress anything!"

"Yeah, right."

"Isn't this what you've been hoping would happen ever since Nell came to live with me?" asked Esa as he searched her face, heartfelt. "That the connection between us would deepen somehow? I think taking her with me could help."

Not much I can say to that, Michelle thought. She wasn't sure this would help them get closer, but if that was what he believed, it was important she demonstrate some faith in him.

"Okay," she said reluctantly. "You've made your case."

Esa grinned. "Very good."

"But she has to check in with me every day."

"She already does that."

Michelle blushed. "Yeah, well . . ." Silence and tension. She cleared her throat. "I should go."

"You didn't drink any of your tea," Esa observed.

"Not really thirsty," Michelle mumbled.

"Tomorrow—"

"Your day, all day."

"That's what I thought. Just checking."

Michelle got up and walked behind him to rinse out her cup and put it in the dishwasher. For some reason, she kept waiting for him to rise, too, but he didn't. He just sat at the table, coffee mug in hand, thinking about God knows what. Michelle took a few steps toward him, wondering if she should touch his shoulder as she said good night. She thought about that shoulder. How muscular it was, and what it was like kissing the skin when they were making love and it was hot. The wonderfulness of leaning her head on that shoulder. She started to take another step, raising her hand, then thought better of it. She'd told him not to touch her. She had no right to turn around and then do the same thing. Hypocrite, she thought.

"'night," she said.

"Good night," Esa replied distractedly. He didn't even turn to look at her as she walked past him. Michelle wondered where his mind was. Perhaps, she thought ruefully, it was still lost in all that silence and tension.

44

Day two on the road with Nell, and so far, so good, Esa thought to himself as he went to collect her from her hotel room, where she was supposedly teaching Ulf to play chess. He wished he could've stuck around to witness that. Instead, he was on his way back from icing his ankle. It had felt a little tight at practice this morning, and he couldn't afford to ignore it before the game against Anaheim tonight. The last thing he needed was a nagging injury.

Nell looked stunned when he'd asked if she wanted to go on the Blades West Coast trip with him. First question: "Is Michelle coming?" Second question: "Will Stanley be there?" After striking out twice, Esa uttered the magic but bitter words: "Uncle Ulf will be there, of course." Suddenly Nell was excited about spending a week with the Blades.

Lou had taken the news that Nell would be hanging out with him better than expected. Just when it seemed like Lou would never stop screaming in Italian, Esa told him it was Ulfie's idea, just to change the subject and perhaps get Lou to make a joke. It didn't work. "You just wait," Lou had sputtered,

pointing a sausage-sized finger in Esa's face. "You just wait."
Esa had no idea what he meant.

It still wounded Esa a little that Ulf continued to be such a
draw for Nell. Esa knew he'd gotten much, much better when
it came to relating to his niece. But there were still all these
words inside him, bunched up tight like a fist, that he longed
to say to her. He still felt, sometimes, like he was outside his
body watching himself talk to her. You made her smile with
that question about her friend Selma . . . that was good . . . He
was constantly grading himself.

He knocked lightly at her door. "Nell?"

"Coming!" she trilled.

The little girl who opened the door had long hair on the
right side of her head and short hair above her ear on the left
side.

"What. The. Hell?"

He slid past Nell into the hotel room to find Ulf sitting
cross-legged on the floor with a pair of scissors in his lap. His
Nordic locks were gone, replaced by a mutant Dutch-boy cut.

"What the fuck did you do to Nell's hair?" Esa yelled.

"We're playing haircutter," said Ulf.

"It's fun," said Nell. "First Uncle Ulf let me cut his hair,
because—"

"Has Uncle Ulf let you see yourself in the mirror?!"

Nell shrank back. "Don't yell at me!"

"I will yell at you, because I know you know better!" He
pointed to the mirror above the dresser. "C'mere. Come."

Nell looked afraid of him as she crept toward the mirror.
She took one look at herself and started to cry.

"See, you big Swedish moron!" Esa yelled at Ulf.

"You came in before I got a chance to finish!"

"Thank Christ for that!"

He turned back to look at Nell.

"I look like a mong!" she howled.

This isn't happening, thought Esa. This. Is. Not. Happening. "First of all, you don't look like a mong. Second of all,
you're not supposed to use that word. Third, calm down. We
can fix this."

"I hate you!" Nell screamed at Ulf. She fled to Esa's room,
slamming the connecting door.

"Great. Just great." Esa walked over to Ulf and picked up the scissors. "I should shove these into your brain. Seriously. What the fuck, Ulfie?"

"I thought it would be fun."

"What the hell do you know about cutting hair?!" Esa turned over the scissors in his hands. "Are these actual hair-cutting shears? What the hell are you doing with haircutting shears?"

"I use them to trim my split ends."

"I can't fucking believe this. Seriously. Pop your head in there, apologize, and then get out of here while I figure out what to do. I'm not kidding."

"Sure, Esa. I'm sorry."

Esa perched on the edge of the bed. The next thing he heard was Nell screaming, "Get out!" at the top of her lungs. Holy shit, he thought. Where was the polite little British child now? He had a hysterical maniac on his hands. He whipped out his cell to call Michelle, and was just about to hit her number when he stopped. If he was serious about getting closer to Nell, this was something he needed to figure out on his own.

He walked into his room. Nell was stretched out on his bed, crying into his pillow. "Go away," she said, not lifting her head.

"I'm not going away." He sat down beside her. "We need to talk."

"I don't want to." She started to cry harder. "You're just going to yell at me."

Esa put his hand on her shoulder. "I'm not going to yell at you. I promise. I was just shocked. Turn over and look at me."

The sight of her swollen, red rimmed eyes tore at him. He went to reach for a tissue but she was already wiping the moisture away with the palms of her hands.

"Look," he began. "I know you're upset. But we can fix this."

"How?"

Think fast, asshole. "We'll talk to the concierge and get the name of the best hairstylist in town. Then we'll go there, and we'll have them cut your hair just like Michelle's. How's that?"

"Michelle's is nice and pretty," Nell said with a snuffle.

"That's right, and now yours will be, too." Esa smiled. "See? Problem solved."

Nell smiled timidly as she sat up. "Am I in big trouble?"

"No. Not unless you do something this silly again."

"Thank you, Uncle Esa," Nell said quietly.

The words trapped deep inside him were slowly climbing their way up to his mouth, determined to be heard. He took a deep breath and started. "Listen, Nell. I need to talk to you about a few things. Don't worry," he said quickly. "Like I said, you're not in trouble or anything like that.

"I know it was hard for you to come live with me. You and I didn't know each other very well, and I know you love Leslie a lot. Before you came, I didn't know anything about little kids, especially little girls, and I was scared! I'm still learning. So that's why it might seem sometimes like I"—he hesitated—"don't know what to say, or why I might ask stupid questions, or do stupid things."

His heart was pounding. "I don't want you to ever think that just because I'm not as fun or relaxed as Michelle, I don't love you. I do, very much. I'm just not very good at saying it, and like I told you, I'm still learning. I need you and Michelle to help me. A lot."

"I know," Nell whispered.

Esa felt tears pushing at the corners of his eyes, and fought them. "I know how badly you miss your mum. I miss her, too. Sometimes I wish we talked about her more, because I think it would help us to feel less sad." He swallowed, cupping her cheek. "It won't upset me if you want to talk about her and cry. You don't have to hold it all inside."

Nell's lower lip trembled as the tears returned. This time, though, she put her arms around Esa's neck, clinging to him. "I miss her so much."

"I know," Esa said, his voice cracking as he held her tight. "I do, too. I think about her all the time."

"Me, too. Sometimes I'm afraid something is going to happen to you or Michelle."

"Nothing is going to happen to me or Michelle. I promise."

"Sometimes I'm afraid that Michelle will never come back and live with us because her dad will stay sick forever."

Chec

285

"Not going to happen," Esa assured her. "Michelle told me he's almost all better."

Nell pulled back to look at him. "And then will you two love each other again?"

The words tumbled back down Esa's throat. He was frozen, probably for too long if the disappointment on Nell's face was anything to go by. "I don't know."

"I hope you do," Nell said sadly. "Those were the best days. Now things feel weird."

"Weird how?"

Nell shrugged. "I don't know. Just weird. It all just feels weird, weird, weird."

"Well, Michelle's been under a lot of stress with her dad," Esa explained, "and I've been under a lot of stress with hockey. So that might be why." Yes, it was only part of the reason, but it was better than lying to her outright.

Nell just nodded, returning to hugging him tight. "Uncle Esa?"

"Mmm?"

"I love you."

Esa swallowed hard, holding her tighter. "I love you, too, Nell." He made a promise to himself: for the rest of the week, he was going to be the one spending every day with Nell. If one of her tribe of uncles wanted to tag along, fine. But she belonged with him, and he wanted her there. There was so much lost time to make up for.

He lightly kissed her temple. "Now let's go get that haircut."

45

"*Oatmeal raisin cookies?* These are pretty damn good."

Michelle smiled as she and her dad settled down on his couch to watch *The Ellen DeGeneres Show*. Her dad used to hate watching TV during the day, but he'd gotten in the habit during his convalescence. The last thing she'd expected was that he'd become an "Ellen" addict.

"Glad you like them."

Her father was finally getting used to a heart healthy diet, and had dropped about twenty pounds. The cough was gone and his blood pressure was on its way down. Depending on their schedules, she and Jamie alternated bringing him to rehab. He was feeling great. Michelle, however, was feeling like hell.

She was exhausted from going back and forth between Queens and Manhattan, and from the daily battles she fought with herself. *You and Esa caused his heart attack. That's ridiculous: he never took care of himself. He doesn't need you here anymore. If you leave something could happen.* Guilt was her predominant emotion. Guilt that her brother had been right, that the warning signs had been there and she'd ignored them. Guilt that she was letting Nell down, that she wasn't there as much, that the reversion of her and Esa's relationship to friendship was damaging her in some way.

It didn't help that her brother continued to be an asshole. If she heard, "Well, if you listened to me, this might not have happened," one more time, she was going to punch him in the face.

Her father reached for another cookie. "When's the kiddo coming back from the West Coast?"

"Two days."

"You seem a little lost without her," her father observed.

"I guess I am. I miss her."

"Just her?"

Michelle closed her eyes. "Daddy, don't. Please."

"I owe you a big fat apology, Michelle. An apology as big and fat as I used to be." He turned off the TV.

"Are you having a stroke? I think you might be having a stroke. Let me call nine one one." She started to get up to get her cell phone from the kitchen table, but her dad reached out, holding fast to the hem of her sweatshirt.

"Very funny. I'm not having a stroke. I'm having—excuse me, had—what's known as an epiphany. Sit back down."

Michelle sat back, unable to take her eyes off him. He'd never used the word "epiphany" before. Maybe he really was having a stroke.

"Stop staring at me like you're waiting for me to keel over," her father said in exasperation, flexing his slippered feet. "People who have strokes speak gibberish."

"You did! You said you owed me a big fat apology!" Her father was unsmiling.

"Okay," she said, slowly reaching for a cookie. "Ellen's gone. I'm all ears."

"I was wrong to tell you I was disappointed in you about the whole Saari situation, passing judgment like that. The more I thought about it, the more I realized: what the hell do I know? You were happy, the kid was happy, the Finn was happy, so I should've just butted out." He leaned over and patted her knee. "The thing is, you'll never stop being my kid, so I'll never stop worrying about you, or wanting to protect you. And given Saari's—Esa's—track record, you have to admit it wasn't nuts for me to worry about you getting kicked in the teeth."

Michelle remained wary.

"But you're a grown woman. If that's what you want, if he's who you want, then I support you no matter what. I just want to ask you one thing."

Michelle rolled her eyes. "Uh-oh. Here it comes."

"As far as I know—and I know daughters don't confide in their fathers the way they do in their mothers, so I might be wrong—you've never been seriously involved with anyone before. Which mystifies me. You're smart, you're pretty—"

"I've always been afraid they'd die on me," Michelle admitted very quietly, her throat clogging with long-suppressed emotion. "I've always been afraid of being the one who's left behind to deal with all the pain."

Her father looked sad. "I thought that might be it."

Michelle wished the TV was on, so she had somewhere to look. "I know it's silly."

Her father put his arm around her shoulder. "It's not silly."

"I feel like it is."

"That's because you're hard on yourself." He looked down at his lap for a long time. "I did the best I could, kiddo. I didn't know anything about little girls. I didn't know much about being real hands-on with you kids, period. Some days it was hard for me to just get out of bed."

"I know you did your best, Dad. Honest."

"I know it was especially hard on you. Don't think I don't know." Tears began spilling from Michelle's eyes as her dad squeezed her shoulder. "I might not know much, but I do know kids need their mothers—or someone who's like a mother to them. Which is what you are to Nell. You know that, right?"

Michelle felt overwhelmed. "I try. She's been through so much."

"She loves you."

"And I love her. I just hope the fact that things have changed between me and Esa isn't confusing her too badly. I'm worried it is."

"So get back with him."

Michelle burst out laughing. "Now you are talking gibberish! We're done." She picked a renegade raisin off the edge of her cookie. "It was stupid, anyway. It never could have worked." She was a teacher; she knew all about concentration. That was what she'd been concentrating on making herself believe ever since Esa said they'd never be romantic again.

"I'm sorry that my stupidity soured this for you, Michelle. If I could take back all my dumbass words, I would."

"Maybe they were meant to be said."

"Don't give me that mystical bullcrap," her father smirked.

"Got it."

"I've got three more things I need to say before I ditch you for Ellen."

"What?"

"I know you love that kid, so if you can handle it, get back to where you belong: living with Nell and Sa—Esa full-time." His eyes shifted away. "I've been selfish, making you go back and forth for so long. It's just that it's been so nice having you around."

"You sure you'll be okay?" Michelle wondered how it was possible for joy and guilt to well up at the same time.

"Yeah, yeah, of course. Hold on a minute." He took a bite of his cookie. "Second thing: I don't see why you can't get back with Esa. He's got to know this whole stupid mess is my fault, right? If you want, I can go apologize to him in person." Her father directed his half-eaten cookie in her direction. "It's important you listen to me, Michelle. It's scary that you never know if the person you love is going to be snatched away from you, that it can happen even when you're young. But the risk is worth it. Trust me."

"*Dad.*" Michelle's voice was shaky. "This is so weird. It doesn't sound like you. To be honest, it's freaking me out a little bit."

"It's freaking me out a little bit, too." Michelle was amused as he took another big bite of his cookie. Ed Beck, Queens original in-between-bites philosopher. "Sometimes a health scare helps you put things in perspective." He shook his head, chuckling. "You would think I'd know all this stuff already after being a firefighter; you see and risk death all the time. But you can't afford to think about it. And even after your mom died, I didn't really think about it that much, I was so wrapped up in my pain. But coming so close myself"—he blew out a deep breath—"you realize life is really goddamn short, kiddo. You have to go for it and not give a damn what anyone else thinks or says. Most important of all, you have to get out of your own way. Don't analyze things to death. Let yourself be happy."

Her father sucked in his bottom lip, always a sign he was trying not to get choked up. "Now, one more thing before I make you go home: your mom's up there in heaven watching everything, and she's very proud of you. She always has been. I just had to tell you that."

"Thank you, Dad."

"No need to thank me." He waved his hand vaguely toward the kitchen. "Now get your purse and get out of here. I need some peace."

Michelle was grinning as she grabbed her stuff, amused by how fast that TV went on and how quickly her dad's eyes were already one with the screen.

"One more thing," he said.

Michelle clucked her tongue. "Jesus, Dad! This is like some bad deathbed skit!"

"Tell Esa thank you."

"What?"

"Just tell him that, all right?"

"All right," said Michelle. She knew it had to do with her; she just hated that it was so cryptic. She sucked at cryptic.

She kissed her dad's cheek. "I'll call tomorrow."

"No, you don't have to call tomorrow." Her dad's voice was distracted; Ellen was sucking him into the vortex. "I'll call you in a few days, okay?"

"Okay. Whatever you say. Love you."

"Love you, too."

Michelle walked out the door, leaving her father and Ellen behind.

* * *

"Look! My hair's just like yours now!"

Nell came spilling into the apartment, a bundle of uncontained energy. Michelle wasn't surprised: the Blades had taken a red-eye flight back to New York from L.A., and Nell had probably slept the whole way. Esa was the one who looked worse for wear, with dark circles drawn under his eyes, his skin a little paler than usual. He also had a five o'clock shadow which, despite his weariness, made him look sexy. Michelle kicked the thought out of her mind.

"I made your favorite scones," she called to Nell, who was in her room unpacking.

"*Utmarkt!*" Nell called back.

"And I'm back for good!"

"Super *utmarkt!*"

Michelle looked at Esa, impressed. "Teaching her more Finnish?"

"*No.* 'Utmarkt' is Swedish for 'excellent.' Torkleson taught her. I wanted to teach her how to say, 'Don't ever come near my head again with a pair of shearing scissors, you Swedish mong,' but I don't think there's a Finnish equivalent for 'mong.'"

Michelle pictured the Swede's giant hand taking a pair of scissors to Nell's head, her beautiful blond hair falling to the floor in uneven sheets. "He didn't."

"Oh yes, he did," replied Esa sourly, shoving his battered safari jacket into the closet. "I almost murdered him. Seriously, what kind of an idiot plays barber with a little girl?"

Michelle winced. "You know how persuasive Nell can be."

"She's eight!" Esa practically yelled.

It was pure impulse: Michelle put a hand on his forearm to calm him. "Relax. No matter what she looked like, she looks adorable now. Little girls play hair salon all the time. It's just usually not a vicious Swedish defenseman who's the other barber." Esa glanced down at where his hand rested on her forearm and gently removed it. Mortified, Michelle took a small step back.

"She wants pierced ears," Esa informed her.

"That's for you to decide," Michelle said coolly.

Esa sighed. "But it's a girl thing," he murmured, closing his eyes as he slowly ran his forefingers along his eyebrows. He stifled a yawn.

"No, it's a *guardian* thing." She was dying to ask him if he'd broken through the wall between him and Nell, but he seemed to be in a very bad mood.

"I could fall on my face right now," he announced.

"Go take a nap."

"I'm physically tired, but I still need to wind down mentally." He paused. "Do you think I might have a couple of those scones?"

"What do you think?"

Esa's mouth curled into a tired smile. "Thank you."

"Apparently, I'm supposed to thank you."

"For what?"

"You tell me. My dad just said to thank you."

Esa opened his eyes.

"What did he mean?" she asked.

Esa shrugged. "I don't know," he said, covering his mouth to yawn.

Watching his back as he retreated into the kitchen, Michelle knew he was lying.

* * *

The entire day felt out of whack. After *very* early morning scones, Esa crawled off to take a short nap. Nell couldn't have cared less about sleep. She'd already recounted most of the trip to Michelle over the phone, but she retold it, this time in greater detail. How she went to Magic Mountain in L.A. with Uncle Esa, Uncle Eric, and Uncle Jason. How Uncle Eric "spewed" after the ride. How she watched the games with Lou and the two of them ate things like fish tacos and Navajo fry bread. How she watched *The Wild and the Free* "with the guys," and they all were upset that Aunt Monica had been possessed by a demon. There was just one thing that made her sad, she told Michelle: "You weren't there."

"Well, I'm here now," she told Nell as they lay side by side on Michelle's bed with sunglasses on, pretending they were at the beach tanning themselves.

"For good? *Honest*?"

"Do I lie?"

Nell chewed on the inside of her mouth for a long time. "No."

Michelle pushed herself up on her elbows, lowering her sunglasses just enough for Nell to see her eyes. "Hey! That should have been a no brainer, m'lady!"

"Sorry," Nell muttered.

"Apology accepted."

Michelle lay back down, wishing spring would get on with it already. She wanted to take Nell to the beach, and enjoy the magnificent terrace, even use the grill out there that Esa told her he'd never touched. She started envisioning all the things she and Nell could do together when Nell slipped her hand in Michelle's.

"I'm sad."

Michelle took off her sunglasses, rolling onto her side so she was facing Nell. "About what, sweetie?" she asked, even though she was pretty sure of the answer.

"I wish you and Uncle Esa loved each other again."

Michelle drew a patient breath, even though her heart had stopped beating. "Honey, we already had this talk. I told you: people can go out and not love each other."

"But you're not going out anymore," Nell accused.

"No, we're not," Michelle said evenly.

"Uncle Esa said it was because of your dad, and his hockey."

Michelle plucked Nell's sunglasses off her nose, placing them atop the tower of paperbacks on her night table. "Yes. And you already knew that, too."

"But your dad is *better* now."

"I know. But it's very complicated."

Nell frowned. "Grown-ups always say that when they don't want to give you the real answer."

"That is the real answer, Nell. Things are complicated. You're a little girl, and sometimes, no matter how mature you are, some things just aren't your business," Michelle replied firmly.

Nell's mouth fell open. "That was mean!"

Michelle remained firm but unapologetic. "Sometimes the truth is mean, honey."

"You sound like my mum! And you're not!"

"I realize that," Michelle said very quietly. "But maybe you need to stop and think a minute about the fact that two grown-ups have said the same thing to you. We've got to have said it for a good reason, right?"

Nell just folded her arms across her chest and stared at the ceiling.

"Can I ask *one thing*?" she asked Michelle sulkily.

"You can try. Go ahead."

"I asked Uncle Esa if you were going to love each other again and he said, 'I don't know,' so that means you might again, right?"

Michelle was stunned. "I don't know." She wished Nell were Hannah, or Marcus, so she could shake one of their arms and say, "What the hell—?"

"But until you do, it's going to be weirdness all-round and I hate it," Nell continued.

"It won't be weird forever. I promise."

But how she planned to make sure that happened remained a mystery.

* * *

This was a better idea, Esa thought to himself as he sat down on a bench near the Bow Bridge in Central Park, waiting for Michelle to arrive. When he'd suggested they meet for coffee at Starbucks after she'd dropped Nell off at school, she'd gestured at the sun outside the kitchen windows as it winked brightly through the lengthening leaves of the trees. "Why sit inside when we can sit outside?" He decided she was right. He probably spent too much time in Starbucks. A Finnish friend told him that one had finally opened at home, at the Helsinki Airport. Finland was getting to be like the rest of the world, fast.

Michelle had gone to a nearby diner to pick up the coffees. She'd looked taken aback by his initial suggestion they meet outside the apartment, but Esa wanted a change of venue.

He spread his arms out along the back of the bench, the phrase "king of all he surveys" popping into his mind. He had no idea where the quote came from, but that was how he'd felt most of his charmed life, until Adam Perry had put it into perspective for him two years ago, at least as far as things went on the ice. Now he lived in Reality Land off the ice as well, thanks to Nell and Michelle, which was okay. He just wished someone had given him a fucking map to follow.

* * *

"Large black for you, small skim milk for me, chocolate chip muffin to split if you want some."

Michelle handed Esa his coffee, sitting down on the bench beside him. His inviting her for coffee surprised her, sparking something in her a little unnerving. She wasn't sure what to expect, especially given his recent coolness. Perhaps he'd changed his mind, and the weirdness she told Nell would soon evaporate would disappear quicker than she expected. She smiled to herself.

She offered him a piece of muffin. Esa shook his head. "You shouldn't eat things like that."

Michelle laughed at him. "You hypocrite! You'll eat the scones and cookies Nell and I bake, but you won't have a piece of this." She shrugged. "Suit yourself."

Esa removed his arms from where they were stretched out along the back of the bench, telegraphing that the conversation was going to be slightly less casual. Michelle understood immediately. The conversation was going to focus on Nell. He started to talk but she interrupted him before he could get started.

"In a minute," said Michelle, surprising herself. "First I want to know why my dad said to thank you."

Esa waved a hand in the air dismissively. "It's not important."

"Clearly it is, considering my father's opinion of you now is very different from the one he had when he left the apartment on Christmas night. Tell me."

Esa sighed heavily. "There was no reason for him to say anything to you."

"But he did. So *tell me*," Michelle demanded.

"Those three extra days in the hospital that his crappy insurance plan didn't cover? I picked up the tab."

"What?"

"You heard me."

"I told you very clearly, 'No help'!"

"And I told you I would be there for you in any way I could." Esa's gaze direct, almost challenging. "You're angry with me, but I don't care. You know how I felt about it: that you were cutting off your nose to spite your face. It was ridiculous for you and your asshole brother to have to deal with that kind of added stress when I have so much money. So I took care of it."

Michelle heard a rhythmic whooshing sound in her ears. It took her a few moments to catch on that it was her heartbeat, growing more and more insistent, not with anger, but with amazement. "How did my dad find out it was you?"

"I don't know. I just wish he hadn't said anything to you."

"I don't know what to say."

Esa took a sip of coffee. "You don't have to say anything."

"You're wrong. I do." Her eyes began welling up. "Thank you."

Esa looked uncomfortable. "You're welcome."

Michelle took a long sip of her coffee, trying to cover how much his sudden discomfort was wounding her. "Now let's talk about Nell."

Esa kicked lightly at some gravel at his feet. "Has she talked to you about the 'weirdness'?"

"Yes. She's a perceptive little girl. She senses there's a disturbance in The Force."

"Good way of putting it," he said, looking thoughtful as he ran his hand through his hair. Michelle noticed it was a little longer than usual. Usually he was meticulous about keeping it the same length. She liked it a little longer, not that she'd ever tell him.

"She keeps asking me when we're going to love each other again," he continued.

We never did, Michelle thought.

"She asked me, too," said Michelle, trying to match the casualness in his voice.

"What did you say?"

Michelle closed her eyes for a moment, letting the breeze play over her face. "I told her things were complicated. She told me that was a cop-out."

"Just like her mother," Esa observed with a clipped laugh, before his face returned to the impenetrable expression she remembered all too well from when she first began working for him. "We gave her false hopes, Michelle. We did more damage than good in showing her how a 'real' family functioned. I should have listened to you on that. I shouldn't have pushed you. Now things are a mess. She watches our every move."

"I know," Michelle murmured. Sometimes Nell reminded her of a cat she'd had as a child: silently appraising her all the time. "I thought we already established this, that the romance element was bad. Isn't that what you told me?"

"I think even our friendliness gives her false hope."

Michelle was struck dumb. Something inside her was beginning to make her feel unsteady.

"We've got to fix this." She felt slightly better when a modicum of sadness crept into his eyes. "Back to more formality, just being employer and employee?"

"And how are we supposed to do that? Find a time machine?" She knew she was being sarcastic, but it just slipped out. "You were the one who said it could never be done," she felt compelled to point out.

"I know. But it's the only way I can think of."

"Do you think it would help if I resigned at the end of the summer?" she heard herself ask.

Esa blinked, incredulous. "Do you want to?"

"Do you want me to?"

"No, of course not! Think of what it would do to Nell!"

"Is it worse than attempting to go even further backward? Isn't that just a new form of 'weirdness'?" Michelle paused. "Yes, it upsets me that we're confusing her. But I don't want to make things worse than they are. We're like two people who have filed for divorce but neither one can afford to move out, except our relationship didn't last as long as a marriage, and it wasn't as deep."

Esa swirled the coffee in his cup, silent.

"I want what's best for Nell," Michelle continued. "If you really think it's possible to go back to the beginning and not weird her out even more, then I'm willing to try. But if that isn't working, then we need to find a different solution."

"It will work," Esa said adamantly. "It has to."

Only for Nell? wondered Michelle. There isn't a small part of you that wouldn't want me to go? Am I that forgettable? She forced herself to move off unsteady ground back to terra firma, where she was in firmer control of her emotions.

"I assume going back to the beginning means minimizing even more time together," she said.

Esa nodded uncomfortably.

"And what are we telling Nell when she asks about that?"

"Revert to the original answer on that, I guess: that you work for us, and you and I shouldn't have gotten involved—"

"—but that doesn't mean we don't love her," Michelle finished softly.

Esa frowned grimly. "Right."

"And our personal lives?" Michelle asked, her right hand slowly crushing the wax paper bag holding the muffin.

Esa hesitated. "I guess that'll go back to the way it was in the beginning as well. Keep things private."

That'll be fun, Michelle thought. "Anything else?"

"No, I guess not." Esa was looking straight ahead as he took another sip of his coffee. "As you know, I have no game tonight, so I'll be home—"

"I know."

He rose. "Michelle?"

"What?" Christ, why prolong this agony?

"What you said about our relationship not being 'as deep' . . . things don't have to last a long time for them to be deep."

Michelle watched him walk away, his outline growing increasingly blurry until he was finally gone from sight.

46

ONE MONTH LATER

Esa strode confidently into his agent's office the day after scoring the second hat trick of his career in a 5-2 smackdown of New Jersey. Far from being a distraction for the team, his lack of a contract had become a distraction for management. General Manager Ty Gallagher and Coach Michael Dante refused to answer any questions about the matter, subtly letting the reporters know the situation was not of their doing. When he saw Michael Wilbon on PTI call Kidco management "idiots" for not already having signed him, he knew he'd be getting a call from his agent soon. He was right: Russ called the next morning. Being old-fashioned, Russ insisted on delivering the news face-to-face.

Esa warmly greeted everyone in Russ's outer office, politely asking his new assistant, Phyllis, to tell Russ that he was here. Russ went through assistants faster than kids went through Happy Meals. He was notoriously difficult to work for: demanding, and not big on paying attention to the clock.

Phyllis told Esa to take a seat. He picked up a copy of *Sports Illustrated*, trying to find some hockey coverage. Out of the corner of his eye, he saw Phyllis checking him out. She was one of those women who fell into the "Very Discreet" category, which made sense, considering who her boss was. Once upon a time, before he lived in Reality Land, Esa would have signaled his interest with a small, sexy smile that held the promise of getting to know each other better. She was certainly good-looking: blond, kittenish, with a cute button nose. There was just one problem: he wasn't interested. He pretended he didn't see her quick sideways glances and returned to burying his face in the magazine he couldn't concentrate on.

Russ's door swung open ten minutes later. Esa rose with a big smile and walked over to the door, ignoring Phyllis's long look at his ass.

"Helluva game last night, huh?" Esa crowed, settling on Russ's couch, crossing an ankle over his knee.

"You were amazing," Russ agreed.

"Yeah, so amazing I want to hear Kidco's offer." Russ was silent. "C'mon, man!" Esa cajoled. "Tell me the suits didn't call you last night with an offer."

"Not a word."

"What the fuck?" Esa wasn't sure he'd ever become this enraged, this fast. "I've been busting my *ass*. They wanted the 'great Esa Saari' back? Yeah, well, unless my coaches, teammates, the GM, and the press have all been bullshitting me, apparently he's been back in full force, and better than ever. What happened to 'They'll all be champing at the bit to get you'? What happened to you telling me that you'd put feelers out, but really, I shouldn't worry, there's no way I'll have to seriously entertain offers from other teams?"

Russ grimaced. "They're flexing their muscles."

"What muscles do they have left to flex?" Esa snapped. "The season has gone great. They do know this shit is affecting team morale, right? They do listen to radio and watch ESPN, right? Great as we've been doing, the uncertainty of my future is always there in the back of my teammates' minds, just like it's in the back of mine. A few of them have mentioned it to me more than once."

"They're all about saving money, Esa. You know that."

"Jesus Christ." Esa laughed bitterly. "Now what?"

Russ didn't look too happy. "There are a bunch of teams prepared to make you serious offers."

"Right, okay, let's hear them," he said offhandedly. Why not? He could use a laugh right about now.

Russ reached for a piece of paper on his desk. "Vancouver, Dallas, Edmonton, and Boston."

"How much?"

Looking distinctly uneasy, Russ reeled off a list of figures, all of which were about the same as he was making now. "Look—"

"No fucking way."

"Listen to me, Esa," Russ said patiently. "This is all preliminary posturing. Kidco knows you want to stay here. They know you don't want to uproot your niece. And they think your playing great might be because you're waiting for them to make an offer."

Esa looked at him like he was nuts. "So you're telling me to just sit and wait them out?"

"Yes. I know that sucks. I'm pissed off Kidco are playing mind games, too, but if they want to take it down to the wire, then fine. I'll let these other teams know that if Kidco fucks you, you're seriously willing to consider their offers. Then I'll go to Kidco and tell them I've got serious offers in hand for you, and that you have no intention of playing it down to the wire with them. So they either make a new offer soon, or else you're going to be signing on the dotted line with someone else the second your current contract expires and they won't have a chance to re-sign you. Sound good?"

Esa nodded curtly. Part of him wished he had a normal job and led a normal life. He knew a lot of people who did, and they were perfectly content. There was just one problem: he only knew how to do one thing, and he only wanted to *do* one thing, and he was already doing it. He knew he'd have to retire from hockey eventually, but that was years away, and he knew that he'd always keep connected to the sport in one way or another. He hated being dicked around, and it made him especially furious that so little thought was being given to team morale by these tightfisted bean counters. We're all just chattel to them, Esa thought disgustedly—chattel that makes them very fucking rich. The more he thought about it, the more frustrated he became. The reality was, they knew they had him by the balls, unless he really *was* ready to walk.

The question was, after all his big talk died down, was he willing to?

*　*　*

"I'd slow down if I were you, mate. You're going to wind up under the table."

Esa glared at Rory and downed his sixth shot of vodka, slamming the empty glass down on the table with a bang when he was done. The two hadn't gone out for drinks together in a long time, and Esa needed to blow off some serious steam. He didn't want anyone else he knew seeing him in his current state of distress. So instead of going to the Hart, he and Rory wound up down in the Village at some bar that Erin had gone to with friends from NYU. It was small, hotter than hell, and packed with students, none of whom seemed to recognize them, which ticked Esa off.

"Balls to that!" Esa declared. "Everyone thinks it's the Irish who have mastered the art of drinking, but it's we Finns! Proof? We have the highest rate of cirrhosis of any country in the world! Ha!" He caught the eye of the overworked waitress, who was scurrying between packed booths. He held up four fingers. She nodded, letting him know she'd seen him.

"You're not drinkin' four more," said Rory.

"Two are for you, asshole."

"I already told you: I'm fine with pint number two."

"It's not going to kill you to do a few shots with your best friend! Unless you're worried you'll never measure up because—"

"Right, right," said Rory with a bored roll of the eyes, "you Finns can drink the Irish under the table."

Esa's shoulders shook with a small burp. "That's right."

"You say it as if it's something to be proud of!"

"There's isn't much else to be proud of in Finland, unless you count fighting off the Russians, vodka, and hockey. Oh, and reindeer meat. And suicide. We have the highest suicide rate in Europe."

"Congratulations! The tourist industry there must be booming."

Esa laughed darkly. "It's so fucking grim there, you wouldn't believe. I knew I wanted to get out by the time I was nine years old."

"Well, you're out."

"Yes, I am. Just pray to whomever it is you pray to that I don't wind up back there."

Rory cradled his head in his hands. "Jesus Christ. D'ya need me to write it on the wall in blood? You know that's not going to happen. You're just ticked off that those pricks are playing mind games—and quite frankly, so am I."

"See?" Esa bellowed. "I told my agent, it's not just affecting me, it's—"

"Lower your voice, for christssake! You never know who's in here."

Esa turned around in his chair, carefully scanning the room. "Maybe it's me, but I don't see anyone in here who looks like a Blades fan," he said as he turned back to Rory. "So relax." He peered past his friend impatiently. "Where the hell is the waitress?"

"Will you just calm the fuck down? It's only been thirty seconds since you ordered, if that! Give the bartender a chance to pour your shots and I'm sure she'll be over with them as soon as she can."

Esa grumbled to himself, enjoying the warmth in his belly. He hadn't been this shit faced in a while. Bad for the team image. Fuck the team image.

"The waitress is hot, don't you think?" he offered.

Rory shrugged. "I guess."

"Oh, c'mon," Esa said with a smirk. "Just because you're married doesn't mean you're dead from the waist down when it comes to appreciating other women. Or are you that whipped?"

Rory's gaze was cold and unflinching. "If you ever say anything like that again, I will punch your oh-so-handsome face in so fast you won't know what hit you."

Esa laughed dismissively. "You would never hit me."

"Don't test me, Esa."

"Because you know you would lose."

Rory took a drink. "It's amazing, you know, how you're an even bigger arsehole drunk than when you're sober. I didn't think that was possible."

Esa gave him the finger. All he wanted to do was laugh and enjoy this feeling of his whole body being intensely alive.

"Ah, here she comes."

The waitress put the four shot glasses down on the table. As she turned to go, Esa tugged on the end of her shirt. "Hey. Hey."

She turned, a false smile plastered on her face. "Yes? Can I get you something else?"

"What time do you get off work?" Esa asked with his trademark smooth smile. He was working his magic. Oh yeah.

Rory groaned. "Please ignore him," he begged the waitress. "We're gonna finish these drinks and then we're going to leave, I promise you. No worries. Thank you."

Esa watched the waitress disappear into the crowd. "What did you do that for?" he snapped at Rory.

"You're drunk, you're embarrassing yourself, you're harassing her, and I don't want to get chucked out of here. That enough?"

Esa downed the first of the four vodkas. "Stop acting like an old lady. They can't throw us out. We play for the New York Blades."

Rory threw his head back and laughed. "That's the best one I've heard all night." He drank one of the shots. "Look, Kidco are bastards, but they're not going to let you go. I can't believe you're seriously worried about this."

"Let's say, for argument's sake, they don't make me a good offer. That means uprooting Nell. Again."

"And leaving Michelle, if she's not willing to move. That's got you all upset, I'll wager."

Esa frowned. "Michelle has nothing to do with this."

"Bullshit. I don't see why you couldn't just—"

"Shut up." Esa downed another shot. "Her father is the one who fucked it all up. Then I fucked it up further. Then it just kept getting more and more fucked up, and now it's beyond fucked up."

"Quite eloquent, Esa. So what if it's 'beyond fucked up'? Look at me and Erin: whoever thought that would work out, eh? If you still want her—"

"I said shut up," Esa repeated sharply.

Rory's anger returned. "Don't talk to me like that, you fucker. I'm not joking here."

Esa smirked. "You want to punch me? Go ahead."

"You know what? This stopped being fun, oh, about half an hour ago. So let's leave."

Esa frowned. "I'm not going anywhere."

"C'mon, you jackass." Rory rose. "I mean it."

"Who are you, my goddamned mother?" Esa downed another shot. "I said I'm not going anywhere. If you want to leave, fine. But for me, the night's still young."

"Suit yourself," Rory said disgustedly, slapping some money down on the table. "Try not to crack your head open or drown in your own vomit, yeah?"

Esa tauntingly held up a shot glass to Rory. *"Kippis."* He threw the shot down his throat.

Rory walked out.

47

Fuck you, Esa thought, as Rory walked out of the bar. His friend was getting on his nerves anyway, being boring and sanctimonious. What he wanted was fun. *F.U.N.* Christ only knew the last time he'd had any of *that*.

He glanced around the bar at the girls. Many of them were beautiful. All he had to do was pick one, walk up to her, and start talking. Women loved accents. They'd ask him if he was from Russia. When he told them Finland, they'd look a little confused. Finland? He was amazed by how little Americans knew about the rest of the world. I play for the New York Blades, he'd say modestly. That's when they'd get that look in their eyes, the one that said, "A professional athlete? Wow." It was amazing, how it took just that one little fact to impress them. He'd offer to buy them a drink. If they were with a girl-friend, he'd politely offer to buy her a drink, too, but it wasn't his job to tell the friend to get lost, at least not verbally. In his experience, the friend always got lost eventually, and he always got what he wanted. Tonight wasn't going to be any different.

He got up, a rush of blood to his head. He held the lip of the table, just for a split second, to steady himself. Rory was a fucking idiot; he was nowhere near drunk. He was halfway down the road to *really* happy. He smiled to himself, but as quickly as the happiness came it was snatched from his body, leaving him feeling bitter. He deserved a night like this. Since August, his life had been one crisis after another after another. That's life in Reality Land, a voice sniggered in his ear. Screw Reality Land.

He carefully assessed the room. A jolt. Michelle? He blinked several times before logic kicked in: Michelle was home watching Nell. But the woman he'd focused on looked like her: small, with short brunette hair and a spunky smile. She was talking to another woman, a tall rangy blonde who held no appeal for him at all.

He took a steadying breath, then made his way over to their table.

"Hi," he said, smiling at the brunette. "I'm Esa."

Her eyes slid warily to her friend's before replying. "I'm Eve."

"Nice to meet you, Eve." He regarded her friend. "I'm Esa."

"Devon."

"Interesting name."

"So's yours," remarked Devon dryly.

Esa redirected his attention at the brunette. "I'm from Finland."

Eve looked impressed, the way Esa knew she would be. "Really? I've never met anyone from Finland before!"

"I take it you're a student at NYU?"

"Yeah, a junior. I'm majoring in economics."

"I play for the New York Blades."

"Wow," Eve said. Devon was doing a very nice impersonation of one of the statues on Easter Island.

"I was wondering: can I buy you ladies some drinks?"

"It's really, really flattering that you want to do that," said Eve, her smile genuine, "but I don't think it's a very good idea: my boyfriend will be back in a minute."

"I'm sorry."

Esa realized he had to be very drunk, because he usually didn't care if a woman had a boyfriend or not. He knew his way around that obstacle. But standing here now, feeling no pain as the room waved at him, it dawned on him that he didn't want to be *that guy*, the drunken asshole who hits on women with boyfriends.

"It was nice meeting you, though," said Eve.

Esa smiled at her. "You, too."

He took his time moving to the bar. One more, he thought. Then he'd go. He ordered another shot, drinking it and turning away just in time to see Easter Island Devon pointing him out to some guy with his jeans hanging off his ass and a Bon Iver T-shirt on. Esa smirked. Asshole may as well have "Super Sensitive Wimp" spelled out in neon lights over his head.

He watched as Eve put a hand on the guy's wrist as if to still him. Smart girl. He turned back to the bar. That's when he felt a tap on his shoulder.

Esa turned. He sighed; it was the Super Sensitive Wimp.

"Help you with something?" Esa said.

"I hear you were hitting on my girlfriend."

Esa longed to tell him it was hard to take him seriously when he had a tattoo of Batman on his forearm, but he didn't. Instead, he smiled apologetically at the douchebag. "Yeah, sorry about that. I didn't know she had a boyfriend when I went over to the table."

"Yeah, well, she does, asshole."

"Glad we established that," said Esa, beginning to turn back to the bar. That's when the guy shoved his shoulder.

Esa felt an eerie calmness come over him. "What's your fucking problem, man?"

"I'm not done with you."

The calmness intensified. "Do yourself a favor, okay? Turn around and go back to your girlfriend right now, and I'll forget you shoved me."

People were watching now, their phones out, poised and waiting for a fight. Esa felt pity for Batman as he tried to play tough guy to the crowd. It was totally pathetic.

"I don't think you heard me," said Batman, his lips drawing back from his teeth in what he probably thought was a snarl.

Esa sighed heavily. "You don't want to do this. Trust me."

The calmness had extended beyond the boundaries of his body, and had possessed the bar. There was a growing sense of anticipation; Esa heard his name being whispered. So, some people did know who he was. Normally, that would be a good thing. Right now, it wasn't, especially if this asshole didn't walk away soon.

"You're drunk off your ass," Batman continued, taunting him. "You couldn't throw a decent punch if you tried."

"You're right," said Esa, holding up his palms in surrender rather than curling them into fists. "So what's the point? Go back to your fucking table."

Batman glared. "I said I wasn't done with you."

"Say what you have to say, and *then* go back to your fucking table."

"I want you to apologize to my girlfriend."

"I already did. Once is enough."

"Do it again." Batman looked around at the crowd again, eager for approval. No one responded.

"You hear me, you Swedish asshole?"

"I'm Finnish," said Esa, sounding blasé. "And by the way, go fuck yourself."

Batman aimed for his face, but even in his drunken state, Esa easily sidestepped it. He was a hockey player and ducking punches while on skates was part of his DNA. Doing it on solid ground, in street shoes, was easy. Esa grabbed his attacker by the neck of his T-shirt and shoved him. "Fuck off before you get hurt. I'm not joking."

Batman nodded curtly, and started pushing his way back through the disappointed crowd toward his table. Then he changed his mind and rushed Esa, throwing another punch. Esa stepped inside the punch, as his father and every coach he'd had since he was ten years old taught him. Before the missed punch finished whizzing by his head, Esa instinctively snapped a right fist to the guy's face. He should have left with Rory.

48

"*I knew you* were an asshole, Saari, but I didn't know you were stupid to boot."

Lou Capesi looked disgusted as he pushed the Sunday morning edition of the *New York Sentinel* across his desk to Esa. Esa had assumed he'd be able to sleep off his brain shredding hangover and feel okay by early afternoon when Michelle got back from taking Nell to the Museum of Natural History, a place his niece never tired of. But he knew he was screwed when the phone rang at ten a.m. and it was Lou, demanding Esa come into the office.

Esa massaged his temples. "I can imagine what it says."

"Read it," Lou demanded. "Out loud."

Esa glared at him as he snapped up the paper. " 'New York Blades star winger Esa Saari spent two hours in police custody after a dangerous scuffle in a Greenwich Village bar that police said was fueled by alcohol. He was released on two thousand dollars bail into the custody of fellow Blade Rory Brady.' " He shoved the paper back across the desk at Lou. "There. Happy?"

"Don't you dare get surly with me, you prick! You're not

one who's going to have to clean up this mess—I am!
angerous scuffle'?"

Esa frowned. "That's an exaggeration."

"Oh, well, that's a comfort," Lou said sarcastically. He
lled open a desk drawer, emerging with a fistful of mini
ndy bars that he tossed on the desk, peeling the wrapping
one of them faster than a monkey attacks a banana, and
oving it in his mouth. "Are you out of your freakin' mind?"
garbled. "This is exactly the kind of shit that drives the
gue insane! They've had a bee in their bonnet for years
out fighting on the ice hurting hockey's image! This is *really*
nna frost their asses."

Esa cradled his head in his hands. "I'm sorry," he said
serably.

"That doesn't cut it."

Esa lifted his head. "What the hell else do you want me
say?"

"Whatever I tell you to, at the press conference I'm setting
for you later today."

"That goes without saying." Esa winced; Lou's deep, boom-
g voice was making the throbbing in his head worse. "Could
u lower your voice a little?"

"No, I cannot lower my voice a little!" Lou screamed, get-
g red in the face. His hands shook as he unwrapped another
ndy bar that he appeared to swallow whole. "This isn't a
ke!"

"I know that!" Esa shouted. "You think I'm proud of losing
ntrol? You think I'm proud that my way of dealing with the
certainty about my future was to get shit faced? I'm not!"

"Yeah, that's really gonna help your case."

Esa actually struggled to his own defense. "Gimme a
eak, Lou. What about years back when there was that story
out all the Blades snorting coke from the Stanley Cup? Did
affect the contract negotiations for any of them? What about
en a bunch of them took the Cup to a topless bar? If you ask
, that's worse than getting into a bar fight!"

"That's irrelevant! Those things happened before people
uld take pictures with their phones!"

"But that's a good thing!" Esa reasoned. "Because when
deos of the fight go up on YouTube today, if they aren't

already up, people will see that the little prick taunted me a
swung at me first! I repeatedly warned him to stop, and
wouldn't. What was I supposed to do? *Take it?*"

"True," Lou muttered. "But the *cops* were called! Th
says something."

Esa's fingers returned to his temples. "Well, I can't undo i

"No kidding, you schmuck. I just hope you're prepared
the shit storm that's coming your way for the next few day
articles about how hockey players are violent on and off t
ice; articles about athletes and booze and drugs; articles abo
overpaid jocks. You're in for it."

"I figured," said Esa, his eyes feeling like they were bei
pushed out of their sockets with forks.

Lou sighed. "Look, I'll do what I can. But don't pull an
thing like this again. I know you're on edge about Kidco a
the contract and all that, but you really don't need to wor
okay? Unless they're dumb as a bag of fucking hammers,
you manage to massively suck in every game between no
and the end of the season, which is doubtful, you'll be offer
a new contract, okay?"

"Okay," Esa replied, not feeling in the least bit comforte
In fact, he felt so miserable he helped himself to one of t
candy bars on the desk.

"Has Nell seen you yet?" Lou asked. "You look like shi

Esa felt shame roll through him. "She's at the Museum
Natural History with Michelle."

"Does Michelle know?"

"I don't think so. She was asleep when Rory and I got ba
to the apartment. I'm sure she'll know by the time they g
back."

"Good luck with that."

"Gee, thanks."

"Hey, take it like a man. If you can't do the time, don't
the crime. She might just be the nanny, but you're the kic
guardian, and she has a right to be angry. She's not suppos
to be the only adult under that roof."

"She's not just the nanny," Esa said to himself quietly.

Lou leaned forward. "You're mumbling. What?"

"Nothing." Esa tried rubbing his forehead, but it on
seemed to make it worse.

"I'm setting up the press conference for four. That okay with you?"

"It's fine."

"Be there half an hour early. And don't forget to wear a jacket and a tie."

"I'm not an idiot!" Esa said angrily.

"Yeah?" questioned Lou, shaking the paper at him. "Well, you sure as hell could have fooled me."

*   *   *

"*Uncle Esa! You* look terrible!"

Michelle glared at Esa as she and Nell walked in the apartment and she watched Nell's excitement while telling him all about the special exhibit they'd seen at the Museum morph into alarm. Michelle knew what had happened because someone had left a copy of the *Sentinel* in the back of the cab. She was furious. She'd had a sneaking suspicion he might be hungover when she woke to a note on the kitchen table that morning saying he had a headache. But this? A drunken fistfight in a bar?

Esa crouched so he was eye level with Nell. "I'm okay. I just had a very late night and I didn't sleep well." He wouldn't look at Michelle. She wasn't surprised: he had to know there was a look of disgust waiting for him.

"Are you sure?" Nell asked.

"Yup."

"Okay." Nell's sunniness returned. "When are you going to come with me to the museum, though?"

Esa smiled. "Soon."

Nell took his hand. "Promise?"

"I promise."

Nell started leading Esa by the hand into the kitchen, stopping at the halfway point to look back over her shoulder at Michelle. "Come have cocoa with us, Michelle!"

"I can't right now, honey. I have to catch up on some e-mails."

"But it'll be fun."

"Seriously, Nell, I have a lot of friends I owe e-mails to."

Nell looked disappointed. "Okay."

Michelle went to her room and flipped open her laptop,

settling down on her bed to write. Nell's unflagging desire fo
the three of them to come together again continued to breal
her heart. Even though she knew they both loved her, tha
wasn't enough, and Michelle worried it never would be. Nel
still watched both of them closely for any sign that might sig
nal a reversion to romantic status. Even though the "It's com
plicated" answer hadn't appeased her, at least she'd stoppe
asking Michelle about it.

She was half an hour into answering e-mail when she
heard a tiny knock at her bedroom door. She smiled to herself
Nell, wanting to bake cookies. "Come in."

The door opened. It was not Nell wanting to bake cookies
Michelle froze. "Oh."

Esa stood in the doorway. "Can we talk?" he aske
quietly.

"Sure." Michelle frowned worriedly. "Where's Nell?"

"On her computer. I guess you inspired her."

"Oh." She thought about the last time he was in her room
and flushed. Right here, on this bed, against that desk . .
God. She hoped the heat in her face didn't betray what she
was thinking.

Esa didn't move. "If you'd feel more comfortable talking in
the living room . . ."

Michelle considered this. "No, it's okay," she said stiffly
"Just—keep the door open."

"Of course."

What an idiotic thing to say, she thought. As if he wa
going to attack her.

She was glad he had the good sense to pull up her desl
chair, not perch on the edge of her bed.

"I'm sorry about what happened last night," he said. "
embarrassed myself, and it was a thoughtless thing to do whe
I'm responsible for a child. I promise you it won't happe
again."

"Okay." Michelle went back to her e-mail. If he though
she was going to go into some kind of lengthy discussion witl
him, he was wrong.

"That's it?" His voice was bewildered. "That's all you have
to say?"

Michelle lifted her eyes to his. "What did you expect me to say?"

"Truthfully? I thought you'd tear me a new asshole."

"It's obvious how I feel, isn't it?"

"Usually you fire at me with both barrels."

"I don't have the energy. Although I do have to say, I'm surprised: I never thought you'd risk messing up that handsome face of yours."

Esa grimaced. "I deserved that."

"You deserve more than that."

"I hated lying to Nell."

Michelle refused to acknowledge the pain in his eyes. "You should."

Esa ran his fingers through his hair. "I have to go back to Met Gar at three thirty for a press conference."

"Understandable."

"Michelle, would you just let me have it?" Esa said tersely. "There's already enough tension between us without adding this to the mix."

"That tension is different."

"Still."

Michelle closed her laptop and put it on the bed beside her. "You want me to tell you I'm pissed? Yeah, I'm pissed. I feel like you completely dropped the ball as an adult, and I feel like it was taking advantage of me as a nanny, and as someone who loves Nell. If Nell had a different nanny, you would never have gotten that shit faced. Never."

Esa's eyes darted away. "True."

"What if this jerk had hurt you?" Michelle hadn't realized how much the thought upset her until now. "What would I tell Nell? God forbid she finds out about this as it is. This is possibly the stupidest, most selfish thing you've done since I started working for you."

"It won't happen again."

"You're goddamn right it won't." Michelle paused, waiting for her anger to abate. "Look," she said, letting feelings of sympathy momentarily catch the better of her. "I understand what you're going through—"

"No, you don't," Esa snapped.

Michelle threw him the best ball shriveling look she coul
manage. "Don't you dare snap at me."

Esa stared out the window. "I'm sorry."

"As I was saying," Michelle continued pointedly, "what'
going on with you and the Kidco brass isn't an excuse for yo
to revert to bad behavior."

"I understand that, believe me," Esa said ruefully, his gaz
still fixed on the window. "And like I said, I'm sorry."

"Good."

"I miss you," he said softly.

"Trying to lure me into bed? Sympathy fuck?"

Esa slowly turned his head to look at her. "I'm not like tha
anymore. You and Nell changed me."

"Yeah, well, whatever," Michelle said brusquely. "You sai
what you had to say, now go. And yes, I forgive you. But if yo
pull anything like this again—"

"I said I won't."

Michelle laughed incredulously, because he actually ha
the stones to sound irritated.

Esa stood and walked to the bedroom door. "I appreciat
your understanding. I appreciate everything."

Michelle frowned harshly. "Don't. Just don't."

Esa nodded, closing the door behind him.

Michelle closed her eyes. She wanted to cry. She was tire
and she felt used, but it was more than that: it was the frustra
tion of missing Esa, too. But she refused to go back to tha
place, not when she'd made so much headway, or so she though
He had no right to say that to me, she thought to hersel
angrily. Just because his head isn't screwed on straight righ
now doesn't mean he gets a free pass to mess with mine. If sh
needed to, she'd make sure he knew that in no uncertai
terms, even if it meant driving the point home repeatedly. For
giveness was one thing; losing your footing was quite anothe

49

You're a moron, you're a fuckup, now just keep your head down and do your job.

Esa had heard this from Lou before and after the press conference, and he heard it from Ty Gallagher and Coach Dante this morning when he made sure to get to practice early. The famously emotional Dante looked ready to haul off and punch him in the face, which was ironic considering the reason why they were calling him a "fuckup." Esa almost wished Dante had taken a shot at him; a physical blow would be much easier to stomach than his coach's disgusted, disappointed expression. He couldn't decide whose gaze was worse: Michael Dante's or Michelle's.

He turned his face up to the hot spray of his postpractice shower, slicking back his hair. Usually, it was one of his favorite feelings in the world, the heat raining down on him. But right now nothing felt good.

What the hell had he been thinking, telling Michelle he missed her? It had surprised him as much as it surprised her, the power of the vulnerability welling up inside him before

he could stop the words from reaching his tongue. He wishe
he could take it back.

He showered faster than usual: Rory and he were going ou
for breakfast; the same Rory who was going to make him pa
the rest of his life for bailing him out.

He went to his locker and dressed. None of his teammate
said anything. He'd apologized to all of them at the beginnin
of practice. He knew that's where it would end. "You owe m
two thousand dollars, you arsehole," were the first words ou
of Rory's mouth as they walked out of the locker room.

"You know I'm good for it," Esa muttered.

"What kind of a twit walks around with nothing but five hun
dred dollars in cash, house keys, and a Finnish driver's license?

"You done yet?" Esa shot Rory a weary, sideways look.
this was what breakfast was going to be like, he wasn't sure h
was in. Then again, he deserved every dart Rory hurled a
him. Still. "Let me know when you're done."

"What'd Dante say to you?"

"What the hell do you think he said?"

Rory shook his head regretfully. "I knew I should hav
dragged you out of that bar. Thing was, I was in no mood t
put up with you. You were being such an arse."

"You're right. I'm an ass. Are we done?"

"For now."

Esa felt his phone vibrate in the front pocket of his jean
and pulled it out with a large frown, assuming it would b
some member of the media who'd gotten hold of his phon
number.

It was Michelle.

"Hi."

"Hi," she said in an eerily calm voice.

Esa tensed. "What's going on? Is Nell okay?"

"She's fine. She's at school, which is good, because we'v
got some major weirdness here."

Esa felt sick. "Did someone break in? Is someone holdin
a gun to your head?"

"Your parents are here."

"What?"

"I know. Please come home if you can. I feel reall
uncomfortable."

"I'm on my way. Just sit tight. *Min rakustan sunua.*" He
turned to Rory as he shoved the phone back in his pocket. "I
can't have breakfast. My parents are here."

Rory looked alarmed. "Esa—"

"I know. I'll call you later, bro."

No way. No fucking way. Esa started running down the
hall.

* * *

Waiting for Esa, Michelle had developed a chant in her head:
*please get home soon, please get home soon, please get home
soon*. The difference between this and most chants was this
one didn't result in relaxation. It was born in anxiety, and the
anxiety remained as Esa's parents sat side by side on the
couch, watching her as inscrutably as two silent, Siamese
cats. Finnish cats, actually. Which made them far colder than
Siamese cats.

When Henry had buzzed to say Esa's parents were in the
lobby, Michelle was stunned. Esa hadn't said anything to her
about them visiting. But what was she supposed to do? It
wasn't like she could turn them away. What a fuckup he was,
she thought.

Michelle greeted them with a pleasant hello when she
opened the front door, immediately struck by Esa's strong
resemblance to his dad. "You must be the nanny," Esa's mother
said to her, looking and sounding unenthusiastic. Esa hadn't
exaggerated their coldness. Or was it smugness? Michelle
thought, as his mother handed Michelle her coat to be hung up.
I'm the nanny, not the maid. His dad seemed aware that there
was a difference: he at least hung up his own jacket.

Esa's mother looked surprised as her gaze traveled a slow
circuit around the comfy living room, finally coming to rest on
Michelle with a mildly appraising smile. "Is Esa here?"

"No, he's at practice. Can I get you some tea?"

"That would be nice."

Michelle went to prepare the tea. Esa's parents were speaking in rapid-fire Finnish in the living room. Then their voices
began to diminish. Alarmed, Michelle popped her head around
the kitchen door. Esa's parents were walking down the hallway toward the bedrooms.

Michelle shot out of the kitchen and was behind them in seconds. "Excuse me: can I help you with something?"

"We want to see Nell's room," said Esa's dad.

"Then you should have asked me, and I would gladly have shown it to you. But you can't just—"

Ignoring her, Esa's mother pulled open the nearest door, revealing her son's room. He was as fastidious as he'd been since Michelle had known him. Even so, they had no right to intrude, even if it was for only a few seconds.

Michelle reached around her, closing the door and pointing down the hall. "That's Nell's room on the left. If you follow me, I'll show it to you."

Michelle did a slow burn as she swept past them. They murmured in Finnish, walking behind her. She had no idea what they were saying, but it sounded disdainful.

She opened the door to Nell's room. It was neat as a pin, bright and sunny. There were plants in the windows, book shelves brimming with books, and a crowd of stuffed animals carefully arranged on her bed. She had a toy box where she kept her Barbies, and a small desk Michelle had painted pink for her. A ballerina music box was the centerpiece of her dresser, bottles of nail polish perfectly lined up off to the side. Nell had stuck a picture of herself and her mother in the left hand corner of the mirror. The picture had only appeared recently.

Michelle smiled proudly. "It's lovely, isn't it?"

"It is," Esa's mother reluctantly agreed. "Though she does seem to have a lot of things."

"Mostly books," Michelle pointed out. *Don't you dare imply she's spoiled, not when her uncle and I have worked so hard to make sure she isn't.* "Shall we have that tea?"

Michelle escorted them back out into the living room, politely bade them to sit, and returned to the kitchen. She called Esa from the depths of the pantry while waiting for the whistle of the kettle to blow. She knew that as soon as she told him his parents were here, he'd stop whatever he was doing and head home. He wasn't an idiot.

50

"I wish I could say this is a pleasant surprise, but it isn't."

Esa's body clenched in anger at the sight of his parents on his couch. There they sat, side by side like two stone castings, while poor Michelle sat in a chair opposite, trying to look relaxed as she clasped a steaming mug of tea between both hands. Esa knew Michelle: she'd no doubt been trying to engage his parents, get them to relax, maybe even go so far as to try to get his mother to smile a few times. She might even have made headway with his dad. But his mother? Doubtful. She'd be too busy sitting there, trying to discern if Michelle "measured up," as if she herself were Finnish royalty.

"You look tired," Esa said to Michelle. He squeezed her shoulder to let her know everything was going to be fine before sitting down in the chair next to hers.

His mother waved her index finger vaguely. "Very nice," she said, indicating the living room. "Not what I expected. I see Danika's hand in this?"

"Yes. She was very helpful. But you're not here to talk about my flat." He bent over, untying his shoes. "So what happened first?" he asked, looking up at them. "Did you see the video of the fight at the bar, or did you read about it? I'm very impressed with the speed in which you got here; you must have caught the first plane out of Helsinki." He placed his shoes to the right of his chair in a neat pair. "This is ridiculous."

"I don't think so," his mother returned coldly. She regarded Michelle with a polite but frozen smile. "This is a private family matter. Would you mind—"

"*I* would mind," said Esa. "Either say what you have to say in front of Michelle, or don't say it at all." Esa slid Michelle a sideways look, worried she might be upset with him for putting her on the spot. But she looked fine. In fact, she looked pleased.

Esa regarded his parents expectantly. "Well?"

"Nell shouldn't be here," his mother declared, "and this bar episode proves it. You're not fit to be her guardian."

"Apparently, my sister didn't agree."

"The only reason I can think of for Danika selecting you as her child's guardian was to stab us in the heart."

Esa chuckled. "How could I forget? Her death was all about you."

Jibes bounced off his mother like rubber bullets on armor. "You seem to have a very short memory, Esa, acting as if you yourself understood why Danika chose you to raise Nell. We were there, too, when her will was read. We saw that horrified, trapped look on your face.

"Perhaps you've been 'behaving' for a while," his mother continued in an imperious manner, "but this fight is a sign that you're still extremely immature. Immature people, especially those who get drunk, should not be guardians of children."

"And yet there you were in London, complimenting me for doing such an impressive job with Nell."

"Perhaps you were. But that was then. Now, the real you is starting to reemerge." She heaved a long, tortured sigh. "We knew this would happen."

Esa turned to Michelle. "Can you believe this shit?" he asked her plaintively.

"Not really, no." Michelle looked extremely upset as she addressed Esa's parents. "I know you think I don't have a right to an opinion, but I do. What I'm getting from this conversation so far is that you've been waiting for Esa to screw up, so you'd have an excuse to just sweep in here and take Nell away."

"Save Nell," Esa's mother corrected with a glare.

"*Take* Nell," Michelle repeated, glaring back.

"You barely saw Nell when Danika was alive!" Esa snapped at his parents. "Know why? Because Danika wanted it that way! I bet you don't even know that. Doesn't that tell you something? Doesn't it tell you something about why she picked me?"

"Yes: that your sister was unstable at the time she had her will drawn up." His mother's gaze was steely. "We told you when Leslie sent Nell to you that we'd be keeping a close eye on you."

"Which amazes me," Esa retorted, "considering the fact you don't like children!"

"You wanted for nothing!" his father spluttered.

"*Esa.*" Michelle's hand shot out and squeezed his wrist, hard. "Don't shout," she said under her breath. "Don't lose it. It's only going to make things worse."

"Right." Esa closed his eyes, and took a deep breath. Thank God Michelle was here. She gave his wrist another squeeze. Esa forced himself to look back at his parents, unable to hide his mystification. "I don't understand. You show up here, no warning. What did you think would happen? That I would just hand Nell over to you? On the basis of *one* screwup? Did you think she'd just pack up and go with you? I'm surprised you didn't try to kidnap her."

His parents' exchanged glances. "Oh, that's good," Esa smirked. "You were going to try to snatch her from school?"

"It wouldn't have worked: the school has permission to release her to only me and Esa," said Michelle protectively. "It doesn't matter if you're her grandparents or not. Even if you tried to claim you had permission from us to pick her up, the school would have been on the phone to both of us to double check."

Esa leaned over and borrowed Michelle's mug, taking a sip of tea. It was one of those soothing herbal blends she liked that he hated, but he was thirsty, and didn't want to leave the room. He just wanted the conversation over and done with.

"We can sue you for custody," his mother said calmly.

Ladies and Gentlemen, Esa thought, please fasten your seat belts as we are now leaving Reality Land and heading straight for Bizarro-ville.

Esa struggled to keep his voice level. "Okay, here's a few reasons why that has no basis in reality at all. One: The time to have sued me would have been right after Danika died; you could have contested her will. Two: Even if you did sue me, then *or* now, the case would be tied up for years, and ultimately thrown out, because it's groundless. You'd have wasted a lot of time, money, energy, and emotion on nothing. Three: I will spend every penny I have, which is considerably more money than the two of you have, or ever will have, fighting you. Four: If you do that, you will lose, and I swear to you that you will never, NEVER, see me or Nell again."

"You've left a trail behind you of news stories and footage," said his father. "Years of being a playboy, out night after night, wine, women, and God knows what else."

"Yeah, and all of it dates back to before Nell came to live with me!" Christ, how long was he going to pay for his past? When it came to his parents the answer was: forever. Maybe if they'd shown the least bit of warmth he and Danika would have turned out differently. But they hadn't.

He leaned forward in his chair. "I'm sorry," he said simply. "I lost control. I don't need you to tell me I was stupid. I know that. As I've made clear to everyone important to me, and to Nell"—he glanced at Michelle respectfully—"it won't happen again.

"It was the wrong way to deal with my uncertainty about my future, and . . . other things. But I can't undo it," he said for what felt like the one hundredth time. "Now can we move on? I have enough shit to cope with without this insanity on top of everything else."

He leaned back, believing the discussion to be over. When he shot a sideways glance of satisfaction at Michelle, the frozen expression on her face made him realize it wasn't.

"Yes, let's talk about that uncertain future that drove you to violence," retorted his mother. "What if the Blades don't re-sign you, and you have to move to another city? You'd uproot Nell *again*? She should have one home until she de-

:ides to go to university. Finland, where she'll lead a happy, normal life."

"A happy life for Nell is wherever Esa is."

There was a stunned silence. Overwhelmed, Esa felt his heart beginning to pick up speed as he looked at Michelle in awe. But Michelle's declaration made Esa's mother look more affronted than he had seen in a long time. She had no idea of the depth of love Michelle felt for Nell, but she was about to find out.

"I agree with you: it was shocking when Nell came here to live with Esa," said Michelle. "He knew nothing about children, and he really didn't want to. He viewed her as one big crimp in his lifestyle. As for Nell, she was still trying to come to terms with Danika's death, and now here she was, being shipped off to an uncle she barely knew."

"My point exactly," said Esa's mother smugly.

"I'm just getting started," replied Michelle. "So if I were you, I'd wait until you hear the whole story before you start passing judgment."

"So rude," Esa's mother said to his father under her breath.

"Blunt," said Michelle. "That's the word you want: blunt. Because in a situation like this, someone has to be." She paused. "I've been here since the beginning, so I've seen the progress Esa has made with Nell. He's gone from being a resentful, terrified bachelor to a loving, caring uncle. His life doesn't make the gossip columns anymore, because making sure Nell is happy and healthy is his priority. Are you hearing me so far?

"Nell has had some emotional ups and downs, and Esa has been there for her. They've gone through many of them together. Have things been perfect? No, and certainly, Esa did make a big mistake this past weekend. But it was *one* mistake, and it in no way put Nell in danger. Tell me: were you perfect parents who made no mistakes? If Esa was still a womanizing jerk out on the town every night, then you might have a case for taking Nell. But you don't."

Michelle's face was flushed with emotion as she took a sip of tea. "Let's talk about Nell," she resumed in an emotional voice. "She was a depressed, frightened, uncertain little girl when she came here. I *know*: I've lived here since the very beginning. That little girl is gone. She loves her school. She's made friends. She likes living in this city.

"Most of all, she loves her uncle. He's everything to her. *Everything.* And the feeling is mutual. Esa adores her, and seeing them together . . ." Tearful, Michelle broke off for a moment. "You'd break Nell's heart if you tried to take her from Esa, and you'd break his heart if you tried to take Nell from him. Their bond goes way beyond having Danika in common. It's loving and intense, and it's growing all the time. So I'd ask you to think twice before you pursue something that is not only ridiculous, with no basis in reality, but something that would only result in your ending any relationship you had with your granddaughter and your son for the rest of your lives."

With that, Michelle got up and walked to her room.

There was nothing left to say; Michelle had said it all. Esa's parents were silent, but it wasn't his mother's usual spiky silence. It was more the absolute quiet that comes when you know you don't have a leg to stand on.

"Would you like some more tea?" Esa asked his parents quietly. "We could even go out to lunch if you'd like. Nell comes home from school around three thirty if you'd like to see her."

"I think, maybe, another time," said his father, not meeting his eye.

"But you've come all this way," said Esa, and he meant it.

"Even so," said his mother. She touched his father's sleeve and they rose. "We'll be talking soon about the summer? Nell visiting Finland?" she asked Esa awkwardly.

"Yes," Esa promised. "I'd want to come as well."

"Why not bring the nanny, too," his father murmured. "I'm sure she's never been to Finland. She'd enjoy it."

"Yes, I'll ask her."

He followed his parents to the door, helping them on with their jackets.

"We'll speak soon," his father said, echoing his mother's words as he squeezed Esa's shoulder, his version of an apology.

"Yes, of course."

He felt more awkward with his mother, knowing she was

e one behind this folly. It was only now, sensing her sadness,
at it dawned on him that one of the reasons she might want
ell was because her own daughter was gone to her forever,
d Nell was the only link left. Or maybe she thought that
mehow, through Nell, she could fix the mistakes she'd made
th Danika. All Esa knew was that this was the first time
'd ever sensed her as being truly vulnerable.

"Are you sure you don't want to stay?" he tried one final
ne. "I could book you into a hotel."

"We've already done that." She hesitated, then kissed him
both cheeks. "We're sorry about your—pain," she said, the
rd not coming to her easily. "All of it. I'm sure everything
ll be fine."

"Call me when you get back, so I know you arrived safely."

"Of course."

His parents departed, leaving a trail of personal remorse
hind them. It was so different to what Esa was feeling,
e gratitude inside him that he needed to pour out to Michelle
ght now. Overwhelmed, he made his way to her room.

51

"They left?"

Michelle was standing at her bedroom window, trying ▌
stem the tears pouring from her eyes when Esa knocked an
entered. She'd spoken to his parents the only way she kne▌
how: honestly. She wasn't exaggerating when she'd said th▌
separating Esa and Nell would break both their hearts. Wh▌
she'd neglected to mention was that it would break hers ▌
well. Esa sat on the edge of her bed. "Yes, they're gone."

"I'm sorry." Michelle continued swiping at her eyes with▌
tissue. "That was very presumptuous of me."

"Don't be silly."

"I'm surprised they didn't want to stick around and s▌
Nell. I was sure that since they'd come all this way—"

"I think you scared them off."

Michelle was clearly horrified. "That was a joke," Es▌
assured her gently. "I thought they would stick around, to▌
but no. Maybe they felt it would be too painful since the▌
wouldn't be bringing Nell back to Finland with them. I dor▌
know."

"Jesus, Esa." Michelle sat down on the bed beside him. "How could they think—"

"I know."

Michelle felt a resurgence of indignity. "Seriously, it looked like they were just biding their time, waiting for you to screw up. Did they really think Nell would just pack up and leave her home?"

Esa paused, looking at her with interest. "Did you mean what you said, how a happy life for Nell is wherever I am?"

Michelle hesitated a moment, then cupped his cheek. If he removed her hand, so be it. "How can you even ask that? Of course I meant it."

Esa nodded, closing his eyes as he put his hand over hers. "I can't thank you enough. You didn't have to do that. You're right: the thought of being without Nell is intolerable to me." He opened his eyes, so blue and clear and startlingly intense. "The thought of being without either of you is intolerable. I want us to be 'a real family.'" He took her hand, twined his fingers through hers. "I love you, Michelle."

She looked down at their joined hands, waiting for a storm to kick up inside her. But it didn't, because this was actually the calm after the storm, the quiet space where she realized that what she'd told Esa's parents about him wasn't only about making sure he and Nell weren't lost to one another. It was about making sure Esa wasn't lost to her, too.

"I love you, too," she said quietly, looking up into his eyes. They looked at each other and both burst out laughing in a release of months of tension.

They were still laughing as they tumbled together onto the bed. They lay face-to-face, gazing into each other's eyes, neither one moving.

"Say it to me in Finnish," Michelle whispered.

"Min rakustan sunua."

Michelle was confused. "I could swear I've heard that before."

"You have. When you called me at Met Gar and told me to hurry home, I said it to you as I hung up the phone. It just came out."

"As natural as can be."

"Yes." Esa slowly ran the pad of his thumb back and forth across her lower lip, occasionally lingering. *Tell me*, he asked with his eyes, looking so deeply into hers she feared he'd guess all her secrets.

Michelle smiled wickedly, and very slowly, very deliberately, took his right index finger into her mouth and began sucking on it, her eyes never leaving his face. Esa inhaled sharply, but then relaxed into it, the way she took each of the fingers on that hand in turn and sucked. But when she took the index finger of his right hand again and not only sucked, but began to move it in and out of her mouth with a naughty look on her face, his breathing changed, his pupils dilated. He pulled his finger out of her mouth.

"You're torturing me."

"Is that such a bad thing?"

"Maybe not."

Agreed upon torture, then. Neither of them moved. They just lay there, looking at each other, smiling secret smiles. Waiting. Who'd do what next? In the meantime, desire was unfurling within Michelle, inch by scorching inch. It wasn't just the way Esa's eyes had latched on to her face with a look of unabashed lust; it was knowing that she'd be the one to satisfy him.

She edged closer to him, planting a series of kisses up his jawline. "How's that?" she whispered, stopping right beneath his earlobe, which she nipped with her teeth. "That okay?"

Esa laughed huskily. "More than okay. Mmm, is this okay?"

He flicked the very tip of his tongue against her earlobe. Michelle's eyes closed as she reveled in the sensation of him pressing against her neck, his hot breath bringing small groans of pleasure to her lips. She reached out, fisting her hand in his still damp hair, that bore the faintest scents of lavender and citrus. She moved her palm to his neck, feathering her fingers there. Michelle smiled to herself as Esa went very still. His skin was thrillingly hot to the touch, but she wanted to feel it more intensely. She lightly lifted her fingers from his neck, snaking her hand up under his T-shirt.

Christ. His skin was burning. Hard muscles rippled beneath the splayed palm of her hand as she moved her hand across his chest. Esa began breathing again, but there was an undercurrent of desperation to it that turned Michelle on. She shoved the material of his T-shirt up, and began feverishly kissing his chest.

"Fuck," Esa whispered.

His own hands came up, cupping her breasts. "Mmm," Michelle purred, the demanding pulse of her heart beginning to make itself known. If Esa's sexy smile was anything to go by, he wanted it as badly as she did: his fingers nimbly unbuttoned her blouse before reaching around for her bra and unclasping it. Michelle watched as he licked the pads of his thumbs, and then put them to her nipples, circling gently. Michelle felt the first wave of pure hunger wash over her as he continued, gently tweaking, then putting his wet thumbs to her again and blowing on the nipples. Michelle arched, pushing her hips against his. She could feel him there, thrilled when he began to gently rock against her, now bringing his face to nuzzle her breasts, his other arm reaching around her to squeeze her ass.

The friction, slow and deliberate, seemed such a simple thing, yet the force of it shocked Michelle. He was scrambling her senses. All she could think about was the ache inside her, how it demanded release, how he was the only one who could do it for her.

Burning up, Michelle tugged at the zipper of his jeans, opening them just enough for her to comfortably slide her hand beneath the waistband of his briefs and begin fondling him. His dick was long and hard in her hand, throbbing with its own pulse. When she circled the tip once with her thumb, spreading the pre-cum over the head, Esa jerked his head up to look at her. "Fuck me," she mouthed.

He growled, roughly yanking her hand out of his briefs before rolling away from her to tear off his clothing. The sight of his magnificent ass, the rock-hard shoulders and back that tapered to a perfect V at his waist, had Michelle quickly doing the same. He rolled onto his back, pulling Michelle on top of him. Michelle lifted her hips, slowly guiding Esa deep inside her. She lifted her hips again, pushing back down on his dick slowly. Then again. And again. Each time she moved up and down, she reveled in the way he filled her, feeling triumphant with each groan and grunt he made. When he put his index finger to her clit and began wildly rubbing her as she rode him, Michelle quickly lost control, crying out her pleasure as her pussy tightened and released around him in a series of intense spasms. Finally, she was spent. Smiling down at him, she grabbed his shoulders and rolled them so he was now on top of her.

They smiled at each other as he began moving inside her, each strike of his hips against hers like two flints creating fire. Faster. More. Was she saying the words aloud or just in her head? Did it matter? Michelle's breath grew ragged as Esa thrust harder and harder, the intensity of her own response signaling another lucky tumble into orgasm. Esa was frenzied now, all taut concentration intent on release. And when he came with an unmistakable cry of pleasure that ended on a laugh, Michelle found herself laughing, too. This was joy. This was crazy. This was love.

52

"Kaunis tytto."

Michelle snuggled closer into the crook of Esa's shoulder for a second before asking him what he'd just said. She knew it must be something wonderful, because he'd said it in such a loving, tender voice. She felt like they were the only two people in the world, and it was thrilling. Anything they desired could happen. It was up to them and no one else.

She lifted her head and looked at him, so handsome even in repose, the sun coming through her windows hitting his cheekbones at just the right angle. His eyes were closed. He looked happy and relaxed.

"What did you just say?" she asked, resting her head back on the pillow.

"Beautiful girl," Esa murmured. "Because you are."

Michelle blushed. "Thank you."

"Why are you thanking me? It's the truth."

Michelle scooched her body a few inches away from his so she could fully take him in. The way the sheets draped perfectly over his slim hips, the sculpted upper torso and arms . . . gorgeous. Beautiful. He was a beautiful man.

"I bet every woman you've ever slept with has told y̶
you're beautiful."

Esa raised an eyebrow. "Does that matter?"

Michelle blushed again. "No."

Esa propped himself up on one elbow, cupping his chin
the palm of his hand. "So . . . Nell?"

"Nell." Michelle rolled onto her back with a smile. "N̶
will be ecstatic."

"When we tell her, I think we should stress that things a̶
permanent and she doesn't have to worry about complicatio̶
ever breaking us apart."

"I agree completely."

"So no matter where I end up playing, you'll be there?"

"Of course." Michelle grabbed his free hand, kissing h̶
knuckles fervently. "I can't believe you even asked that! Y̶
and Nell are my home, Esa. Not some physical locale." S̶
pressed her lips to the hollow of his collarbone, moving up
his neck, and then cheek. "Do you know how much I lo̶
you?"

Esa laughed. "Bet you never thought you'd be saying tha̶

"God, I hated you," Michelle recalled with amusement.

"You *wanted* to hate me," Esa corrected. "But you didn̶
And it bugged the hell out of you."

"You have to admit, you were pretty clueless. Selfis̶
even."

"I admit it completely," Esa said without hesitation. "B̶
you were still attracted to me."

"Egomaniac!"

"Just stating the truth," Esa insisted plainly. His ha̶
brushed her breast, sending a shiver of pleasure through h̶
body. "It was the same way with me: I was attracted to you, b̶
I didn't want to be. It didn't seem right. And you were
bossy. It bothered me that I liked it a little."

"I'm still bossy."

"And I still like it."

Esa kissed her forehead, then let out a small groan of m̶
ery. "I almost wish we didn't have a game tonight."

Michelle was surprised. "Seriously?"

"Sometimes it's hard to maintain absolute focus with th̶
ax hanging over my head. If I fuck up, blame is placed squar̶

my feet because of all this contract crap—or lack of one, I ould say."

Michelle smoothed back his hair. "Maybe focusing on mething positive could help you concentrate?" she sugested tentatively. "Like . . . thinking about you, me, and Nell ally being a family?"

Esa cheered a bit. "I wish it were that simple. But it cerinly can't hurt."

* * *

had been a tough game. The Blades and Philly traded goals r three periods, leaving them tied 3-3 at the end of regulaon. With so few games left in the regular season and the two ams tied in the standings as well, the winner would likely d up with home ice advantage all the way through the playfs. Philly seemed willing to play it close to the vest and take eir chances in a shoot out. But before overtime even started, oach Dante had told them to go for it. Esa took him at his ord.

Esa's line took the ice after a Philly shot had been deflected to the netting, leading to a face-off in the Blades' zone. ory was tossed from the face-off, and Esa took the draw. ancing back at Eric Mitchell before settling to take the ce-off, Esa sensed they were on the same page. If he won e drawback to Eric, he was definitely going to go for it. The illy center dawdled for a few seconds, but the linesman rked for him to put his stick down. The moment his blade t the ice, the linesman dropped the puck. Esa, anticipating e drop, caught it in midair and swept it back to Eric in the ft corner. Eric gathered the puck on his backhand and lofted e puck toward center ice.

The moment after he'd won the draw, Esa had taken off. here was only one thought in his mind: end this game now. e didn't bother looking back to see if Eric had lobbed the ick down the ice. He *knew* where the puck would be. He was ght. Skating faster than he'd ever skated before. Skating the ay he'd dreamed of all those years playing on ponds in Helnki, he gained a step on both Philly defensemen. Gathering e puck on the Philly side of center ice, Esa had a stride on eryone else. He knew no one could catch him.

Despite their desperation, the Flyer defensemen couldn't
close the ground. In fact, Esa pulled even further ahead.
When he crossed the Philly blue line, he looked at the goaltender who'd shuffled out a few strides past the top of the
crease and was slowly backing up, in sync with Esa's stride
forward. Esa's mind raced through all his shots against this
goaltender. High to the glove side twice. High to the stick side
once. Esa knew the goalie was thinking the same, despite
there being only seconds for both of them to think. *He's ready
for a shot.* When he reached the slot, Esa faked as if he would
shoot, and then pulled the puck wide to his forehand side. The
goalie froze for a moment, anticipating a shot high to either
side. But he was good. When the shot didn't come, he'd gone
into the butterfly and kicked out his left pad, covering the bottom of the net. But Esa knew he'd have to go high: with the
puck on his forehand, he lifted it over the outstretched leg pad
into the back of the net. That's when he knew.

* * *

"*Twelve point five* million, three years. Not bad, considering their original offer was nine million. I think we should
take it."

Russell had given Esa the thumbs-up as he wrapped up his
call with Kidco, grinning across the rectangular divide of
his desk.

Esa wasn't sure who would be happier with a guaranteed
three more years in New York: him or Michelle. He knew
she'd meant it when she said she'd go wherever his career took
him, but he was relieved for both their sakes that they were
staying put. This was where her family was, and Nell finally
thought of Manhattan as "home." The idea that she might
have to be uprooted—again—killed him.

He and Michelle hadn't yet told Nell the good news that
they were back together. Life had been a little crazy the past
few days, and they wanted breaking the news to her to be special. Michelle had ordered a custom ice cream cake from Ben
& Jerry's in Nell's favorite flavor, triple caramel chunk. Esa
was going to pick it up after he was done with Russ. They
would tell her tonight after dinner, and celebrate.

Russ put two fingers in his mouth and whistled. "When

are you? I just gave you the best news of your fucking life and you're spacing out on me?"

"Second best news," Esa said with a grin.

Esa's agent looked confused for a minute, then broke into a big smile. "The niece, huh? Everything's turned out well?"

"Everything has turned out great. Better than I ever could have dreamed."

"Then you have a lot to be grateful for."

"Believe me, I know it."

"So." Russell tapped a pencil on his desk. "We're accepting the offer?"

"Yeah!"

"Good man. I'll wait until the end of the day tomorrow to call them. We don't want to look over eager, and it won't kill those bastards to wait. Fuck 'em. Let them suffer with a day's worth of bad press and see what it feels like to sweat it."

"I agree." Esa went toward his agent as the older man came out from behind his desk to embrace him.

"Congratulations, Esa. You deserve every penny. Now go out and celebrate the way only you can."

"Oh, I will," Esa assured him. "And believe me, it's going to be the best celebration ever."

53

"Something weird is going on. Tell me!"

Michelle loved how animated Nell's face was as she peered back and forth between her and Esa at the dinner table. Dinner was done, and the ice cream cake was just waiting in the freezer. All that was left was to surprise her.

"What do you mean, 'weird'?" Michelle asked innocently.

"You guys were teasing me and stuff, but in a fun way." It was true: a lighthearted mood prevailed at dinner. It was unavoidable. But Michelle was glad it also served another purpose, that of easing Nell back into the change of status in her and Esa's relationship. She took it as a good sign that Nell didn't seem anxious. Instead, she seemed pleasantly suspicious.

"You were *both* weird," Nell insisted, "but in a good way." She scrutinized both of them for a long time. "This is good weird," she speculated. "Right?"

"You'll see," Michelle said mysteriously. "We have a surprise for you."

Nell clasped her hands together in anticipation. "Is it a dog?"

"Uh, no," said Esa, while Michelle covered her mouth and ▸oughed to keep from laughing.

Nell looked disappointed. "Oh."

"I'm sure you'll get a dog one day," Michelle told her. "But ▸r now, close your eyes."

Nell closed them, bouncing a little in her chair. "This bet-▸r be good."

It was too bad Nell couldn't see Michelle quirk her right ▸ebrow. *"Excuse me?"*

"I meant 'I hope it's good,'" Nell amended.

Michelle crossed the kitchen and removed the giant cake ▸ox from the fridge. Jesus, the thing weighed a ton! She was ▸tra careful as she placed it on the counter, removing the ▸ake from its box. The last thing she wanted was to drop it and ▸ave the top be ruined. "Your eyes better be closed," she ▸lled out to Nell.

Michelle tiptoed gingerly as she brought the cake to the ▸ble, excitement feathering up and down her arms. *Please let ▸r like it. Please let her be happy.*

"Okay, open your eyes!" said Esa.

Nell's eyes popped open.

"We had it made special for you—triple caramel chunk!" ▸ichelle exclaimed. "Read what it says!"

"Out loud!" Esa added.

"'Nell plus Michelle plus Uncle Esa equals a Real Fam-▸y.'" Nell looked up from the cake, dumbstruck.

"What do you think?" asked Michelle, so excited she was ▸pping impatiently from foot to foot like a little kid.

Nell grinned. "Does this mean you two love each other ▸gain?"

"Yes," said Esa. "For good. Forever. No complications, we ▸romise."

"Are you getting married?" Nell squealed.

Esa looked questioningly at Michelle, who lifted her palms ▸p with a jerk, looking back at him wide-eyed. You expect me ▸ answer that? she thought. No way.

"Soon," Esa answered. He shot a look to Michelle to see if ▸is answer was okay. She gave a small nod of approval.

"But why not now?" Nell pressed.

Esa hesitated.

Please don't let him say "It's complicated," Michelle prayed. Not after promising her they were done with all that. Please.

"I have to search for the perfect ring," he said.

"I can help."

"I'll definitely need your help," Esa assured her.

He smiled across the table at Michelle, who was so happy she thought she might break out into a dance. Never in a million years did she imagine that this was how her life would turn out. No, there was something wrong with that sentence. Never in a million years did she imagine this was how her life would *start* out, the well-rounded one she'd always hoped for.

"I love you guys!" she proclaimed.

"I love you!" said Esa.

"Me, too!" said Nell loudly. "Now can I have some cake?"